THE DEAD DON'T DRINK AT LAFITTE'S

SEANA KELLY

This is a work of fiction. Names, characters, places, and incidents are either products of the writer's imagination or are used fictitiously and are not to be construed as real. Any resemblance to actual events, locales, organizations, or persons, living or dead, is entirely coincidental.

NYLA Publishing

121 W. 27th St., Suite 1201, NY 10001, New York.

http://www.nyliterary.com

ONE

Ghosts, Amirite?

I enjoyed ghost stories as much as the next werewolf. I'd assumed, though, they were just that—stories. Something to make your heart beat faster and your skin prickle with unease. Tales told by the fireside, evoking ancient, unnamed fears and causing our eyes to seek out shapes in shadows. Turned out I was wrong.

A colorless, almost transparent woman who seemed vaguely familiar glowed in the moonlight. She gesticulated wildly, blocking the dark path to The Slaughtered Lamb, my bookstore and bar currently under renovation. Silently shouting, eyes filled with urgency, she flickered in and out of existence. I moved forward, straining to read her lips, more concerned than scared.

Cold air chilled my skin, damp from running. I caught *no* and *vampires*. Mostly, I was onboard with that sentiment, but my boyfriend—a stupid term for a gorgeous British man who appeared to be about thirty but was actually hundreds of years old—was a vampire.

While I contemplated how I was supposed to refer to Clive, even in my own head, the woman shot forward and clamped a hand around my wrist. She was a ghost. I'd swear it, and yet I felt her cold fingers digging into my skin. Her filmy image became a shade more solid at the contact and I heard a whisper of words.

"They're coming! He'll be killed. Go!"

Understanding without a doubt that she meant my manfriend Clive, I tore my arm away and sprinted the four miles to the vampires' nocturne in Pacific Heights. There was unrest amongst the vamps. One of Clive's people had recently shown herself to be an enemy, working against him, trying to exact revenge for a dead lover. Clive had been investigating, to determine if others in his nocturne were plotting a coup attempt. He'd routed out two with an allegiance to her but suspected there were more.

Dodging trees and startled rabbits, I raced through the Presidio, a fifteen-hundred-acre park that was a former military post. Why had the ghost looked so familiar? I couldn't put my finger on it. *They're coming*, she'd said. Emerging from the park onto Pacific Avenue, I had to slow to human speed. I was almost there, four minutes tops.

Rounding the last corner, I slowed at the looming wrought iron gates. The vampire standing guard pretended not to notice me, but at my growl grudgingly stepped out of the way, allowing me to speed across the courtyard. Before I had a chance to touch the door, it swung open, Clive's butler already there.

"Where is he?" I shouted, racing past and skidding to a stop in the foyer.

"Who?" he responded after a moment.

I knew the vampires loathed me, considered a werewolf no better than a stray mongrel, but I wasn't putting up with his bullshit. Long, razor-sharp claws sprang from my fingertips as my eyes lightened to wolf gold. "I will shred you, you pompous ass! If anything happens to Clive, I'll be back to slice the smug off your face."

"Sam?"

I spun and there he was, burnished hair glowing in the light, chiseled features, cool gray eyes assessing me. The door closed behind me as Clive waited, amusement coloring his expression. Retracting my claws, a skill I'd recently mastered, I crossed to him.

"You're okay?"

"As you see. Why did you think otherwise?" Taking my hand, he led me over the marble floor toward the library. "And how was your lesson with Lydia?"

My shoulders slumped. "Miserable." Lydia was the mother of my right-hand man Owen. She was a powerful wicche who had trained all her children. I was coming into my magic late in life, but we were hoping she'd be able to teach me as well. So far, I'd proven to be a failure at all things wicchey.

He closed the door of the library behind us and waited for me to explain. I crossed the room to my window seat. He'd had it built for me. It was mine.

"Tell me all about it and why you raced home searching for me." He followed, settling in next to me.

Studying him, I made sure he wasn't hiding an injury. "You're really fine?"

He kissed me softly, tenderly, until I'd almost forgotten all about my horrible magic lesson and the ghost who'd scared the crap out of me. "I am," he finally said.

"I don't understand what that was about then." That's what I got for believing random apparitions.

"Tell me what you were up to while I slept." He leaned back and pulled me to him.

"Before or after I ruined another of Lydia's pots?"

Taking my hand, he squeezed. "I'll have a new set of cookware delivered tomorrow."

"It's not for you to replace. I'm the one whose potion turned into a toxic sludge that hardened into volcanic rock." Thunking my head against his shoulder, I continued. "Owen walked in, wondering what the horrible smell was. I saw it, Clive. Horrified pity passed between Owen and his mom. I'm a failure as a wicche."

"Nonsense. We haven't found your gift yet."

Snorting, I flopped back on the window seat cushions. "A kitchen wicche, I most assuredly am not. Owen and his mom even did this cool incantation over me to open up my powers and make them manifest. P'fft. That worked real well."

I'd learned recently that I, like my father and grandfather and many male grands before me, was a born wolf. I hadn't been mauled by a werewolf and turned. Well, I had been, but the reason I'd survived prolonged torture was due to the werewolf genes that my mother, a wicche, had kept suppressed with a protective amulet. The necklace had been stolen a few weeks ago. Latent talents had begun appearing. Or not, as the case was clearly becoming for any inherent wicchey skills.

"Just as well. Kitchen magic would be wasted on me." Lifting my hand, he pressed his lips to my palm. "I still don't understand why you thought I'd been hurt."

Oh, right. "I was jogging home by way of The Slaughtered Lamb to check on progress."

"I wish you'd borrow one of my cars. There are many and you'd be better protect—"

I kissed him quiet. "Nope. Those are your cars, not mine. I'm already living in your fancy mansion while my place is being remodeled," I said, in reference to my small apartment in the back of The Slaughtered Lamb. "I even went along with you calling the fortune you spent on this necklace a gift," I added, patting the stunning, spelled replacement for the one my mother had made.

This one didn't hide me, as hers had. It protected my mind from my psychotic aunt hell-bent on retroactively aborting me. My mother was a Corey wicche—an ancient and powerful family of wicches—who had fallen in love with and married a werewolf. My aunt considered that union a blasphemy and their daughter an abomination that needed to be destroyed. She'd been doing her damnedest to turn my own mind against me, ergo the new protective necklace around my neck.

"Hell, you bought me a whole wardrobe to make up for the crappy jeans and t-shirt collection I lost when the wolves destroyed my place. I draw the line at expensive sportscars I don't need. I have legs and I like to run. Werewolf, remember?"

"Vividly."

Smirking, I continued. "Anyway, I was jogging down the path to Land's End and ran into a ghost."

Clive furrowed his brow, studying me. "A ghost?"

"Yep. At first, she flickered in and out, waving her arms. When I got close, she—" Like a flash, I remembered where I'd seen her. "She was the second wolf. The one I'd gone out into the ocean to rescue. When I got shot?"

"Yes. I remember." His hand tightened around mine. "This was the ghost of the woman who had been murdered and dumped in the water in front of your bar?"

"I think so. She'd been torn up before she'd been murdered and her body had been in the water for a while. I can't be positive, but it *feels* right. Anyway, she grabbed my arm and said, 'They're coming. He'll be killed.'"

"We'll come back to the ghost sighting in a moment. How do you know she meant me?"

I opened my mouth and then stopped. Huh. "No idea. She never said your name. Your face popped into my head and I ran back to save you."

"Thank you for that," he said, grinning.

I shrugged, feeling stupid for racing in, ready for battle, only to find everyone safe and sound.

"Back to the ghost," Clive said, rubbing his thumb over my knuckles. "Have you ever seen a ghost before, communicated with one?"

"Nope. First time. Maybe she was grateful I'd tried to help?"

"Perhaps."

A knock sounded at the library door. I tried to extract my hand from his before one of his vampires saw us. They'd never show the disdain they felt for me in front of Clive. They feared him too much. All bets were off, though, when Clive wasn't around.

He didn't let go of my hand, freakishly strong vampire. "Come," he called.

Russell, Clive's second, stepped into the room and closed the door. He was a tall, handsome Black man, who seemed born to the formality of vampires—until you got to know him. "I've received a call from a visiting party from New Orleans."

"Have you now?" He shared a look with me before focusing on Russell again. "Isn't that interesting."

"Sire?" Russell's dark eyes moved back and forth between us.

Clive rose from the window seat, pulling me along. Leaning over the coffee table, he swiped through a tablet until classical music was playing throughout the room and then motioned for Russell to move closer. "Sam was telling me that a ghost waylaid her to say—and I quote—'They're coming. He'll be killed.'"

"Ghost?" Russell appeared confused. "A ghost told her?"

"Yes. When are they due?" Clive dropped my hand and began to pace.

"Tonight. Lafitte's people requested, quite politely, an audience with you." Russell spared me a wary gaze before crossing to the fireplace to speak with Clive. "If you believe Lafitte is moving against you, we can get you out."

Expression incredulous, Clive said, "You'd have me run and hide?" Shaking his head, he patted Russell on the shoulder. "No, old friend, that I will not do. We will meet the envoys, take their measure, and if they lift a hand against us, we will slaughter them all. Afterwards, we'll send their remains back to Lafitte in a box with a bow."

Russell glanced at me and then leaned in closer to Clive. "Sire, perhaps we should—"

"No. We let them come. I am very interested in who arrives, and even more interested to see if any of our own nocturne fight with them against us. Leticia has allies I've yet to ferret out. Tonight will let us know exactly who our enemies are." Patting

Russell's arm again, he added, "Trust me. It's better this way. We'll know who stands with us and who has betrayed their oath."

Russell nodded. "Yes. You're right." He held out a hand for Clive to shake. "I'll speak with Godfrey, but no one else. If the three of us can't take them out, it has been an honor to be your second."

Shaking Russell's hand, Clive said, "The honor is mine. If I don't survive the night, you know what to do."

"Yes."

"Good," Clive nodded. "Go then and prepare."

When the door closed behind Russell, I stalked over to Clive and drilled a finger into his chest. "What the hell is this 'if I don't survive' bullshit? You're not dying. And there are four of us, not three!"

Clive was shaking his head before I stopped talking. "No. This is vampire business. I won't have you hurt because of political maneuvering. Stay with Owen. He'll take care of you."

When he tried to pull me close, I shoved him back. "That's who you think I am? The going gets tough and I need to be protected? Screw that! I'm not hiding anymore, remember? If there's a fight, I'm in it. The *four* of us are going to wipe the floor with those New Orleans usurpers."

Studying me, he shook his head. "I can't lose you. I won't. You're stronger, yes, but you're still learning."

"Clive." I moved forward, resting my hand on his chest. "I love you, but I will kick your ass if you ever say anything this stupid again." When he opened his mouth to respond, I moved my hand to cover it. "No. We're in this together. Whatever it is, we're together. Battling syphilitic zombies or moonlit strolls. Good, bad, or insanely weird, it doesn't matter. Partners, okay?"

He kissed my palm before moving my hand. "Point taken. Are you sure you're up for a vampire bloodbath?"

"That's my favorite kind of bloodbath."

Shaking his head, he twined his fingers with mine. "Do the zombies have to be syphilitic? Being zombies isn't enough?"

Shrugging, I swung our joined hands. "Seemed worse. So, we have visitors coming and I need to change."

Clive raised his eyebrows and surveyed my hoodie, threadbare jeans, and running shoes. "I like it."

"Nope. I need to score higher on the badass scale." Lifting our joined hands to my lips, I kissed his fingers. "You, Russell, and Godfrey go work out the battle plan and then let me know my part. I'm going to go dive deep into that closet you keep adding clothes to and find something that says, *I will fuck you up and then giggle as I lick your blood from my fingers.*"

TWO

I'm Not Insecure. You Are

Clive found me almost an hour later, freshly showered, blown dry, made-up, wearing a robe, and hunting through the closet in the sidepiece's bedroom I'd been given when I'd first moved in. It held an insane amount of clothing, so much so that some had migrated over to the closet in the bedroom I now shared with Clive.

So far, I'd found a pair of black leather pants and motorcycle boots, but I was still weighing my options. Should I lull them into a false sense of security by appearing soft and harmless or would it be better to earn a modicum of respect at the jump by appearing battle ready?

I was sorting through tops in the depths of the huge closet when I felt his presence at the door. "Quick question. What are you wearing?" Turning, I found him leaning on the door sill, heat in his eyes as he watched me. "None of that, mister. We've got a melee to prepare for."

Grinning, his eyes traveled over me as he drew near. "I'm sure there's time enough for both," he said before pulling me into a deep, scorching kiss.

When his hand trailed down to untie my robe, I disentangled

myself. "If we survive this night, we'll meet back here for closet sexy times. Right now, I need to get ready."

Sighing, he leaned against the built-in shelving at his back. "If we don't live, do you really want to give up our last chance to be together?"

He tried to sound glib, but I could hear the worry in his voice. He didn't think I was strong enough to take on a roomful of vampires. I'd have to prove him wrong.

"If you're staying, help me with what to wear. Will the New Orleans vamps be dressed in suits like the rest of you weirdly formal guys?"

He shrugged, his eyes traveling over me as though trying to memorize me. "Undoubtedly."

"So I should go the opposite, right?"

"You're thinking running shorts and a tank top?"

"Ha. I was considering the badassery of leather pants and motorcycle boots," I said.

He nodded slowly as he ran a hand down my arm, found my fingers, and squeezed. "Wear whatever you wish. I know you're determined to fight tonight. I'm trying to make my peace with that decision. Stay close to me, though." Kissing my cheek, he turned to go. "I mean it, Sam. You'd best survive or I'll be quite put out."

Deciding that since I wasn't a vamp and would be seen as a nonentity anyway, I went with a softer, more unassuming ensemble for tonight. The leathers would need to wait until I picked up a few things. So, clad in soft, worn jeans, running shoes, and a sea green cashmere wraparound sweater, I trotted down the stairs to the foyer.

"Sam?"

Turning, I found Clive and Russell standing together, wearing matching expressions of boredom. "Hey. I heard you had visitors coming," I said in a normal voice, hoping any straining ears would assume we knew nothing about what was coming.

"Yes. I'm afraid our dinner plans will need to be postponed until they leave." Clive held out a hand and I went to him.

"I doubt they'll stay long, Sire," Russell said. "My guess is that they will pay their respects and then leave." Russell's gaze bore into mine. "Miss Quinn, are you sure you wouldn't rather check on The Slaughtered Lamb's progress? I can assure you, tonight will be tedious, filled with posturing under the guise of fawning."

"I appreciate the warning," I said, patting his shoulder. "But I'm sticking."

He gusted out a sigh, his dark skin glinting in the low light. "As you wish."

The butler came out of a side hall and went to the double doors, throwing them open. "They are arriving, Sire."

Three black Town Cars drove into the courtyard, their windows dark. Clive's security team surrounded the cars and opened their doors. The first out was a gorgeous woman. She had skin darker than Russell's, closely cropped hair, large liquid eyes, and a body designed for runways. Bucking tradition, she wore a long, form-fitting magenta dress. Men wearing black suits that might have been fashionable in the 1800s filed out of the cars around her, but she drew all eyes.

I heard a strange barely audible sound beside me and realized that this woman wasn't a stranger to Clive or Russell.

"Lover, it's so good to see you again." Her voice was a deep purr. Holding out her arms, she walked straight to Clive.

He welcomed her with an embrace and a kiss that lasted far too long. "Amélie, what a lovely surprise. I didn't realize you were now residing in New Orleans. Last I heard, you were somewhere in Europe."

The men she'd arrived with stood behind her, clearly ceding authority to her. A few glances cut my way before trailing off, disinterested. Twelve with Amélie. Was that a lot or a normal number for a visiting party? They didn't seem too menacing, but vampires, unlike werewolves, usually weren't muscle-bound. Their threat was less obvious.

Amélie had plastered herself to Clive. "That was ages ago. I've made Louisiana my new home." She ran her hand appreciatively down his chest. "I'm hurt you weren't keeping tabs on me."

He tightened his arm around her waist. "I assure you it was in self-defense. I'm still nursing a broken heart."

Her laugh was a throaty invitation to her bed, and one Clive acknowledged with dark eyes.

"Welcome to the San Francisco nocturne." Russell bowed his head. "Please enter and allow us to slake your thirsts."

Clive and Amélie entered first, still wrapped around one another. All of Amélie's men followed in their wake, trailed by Russell and Godfrey, Clive's third. Godfrey looked like a British rake on loan from a historical romance, with chiseled features, light brown hair, and a ready smile. I was left standing in the courtyard, forgotten. One of Clive's vamps smirked at me as he walked back to resume his post at the gate.

"Sam, do come along." Clive's voice called from deep in the house.

Excellent hearing meant I also picked up Amélie's rejoinder of, "Oh, must we? I hate the smell of wet dog."

The ensuing laughter, both inside and outside the house, hurt. Recognizing the sound of Clive's chuckle adding to the others felt like a knife in the gut. It was theater, though, and I had a role to play. I didn't want to be the beaten dog with her tail between her legs. I wanted to rip out their throats, starting with Amélie. Instead, I would meekly join their party, following Clive like a grateful stray. I'd agreed to stick close, so I would.

I found them in the large salon. The walls were a dull gold, the floors a deep mahogany covered in rich Persian rugs. The furniture was of the delicate, antique, and very expensive variety. More of Clive's vamps joined the soiree. They were milling about, speaking in hushed tones, but it was more theater. All attention was on Clive and Amélie.

Stationing myself a little behind and on the opposite side of Clive from Amélie, I did my best to become invisible. I stared vacantly ahead, as though waiting for my master to recall my existence and give me a command. As Clive paid me no mind, the others quickly forgot about me as well. Servers snaked through the room, carrying trays of cut crystal wine glasses filled with blood.

Amélie threw back her head and laughed at something Clive said. Singing loudly in my head, I hadn't heard what prompted it. I was trying desperately to keep the snarl from my lips and the growl from my throat every time she rested her hand on his arm or called him lover. The other vampires pantomimed normal behavior, drinking, murmuring, nodding, but they were taut as bowstrings. Waiting.

I felt the tension in the room change before I could identify why. Once I started paying attention again, I realized that Amélie's men had subtly taken up positions around Clive, hemming him in, cutting him off from Russell and Godfrey. They were about to attack, and she was their diversion.

I grabbed Clive's arm. When he glanced back at me, eyebrows raised in mild surprise, I yanked him down right as a sword swung over his head where his neck had been a moment earlier.

Eyes turning vamp black, he gave me a hard kiss and then blinked out of sight as the vamp holding the sword had his head ripped off his body. Blood splattered across Amélie's dress. She stood frozen, one vamp down and turning to dust as another head went flying. That moment of shock made me hesitate. I should have killed her. Lord knew I'd dreamed of little else since they'd arrived, but if she'd been used, unaware of the plan, she didn't deserve true death.

Out of the corner of my eye, I saw a vamp fly at me, eyes black, fangs glistening. It was one of Clive's. The smirker. Long and razor-sharp, my claws sprung from my fingertips. Vampires were fast, but so was I. Before he could touch me, I'd raked my claws across his neck, slicing off his head.

Russell and Godfrey had their hands full, taking on two each. I couldn't worry about them, though. I had vamps to kill. Two flew at me and I spun, arms out, claws digging through their torsos. They each stuttered to a stop, hands flying to their chests. A split-second of fear slid over their faces before they both shot forward. I leaped straight up, landing behind them, and then slammed them both face down on the floor. As they struggled, I made short work of carving through bone and gristle. Three down.

Dust and clothes littered the floor of the salon. Russell and Godfrey were bloodied but still fighting, while Clive blinked in and out of sight, taking down one after the other. Retracting the claws on my right hand, I grabbed for the fallen sword and came up swinging, halving one vamp from hip to shoulder. A vase flew over my head, which seemed odd. Who was throwing vases?

I scanned the room searching for magenta, and didn't find it. Had Amélie run? A body slammed into my back, making me stagger forward. When I spun, I found nothing but settling dust. Godfrey needed to pay attention to where he was flinging dying vamps. Clive, Russell, and Godfrey were battling their way through the few remaining vamps in the room.

When one ran for the door, trying to escape, I swung, letting the sword sail. It pinned the retreating vamp to the wall. As he scrambled to free himself, I ran to him and shoved the sword farther in to keep him in place and then slashed my claws through his neck, sending his head rolling.

It came to a stop near a glossy black shoe connected to the vamp who'd appeared in the doorway. I'd barely registered his arrival when he had a gun at my temple. *Well, shit.*

Clive's shout of "No!" made the vamp with the gun smile.

"Should have thought of that before you decided to kill

everyone. Now, my remaining friends and I are walking out of here, unless you'd like your dog's brains splattered all over this wall." He'd found Clive's weak spot.

Clive kept a squirming vamp pinned under his foot. His gaze rested on me a moment before returning to the gunman.

"What kind of sorry-ass vampire carries a gun?" I asked. He hated Clive. I could feel the loathing pouring from him. Who was he?

The vamp smacked the gun across my forehead. A flash of black accompanied the pain, but it had been done casually, without rancor. He cared about me only as much as my death might hurt Clive. It was Clive's true death he wanted.

I could feel his emotions like an itch in the back of my brain. Only Clive writhing on the floor in agony would please him. He dreamed of killing Clive slowly and with extreme malice. One of the vamps Godfrey had been fighting tried to break and run. Godfrey tackled him to the ground, while Russell kept his trapped against the wall, unable to move. Clive's wriggled under him but then froze when Clive glanced down.

The vamp with the gun took advantage of Clive's distraction. I could hear his thoughts. When he angled the gun to take aim at Clive, I sprang, taking him down. A second later, he was on the ground, me sitting on his chest and his gun under my jaw.

He wanted to pull the trigger but couldn't. I stared into his eyes, ignoring the crashing behind me. It was like an Alpha challenge. It shouldn't have worked. He was a vampire, not a werewolf. It hadn't been a conscious decision. Head pounding, I felt his intent and overrode it. I could feel his brain fluttering under the pressure. He didn't want to give way, but I wasn't giving him a choice.

The quiet grunts of vampire battle surrounded us, but I ignored them. There was one battle to be won right now. This one. I was not going down like this. The black drained from his eyes, leaving brown irises filled with fear. His mind struggled in my grasp as I tightened my hold, slid mental claws in, and shredded. When his eyes went blank, I reached up, wrapped my hand around his, and guided the gun under his own jaw. One more mental shove caused him to pull the trigger. I closed my eyes as blood sprayed.

Wiping my face, I was consumed with one thought: How the hell had I done that?

THREE

Dust to Dust

"Sam!" Clive pulled me up, fear written on his face, eyes back to stormy gray. Running his hands over my blood-spattered body, he checked for damage.

"It's not mine. I'm fine." My vision narrowed, black encroaching. No, no. No passing out. That would negate all my badassery tonight. "I'm fine. The blood's not mine. No one touched me."

As he stared at me, emotion drained from his expression. Face blank, he turned away.

"Wait, are *you* okay?" This wasn't like him, neither the panic nor the blankness. "Were you hurt?" Vision narrowing to pinpricks, I tried to appear normal, leaning against the wall, bracing my knees. I was not passing out.

Absently, he replied, "I'm perfectly well."

I'd gone blind. My head was still pounding, but I was upright and conscious. I didn't feel faint. What was going on? I wiped at my eyes as I heard Clive's footsteps move away from me, toward Russell and Godfrey. Had the vampire's blood spattered in my eyes? My heart raced. Had undead blood made me blind?

"How many of our own?"

"Sire," Godfrey began. "We counted eight from our own nocturne who fought on their side."

And then the pounding in my head eased and they all swam back into sight. It was as though the lights were slowly turned up, dispelling the dark. I'd worry about this later. There was already too much tension in the room. I didn't need to add to it, to Clive's worry, when I didn't even know what that was. Pushing off the wall, I moved into the room, hoping everyone was too preoccupied by death and mayhem to notice whatever was going on with me.

"Eight more." Clive made his way to the fireplace, walking over the dusty remains and scattered clothes of the twenty truly dead vampires who littered the salon floor. A couple hadn't turned to dust in death. Huh. They were headless corpses. Where were the—oh. The heads had rolled or been kicked to the edges of the room. I'd need to ask someone why we had dust and corpses. Later, though.

Clive gripped the mantle and bowed his head. "And the others? No one came to fight on our side. Have they all betrayed me?"

Russell and Godfrey shared an uncomfortable glance. "We don't know, Sire."

"Perhaps you could search the house for them. Find out why they left us to be slaughtered."

Russell and Godfrey rushed from the room.

"You guys are pretty quiet fighters," I began. "Other than whoever was throwing vases, it was a mostly silent brawl. Maybe they didn't know it was going on." I doubted it, but I'd say anything to take away the sorrow weighing him down.

"Do you think they're sitting in their rooms, watching TV?" He snarled. "Reading a book?" The mantle cracked under the pressure of his hands. He turned, his expression ravaged. "I called them, Sam." He tapped his temple. "I called them to us, and they ignored the summons. My people abandoned me."

"Not all of them. Russell and Godfrey are still loy—"

"Two? This nocturne had forty-four members not a month ago. We're one of the largest in the world. In the last two weeks, ten have been given true death for actively working against me. The rest have apparently fled." He sat heavily in a nearby chair.

"Well—"

"And you almost had your head blown off, not fifteen feet from me." He glared, as though it was my fault.

"Hey, I dealt with him." I studied the gun sitting in a pile of dust and wondered. "Not entirely sure how I did that, but the point is, I'm standing here fine and dandy. So, you have three people who are loyal to you, not two."

"I remember him. He was no one, someone who'd requested to join the nocturne and had been refused. It's common enough. I didn't like his attitude and politely sent him on his way. Is this our future? Everyone with a perceived injury will come after you to get at me?" He ran his fingers through his hair in frustration, not realizing they were covered in dead vamp dust. "I tried." He turned to me. "To get into his mind, to debilitate him with pain. I couldn—"

Godfrey ran into the room. "Sire, we've found them. They've been poisoned. The traitors locked them in the safe room. They couldn't respond to your call. Two will likely need to be given true death, Matthew and Jacob. They're too new to have the defenses needed to overcome the effects. The rest are either vomiting up the tainted blood or unconscious. We're not—we don't know how many more we might lose, Sire."

Clive rose. "We are unguarded tonight. Those swearing to protect the nocturne and myself are here among the dead. Secure the gates, check security, and then lock up the house as well as you can. We have no idea if this was the entirety of the visiting party or if a second wave is about to hit us." He studied the scattered clothes. "Did we get them all or did any escape to tell the tale?"

"Amélie," I said.

He glanced at me, surprised, as though he'd forgotten I was in the room. "What about her?"

I gestured to the ground. "No magenta dress."

"Of course." He turned to Godfrey. "Go. Secure our home. Amélie may be back with more."

Godfrey raced past me as I moved closer to Clive. There was something wrong with him. Yes, we'd been attacked, but I'd seen him under pressure before. Had he been hurt? Was he poisoned too? He seemed to be vacillating between rage and emptiness. Russell and Godfrey had noticed as well.

"Did you drink any of the blood tonight?" I moved in closer.

He glanced up from his study of the salon floor. "Yes, of course."

"Maybe you should stick your finger down your throat or something." His weird calm was freaking me out.

He blinked and then focused on me again. "Don't be ridiculous. I haven't been poisoned."

"Should I slap you?"

His brows drew together as his focus turned back to me. "For kissing Amélie? You know I was—"

"No. Well, yes. That too. But to snap you out of whatever fog you're in. Three-quarters of your nocturne are loyal and have been hurt, and yet you're standing here, staring at the carpet. I don't want to tell you how to do your job, but—"

"He meant to kill you. He had a gun to your head and I froze. In that split second, the long and happy life I'd envisioned spending with you disappeared and I saw myself standing over yet another grave. I tried reaching for his mind, but I couldn't touch it. I was failing and you were dead."

I grabbed his hand and squeezed hard. "But I'm not dead. I'm not fragile." Ignoring the temporary blindness, I unleashed the claws on my free hand and said, "Werewolf, remember? I killed five vampires tonight. You don't need to worry about—"

"But I did. I was so consumed with fear over losing you that I froze. I'm Master of this City and I froze. Even now, I know the choice I need to make. I have a responsibility to this nocturne, to all the supernaturals in this city. That responsibility supersedes any tender feelings on my part. I know this and yet the idea of giving you up cores me and so I stand here desperately searching for a different answer."

"Sire, the gates have been locked. I contacted Megaera. She said she was willing to perch on the roof and keep an eye out for us." Godfrey bowed, a wary gaze on his master.

Megaera was a friend and one of the Erinyes, or Furies you may have read about in Greek mythology. She and her two sisters were winged goddesses of vengeance. She was a good choice for the job.

Clive nodded at Godfrey. "Perfect. No one will get past Meg and I'm sure she misses the consequence-free slaughter of her youth. Tell Russell I'll be right down."

Godfrey departed, leaving Clive and me struggling, grieving a breakup that hadn't yet happened.

"Clive—"

"Why don't you go get some sleep while I deal with my people." The exhaustion in his voice broke my heart.

"Please. Let's talk about this." I needed to smack him upside the head and dislodge this dumbass idea of his.

"Later. They're suffering," he said as he walked out the door without a backward glance.

"But so are you."

I didn't follow him downstairs. He needed time with his people, and they needed time away from me while they healed. The vampires suffering in the basement may have been loyal to Clive, but they wouldn't have shed any tears if he dumped my ass. I considered going to the Slaughtered Lamb, but it was still under construction. There'd be no place to sleep and my wards hadn't yet been rebuilt. Like it or not, I was staying put.

I went to the bedroom I'd been given when I first moved in and tried not to think about the resignation in his eyes, the sorrow in his voice. I hadn't gone through hell to be with him only to give up that easily. We could make this work. If our biggest problem was him loving me too much, did that really count as a problem?

Locking the hallway door and closing the one adjoining our bedroom suites, I went to the bed, intending to lie down before remembering I was covered in blood. Detouring to the bathroom, I stripped off my clothes and jumped into the shower. Steaming water sluiced off my cold, blood-spackled skin. I scrubbed off layers, trying to get clean, attempting not to think of the vampires I'd given their true death.

Wrapped in a warm robe, I went to the closet. The leather pants and motorcycle boots still laid on a bench. Clive and I had promised to meet back here for sexy times if we survived the night. Instead, he was nursing his vampires back to undeath and I was alone, waiting to be dumped.

It hit all at once. Breath uneven, as my body trembled. Second best and alone. I'd forever be an afterthought. Abandoned. He'd said he loved me and yet here we were, him unable to conceive of a future where I stood at his side. I'd battled with him, killed alongside him, and still I'd never be enough. I'd never be good enough. I was pathetic. Alone.

Blinding pain stabbed me. I dropped to the floor of the closet, my robed arms over my head, blocking out the now too-bright light. It was too much. What was the point? I'd tried so hard and yet was all alone again, abandoned and unloved. An abomination.

Abomination?

I sat up fast, ignoring the spinning in my pounding head and grabbed my necklace. Abigail was worming her way in. She'd found me vulnerable, exhausted, shaky, and she'd pushed into my thoughts, trying to break me. With a Herculean shove, I evicted my psychotic aunt from my mind. She wanted me dead, but I wasn't going to follow her mental breadcrumbs to suicide.

Standing up, head hammering, I let the robe drop and dressed to go out. I wasn't staying here. I needed to get away from vampire drama, clear my head, and figure out what I wanted to do. Not Clive, not Abigail. Me.

After lacing up my running shoes—the ones not covered in blood—I wrapped a scarf around my neck, pulled a knit cap over my damp hair, and zipped myself into a fleece-lined hoodie that was perfect for cold, foggy San Francisco nights.

I overrode the alarm at the front door and stepped outside. Well, if there really was a second wave coming, I guess I'd be the front line.

Silence.

Good enough. I checked my watch. How was it possible that it wasn't even midnight yet? This was already the longest night ever and it wasn't over.

"And where do you think *you're* going?"

I jumped. I'll admit it.

Huge, heavy wings beat at the air once, twice, and then Meg landed lightly in front of me. She had long, wild hair and gray, scaly skin that absorbed the blood upon whom her vengeance was wrought. She wore black, because her clothes, unlike her skin, showed blood stains and black forgave so much.

Crossing her arms, she barred the way. "Well?"

"Hey, Meg. It was nice of you to come help the vamps." I jabbed my thumb back at the mansion door. "We had a bit of a bloodbath—dustbath—whatever. Which reminds me, do you know why some vamps leave corpses? It seemed insensitive to ask at the time."

Meg's fingers drummed on her arms. "I only agreed to guard the house because you were in it."

"Aww, that's sweet. But I thought you were forbidden from intervening to help me." That one still stung. Meg had known all along who had been trying to kill me a couple of weeks ago and had kept it to herself because she'd been forbidden by someone bigger and stronger—no idea who—from helping. It's not like Meg and I were best buds, but I thought we were friends. She'd sat her goddess ass on my barstool almost every night for years and then she'd stepped back and let whatever was going to happen to me happen. Yeah, I was still smarting over that one.

"Do you think I care what vampires do to one another? They're already dead. They should lie down and spare the rest of us the grief."

Not that I hadn't occasionally had the same thought myself, I was still surprised by the sentiment from Meg. "I thought you liked Clive."

"He has been a good Master of this City, so I don't dislike him. I just don't care."

Oh. "Then why did you agree to protect them?"

"I didn't. I agreed to protect the house from attack because you were in it. That Godfrey was very specific that you had survived a vampire battle but needed my protection to keep you from further harm."

"Wow, manipulative much?" I shook my head, disgusted with the lot of them. "So, Sam's a mongrel dog and an embarrassment to their Master unless she's handy for securing a goddess guard." I wanted to march back in there and knock some fanged heads together. Assholes.

"As I said, they need to remain dead and stop bothering the living. As to your question about the dead, the young ones— those who have not been vampires long—leave desiccated corpses. The old ones turn into the dust that should be in their coffins."

Made sense. "Okay, Meg. I'm outta here. Keep an eye out for a beautiful Black woman in a bright pink dress. She's trouble. I, on the other hand, have had more than enough vampire shit for one night. I'm off to beg Owen for the use of his couch."

"I have a couch."

"And I'm sure it's a nice one." I motioned to the house. "I'm sorry they misled you. It would be nice if you kept an eye out, though. I love Clive and Russell's a good man. The rest?" I shrugged.

"I have a couch," she repeated, her black eyes staring into mine.

"Yep. Heard you the first time." I stuffed my hands into my pockets, trying to remember where Owen lived. Did I know? Would he answer my call this late?

"You don't need Owen. You can stay with me tonight. For as long as you need."

"Oh." Feeling pinned under her goddess gaze, I smiled weakly. "Thanks. I'd appreciate that."

"Good." She reached out, pulled me into her arms, beat her wings, and we were off.

"Wait! What about guarding them?"

Heavy wings beat the night air. "If it means that much to you, I'll ask Horus to watch the house. He owes me."

FOUR

The Only Way to Fly

W ith every beat of Meg's wings, the earth dropped farther away. She held me in an iron grip, so I wasn't worried about falling. It was more that I lacked the desire to fly without a plane surrounding me. Meg clearly didn't feel the cold, but the icy wind whipped tears from my eyes and set my teeth to chattering.

The harbor lights remained on my left, so we were flying east across the city, angling a little to the north, toward Fisherman's Wharf. We'd barely cleared the white spires of Sts. Peter and Paul Cathedral when Meg stopped beating her wings, gliding down to a tall, narrow, derelict church, sitting in the shadow of the behemoth cathedral blocking it. She alit on the roof beside the bell tower and shoved me over the half wall.

Once back on my own feet, I studied the five-foot square bell tower. The wood was rotted, holes leaking hazy light from the foggy North Beach neighborhood around us. A trapdoor under where a huge bell should have been hanging was flipped open, a ladder leading into the depths of the church.

Pointing up into the empty bell tower, I said, "You're missing something."

Meg tipped her head back to take in the dark, empty interior of the spire and shrugged. "I was constantly hitting my head on the damn thing. What do I need a bell for?" She pulled out her phone, swiped through contacts, tapped Horus, and then walked to the hole in the floor and dropped through.

Not having wings, I chose the ladder route. I ended up on a rickety catwalk that traversed the exposed interior beams of the church. The narrow walkway bounced and creaked with every step I took.

"I swear, Meg, if I fall to my death in this joint, I'm haunting you."

"I wouldn't recommend using that. The wood is old. Termites had eaten through most of it before I bought the place." Meg's voice floated up to me from somewhere near where an altar should be.

I stopped abruptly, gripping the narrow rails on either side of me, afraid to take what might be my last step. "Meg? I'm super not cool with this. If you wanted to kill me, you could have dropped me while we were flying over the city."

I heard a sigh with a muttered, "Bitch and moan."

"Some of us don't have wings."

The catwalk jolted. My stomach dropped and I knew my time was up. Before my life could pass before my eyes, her arm wrapped around my middle and we dropped fifty feet to the floor of the church.

When Meg let go and stalked off, I gave myself a minute to be grateful for my return to the ground. Most of the pews had been removed, creating a kind of living room area. The altar was gone, a large bed in its place.

I pointed to her open-air bedroom. "Isn't that kind of sacrilegious?"

Meg glanced where I pointed but didn't respond, continuing to work in a makeshift kitchen in what would have been a side chapel.

"And using a hot plate in a wooden death trap seems super unsafe too."

"Bitch, bitch, bitch. I'm sorry I offered you my couch." Meg brought me a mug of something that smelled deliciously chocolatey.

I took the oddly pristine mug—given the dark, decrepit building we were standing in. "Thank you for the cocoa and sorry about the complaints. It's been a night."

Flinging a dusty sheet off a beautiful leather couch, she nodded her acceptance and sat down. "I don't come here every day. The covers keep the furniture clean." She waved an arm up. "I vacuum and fly up to deal with cobwebs, but there's only so much I'm willing to do for a place I rarely stay."

I moved another sheet and sat in a lovely, overstuffed chair. "So, how did you end up living in a church?"

Meg shrugged, taking a sip of the whiskey she'd poured herself. "I like it here. After they built the cathedral next door, they decommissioned this one. I bought it before it could be torn down and turned into a blacksmith shop or a livery stable. The original Peter and Paul was built in the late eighteen hundreds a couple of blocks away. It burned in the 1906 earthquake. They built the one you see now a decade or so later as its replacement."

"Does 'decommissioned' mean this isn't holy ground?"

Meg smirked before taking another sip. "Theoretically. There needs to be a deconsecration ceremony on the site by a priest. I may have scared such a priest away, leaving my home firmly situated on holy ground." She pointed toward her bed. "It's not a church anymore. I can put my bed wherever I want. The fact that it remains holy land means demons and assorted dark dead-lies can't get to me here."

"Nice." I wondered if I could trick a priest into accidentally blessing the Slaughtered Lamb to keep demons away. Then again, that might mess with my half-demon cook Dave's ability to make me cookies on the regular. Never mind. Totally not worth it.

She slid a sheet off a dark wood coffee table and put her feet up. "Now, why are visiting vampires attacking our locals?"

I related the entire evening, starting with the ghost's warning. I could use some goddess insight into whatever the hell was going on.

"Sounds like typical vampire power plays and politics. They expend too much energy on etiquette and replicating social constructs put in place hundreds of years ago by 'cursed denizens of the night.'" She air-quoted that last part. Crossing her legs at the ankles, she continued, "When was the last time you saw a mob with torches and pitchforks? They don't have to run through sewers and suck on rats anymore. No one even believes they exist. It's probably the forced living arrangements that's bred the unending animosity," she scoffed. "Just let them all have their own apartments. Most drink bagged blood at this point anyway."

I thought about it. "Good point. Why do they live in upscale frat houses?"

"They're a community built on power and treachery. If they were allowed to go off and live their best undeaths, how could they threaten to overpower one another? All that bowing and scraping can be addictive." She winked at me. "Take it from a goddess."

Nodding, I sipped my cocoa. Clive sure did get a lot of bows in his daily life, but I didn't think he enjoyed it as much as Meg believed. He was happier and more relaxed when we went out alone, without the scraping and bowing.

"Now, tell me about this ghost that warned you."

I explained about the apparition blocking my path, her filmy image blinking in and out of sight, the way she grabbed my wrist in order to be heard.

"She gained strength by touching you?" Meg stared intently at me.

Shrugging, I replied, "Seemed to."

"I think," she began slowly, her fingers tapping against the side of her whiskey glass, "that you're wasting your time training with Owen's mother."

"Wow. Don't pull your punches, Meg. Give it to me straight." Yeah, I was a failure as a wicche. I didn't think this was the exact time we needed to get into that, though. I much preferred picking apart the vamps and analyzing what was wrong with *them*. Why did we have to move on to me?

She rolled her eyes. "I'm saying I think your gift is necromancy, which isn't something Lydia can help you with."

"Necromancy? As in raising the dead?" Eww. What the hell was I going to do with a bunch of zombies? As superpowers went, that one sucked.

"As in speaking with and influencing the dead. You saw and were able to communicate with a ghost, one who became stronger when she touched you. Because of her warning, Clive is still enjoying his undeath. And I believe it's your innate ability to influence the dead that allowed you to get into the mind of the vampire with the gun and push him to shoot his own head off."

Meg finished her drink. "Considering the time you spend with vampires, I'd say necromancy is a gift, indeed."

My phone buzzed. Patting my pockets in search of it, I found it in my hoodie.

Clive: Where are you?

Me: With Meg

Clive: …you're on the roof?

I snickered.

Me: Sorry to break it to you, but Godfrey got Meg to help by saying she'd be guarding me. When I took off to find a couch not in your house, she followed. Soooo, no Meg. She called Horus to take over, though.

Clive: I see.

That was it. *I see.* No follow-up apology for being a dick and threatening to dump me. Dots finally appeared.

Clive: I was hoping to talk with you tonight. Where are you?

Me: I'm at Meg's and I'm not telling you where that is. I fought with you. I killed 5 vampires and you're all 'Oh, I can't be with you because…' who the fuck knows?

"You know, it's quite rude to text when someone is sitting with you."

"Shut up, Meg."

Me: AND Meg thinks I was able to fuck with that last vamp and make him blow his own brains out because I'm a necromancer. So, remember that the next time you plan to dump me. I'll force you to skip and whistle in front of your little vampire friends!

Clive: That's a disturbing yet effective threat. Answer your phone.

A second later, it began to ring. I hopped up and walked into the shadowy back of the church before answering. I knew Meg could still hear—probably both sides of the conversation—but it felt more private. Sliding into the last pew, I hit answer.

"What?"

There was a long pause. "I'm aware I've screwed up badly and am prepared to grovel in whichever form you'd prefer."

"What if that form takes the shape of you shaving your head and always walking three steps behind me?" I heard Meg snort but ignored her.

"I'd say I'd rather walk through life at your side, but if that's what you need, I'll consider it. I would at least enjoy the view."

I did have a good ass. It was all the running. "So, if you're not calling to let me down easy, why are you?"

"Because I wanted to hear your voice."

Meg made a retching sound.

"So, what was all that about, anyway? Why is New Orleans trying to kill you?"

"I don't believe the entire city would like to see me dead. Lafitte, however… he believes a competition exists where there is none."

"Because you could wipe the floor with him?"

"One of many reasons, yes."

"So why send his people to get slaughtered?"

"That is the question. Amélie doesn't usually align herself with the weak. Unless, of course, she's planning to take over the city."

"Can you do me a favor?" I asked.

"Anything,"

"Can you check the house, make sure there aren't any stray vamps that Amélie may have planted somewhere, waiting to slip out of the shadows and whack off your head. As it could be San Francisco she's set her sights on."

"I had the same thought and have already checked security footage. Amélie left through the front door and drove off in one of the Town Cars. For safety's sake, though, Russell, Godfrey, and I checked every inch of the house. That was when I discovered you weren't in our room."

"I needed out."

"Understood. Are you staying there tonight?"

"Yep. It's a really nice couch, so I'm good."

"Meg," he pitched his voice louder, "I expect you to protect her."

"I don't answer to you, vampire." She paused. "But I wouldn't have taken her if I was planning to abandon her. Go away now. Let her sleep."

"My hostess has made it clear that she finds all this texting and phoning in her presence rude, so I should hang up now."

Clive sighed. "All right. If you need me, call. I know where Meg's church is. Make sure she tells you how to get out before she falls asleep. She sleeps like the dead and you can't fly out the bell tower as she can."

"Okay."

"And I love you."

Smiling in the dark, my heart gave a kick. "I love you too."

"I'll see you tomorrow, yes?"

"Yep."

"Good. Tonight's attack must be answered. I want to see you before I leave for New Orleans."

FIVE

Of Trapdoors and Tunnels

Oh, hell no. If he thought he was going to New Orleans and waging war without me, he was sorely mistaken. I was the perfect secret weapon for dealing with vampires.

"I left you a blanket and a pillow. Do you need anything else?" Meg was standing by the couch, hands at her hips as though daring me to ask for something more.

"Um." I glanced around the shadowy church. "Please tell me you have a bathroom." She never used the Slaughtered Lamb toilet. I had no idea if goddesses even used toilets.

She pointed into the dark recesses of the left side of the church. "Over there."

"Thank goodness," I sighed.

"As for how to get out, follow me." Meg led me past her bed to an ancient organ. Pipes of varying lengths and widths rose up the back wall. My fingers itched to play a chord on the keyboard, to see if sound still boomed from the pipes.

Meg followed my gaze and said, "It doesn't work. Hasn't for decades."

Bummer.

"But this tunnel was put in for the repair of the organ, so it still serves a purpose." She flung open a trapdoor in the floor next to the organ. "There's a small storage room down there with tools and spare parts. On the back wall is a door. It leads to an earthen tunnel under the church. At the end of the tunnel is a storm cellar door. The lock is on this side, so you can get out. If you try to come back in some other time, you'll find it locked. If you need to break my lock to enter, please replace it."

"Of course."

Meg nodded, kicked the trapdoor closed, and strode to her bed, pulling a tunic with a long slit down the back over her head. It took me a moment to realize what I was seeing. Her wings were folded in, acting as a kind of long, feathery cape running down the back of her body. As I had no desire to see Meg naked, I turned my head, studying organ pipes and carvings on the walls as I made my way to the side chapel.

The bathroom, thankfully, turned out to be surprisingly modern. Maybe the supernatural construction crew who were working on my bookstore and bar had put in her bathroom. She had a massive shower with multiple heads, which made sense, as Meg had huge wings that needed to be cleaned as well.

I found a couple of extra toothbrushes still in their packaging. I took one, brushed my teeth, used the facilities, and then opened the bathroom door, finding the church in darkness. Night vision was darn handy. I tiptoed to the couch, pulled off my boots, and stretched out, wrapping myself in her spare blanket.

Damn. I'd forgotten to ask Meg about the temporary blindness. Maybe she had some insight for me. "Meg?" Nothing. Louder, I said "Meg?" Her snores were the only response. Bone weary but unable to turn off my brain, I tossed and turned. Images of gorgeous, perfect Amélie draped all over Clive, kissing Clive, warred with the damage a bullet can do to a person's head. Blood and gray matter exploded over and over in the dark behind my closed eyelids. And then again, Amélie of the perfect body and unmarked skin. She commanded the respect of all the vampires in the room. No one sneered at her or whispered insults.

When exhaustion finally won, I fell into a nightmare-laden sleep.

I awoke in dim light to the sound of Meg's snores. There was a loud crashing outside the church. Tensing, I prepared for another battle before realizing it was the sound of a garbage truck. I reached into a boot and pulled out my phone. It was a little after seven in the morning. I'd slept a couple of hours at the most. I considered rolling over but knew I'd never fall back asleep.

If Clive was planning to go to New Orleans, I was going with him, which meant I needed to prepare. After using the bathroom and the toothbrush again, I put on my boots and made my way to Meg's bed. I'd much rather be flown out of here than crawl through a tunnel.

Her sheet had fallen to her waist, leaving her gray, scaly torso exposed. Averting my eyes, I said, "Meg." There wasn't even a hitch in her snoring.

"Meg!"

Still nothing.

Gaze on the carved wood around where the tabernacle should have rested, I reached out a hand and shook her shoulder. "Wake up, Meg!"

Not even a stutter in her breathing.

"What if I were a demon or some serial killer? Are you going to lie there and let me cut you up?"

When I unleashed my claws to make my point, her eyes flew open and her hand wrapped around my wrist, crushing it.

"Ow, Meg. Stop it! I just wanted a ride out of here."

She released my hand and rolled over. "Use the tunnel," she mumbled before falling back to sleep.

Damn. I went over to the cleverly concealed door in the floor. After a moment of study, I found a release and flipped open the trapdoor. There was a ladder, but the wood was rotted, so I jumped the ten feet down, landing easily.

Oh, yuck.

"Couldn't dust down here, could you!" The walls and ceiling were spun with cobwebs. Great. Where there were webs, there were spiders, an army of spiders.

Arms extended, I brushed away white, sticky threads and ducked under huge knots containing bug parts, eventually finding the side room. A wispy apparition was there and then gone.

"Hello?"

The ghost didn't reappear.

Wishing I had a moment to study the antiques, I instead searched for the tunnel door. Nothing. On the second pass, I shoved aside storage boxes and found the door to a crawl space. Lovely.

I couldn't find a release mechanism like the one on the trapdoor up in the church. There was no handle. Grabbing some type of long, metal tuning device from a nearby shelf, I wedged it into the groove outlining the door and tried to pry it open. When I heard a metal squeak, I stopped and tried the other side. One good jab and the door lurched open on hinges I'd accidentally stretched.

Squinting into the dark, I could make out the earthen walls of a tunnel that was thankfully larger than the door. I hadn't been relishing the idea of crawling through who knew what in order to get out of here. Duckwalking through the door, I breathed in the cold, rich smell of dark soil.

This tunnel wasn't as well used as my own tunnels to the Presidio and Mount Tamalpais. It appeared as though no one had used it in a century, which dmay have been the case. Mine were used every month when I shifted to my wolf form and needed a secluded place to run far from human eyes.

The tunnel wasn't long. It was a small church. Light trickled into the dark through small gaps in the boards of the storm cellar door. Instead of a lock, though, there was a rusted U-shaped bar securing the door to the frame. The bar didn't want to pull free, having rusted into the hasp. I could have pulled the whole works out of the wood but didn't want Meg to bitch at me about replacing the door. So instead, I slowly worked the bar back and forth until it finally broke free.

I pushed up the door a few inches to see if the exit was clear. It wouldn't do for joggers to watch a strange woman emerge from under a condemned church. Conveniently, the door was located behind a huge bush, blocking me from view. I hopped out and dropped the door back into place. When I glanced down at myself in the bright morning light, I had to repress a shudder. My beautiful new clothes were a wreck, covered in cobwebs, dirt, and rust shavings. Damn. I'd need to swing by that haunted house I was currently calling home to shower and change. After that, I needed to find Owen, my wicche friend and assistant, as well as Dave, my half-demon cook. If I was going to New Orleans with Clive, I'd need them to oversee the reconstruction of the Slaughtered Lamb.

It was after eight when I made it back to the iron gates of Clive's mansion. Locked. I tried to disarm it, but they must have changed the code. When I pushed the button, Norma, Clive's human assistant who took care of daytime issues, didn't answer. She always answered and released the gate for me. I leaned on the button for an annoyingly long time and waited. Nothing.

My phone buzzed in my hoodie pocket. I fished it out and checked.

Clive: If you return during the day, all the doors are locked. You should go for a swim before we wake.

The text was time stamped hours ago. Why was it coming in now? And why was he suggesting I go swimming? That made no—oh. Last week we'd gone to the pool house to get away from everyone. When we were curled up by the fire, watching the flames dance, he'd said there was a passage behind the stones of the fireplace that led to his room in the big house. He'd wanted me to know in case I ever needed to escape. I was pretty sure that text meant I should use the passage to break in.

Studying the design of the gates, I decided not to attempt scaling them. There was a huge eucalyptus tree outside the far side of his property. I could climb that and drop in over the fence.

I followed the high stone wall around the estate. The tree was on a small side street. I waited until a dad pushing a stroller up the steep hill passed and then quickly jumped to a low branch and scrambled up the tree.

When I saw no one nearby, I ducked out from under the sparse leaves, got as close to the wall as possible, and jumped over, landing on bent knees and rolling with the momentum.

Glowing white in the early morning light, the nocturne house bore a troubling resemblance to a grand mausoleum. Which, given the number of dead people in it, was probably not too far from the truth.

Detouring from the mansion, I headed for the pool house. It was a small-scale model of the main house, mirroring its impressive formality. For a pool house, it seemed a bit much, but vampires were all about haughtiness.

The door was unlocked. Letting myself into the dim main room, I closed and locked the door behind me. Stilling, I slowed my breath and opened my senses. Nothing. Vampires emitted a low almost-hum, even when it was daylight and they were dead to the world. I'd only recently been able to sense it. I'd assumed it was because I'd been spending so much time amongst them. If Meg was right, however, it might be a talent for necromancy that accounted for my ability to sense them. Either way, I knew I was alone.

It hadn't struck me earlier when I'd been here with Clive, but the style of the fireplace didn't fit the house. I'd have expected marble, like the fireplaces in the main house. This one was a mosaic of sea glass, the mantle a thick slab of light gray wood. It didn't match the stuffy aesthetic vampires preferred. It would be more at home in the bedroom he'd redecorated for me than this pool house.

I searched all around the edges, trying to find a release. Clive had said there was a passage from here to the big house. There had to be a door to the passage here somewhere. It struck me that my life was becoming more and more like a Nancy Drew novel, vampires and ancient Greek goddesses aside.

Twenty minutes later, I dropped to the couch in defeat. I'd touched, tapped, and pushed every inch of the fireplace and mantle. My hands and the knees of my jeans were covered in soot. What was I missing?

I studied the sconces on either side of the fireplace and then the design of the room. They matched the style of the fireplace, not the room, more whimsical than austere, so they must have been a recent addition. I jumped up from the couch and ran my hands over the sconces. There was an old film I'd seen as a child. The story was set in a spooky house with a secret passage that was revealed when a sconce was pulled. Hoping I wasn't about to break a light fixture, I pulled on the sconce to the right of the fire. It didn't move. When I tried the left, though, I heard a quiet pop right before a narrow panel of wall between the fire and the light slid open.

SIX

The Calm Before the Storm

Leaning into the narrow passage, I could discern nothing beyond the first few stone steps. With one last glance over my shoulder at a perfectly comfortable place to spend the day, I instead stepped into the passage and made my way deeper into unrelieved dark. The panel slid back into place, cutting off my only source of light.

I made my way down the narrow stairs. Night vision couldn't help in complete darkness, so I trailed a hand along the wall as I walked. Unlike Meg's, this one was at least a finished passageway. A short uphill and uneventful walk led me to another narrow set of stairs, this one much longer than the first. When I made it to the top, I found a solid wall, no doorknob to turn, no sconce to pull. Running my hands over the passageway, I found a keypad. When I hit a button, numbers lit up.

I needed a code to get in. I tried the key code for the front door alarm. Nothing. Okay, Clive had sent me here, assuming I could find the passage and get in. That being the case, the code had to be something I'd guess. I tried my birthday. No. Not knowing his birthday, I tried other numbers at random: the street number of his house, his cell phone number, mine. I was getting ready to go back to the pool house and wait until dark when another number popped into my head.

I keyed in the date of the first time we'd made love. The keypad turned green and the wall in front of me slid to the side, revealing Clive's bedroom. Romantic fool. I made my way across his room to the bed. The panel slid closed behind me. I needed to wash the grime and spiderwebs off before I touched him, so I contented myself with dropping a chaste kiss on his forehead. One of his hands, palm up, seemed to be reaching into the empty side of the bed, searching for me. My throat tightened at the sight.

I tiptoed to the adjoining bedroom. He'd had the room decorated in blues and greens, the colors of water intended to relax and comfort. He'd wanted to replicate, as much as he could, the ocean view I had at The Slaughtered Lamb.

One long, hot shower later, I was feeling more human. Dressed in silky pajamas, I slid into bed with Clive, plugging in my phone before it died and setting the alarm for the early afternoon. If we were heading to New Orleans, I needed sleep and time to arrange things with Owen and Dave.

When I snuggled into Clive, his searching arm wrapped around me. Most vampires can't move during the day. Clive was old and powerful enough to move or talk if it was an emergency, but it took a great deal out of him. Resting my head on his chest, the fears and anxieties plaguing me the night before disappeared and I was able to drop off almost immediately.

When my alarm buzzed, I awoke with a groan. It had been such a lovely dream, Clive and I dancing on a rooftop, bright stars blanketing in the night sky. I tried to roll away, but Clive wouldn't release me. Running my hand up and down his broad chest, I kissed his jaw.

"You have to let me go now."

"No." His slow voice rumbled in the silent room.

"I'll be back. I promise. In fact," I said, sneaking out from under his arm, "I'm going to New Orleans with you." A low grumble sounded from the bed, but I was already headed back to the other room so I could dress and pack.

Checking my phone for the weather in Louisiana, I filled a medium-sized bag, not knowing if we'd be doing casual, stealthy things or formal vampire meet-and-greets. When I was dressed and done, I sent texts to Owen and Dave, asking them to meet me at The Slaughtered Lamb.

The jog to my bookstore and bar was uneventful. After last night, it was appreciated, even though I couldn't stop bracing for an ambush. I hadn't seen the place in a few days. When I hit the bottom of the stairs, standing between the bookstore and bar, I was swamped with emotion. Randy—who'd given me my neck-to-toe scars and just as many that couldn't be seen—and his wolves had literally torn apart my beautiful home. They'd destroyed everything they could get their hands on. We'd had to gut it and start again.

Seeing it now, with the rich mahogany floors replaced, the bar rebuilt and gleaming, the etched-glass mirror in place, it felt like a miracle. What they'd done had been burned away and The Slaughtered Lamb was rising from the ashes. I was home.

Light steps sounded behind me. Turning, I found Owen Wong, my best friend and wicche extraordinaire. "What happened to the blue streaks?" Owen was gorgeous, my own personal Chris Peng, but his naturally black hair had had deep blue streaks not twenty-four hours ago. Wait, his piercings were gone too.

"Oh." He ran a hand over his hair, his gaze avoiding mine. "The place is really coming together." He turned into the bookstore. "I was hoping the bookshelves would have arrived by now, but I guess not."

"Owen?"

His shoulders dropped. "Fine. I'm meeting George's family tonight. I mean, I've met his sister Coco, but this is the whole family. Mom, dad, grandparents, brothers." He stuffed his hands in his pockets. "I'm trying to make a good impression."

"Honey." I pulled him into a tight hug. Hugging was new to me. I'd avoided touch for seven years, since—well, I had. Clive was changing me. That, and I'd killed my rapist. That helped too. "How could they not love you? Any family would be lucky to have their son dating a guy as fabulous as you."

Squeezing me, he breathed, "Yeah?"

"You're smart and kind. You're an incredibly skilled wicche." I leaned back and grabbed his face. "You're a stunner. People stop on the street to watch you walk by. But," I said, ignoring his blush, "the most important selling point is that you love and respect their son."

Owen gave me a tight smile. "I'm not a dragon, though." He stared out the window wall at the ocean waves slamming against the glass. "We've been talking about moving in together. We spend most of our nights together already, but we want to make it official, get a place that's ours."

Grinning, I patted his shoulder. "I approve."

Heavy footfalls sounded on the steps and Dave appeared a moment later. Dave was a half-demon with naturally dark red skin and full black, shark-like eyes. He stood well over six feet, with broad shoulders and a muscular physique. Since he'd come from dealing with humans, he was wearing his usual glamour, that of a Black man in his thirties. His head was bald in either guise. I had no idea of his real age. Given comments that he or Clive had dropped over the years, though, I thought he might be closer to Clive's age than my twenty-four years.

He stared at Owen a moment. "Why are you less shiny than usual?" Dave wasn't overly concerned with feelings. It could have been the demon in him, but I think it was just his own flavor of grumpy guy.

"I'm meeting George's family tonight," Owen said.

Dave nodded, giving Owen a once-over. "You'll be fine, kid." He walked through the bar to the doorway into the kitchen. "Good. He got the stove I wanted, with the pot filler." He went into the kitchen, leaving us alone in the bar.

"Come on," I said to Owen. "We'll never get him back once he starts playing with the new appliances."

We found Dave crouched in front of the oven, door open as he peered inside. Studying the new kitchen, I forgot what I was about to say. It was almost done. The cabinets were a soft, blue gray. The island in the center had its own sink. It was the countertops, though, that drew me. They were a river of shimmering oceanic blue and green running over the island and around the room. A slate tile backsplash brought in hues of gray, blue, and black. The floors were the same color as the mahogany wood in the bar, but they didn't feel like wood.

Fingers skating over the countertops, I asked, "Is this glass?"

Dave closed the oven door and strode to the refrigerator. "Concrete. I considered glass, but it felt too fussy. Concrete can take stains and finishes well. I thought you'd like this one."

"I do. It's beautiful."

Owen hopped up on the counter and watched us, clearly not as interested as we were.

"And what are the floors?" I asked, tapping a foot.

"Cork," Dave said. "They're softer than standing on wood or tile for long periods. They're also eco-friendly and easy to clean. We don't have to worry about sun fading down here and the sealing process is pretty easy."

He shrugged, continuing, "You said I could design the kitchen." Slamming the fridge door closed, he studied me. "Well?"

Piece by piece, room by room, I was getting my home back. Tears pricked behind my eyes. Instead of answering with a too-tight throat, I crossed the kitchen and hugged him. Hard.

Patting me awkwardly, he said, "Fuck, Sam, it's a kitchen. Dial it back."

Shaking my head into his muscled chest, I hugged him harder.

"You know what I've always liked about working here, Sam? No tears and no hugs."

Laughing, I released him. "Sorry."

"That vampire is making you soft," he said, patting my shoulder with a heavy hand.

"Not that kitchen appliances aren't fascinating," Owen began, "but why are we here? You made it sound more important than a construction site walk-through."

"Right. Sorry. Got distracted. I'm getting my home back."

Owen's gaze softened. "It's a good home, and they don't get to destroy it."

Nodding, I swallowed down unshed tears. Mirroring Owen, I hopped up to sit on the counter. "So, last night was pretty eventful."

Dave leaned against the island, eyebrows raised. "I didn't hear anything."

"Yeah, well, anyone who could have talked is dead."

Owen and Dave exchanged a glance. "Explain," Dave said.

"TL;DR: Vamps from New Orleans visited the nocturne last night, intending to kill Clive. About eight of Clive's own people fought on their side. Clive, Russell, Godfrey, and I killed them all." I enjoyed the stunned silence. That's right. I was a badass. "Except for Amélie. She got away."

Dave surged forward. "What the fuck are you talking about? I haven't heard anything about an attack on the city's Master."

"Telling you now." I doubted it was the type of news vamps wanted publicized.

"And what do you mean, you fought vampires too? What was Clive thinking?" Dave paced to his new stove and back. "How many New Orleans vampires attacked?"

"Twelve of theirs with eight of ours. Amélie was the NOLA leader and huge distraction. I guess she's one of Clive's exes. She was all over him while her vamps moved in."

"Where were you?" Owen asked, his face unnaturally pale.

"Standing right next to him. I pulled him out of the way as a sword sailed through where his neck had just been. He—"

"You run, Sam. That's what you're supposed to do when

vampires start brawling." Dave threw his hands up in frustration. "How are you even still alive?"

Kicking my legs out, I barred Dave from passing me. "Hey. I'm the one who talked to the ghost and got the tip about an attack. I'm the one who alerted Clive and then saved his neck. I killed five of the vamps myself, so *you* dial it back. I can take care of myself."

While Dave glared at me, Owen sputtered, "Ghosts?"

Turning to him, I shrugged. "It was only that one, but Meg thinks I might be a necromancer." Pausing, I glanced between the two of them. "This weird thing happened in the fight. A vamp pulled a gun on me, had it aimed right at my head to mess with Clive, to get him to stop killing everyone. Well, I got him pinned and then I slipped into his thoughts and forced him to blow his own brains out. So I'm thinking Meg is probably right."

Dave grabbed the ankles I still had blocking his way and yanked. I slid off the counter, almost slamming my head on its edge. He caught me, hauled me up, and then deposited me back on my feet. "And that's how easy you are to kill."

The move was sudden, out of nowhere. I reacted without thinking, punching him in the gut. He didn't even blink, whereas my hand felt like I'd broken a few bones. "I'm not fragile, damn it! You don't get to tell me what I can and can't do. I'm not hiding anymore." My chest constricted, thinking of what I'd had to fight my way back from. I could defend myself now. I wasn't a victim anymore.

Drilling a finger into Dave's chest, I shouted, "I fought, and I killed them before they could hurt me. No one gets to hurt me, not even you!" My breathing was ragged, but I couldn't seem to calm down.

Arms slid around me. I flinched, but then Owen's low voice was in my ear. "Shhh. It's okay. He'd never hurt you." Owen's voice turned hard. "Would you, Dave? He's worried about you. Right?" Owen ground out.

I was glaring but felt my eyes filling with tears.

"Ah, shit. Don't do that. No hugging and no tears. I already said that. Fine!" He threw his hands up and stalked away. "Go get yourself killed playing with vampires."

"He doesn't mean that, either," Owen said.

"Yes, I do," Dave growled.

Blinking back the tears, I patted Owen's arm and moved away, shaking off memories that tried to choke me. "I'm glad you feel that way, because that's why I asked you to meet me. Clive is headed to New Orleans for some payback, and I'm going with him. I need you guys to oversee the Slaughtered Lamb renovations for me."

"What?" Dave roared.

SEVEN

In Which Sam Tests the Limits of a New Power

Dave bellowed while Owen tried to quietly get me to see reason. I knew both were coming from a place of concern, so I thanked them for taking care of my baby while I was gone, wished Owen well on meeting the parents, and then took off before Dave singed the new flooring with his anger. He worked on keeping his rage in check, hence the cooking, but I'd pushed him out of his grudgingly self-imposed Zen space today.

I, on the other hand, had a vampire that needed convincing. The nocturne was a few miles from my bookstore and bar. I was able to run through the Presidio, a hilly park located at the northern tip of San Francisco and straddling the bay and ocean with the Golden Gate Bridge jutting out from its tip.

I could run faster in the Presidio than in the streets, so I made it to the nocturne quickly. It was still about an hour before sundown, but I had keys with me this time. The house was dark and quiet. Instead of heading up the stairs to Clive, I went down the main hall toward the kitchen. I'd had nothing to eat since sometime yesterday. Wolves have a faster metabolism, so I was feeling hollowed out and ready to pounce on the first rabbit I happened upon. Luckily, a kitchen made the search for food easier.

I was the only one in the house—besides Norma—who ate. As she didn't seem to be here, all the glorious food was for me. I walked through the butler's pantry, with tall, black cabinets and white marble counters, into the main kitchen. They weren't big on keeping snacks for me in the cupboards, but I could usually find something good to eat in the refrigerator. Clive forced them to have food for whenever I might be hungry.

Most of the fridge held bagged blood, but a couple of shelves had been reserved for food. I found leftovers of sliced ham, crispy potatoes, and Brussels sprouts. There was even some chocolate cake in there. Clive knew me so well. I piled a plate, stuck it in the microwave, and was stuffing my face when Clive strode in.

"I heard the microwave's beep and figured I'd find you here."

I waved the potato at the end of my fork at him and then popped it in my mouth with a smile. "Must eat," I said after swallowing.

Sitting next to me, he reached out and ran a finger down my cheek. "Is this the first you've eaten today?"

I nodded my agreement, forking in pieces of ham and Brussels sprouts.

"I made sure there was food stocked in the pool house. Why didn't you eat earlier?" He ran his hand over my hair. "You've lost weight since yesterday. Your face is thinner."

Swallowing first, I said, "I know. I waited too long, but I've been kind of busy."

"True." He rubbed my back as I tried to slow my shoveling into ladylike bites. "Can you continue to stay with Meg while I'm gone?"

I shook my head.

Eyebrows raised, he watched me a moment. "Why? What did you do?"

Swallowing again, I said, "Why does it have to be me?"

Chuckling, he kissed my cheek.

Even though there was still more food on the plate and I desperately wanted that chocolate cake in the fridge, I put down my fork and turned to Clive. "I'm going with you." At his blank stare, I added, "New Orleans. I'm going with—"

"No, Sam. You're not." Clive's face hardened. "You're staying here. You're staying safe."

"Oh, yeah. It's super safe around here. Remind me how many times I almost died in the last month." Before he could speak, I continued. "Not again, Clive. I'm not going to have this argument over and over. I'm your partner. We work together. You can't hide me in a tower and then run into battle on your own." I poked his shoulder. "You already owe me a lot of groveling. Do you really want to add to that tab?"

Sighing, he took my hand. "Is it so wrong that I want to protect you?"

"Of course not. I want to do the same for you. The problem is when you decide for me what I can and can't do, where I can and can't go. You're my love, not my jailer. Besides, I have talents that are uniquely useful, given the purpose of your trip to NOLA."

Grinning, storm gray eyes heated. He kissed me soundly. "Yes, you do."

"Quit it. I've got chocolate cake in the fridge screaming my name."

When he stood up, I shoveled the last of my dinner in. He returned a moment later with a slab of cake and a napkin.

"I wasn't going to eat the whole thing."

"Might as well. We're leaving for New Orleans soon and you could use the calories."

"When?"

Returning to his chair, he watched me eat. "Tomorrow night. I need to call in some favors. I can't leave the nocturne vulnerable in my absence. If I'm able to convince one or two friends to stay here while I'm gone, it will change the strategy. If no one is able to fly here on such short notice, I'll need to leave Russell and take Godfrey." He tapped his finger on the table, lost in thought. "I don't want to leave him in charge of a house that could have more traitors."

"Let's find out, then."

Lifting his head, he focused on me. "How do you suggest we do that?"

I took another bite and thought about how to explain it. "I think part of the reason I was able to pull you out of the way before the sword chopped off your head is because," I whispered, "I was picking up on emotions in the room. You know how—maybe you don't—anyway, wolves can scent lies. I think —if Meg is right about my having latent necromantic talents—I think I was picking up on the emotions of the vamps, like wolves do.

"Mostly," I continued, voice still low, "I was singing in my head, trying not to hear Amélie and all her 'lover' talk. I noticed the tension in the room spike and started paying attention. I felt anger, excitement, and fear all jumbled together, gaining strength. When Amélie pointed to a painting on the wall, drawing your attention away from the group that formed around you, I heard—at least I think I heard, 'Now!' and that was when I pulled you down. I didn't know it would be a sword, but I knew someone was about to try to kill you."

Clive listened intently, a gleam in his eye. "Is that so?"

"So, I was thinking, maybe we could run a sting on your vamps. Call them into the library, one by one, talk to them, ask them some questions, how they're doing, and the whole time I'll be sitting in the window seat pretending to read, but listening. If I pick up on any 'Die, Clive, die' thoughts, I can let you know."

He whispered into my ear, "Yes. We'll practice your formidable skills on all my people, starting with Russell and Godfrey."

Shocked, my voice little more than a breath at his ear, I said, "You don't trust them?"

"When you're done here," he said at a normal volume, standing, "I need to talk to you about what you'll do while we're gone. I'll be in the library."

"Mm-hm," I hummed through a mouth full of cake as he kissed the top of my head and left. I ate the last bite, dealt with my dirty plates, and braced for what was coming.

I found Clive with Russell and Godfrey, speaking in quiet voices in a small seating area closer to the window seat than the door. They all glanced up when I entered. Clive's expression was blank, Russell's concerned.

Godfrey, unlike the other two, broke out in a huge grin. "And here she comes, our resident stone-cold killer! How many did you take out last night? Three? Four?"

"Five," Russell said. "And you should have run as soon as it started. You alerted us to the threat. You'd already done more than your share. You could have been killed last night." He focused on Clive. "She shouldn't have been allowed to stay. This doesn't concern her."

I had opened my mouth to argue when Godfrey began laughing. "Don't be an idiot. She saved our lord and master."

Expression hard, Russell's eyes flicked over Godfrey and landed on me. "If he hadn't been trying to protect you, he'd have sensed the attack. You were a liability." He turned back to Clive. "I apologize, Sire, but she shouldn't be living here. It's too dangerous."

"Sam stays because I want her here," Clive said in a tone that shut Russell up and wiped the grin off Godfrey's face.

Both men, almost in unison, bowed their heads and murmured, "Sire," in apology.

Turning to me, Clive said, "I need to finish here and then I want to discuss where you'll go while I'm gone. As much as I hate to admit it, Russell is right about one thing. This nocturne is not safe for you without me." He gestured to the window seat and then returned his focus to his men.

I walked over to the window like a good, obedient little werewolf and crawled into the corner of the heavily cushioned bench.

Clive had even had draperies put in so the seat could be separated from the rest of the room. I'd wanted a window seat ever since I'd first read *Jane Eyre*.

Leaning back on the cushions, I curled my legs under me and adjusted the curtain, so it blocked my head. I wanted to be able to close my eyes and concentrate, without it appearing odd, even though Godfrey and Russell were sitting with their backs to me.

Head tipped to the side against a pillow, I let my limbs go slack and tried to do what I had done the previous evening in the wrecked parlor across the hall. Not knowing how I had done it, though, I had no idea how to replicate it. I concentrated hard, trying to hear beyond what was being said. Nothing.

Maybe Meg was wrong. Maybe this wasn't a talent of mine. Except I had felt their emotions yesterday. I'd heard their strongest thoughts. It had been during a state of high emotion, though. Did I need to be in a fight or flight situation in order to access the skill? That would be inconvenient.

And then I noticed something. Behind the dark of my eyelids, I noticed a pinprick of cold green that throbbed in time with Godfrey's words. I focused all my energy on that green light, envisioning diving deep, immersing myself. Pain shattered my thoughts, as though I had slammed my head into a wall of green cement. And then I heard it. It was an almost subaudible whisper that ran alongside his spoken words.

Minds are chaotic and Godfrey's was no different. He was thinking the words he was saying, but he was also annoyed that Russell was so conservative with his responses to Clive. He wanted him to be less restrained. He and Russell were Clive's most loyal people. They shouldn't have to measure every single word.

Godfrey thought Clive was acting strangely. His tone with me was all wrong. He loved me. Godfrey saw it shine in his eyes whenever he talked about or even thought about me, and yet he was cold and dismissive, sending me to the window seat. And I'd gone without an annoyed snarl. Something was off.

"Godfrey, I'd like your thoughts on my going to confront Lafitte," Clive said.

"You can't go alone, Sire. I have every confidence that you could take out the nest on your own, but I don't think it would be wise to attempt." His thoughts ran right along those lines, but he worried about losing Clive. They'd been together, off and on, for hundreds of years. He didn't want Clive hurt, or worse, killed.

"If I chose to take a small party of people with me, who would you suggest?" Clive asked.

Me! The thought felt like a shout. "With all due respect to Russell, I think the nocturne needs him to stay. The others like me, but they don't fear me the way they do him. I think he needs to stay to keep this house together." He paused. "I ask instead, Sire, that you take me. I'm not as needed here and would consider it an honor to act as your shield." His thoughts ran right along with those sentiments, although internally he questioned Russell. He wondered how Lafitte had turned so many in the house if Russell were not in some way complicit. It hurt to think it, but he was suspicious and therefore didn't want Russell at Clive's back.

"Is there anyone else in the house you think should travel with me?"

"Her," Godfrey said. "She fought like she's been training for years. And the best part was they hadn't expected it. I saw it, that split second of shock when she pulled you out of the sword's path and unleashed those knifelike claws of hers." He paused, relaxing into the subject, his voice taking on the ease of recounting a great story. "They were so bloody smug, thinking they could throw Amélie at you. They actually thought a woman would distract you from an attack."

"Yes, they did," Russell interrupted. "I was wondering about that as well. Amélie, Lafitte, many of the vampires who attended last night have known you for a very long time. Where was the respect—as Godfrey said—the fear of you last night? He's right.

They walked in here thinking they could dangle Amélie in front of you like a cat toy and then take you out."

Concentrating on Russell, I mentally tried to burrow into his words as he spoke them. The pain in my head increased, but I finally broke through. Worry. Russell was outraged at the lack of respect the New Orleans vamps had displayed the previous evening, but beneath that was fear for Clive. Clive had built a deservedly towering reputation in the vampire community. It was what kept smaller threats away, what drew a huge panoply of supernaturals to their city and made their lives here comfortable. If Clive's reputation were decaying, the attacks would increase. Why, though, had his reputation diminished? Leticia. She must have been betraying him for years, whispering to whomever would listen, that he was ripe for attack. Russell hoped that he would be the one to give her true death.

"Do you agree with Godfrey that Sam should come with me?" Clive asked.

"No. This is vampire business. She has no place in the middle of this."

"Come on," Godfrey interrupted. "Don't be such a prig. A surprise is always valuable in an attack and she held her own. Plus, we know she's loyal. If not for her, our master might be minus his head today."

The room went deathly quiet.

Godfrey, realizing what he'd said, was desperately trying to figure out how to smooth it over. Russell was barely holding on to his need to crack his hand across Godfrey's mouth. This, talk like this, was what had been tarnishing Clive's reputation.

"Do you honestly believe," Clive began, "that group last night would have beheaded me if not for Sam?"

Outrage rolled off Russell, whereas Godfrey gave off the sour scent of fear.

"I spoke out of turn, my liege. Please accept my most sincere apologies for intimating that you could not have killed everyone in that room single-handedly. Of course, a mere wolf did not save you. I was—" He swallowed. "I was suggesting that she go with you as she's an unexpectedly good fighter and an acceptable risk."

He threw that last phrase in to test Clive. Godfrey couldn't get past the fact that Clive wasn't behaving normally. Even if it cost him a couple of weeks in a cell downstairs, he needed a better handle on what they were dealing with. They'd been discussing me as though I weren't in the room, and no snarky comments had been thrown at them from the window seat. Something was very off.

"You believe Sam to be an acceptable risk in this fight?" Clive asked, his voice bored, as though merely asking a follow-up question as a conversational habit.

Surprisingly, it was Russell who roared *No!* in his head. Oh, I heard it now. All of Russell's talk of leaving me out of vampire fights, making me stay in San Francisco when they left, was because he feared for me. He knew I was the most vulnerable of us and he feared how Clive would deal with my loss. He'd noticed subtle changes over the years, ever since Clive had started visiting my bar every month. Russell saw it as Clive regaining some of his humanity. He worried others saw it as Clive losing his edge.

EIGHT

Wait, You're How Old?

I set down the book I'd been gripping and flicked my fingers. Clive must have noticed because a moment later, he said he needed to make a call and sent them away. Once the door closed after them, Clive swiped through the tablet on the coffee table. Soft classical music filled the room. He came and sat next to me.

"Were you able to pick anything up from them?" Clive asked, taking my hand.

"Actually, I was."

He turned to study me, pride shining in his eyes. "Truly?"

"It took some work, but I got it."

Clive waited, his body tense, as though preparing to be slammed by yet another betrayal.

"Godfrey is worried. We're not behaving normally. You were cold. I didn't call you out on it. I followed directions like a good little wolf. He knew there was something going on with us but didn't know what."

Clive relaxed a fraction. "Nothing else."

"Well…"

At my pause, he stiffened. "What else?"

"He's wondering if Russell is involved in the attack. He can't see how Lafitte—or Leticia, for that matter—could have turned so many in the nocturne without Russell's help. The thought angered and saddened him."

Clive stared down at our joined hands, his thumb running over my skin. Body braced, he turned to me. "And Russell?"

Russell was one of Clive's dearest and most trusted friends. If I had bad news for him, it would take him out at the knees. "It's not Russell."

"Are you sure?"

"Yes."

The tension in his body drained. "How do you know?"

Squeezing his hand, I said, "Because he cares for you. His entire focus was on protecting you. He wants me out of the nocturne because he thinks it's too dangerous for me and he worries what my death would do to you."

Clive nodded slowly, staring at our hands.

"Like Godfrey, he doesn't understand how people who know you, people like Amélie and some of the others last night, aren't afraid of you. According to Russell, you're viewed as quite the scary son of a bitch and yet here these people come, acting as though killing you will be easy. He's offended on your behalf and utterly baffled by the lack of fear."

"Yes." Clive almost slumped against the back of the window seat. "That reputation was hundreds of years in the making. Why has it eroded?"

"Russell thinks Leticia has been whispering for years." I paused again, not wanting to tell him the next part. Did I have to?

"What is it, Sam?"

Fuck it. "He worries that your feelings for me have made you appear weak, and he wonders if more will attack because of it." I wasn't going to play games to keep him. Either he wanted to be with me or he didn't. He needed to know that Russell thought more trouble was on the way.

Lifting our joined hands, he kissed my fingers. "Whereas, I have had an epiphany."

"Have you?" Hope bubbled at his 'whereas.'

"Like Russell, I had the same thought when Lafitte sent a band of twelve to take me out. Twelve. I didn't know whether to laugh at the attempt or be horrified that my reputation has dropped so precipitously. My first thought was Leticia. She had ties to Lafitte, as Étienne, Lafitte's brother, had been her lover for years. Executing him after he defied me and left you unguarded—that kelpie could have killed you—is what originally set her against me."

"Executing him for me."

"No. I—oh." He thought a moment. "Yes, you're right. It could be interpreted that way. I gave him true death because he made a habit of disobeying me, treating my commands as suggestions. He was an arrogant, swaggering peacock who believed himself to be far more intelligent and powerful than he was. But, yes, his final act of disobedience was precipitated by my telling him to guard you."

His expression softened. "You were so young and so very scared. You'd lost your mother, been tortured by that wolf, and then your uncle had dumped you here, in a new city where you knew no one." He shook his head. "You had begun to see past the trauma to a new life, had come up with the plan for your bookstore and bar. The Slaughtered Lamb was still under construction; no wards were in place. I could see you trying so hard for independence but quailing under the combined weight of fear and loneliness."

Resting my head on his shoulder, I said, "And I thought I was doing such a good job of seeming tough and capable."

He wrapped his arm around me and stretched out his legs. "You were both of those things. Now, even more so."

"I'm a badass."

"Indeed."

"So, does this change your plans, knowing Russell and Godfrey's thoughts?"

"Not unless—" His phone began to ring. "Not unless I receive this phone call." He hit answer.

I expected him to move to a different part of the library, but he didn't. With one arm still around me, he spoke with a woman named Liang. She had a British accent as well. Their voices were lovely, lulling me. Eyes closed, I listened to both sides of the conversation. Clive explained what was going on with great candor. Liang seemed as shocked as Russell that Lafitte had attempted to have him killed.

Clive asked if she'd be willing to come to San Francisco to watch over his nocturne while he went to confront Lafitte. She said she was in New York and would book a private plane and arrive this very night. I could feel Clive's body relax, knowing she was on her way.

"Will you be taking Russell with you?"

"Yes."

"Too bad. I've missed him. I don't believe we've spoken since…"

"Hong Kong," Clive finished for her.

"Yes, Hong Kong. You and I had such a lovely time there." Her voice had changed. It wasn't the cartoonish seduction of Amélie, but there was a wistful nostalgia that spoke of remembered romance.

I sighed. Another ex. Clive kissed the top of my head, acknowledging my chagrin.

"It will be Russell, Godfrey, and my particular friend Sam."

I rolled my eyes. He was breaking out the Jane Austen phrases to cheer me up.

The woman said something, but I wasn't listening. 'My particular friend.' I liked that better than boyfriend.

"Yes, she's right here. I'm being glared at; not sure why."

"I look forward to meeting her," she said. "So, is she wearing any special jewelry?"

He held up my hand and studied my naked fingers. "Alas,

she is not. I'll need to fix that." He pulled my hand to his lips and kissed my ring finger.

I gave him a squinty-eyed study. Was he joking? If that was his idea of a proposal, I was going to punch his junk.

Clive winked at me and continued his conversation. The change that had come over him since she called was remarkable. The attack had thrown him. It wasn't the possible threat, as we had disposed of the NOLA vamps quickly. It was the underlying lack of respect for him. His own people had sided against him. Liang's phone call could not have come sooner.

They said their goodbyes and then Clive disconnected and grinned at me. "Liang is coming."

"So, I gathered. Another ex, huh?" I said, pretending disgruntlement.

He twisted, pulling me down on the cushions and dropping kisses over my jaw, before landing on my lips. Clive's kisses drove all thought from my head. When he eventually pulled back, he grinned down at me. "Yes, another one. But think of all the practice time I've put in so I can be at my best for you."

"I'd rather not think about the practice time," I managed, my breath still uneven.

He nodded. "Fair point." His expression changed, growing more serious. "I'm older than you imagine. I told you I'd once met Shakespeare, and because of that, you seem to have placed my human existence in the Elizabethan Age. I was, however, enjoying my undeath long before Elizabeth took the throne."

He paused, searching my face. "I was alive when William invaded England."

"William?" I thought for a moment and then my eyes flew wide. "The Norman invasion? 1066? That William?"

"Not if it's going to horrify you." Clive lay beside me, his head propped on his hand, giving me time to process the fact that my fiancé was almost a thousand years old.

"Wow. Rob the cradle much?" I poked him in the ribs, grinning.

He ran a finger down my nose, across my lips. "It is a problem, but if I didn't rob the cradle, I'd be limited to a few undead beings in the world." As I contemplated that, he added, "Most of whom I've already dated."

A thousand years. He'd lived through ages. It was unfathomable. Not to have read about history, but to have lived it. "I have so many questions."

"And we have our very long lives to discuss them."

I grabbed his face and brought him down for a long kiss. His age, the exes, it didn't matter. What mattered was us, together. What were the chances? A person from another age, another part of the globe, and yet we found each other here and now. I would never stop being grateful for the gift the universe had given me.

When we came up for air— "Hey, do you need to breathe?"

"No. It makes the living feel more comfortable, so it's become a habit."

"Huh. Anyway, shall we bring out your dead so I can try my new party trick on them?"

He gave me one last hard kiss and said, "Yes, let's."

Russell and Godfrey brought in each of Clive's vampires, one at a time. I was back in my window seat, reading. After the third interview, my head was pounding so hard, I thought I'd throw up.

When that vampire left, I pushed the curtain aside and told Clive I needed a break.

He was at my side a moment later. "What wrong? Is he one of them?"

Eyes shut tight, I willed my stomach to settle. "Can I have a glass of water? I need a minute."

His thumb brushed over my forehead, sweeping the pain away. I'd forgotten. Clive could torture, causing horrendous pain with his only mind, but he could also take someone's pain away. Slumping against the cushions, I breathed easily for the first time since I started my foray into espionage.

"I hadn't realized this caused you pain. You should have said something earlier."

Blinking my eyes open, I marked the concern etched in his features. "I'm okay now. It started with Godfrey and Russell. I hoped that it would get easier with practice, but instead it gets worse with each new vamp. I need a few minutes before we begin again."

"Now that I know, I can keep part of my mind focused on relieving your pain as I question them. I'm sorry to ask it of you, but we need to know who else is acting like a cancer in this house." He stood when Russell walked in holding a glass of water.

"Are you all right, Miss Quinn?" Russell asked, glancing quickly at Clive. A couple of mother hens, these two.

"I'm fine. A sudden headache, but Clive has taken away most of the pain." I took the glass from him and drank it down.

He took the empty glass and murmured about getting me more as he left the room.

"I'm okay. Really," I said to Clive, who had yet to relax. "I think I need to talk with Lydia. I know she's not a necromancer, but maybe she knows why I'm getting these splitting headaches."

"Good. Yes, that's a good plan." Relieved at finding a possible solution, his brow finally cleared. "Even if she's not familiar with necromancy, she may know someone who is."

Russell returned with another glass of water. I drank half and then placed the glass on the windowsill to finish later. I didn't need to push into his brain to know he was worried about me. I gave Clive a questioning look. If Russell was loyal, shouldn't we tell him what we were doing?

Clive must have been thinking the same thing because he nodded at me, patted my leg, and then stared into Russell's eyes. Clive could project his thoughts into his people's heads. They couldn't speak back that way, but they could hear him.

Russell's expression changed from concern to shock before becoming completely blank. "I see," he said.

"I'm sorry," I said, assuming he was pissed off I'd been spying on him.

He leaned forward, his lips at my ear. "Never be sorry for protecting Clive. I have sworn my life to do the same." His voice was barely a breath of sound. "I am pleased that you have set his mind at ease and that you have a defense against us. He needs you. Therefore, your safety is my charge."

I patted his arm. "Thank you for that, but I'm more than a little uncomfortable with the swearing of life and loyalty. I'm no one's liege. You guys do your thing and I'll try to do mine from the sidelines, sneaky-like."

He crouched so we were eye to eye, a grin splitting his dark, handsome face. "This isn't some colonial racist bullshit," he said, repeating a line I'd used when I first met him. Clive had been shocked at how I'd viewed the bowing and 'sires.' He'd said vampire society was based on a kind of ancient feudal system, one of vassals and lords. It all still made me super uncomfortable.

Russell told me later that he'd heard me berating Clive through the bedroom door and had laughed like hell—on the inside—as he'd walked down the stairs.

Russell reached out and took my hand before bowing his head over it. "My lady, I vow on my life to keep you safe." When I tried to pull my hand back, he held on tight. "No matter how much that makes you squirm." He laid a chaste kiss on the back of my hand and stood. "Now, do you need more time, or should I bring in another one?"

NINE

Bring in Your Dead

"Sire." Godfrey inclined his head. "I have Jonathan for you."

With Clive controlling the pain, I slid into Jonathan's mind easily. He resented being summoned and especially hated that the werewolf whore was still around. Adjusting the book in my grip, I pointed to this one. Clive drummed his fingers on the arm of his chair and stared at the vamp. After a moment, the vamp threw an arm over the back of the couch, feigning ease while worrying that Clive knew something.

"Explain," Clive said.

"Explain what, Sire?" His mind was a frantic jumble, trying to figure out what Clive knew and how he could survive this meeting.

"Explain your disloyalty to the nocturne and to me." Clive's words were spoken with an indifference that was at odds with his eyes turning vamp black.

"Sire"—The man's voice pitched higher this time—"I was locked in the cell and poisoned with my nocturne. I didn't fight against you. I have sworn my loyalty to you." He'd spoken to no one. How could Clive possibly know he'd been aware of the NOLA attack and the poisoning? He couldn't. This had to be a bluff.

I'll admit it, the 'werewolf whore' thing pissed me off, but that wasn't why I put my book aside and moved to the center of the window seat. I knew there was no way I could give signals for all of this and I knew this vamp would be dead soon anyway, so I tipped my hand.

"Come now, Jonathan. Do you really think Clive is unaware of your plotting?"

It was lovely to watch. The vamp glared over his shoulder at me and then turned back to Clive. He barely held his tongue on the *fucking cunt* that wanted to fly from his lips. He was confused, though, as well. How could we know anything? Had someone talked during the battle the night before?

"Clive knows," I continued. "Quite a cowardly traitor, aren't you? Too weak to fight outright like all your slain comrades, but willing to lean against a wall while members of your nocturne were fed tainted blood, blood you knew not to drink. You watched them double over, their insides being dissolved like acid. You watched the young ones clutch their stomachs, their backs bowing, blood foaming at their lips. You watched and did nothing."

Caught between pleading his innocence and tearing my throat out, he sat silently, unsure of what to do. If Clive truly knew all of this, how had he not already been given his true death?

"The only question I have at this point," Clive said, his voice arctic, "is were you working directly with Lafitte, or someone else in his organization?"

"I'm working with no one, Sire." His words had taken on a pleading quality. How quickly he'd moved from arrogance to submission. "Leticia was trying to drum up support for a coup, but I never went along with it. I heard her dead mate was Lafitte's brother, but I didn't know him. I've only been here a few months. I'm not a part of this. These were your own people who plotted against you, not me." He remembered meetings with Richard, the sneering vamp on guard duty.

Richard had given Jonathan the history. Clive had killed one of their own, the younger brother of a master vampire, no less, and over a fucking wolf. He'd used vampires to guard a dog. Clearly, Clive was losing it. That's what Leticia had said. Sometimes the really old ones begin to devolve. Clive's sick wolf perversion was a sign.

"You knew what was being plotted but did nothing," Clive said. "And you believe that proves your innocence?"

"*I* didn't do anything. You can't blame me for what others do." Desperate now, he wondered if Clive was as deadly as he'd always heard. He wondered, too, why he'd believed Richard and the others when they'd said Clive had grown weak.

"You'll find that isn't true." Clive turned his attention to me. "Do we need anything else from him?"

Jonathan scrambled, glaring over his shoulder again. "Her? The whore dog shouldn't have a voice here! She's been feeding you lies about your own people. You honor her and wonder why your vampires are revolting!" He was so agitated, I wasn't sure if he was going to start raging or crying.

"You guys are revolting, all right," I snarked.

I knew the second he broke his chain. He flew over the couch, eyes black, fangs out. I moved even more quickly. My hand, razor-sharp claws extended, was already sweeping through the air as he came at me. A fine mist of blood and then his head was rolling across the floor. A moment later, dust settled where his head and body had fallen.

"I wanted to do that," Clive said.

I wiped my sleeve over my face, damp with tiny blood droplets. "You can get the next one."

"Deal."

Russell walked in a moment later. "Yes, Sire?" He glanced around room, no doubt searching for Jonathan, before his gaze settled on the floor. "I see. Would you like to continue in this room, or shall we move the meetings to your study?"

"We'll stay here," Clive responded.

"Would you like this cleaned up?" Russell eyed the vamp remains and then me, a new gleam in his eye.

"I think I'd like Jonathan left right where he fell, at the feet of the woman who killed him. For everyone's safety, they need to know who they're dealing with when they disparage her."

"Not to mention," I added, "it'll throw them off even more when they walk in and see the remains of a dead vamp." Grinning, I curled my legs up on the widow seat again and picked up my discarded book. "Send in the next one, Russell."

"As you wish," he said with his head inclined.

In the end, Jonathan was the only traitor left in Clive's nocturne, although most of them hated my guts and resented the hell out of having me in the room and at their backs. The ones who came in after the appearance of the Jonathan dust pile eyed me more warily. So, there was that.

After the last left, Clive received another phone call. We'd had to stop the interrogations twice for other phone calls. The conversations were brief and strikingly similar. Each said he could be on a flight that night. The one he was speaking to now wanted to come, but his second had been given true death, so he'd rather not leave his nocturne in the hands of his third.

"If you need me, though, I'll be there. We're not under attack. My second was taken out over an old grudge with his maker that had been festering for a few hundred years. My third is quite strong."

"Yes, Salma is strong enough to be anyone's second. It's a testament to you, Mateo, that she's chosen to stay as your third," Clive said.

"True."

"Thank you for returning my call and for the offer, but I've received calls from a few tonight. My nocturne will be well-protected. Your support, though, will not be forgotten. My sword is yours when you need it," Clive said.

"My call was not the first, eh? Who beat me to it?"

Clive grinned, a weight being thrown off. "Liang is already

on her way." He checked his watch. "She should be landing in a couple of hours. And Rémy and Cadmael have each volunteered to back her up."

"That's quite a group. I'm sorry I'll miss it."

Clive chuckled. "Actually, so am I."

"It sounds like things will be well in hand. If you need me, though, you have only to call."

After Clive hung up, he grinned at me. "They're coming."

"So, I heard. Who are Rémy and Cadmael?"

"Friends. I met Rémy in the late seventeen hundreds in Paris. Remind me to tell you that story someday. It was quite harrowing. Cadmael is ancient, even by vampire standards. He was a Mayan warrior in life. He is a very private man who befriends few. I am privileged to count myself among those few."

He stood. "Go rest. You're exhausted. What you did today was"—he searched for the word—"astounding. You had a feeling you might be able to read a vampire's thoughts and then succeeded in doing exactly that over thirty times in a row." He kissed my forehead. "Go rest that poor, tired brain of yours while I coordinate with Russell and Godfrey." He checked his watch again. "Liang should be arriving by three. If you're still awake, I'll introduce you. Otherwise, it can wait until tomorrow."

I wanted to fight him on it, wanted to be in the planning meeting, but he was right. His efforts to relieve my pain had definitely helped. I wasn't vomiting, after all. There appeared to be only so much that could be done, though. So, with a pounding head and heavy limbs, I climbed the stairs, longing to crawl into a soft bed in a thankfully lightless room.

I'd had every intention to get up at three to meet Liang, but I slept soundly until midmorning the next day. Clive was in bed with me, his arm slung around my middle. I slid out of his hold, showered, dressed, and checked my phone. One missed called from Owen. Perfect. Exactly who I needed.

Thankfully, he was willing to do what he'd been threatening

for years: help me shop. I wanted to mess with their preconceived ideas of me. Vamps liked to refer to me as Clive's scarred stray. Well, screw that. I was a warrior, not an abused dog waiting for the boot.

Owen met me downtown and I used the black credit card Clive had given me. Since I was purchasing badass gear for a vamp operation, it seemed only fair for him to foot the bill. That, and the clothes were really stinking expensive.

Hours later, arms weighed down by expensive crap, keys gripped in freshly manicured fingers, bag handles tangled around wrists, I thanked Owen and keyed in the security code on the gate. Once through, I kicked it shut and attempted to wave goodbye. Getting through the front door was trickier. It involved a code and a key.

When the light turned green and the door opened, I breathed a sigh of relief. Once in, I shut the door, pausing to listen. Silent as the grave. Huh, I thought someone would be moving by now. Taking the stairs two at a time, I made my way quickly to the third floor. I had a moment as I was passing through the second-floor landing, the house pitch black, when I knew someone was watching me. I didn't stop to investigate, as I was currently hampered by shopping bags. Strangers could wait until my armor was in place.

I went to the door of the bedroom I'd been given when I first moved in, bypassing Clive's door. If he was still sleeping, more power to him. I wanted to get cleaned up and changed before I had to meet yet another of his exes and then board a plane to certain death.

The room was empty. I turned on the lights, locked the door, and dropped all the bags on the bed before shaking out my arms. I went through the passage to Clive's room. He was still abed. After dropping a kiss on his nose, I went back to my room, unbagged everything, and tried to decide what I should wear tonight. Should the badassery begin now?

While showering, I was still running through clothing

options. The shower was filling with steam when strong arms slid around my waist. I had a moment of panic, before Clive's scent hit me. He always smelled like lemons and fresh linens dried in the sun. He smelled like love and home.

"We'll need to be fast. Clive will be up soon."

His fangs glided down the side of my throat, causing tectonic plates to quake. His hands spread out over my soapy stomach, one hand gliding down between my legs while the other palmed a breast. His lips were driving me crazy, running along my neck, sucking at my earlobe, as his fingers plucked at my nipple. I was ready to come undone when he spun me around, pressing my back against the tile, his mouth coming down hard on my own.

He felt so good, so solid, I couldn't stop running my hands over his chest and abs, over his shoulders and down his back. As our tongues tangled, I reached down to grip him hard. I wanted him inside me now.

He spun me back around, ran his hands down my arms, and lifted them, curling his fingers over my own, asking me to grip a narrow stone shelf. He glided his slick hands all over my body before they landed on my hips.

"Don't move your hands," he said as he pulled my hips back, stretching out my arms.

I could feel his erection as he leaned over me, hands at my breasts, fingers rolling my nipples. One hand flattened against my stomach, pulling me closer to him, lifting me to my toes. Pushing my legs apart, he plunged in, one long stroke that caused earthquakes to erupt. The hand on my stomach held me up while his other gripped my hip, keeping me in place.

He slid out and then slammed home. Legs trembling, I gripped the shelf, absorbing every inch of him. He drove in again and again as I pushed back to meet him. My brain shut off as wave after wave of sensation capsized over me. When I thought I couldn't hold on a moment longer, he leaned over my back, sunk his fangs into my neck, and I shattered.

Muscles like melted wax, I would have slumped on the tile

floor if Clive hadn't caught and held me against him as hot water rained down on us. "Standing and walking are out of the question. You'll need to carry me everywhere."

A moment later, I was on his shoulder in a fireman's carry. I huffed out a laugh. It was all the energy I could spare. He handed me a towel as we left the bathroom. Carpet flashed by and then he stopped.

"Why is your bed covered in clothes?"

"I—"

"Never mind. I don't care." He carried me through the passage to the bedroom we'd been sharing for the last few weeks and tossed me down on a warm, rumpled bed.

He was a god standing over me, body hard and ready, gaze heated as it trailed over me. And then he dropped to his knees beside the bed, pulling me to the edge. Kisses trailed up my inner thighs as he spread my legs. His mouth was on me, teeth and tongue devouring me. My core clenched as his mouth dragged a groan from me.

Hands gripping his hair, I writhed, opening to him, desperate. When the orgasm began to rip through me, Clive stood, pulling my hips up off the mattress. Firmly in his grip, he slammed into me, pumping relentlessly. Back bowed off the bed, I tried to keep up with him.

"Touch yourself," he growled.

When I did, he was the one groaning. I came a moment later, Clive right behind me. Still gasping for breath, tremors running through me, I felt the bed move as he laid down beside me. An arm wrapped around me and he pulled me close, feathering kisses over my shoulder.

My body was lax and headed toward sleep when I remembered our guests. "I don't need to move anytime soon, right?"

"No. The formal introduction of Liang, Cadmael, and Rémy to the nocturne won't be until nine. I need to meet with Russell and Godfrey prior to that to finalize our plans. The only thing you need to do," he said, stroking my waist and hip, "is pack a bag and be in the study at nine. We'll be heading to the airport after that."

Knowing it was going to be a long night, I set my alarm and dropped off immediately. When it went off an hour later, all I wanted was to roll over and go back to sleep. As I had a few powerful friends of Clive's to meet, including an ex, I instead got my groggy ass up and went back to the shower. After blowing my hair dry, I put on some mascara and lip gloss, hit the closet for undies, and then stood in front of the bed, weighing my clothing options.

Deciding I should save my middle finger wardrobe for New Orleans, I chose a long narrow ombre sweater dress. The soft knit was a deep burgundy at the V-neck that gradually transitioned to black. I put on a pair of glittery black earrings I found in my jewelry box. I hadn't seen these before. Clive kept slipping new clothes and jewelry into the closet as though I wouldn't notice.

When I first moved in a few weeks ago, there'd been a couple of drawers, a few shelves, and one bar of clothing for me, as I'd lost everything when The Slaughtered Lamb had been destroyed. Now, almost the whole walk-in closet was full and I'd spent much of the day shopping for more, albeit decidedly different, clothes. It was nuts.

I was focusing on that because I didn't want to think about how much of my chest and legs were revealed in this dress. It wasn't that it was cut low or high. It was that I'd spent the last seven years keeping my scars covered, neck to toe. Exposing them was very difficult for me. Yes, Clive had said he thought scars were sexy, but the rest of these vamps saw me as the abused stray dog their master had taken in. They were all just waiting for me to pee on the carpet.

I checked my watch. *Suck it up, Sam.* It was time to meet our guests.

TEN

Do All the Exes Have to Be Gorgeous?

The upper floors were very quiet, not that vamps are a rowdy group by nature. Everyone must have already been in the study. Taking a deep breath, I tried to steady my nerves. Given the choice, I'd rather reprise my role as the dead eyed pet standing behind Clive and bracing for an attack rather than an evening being cordial and presented as his particular friend.

Pausing on the last stair, I blew out a breath. If I went in now, they'd all hear my heart racing. I needed to chill. If I couldn't do it now, how was I going to make enemy vamps believe I was a stone-cold killer? It wouldn't matter how tough I dressed or behaved. My rabbit pulse would give me away.

Closing my eyes, I went to my happy place—the window seat in Clive's library. I imagined the twilight sky filling the window, me cuddled up against the cushions with a soft blanket wrapped around me, a book in my hand. It was lovely and I could feel myself relaxing into the vision.

When I opened my eyes, Clive was standing in front of me. I'd known he was there. His scent meant safety. Of course, the way his gaze roamed over me caused my pulse to pick up again. "Quit it."

"You're stunning," he said. "And what should I quit?" He

took my hand, pausing to notice the nail polish, and helped me down the last step before dropping a soft kiss on my lips.

"Stop that. I don't want everyone in that room to hear my heart racing," I whispered.

"Ah. I'm not sure if this is better or worse, but we could hear it when you were up in our room. Come," he said. "I have some friends I want you to meet."

Low murmurs filled the room. Three people stood together in the center, drawing furtive glances from the rest of the room. Like Clive, there was something magnetic about each of them. The woman was breathtaking, with a perfect oval face that almost glowed, eyes a golden brown, and glossy black hair that barely brushed her shoulders. She was a goddess and Clive's ex. Awesome.

The men were very different and yet each commanding in his own way. One was fair-skinned, with close-cropped dark hair, and a trim mustache and beard. He was shorter than his two companions. The third of the party was tall and raw-boned, brown skin like aged leather drawn tight over prominent cheekbones. His nose was crooked, as though it had been broken numerous times. Long, dark hair was tied and braided down his back.

All three turned toward us as we walked across the room. Russell appeared with a tray holding four etched crystal goblets filled with blood and one with some kind of wine. I wasn't much of a wine drinker, but this seemed more posh than a soda over ice.

"Thank you, my friends. You are most welcome to this nocturne. What is mine is yours," Clive said very formally.

When they took a drink, I lifted my glass to do the same but stopped when I noticed the bubbles. I sniffed it and then grinned at Russell, who stood nearby. He'd given me cherry cola.

"What's yours is ours?" asked the shorter man in the middle as he leered at me.

"Rémy, don't make me stake you in my study. I'm fond of this rug," Clive said.

Rémy laughed good naturedly while the other man shook his head in what appeared to be centuries of forbearance.

"May I introduce Samantha Quinn," Clive said, his arm around me. "Sam, these are three of my dearest friends. Liang, whose heart is as true as her sword. Rémy, whose mind is as sharp as his libido is legend. And Cadmael, who barely puts up with any of us, but is more powerful than all of us."

Each nodded in turn as Clive introduced them. Liang appeared curious, whereas Rémy seemed to find me amusing. Cadmael, though, was having none of it. His disdain—either for me or for Clive's relationship with me—was stark.

"Have any of you visited San Francisco before?" I asked. When Clive rubbed my back, I realized my mistake. They were centuries old. There probably weren't many places they hadn't been. This is what came of my trying to make small talk.

Cadmael gave one short nod. Rémy smirked and raised an eyebrow as though asking, 'What do you think?' Liang inclined her head and said, "Yes. I lived here for many years."

"I'm very happy to have you all visit us again. I hope your rooms are to your liking," Clive said.

Both men shrugged and drank, clearly not interested in the room question. Liang, though, gazed meaningfully at Clive and said, "I preferred the one I had last time, but the one I'm in now is lovely."

Clive's hand gripped my waist a little tighter. "We've had that room redecorated. Sam is using it now."

Rémy's attention had been caught with that comment, his expression incredulous. "You have a werewolf living in your nocturne? And you're surprised your people staged a revolt?" He shook his head. "I know you have always been the more liberal-minded of us, but even for you…" He let the comment hang, finishing off his glass of blood.

Liang regarded me like an unsightly problem before focusing on Clive. "It does seem ill-advised."

The grip on my waist tightened, although Clive appeared as relaxed as ever. "Yes. Russell and Godfrey expressed the same concerns. I'll tell you what I told them. This is the twenty-first century, not the tenth, not the fifteenth. This is a unique city. We have hundreds of different kinds of supernatural creatures: gods and goddesses, wicches and demons, water and land fae, vampires, and one werewolf. I am Master of this city and all who dwell in it. If you have a problem with Sam, come at me, bro."

I almost snorted up my soda. He winked at me, finishing his glass.

"It sounds as though they did," Cadmael said.

"And look how well that turned out for them," I put in. Why did everyone assume I was a huge liability?

Cadmael's lips turned up on one side, somehow making him more terrifying. "Is it true that some of the dead were your doing?" he asked.

I nodded.

Rémy and Liang studied me with unflattering surprise.

"Was Amélie found?" Liang's full focus returned to Clive.

He shook his head. "No. I have people searching. We won't know until we arrive, but she's most likely back with Lafitte."

"He has to know you'll retaliate," Cadmael said.

Clive shrugged.

Cadmael turned his attention to me. "You had time to transform before they were all killed? I thought wolves took longer to do that."

"Oh, well," I glanced at Clive. Were we laying our cards on the table? He regarded me blandly. I guess it was up to me. I studied my nails mournfully.

"Sam?"

"It was my first manicure." Grimacing, I handed him my glass and unleashed my claws.

When Liang and Rémy took a step back, Cadmael moved

forward. "Apex transformation? How are you—what's your last name?"

"Quinn," I said, retracting the claws. Yep. Manicure gone.

Cadmael threw his head back and laughed. "Only you, my friend."

"To be fair," Clive began, "we only discovered the story quite recently."

"Of course," Cadmael murmured, clearly dubious.

"How do you know so much about werewolves?" And was he saying he thought Clive was only interested in me because of my lineage, because of what I could do? I tried not to let the hurt take hold. Clive loved me. I was sure of it. Of course, Cadmael had known Clive for centuries longer than I had.

"Clive is not the first of our kind to dabble with wolves. In another age, I had a pack at my command."

I bristled at his words, wanting to rake my claws across his smug face. Clive wasn't dabbling with or commanding me, the asshole. Cadmael, not Clive. I side-eyed Clive, though, just in case.

"Cadmael," Clive began, "you have had my friendship and respect for a very long time. I know exactly what you are doing, though I doubt Sam does, not knowing you as I do. If you continue down this path, our long and storied friendship will be coming to an end tonight. Think carefully."

I hadn't seen them move but Russell and Godfrey were suddenly flanking us. Faces impassive, they gave no sign of agitation, but their presence at Clive's back spoke volumes.

Rémy grinned, watching the drama play out. Liang, on the other hand, appeared concerned. Well, her face was blank, but her eyebrows were slightly raised in what could be construed as concern.

The lingering good humor on Cadmael's face fell away. "I don't like it."

"Understood," Clive said.

"They're animals," Cadmael added.

Although the other vampires in the room feigned disinterest, all focus was on our small group of seven.

"She, not they. I'm not attempting to change your mind regarding all werewolves, although it is quite outdated. I am asking that my friend show my mate the respect due her, regardless of her bloodline."

That was the first time Clive had used the word 'mate' in reference to me. Vampires around the room stilled.

"And if I refuse?" The tension amped up.

"Then I will thank you again for making the trip and have a car take you back to the airport. I will be sorry to lose your companionship." Clive's arm around me felt like steel.

"For her? You'd betray an ally for her?" Cadmael's voice dripped with disdain.

"I betray no one. I do, however, love someone. You're the one causing a rift because of it. So, let me ask you the same question. For that? You'd betray an ally because of centuries-old bigotry?"

Cadmael ignored the question, searching Clive's face. "You're sure?"

"I am."

I held my breath, waiting to see if I'd lost Clive the friendship of the most powerful vampire in the room.

"Fine."

Rémy laughed, slapping Cadmael on the back. "That was fun."

"Quiet, Rémy," Liang said. "Clive, we'll watch over your nocturne, as though it were our own. You have my word." Turning to me, she held out her hand. "Samantha, it was lovely meeting you. I'm sorry about the manicure. It was a beautiful color."

"Thanks." I felt a little stupid worrying about my nails, but I was glad someone had noticed before the polish disappeared.

"You should go to the airport soon if you want to land and make it to the townhouse before daybreak." Liang checked her watch.

"Yes. You are correct, as usual. Ladies and gentlemen," Clive pitched his voice louder, even though everyone in the house was already listening to his every word, "I am leaving this nocturne in very capable hands. They will be in contact with me if there is a problem. Lafitte and his people chose to start a fight. We are going to finish it. I don't recommend visiting New Orleans anytime soon. The air will be thick with dust."

The shout of "War!" sounded like a crack in the room. Clive raised his glass, a toast to his people. We left shortly after to collect our things.

Once back in my bedroom, I headed straight to the closet to change out of the dress and into my badass bitch wear.

"Sam?"

"In the closet. Jacket or no jacket?" I asked as Clive walked in.

He stopped in his tracks, a number of emotions playing over his face, only one of which I could identify: lust. His gaze traveled leisurely over me, pausing at the strip of stomach visible between my low-cut leather pants and my skintight top. The slick material appeared to have been poured on. The top had a high neck and long sleeves, but I'd left a line of my scarred abs on display. I had tank tops packed. I was going to show my scars.

"We'll need to postpone until tomorrow," Clive said, his voice a deep rumble.

"What happened?"

"That outfit happened." Moving forward, he ran his hands over my black-clad body before they came to rest on my ass. Pulling me toward him, his mouth came down hungrily on my own. I gave as good as I got until he flicked open the button on my pants.

Pushing at his shoulders, I came up for breath. "No, no. We're leaving. We have vampire asses to kick."

"I've got werewolf ass to bite. I'll be very busy for the rest of the night."

When he reached for me again, I ducked under his arms and out of the closet. "No. Have you already forgotten that vampy 'War!' bark downstairs? We have a plane to catch."

"First, that word. Second, we don't bark," he said, following me out. "Third, we don't need to catch it. It's my plane. It waits for me. Fourth, we have a date. After Lafitte and his people are destroyed, you're wearing that and we're meeting right here." He held out his hand. "Deal?"

I pretended to go for his hand, and at the last minute dropped it to stroke him through his trousers. His eyes went vamp black and before I could blink, he had me pinned beneath him on the bed.

"Playing with fire, little wolf," he murmured as he kissed along my jaw.

A knock sounded, making me flinch.

"It's Russell. He's been standing in the hall, trying to decide when it was safe to knock." His lips found a spot behind my ear that drove me crazy.

"What?" I whisper shouted. "Get off. That's so embarrassing. He's standing out there waiting for us to cut it out?"

"Yes." Russell's voice floated through the door.

Clive rolled off me. "You're getting a pay cut," he said toward the door.

"I apologize, Sire, but we really do need to leave if we want to get to the townhouse before daybreak."

Grabbing my suitcase, I went to the door and opened it for Russell. He stood, stoically putting up with our shit. "Sorry," I said, as I dropped the bag by the door, remembering the original question I'd asked when Clive had arrived. I went back for a long leather trench coat. It was overkill for Louisiana in the fall, but it went with the outfit, so I might as well bring it.

I found Russell still standing in the hall, Clive at the door speaking quietly with him. Russell held my bag. "I've got that," I said, reaching for it.

Russell shook his head. "You need to get used to the role, Miss Quinn. Disdain for underlings is a hallmark of our creed."

"I'm not a vampire and you're not my underling." What kind of craziness was this now?

Russell allowed himself a brief grin. "Thank you, but you are the Master's woman. Even if they didn't already know that—which I can assure you, they do—his scent is all over you."

I could feel my cheeks reddening.

"They'll expect haughtiness," he continued.

"Won't they be disappointed then," I snapped as I reached for my bag. He let go. I had both men's attention as I stood with a suitcase in one hand and a leather coat in the other. "I'm not who they expect. That's to my advantage. They won't know what to make of me right up to the moment I take their heads." I stared both men in the eye. "I'm not the pampered bed ornament of the moment. If that's what they're looking for, they'll never see me coming."

Clive closed the door in Russell's face.

"Sire, please." The defeat in Russell's voice made Clive grin.

"We'll be right down. We'll beat the dawn. Now, go away." Clive cradled my face in his hands, thumbs brushing back and forth over my jaw. "You," he said as he kissed me. "They'll never understand." Another kiss. "You're right. They won't see you coming." Kiss. "Now, let's go kick some vampire ass."

When he reached for my bag, I held on. "Mate's privilege," he said, and I relented.

When we turned the last corner to descend the stairs to the main floor, we found Godfrey and Russell waiting at the door with Liang, Rémy, and Cadmael.

Russell gave a short bow, which I'd come to realize he only did when we had an audience. "Sire, the car is ready. May I take your bags?"

Clive handed them off, thanking Russell. The exchange caused Liang's eloquent brows to rise. The first time I'd visited the nocturne, I'd noticed all the vampires bowing and scraping to Clive while he sailed past them, a king receiving his due. Needless to say, I'd given Clive a hard time about it. It warmed me now whenever he thanked someone.

Godfrey walked out the door with Russell, leaving Clive and me alone with his friends. Rémy wiggled his eyebrows at me. "New look? I approve."

"Smart," Cadmael said. "I hear she scored the first kill, right in front of Amélie. They know she's lethal. There's no point in trying to make her seem innocent. This," he said, pointing to my clothes, "is a middle finger to Lafitte and his fetishizing of Old World elegance." It was the most I'd ever heard him say. Judging by Rémy's expression, he'd found it surprising as well.

"I'm not one of you and I'm not trying to be," I said. "If they want to start something with me, I'll handle it."

"Yes," Liang began. "That's the right attitude to have. There are strict lines of etiquette in our society. Lines that will get you killed if you blur or cross them. You're not held to our rules. You're something else entirely. Use that to your advantage."

Clive went to his friends, one after the other, and pressed his forehead to theirs. It was brief and was repeated with no one else in his nocturne. It must have been some kind of sign of parting amongst equals. I'd need to remember to ask about that.

I offered my hand. Liang paused a moment before taking it, which told me I was probably making a vampire faux pas, but whatever. Rémy shook longer than was considered polite, and Cadmael barely touched me before he dropped my hand. It was enough, though. Clive was right about Cadmael being stronger than the rest put together. Touching him had been like stabbing a fork into an electrical socket.

As we walked through the door, Clive growled, "Stop staring at her ass." He didn't specify who he was talking to, but I had my suspicions.

ELEVEN

The Big Easy

The four-hour flight was unremarkable, although flying in a private plane was even better than I'd imagined. Russell and Godfrey sat at the front of the cabin, taking positions on either side of the cockpit door. I guessed if anyone came through that door intent on killing Clive, they'd both step forward. I needed to get used to that, the almost casual way in which Clive's people put themselves between him and danger.

Clive, for his part, spent most of the flight on his phone, which I guessed you were allowed to do if it was your plane. He led others though byzantine conversations with the express purpose of learning more about our enemy. It was masterfully done. I had no idea if the people he was talking with understood what he was mining for, but I doubted it.

His tone and cadence, his choice of words, everything he said projected boredom and a desire to waste time while stuck on a flight. When they eventually asked where he was headed, he still didn't tell them outright, saying only that he needed to visit one of his properties. It wasn't until much later that he dropped a hint that pointed to New Orleans. Each picked up the hint and led the way to a conversation about Lafitte.

The second time it happened, I rolled my eyes at him and

reclined my seat. Maybe I could get a power nap in. Clive tapped a button on his console, dimming the cabin lights for me. I slept better when Clive was by my side, even talking on the phone in the next seat. His scent allowed me to relax in a way I never did alone. A year ago, sitting in my then very secure apartment behind The Slaughtered Lamb Bookstore & Bar, there was still a part of me clenched, bracing for a threat. It made no sense. Even now, when I knew we were about to be attacked, I slept like a baby. I heard Clive's voice and knew I was safe.

A finger stroked down my nose. I opened my eyes what seemed like a moment after I'd closed them and found Clive's face near mine. "Wake up, sleepyhead." He'd reclined his seat and was watching me in the dark. "We'll be landing in a few minutes."

I popped out of my seat to use the restroom and put on my game face before we got off the plane. Whether they made themselves known or not, vamps would be watching us. Thankfully, when I studied myself in the mirror, I didn't find creases on my face or dried drool. I looked exactly the same as when I stepped on the plane. I must not have been out long.

When I went back, I found Clive, Russell, and Godfrey in an intense conversation. "Sam," Clive said with an arm extended, inviting me to join them. I sat beside him.

"As you all know, I spent most of the flight speaking with those who share an acquaintance with Lafitte. What I've learned is that Luc, his unofficial second, disappeared almost a year ago."

"Why unofficial?" I asked.

"Luc doesn't want the responsibility," Russell responded. "He's a behind-the-scenes master tactician. He's the advisor, not the leader."

"Exactly," Clive said. "If Lafitte has been without his advisor for a year, the only thing surprising about this whole situation is that he waited as long as he did to attack. He has little impulse control. And although he believes himself to be vampire royalty, he's..."

"Not exceptional," Russell finished.

"No," Clive agreed. "But if Luc is no longer holding the reins, who is?"

"Amélie?" Godfrey guessed.

Clive tapped his finger against the armrest. "Possibly. She's ambitious and smart. When their attack fell apart, she ran." He sought out my hand while he thought.

"Leticia?" I asked.

"She most definitely played a role, but why lay so much store in her word, given her grudge against me?"

"The 'not exceptional' thing?" I asked.

Godfrey grinned. "He was always content to rule New Orleans. What's changed?"

"That's the question, isn't it? If Luc is truly out of the picture —and we need to confirm that—who pointed him at me?"

We all felt the plane's change in altitude and went back to our seats to strap in. A few minutes later, we were on the ground and taxiing to a small hangar away from the main terminal where an SUV with blackout windows waited.

"One of my people was already down here overseeing some minor repairs on the townhouse. It's made opening the house for this visit easier," Clive said.

The driver was waiting by an open back door when Clive and I descended the stairs from the plane. He bowed deferentially to Clive and then nodded to both Russell and Godfrey. He didn't spare me a glance. Was that because he was being discreet, not knowing who I was and why I was there, or was I beneath his notice?

"Daniel, is everything as I've requested?"

"Yes, Sire. The townhouse has been readied and your guest has arrived."

"Good," Clive said, as he ushered me into the SUV. Russell

took the passenger seat in front and Godfrey slid into the third row behind Clive and me.

"Any problems?" Russell asked.

"Not really a problem." The driver dipped his head in respect when he spoke to Russell. "But I have noticed more of Lafitte's people in the neighborhood."

"Has anyone approached you about this visit?" Godfrey asked.

The driver shook his head. "It's been quiet. Well," he paused, glancing in the rearview mirror at Clive, "was quiet until your guest arrived."

"What guest?" I whispered to Clive, who merely smiled in response.

Letting it go for the moment, I stared out the window into the dark and prayed we'd all make it out, that in a few days we'd be back in this SUV on our way home. Eventually, I started paying attention to the neighborhoods we passed, the little houses lined up shoulder to shoulder. It was the wee hours of the morning, but as residential gave way to industrial, I noticed more lights illuminating the surrounding area. I'd had romantic ideas, based on books and films, as to what New Orleans was like. This wasn't it.

When we exited the main highway and drove farther into the city, I realized how wrong my initial impression was. Those stories in my head came alive. So different from San Francisco, I felt like I was moving through a different world, another era.

"The townhouse is in the French Quarter," Clive told me. Pointing, he added, "That's Bourbon Street."

I whipped my head around but missed it.

Patting my hand, he said, "You'll have time to sightsee." The SUV slowed. "We're a short walk from the center of the Quarter."

The driver turned onto a wide boulevard lined with live oaks. The sign read *Esplanade Avenue*. Creole cottages stood side by side with multistory American townhouses and French colonial homes. Squinting, I tried to study a hazy white vapor on the balcony of one of the houses, but it was there and gone as we drove past. Glare on the window or a ghost?

I wanted the car to stop so I could study each house and any hazy apparitions I might find. Instead, we pulled up to a light gray townhouse with sage green and white trim. The second and third floor balconies were wrapped in a filigree of sage green wrought iron scrollwork.

White lace curtains hung in the windows. Stained glass magnolias filled an inset in the front door. The ceilings of the upper balconies displayed intricate medallions that drew the eye. A live oak stretched its broad branches, protecting the house. It was heartachingly lovely.

Russell exited first, studying the street before pulling open Clive's door. Clive took my hand and pulled me out with him, with Godfrey right on my heels. Each of us stood silently, listening, or in my case reaching out for nearby vampires' thoughts. We were clear. Apparently, we all felt it because we were moving again a moment later.

Clive squeezed my hand. "Before you meet our guest and wonder if I've lost my mind, remember, I may have given in to you joining us, but I will *not* allow anything to happen to you."

The driver went to the back of the SUV to retrieve the bags while we headed for the front door. The entryway had hardwood floors topped with a long carpet that ran the hundred or so feet to the back of the house. The rug was dark with that same magnolia pattern from the front door. Wide doorways opened off the entry hall leading to sitting rooms, a study, and a powder room. The ceiling soared above us, with huge carriage house pendant lights hanging from the ceiling.

It was all a blur as Clive strode to the back of the house. I wanted to stop and study every portrait on the wall, the exquisite antique furniture, the grand crystal chandeliers in the sitting rooms we passed, but Clive was still holding my hand and clearly had a destination.

Overwhelmed by what I was seeing, I hadn't been paying attention to what I was hearing: scary music. How odd. Did they have their own scary music soundtrack going all the time? The idea had me grinning as we passed a gorgeous dining room and turned into the last room at the end of the hall. An airy white cupboard and black marble kitchen stood to the right, with a homier family room to the left. The source of the music became apparent when a scream ripped through the room. On a massive flat screen, a killer with a long knife stabbed a woman in surgical garb.

"The special effects suck. Where's all the blood?" A voice sounded from the couch, although I still hadn't seen anyone.

Clive turned on the light and moved to the end of the couch. "Stheno, thank you for coming."

A woman sat up. She had olive skin, a long, thin nose, and a full head of black corkscrew curls that fell to the small of her back. Light, golden brown eyes glowed with intelligence. She wore a black yoga pants, thick fuzzy gray socks, and a black oversized hoodie with the words *Abandon all hope, ye who enter here*. She was stunning, even in sweats, but I felt a chill run down my spine.

"You promised me snacks and premium channels, *including* porn. Instead, I've got basic cable and a bowl of fruit. What the fuck?" Her curls swayed as she spoke.

"I apologize. We'll have this fixed tomorrow." He eyed the pizza box on the coffee table. "I trust you were able to order in what you needed."

"Yeah, and I'm adding it to your bill," she huffed.

"Understood."

Her gaze traveled over the other three of us, landing on Russell. She bobbed her head, curls swinging. "Hey."

"Stheno, it's good to see you. We'd heard there had been some trouble at your sister's birthday party. We were pleased to hear everyone survived." Russell had a glint in his eye I didn't understand, but then again, I had no idea who this woman was.

She fell back onto the couch, cackling. "Damn, that was a fun party. We caused a couple of," she air-quoted, "*natural disasters.* Euryale promised she'd wait another hundred for the next one."

"So the reports were true?" Godfrey asked, a grin splitting his face. "That tsunami was you?"

Stheno scoffed, "No, that was her." She paused a moment, lost in thought. "Or it could have been Cymi. Both of them had been drinking for a week straight before I got there." Rolling her eyes, she added, "I always get blamed for the destructive shit."

"You have a reputation," Clive said.

"Yeah, I guess." She turned her attention to me. "You're not a bloodsucker."

"No, ma'am." I still had no idea who I was dealing with, but if she could cause tsunamis, I was going to show the proper respect.

She stood, sniffing. "Wolf." She paused, thinking. "Not only wolf…" Her eyes shot to Clive before she threw back her head, howling with laughter.

"This is my mate, Samantha Quinn," Clive said.

That sobered her up quickly. "Mate? Well, well. This should be interesting."

"Has there been any trouble since you arrived?" Clive inquired.

"Your driver's a dick. The liquor cabinet's a joke. And fruit." She gestured toward the front of the house. "If you're talking bloodsuckers and assorted baddies sneaking in, nah. It's been quiet. Now that you're here, maybe I'll start seeing some action."

Putting her feet up on the coffee table, she shoved the pizza box with her heel and said, "Wolf girl, there's still a piece or two left."

"Sam. And I'm good."

"No, you're not. You're hungry. I can feel your stomach churning from over here." She pinned Clive with a glare. "If you're going to hang with a live one, you have to feed her. Go on," she said to me, her voice kinder. "Eat."

Clive's hand ran down my back. "I'm sorry. I should have made sure there was food on the plane."

Moving to the chair adjacent to the couch, I sat and spun the box toward me. "You're right. I am hungry. Thank you. But Clive," I said, as I picked up a piece, "I can feed myself. That's not your job."

The driver came in, carrying our bags. "Sire, the vehicle has been garaged and the house secured. Dawn is near. I'll take your bags to your rooms and then ask that I might retire."

Clive nodded. "Do so."

Stheno pointed down the hall toward where the driver had retreated. She mouthed to Clive, "Asshole."

"Russell," Clive said as he walked to the main hall, "check the alarms and locks while I have a conversation with Daniel."

"I can deal with Daniel, Sire," Godfrey volunteered.

"Good. I need to make a phone call."

The three vamps took off, leaving Stheno and me alone. She eyed me as I ate, but I was too hungry to care. I felt like I should know who she was. Stheno and Eur-something. Sisters. Long-lived if they could wait a hundred years between parties. Natural disasters. What was I missing? She watched me with golden eyes, her curls swaying.

It hit all at once and I almost choked on the pizza I was chewing.

"Got there, did ya?" She chuckled, taking a sip from the beer bottle on the table.

"Um." I averted my gaze. "Aren't you supposed to wear dark sunglasses or something?"

She snorted into her beer. "What am I, a teenager? I don't shoot my wad at every pretty face."

I struggled to swallow. "Eww." I couldn't help it. That image.

Snickering, she winked at me. "I only kill the people I intend to kill. Relax. As of right now, you're not on that list."

"Super." I dropped the uneaten slice back in the box. Our guard was a gorgon.

TWELVE

So, Is Horror Like Porn for Vampires?

I finally found Clive on the top floor. The master suite occupied half the third floor, with a large sitting area and a delicate crystal light fixture hanging from a soaring ceiling. Clive was sitting on the side of the bed, talking on the phone, so I went exploring. The attached bathroom had a walk-in shower as well as an oversized tub. The walls and cabinets were a warm, buttery off-white. The floors and countertops were a light blue-gray stone, a color echoed on the walls of the bedroom. It was a restful oasis.

The bed was a cloud of white bedding and pillows, surrounded on all sides by windows overlooking the garden in the backyard. Windows. Hmm. I got Clive's attention and pointed. He checked his watch while still talking on the phone, and then held up a finger for me to wait. Not a minute later, a panel slid down from the ceiling, blocking the windows from the rest of the room. It was on a timer, like the ones at the nocturne back home. Handy.

I grabbed my bag and went into the palatial bathroom to change and clean up for bed. When I went back into the bedroom a few minutes later, the room was dark and silent. I checked the door to make sure the lock was engaged. A lock wouldn't keep anyone out, but it would cause them to make noise breaking through it. That was all the time we needed.

I slid into soft, cool sheets and settled in. A moment later, Clive's arm snaked around me, pulling me to him. Questions about who was really behind the attack and why looped through my head. I worried I wouldn't be able to sleep, but I needn't have. Clive's solid presence at my back, his scent in my head, allowed me to relax in a way nothing else did and I tumbled into sleep.

When I awoke, it was early afternoon. Clive would sleep for a few more hours. It was hitting me how certain times of the year meant more time with him. Winter, with its shorter days, was my new favorite season and summer my least.

While he was dead to the world, I showered, dressed, and got ready for our first full night in New Orleans. Chances were we'd be fighting off vamps tonight. I pulled my e-reader from my bag and intended to wait for Clive in one of the pretty sitting rooms I'd passed when we'd arrived. I knew not to wander around a new city possibly filled with vampire helpers who'd be over-joyed at finding me on my own. Yes, I could fight, but could I win if I were attacked by a group? Or worse, if I were taken and used as a blackmail tool?

I hit the kitchen for food first. Stheno was right. There wasn't much here. A bowl of fruit sat on the counter. I went to the refrigerator and found bags of blood, some cheese, a stunning display of condiments, a tomato, a carton of milk, eggs, and that was it. Clearly, they'd given the task of stocking the fridge to someone who'd stopped eating long ago.

I searched the pantry closet. Like the refrigerator, it was mostly empty with a few odd items: a box of matzo crackers, a sack of rice, a package of cornmeal, a canister of five-minute grits, an assortment of barbeque sauces, cans of baked beans, garbanzo beans, green beans, and black beans. It was as though the shopper pulled items indiscriminately from the shelves.

"Ridiculous, right?"

I didn't jump, but it was a close thing. I had scented Stheno a second before she spoke. "It's like he has no idea how food works." I was baffled. "They were alive and ate at some point, right? It doesn't make sense."

"That"—she pointed into the open pantry—"is a fuck you for making a high and mighty bloodsucker shop for a werewolf. I'd only agreed to guard you a couple of hours before you showed up. This stuff was already here."

"Oh." I nodded. "That makes way more sense. They hate me. I couldn't figure out who would be stupid enough to piss off a gorgon."

"I'm not much for kitchens. Can you turn any of this into actual food?"

I thought about it. "There are eggs. I can make us a couple of cheese and tomato omelets."

"Perfect. You do that and I'll make the coffee. I know how to use the—wait." She ducked her head back into the pantry and growled. She moved to the refrigerator and slid open the freezer drawer to find it empty. "Motherfucker."

"What?"

"No coffee. Son of a bitch. It was probably that asshole driver." Her expression turned speculative. "I think it's time I put the fear of me in him."

While Stheno plotted, I cooked. Omelets were fast and easy, so I cut up some apples to go with them. I brought our heaping plates to the island where a couple of stools stood. There was no coffee, but Stheno found a bottle of bourbon somewhere. I opted for water.

"Good," she said when she had swallowed her first bite. "So, what's a nice girl like you doing with a cold bastard like Clive?"

I swallowed and said, "Twue wuv."

Scoffing, she took another loaded forkful. "Right."

"It's true. I love him." I didn't know what it was about Stheno, but like Clive, I felt totally safe with her. Which was ridiculous, considering.

"Why? With him, you can kiss the sun goodbye." She took a sip of bourbon. "You'll constantly be dragged into their scheming, homicidal bullshit. No kids." She studied me a moment. "Are you immortal? Yeah, werewolves are, aren't they? Shit, I can't keep all this crap straight."

"I'm up and the sun is out, so I still have it. Clive has helped me out of plenty of werewolf and wicche bullshit, so it seems only fair that I do the same for him. We're in this together." I took a sip of water. "No kids for me anyway. I have to change with the moon. On the immortal thing?" I shrugged. "I doubt I'll live long enough to find out. I have an aunt who wants me dead. Quite badly."

"What'd you do?" She continued eating.

"I was born."

She laughed. "I could see how that would piss her off."

"Honestly, I'm really not sure about any of it. Werewolves can live forever, but I'm half wicche. Then again, I'm a descendent of the original line of werewolves and my mother's family is old and powerful as well." I shrugged again. "And I could get jumped by a pack of vampires tonight, so what difference would any of that make?"

We were quiet as we finished eating. When I picked up her empty plate and took it to the sink to rinse off, I finally asked the question that had been bugging me. "Do you know Meg?"

"Meg?"

"Sorry. Megaera."

Stheno scraped the legs of the stool against the floor as she pushed away from the island to watch me load the dishwasher. "Unfortunately. It's been almost a millennium since I laid eyes on the old buzzard. Why?"

"She's a friend." Sort of. She'd let me sleep on her couch. That probably meant something. "Do you know who her boss is?" I wanted to know who had ordered her not to help me when my aunt was trying to kill me.

"If she's a friend, why don't you ask her?"

"I did. She wouldn't tell me."

"Now that sounds like Megaera. Actually care about someone? No. Secretive, vindictive bitch? Oh, yeah."

Feeling disloyal, I tried to defend her. "She let me sleep on her couch. And flew me across San Francisco to keep me safe from vampires."

"Uh huh, and I bet there was no ulterior motive for doing any of that." She finished off the last of her bourbon. "Listen, kid, I don't know why, but I'm feeling protective of you. There are dozens of bloodsuckers here who would cheerfully tear you apart to get to Clive. I think you should take off and let the bloodsuckers kill each other."

I closed the dishwasher door, wiped off the counter, and then hopped up on it. Stheno deserved my full attention. "Thank you for the protective feelings. Really. I can't leave, though."

"Why not? I can only protect you in this house. Once you walk out that door, there's nothing I can do." She may have sounded irritated, but I could tell it was masking concern.

I went with my gut. "I've been hiding most of my life. Running from the aunt who wants me dead, then from the wolf who did this," I said, lifting my shirt to reveal the extensive scarring on my stomach. "I'm not hiding anymore. Clive and I are in this together."

Stheno wandered back to her couch. "You shouldn't trust us, kid. Me, Clive, Megaera. We're old enough to have more reasons than you could guess for why we do what we do, and virtually all of them are self-serving. We've lived this long because we lie and manipulate and put our own interests first. Always." She flopped down on the cushions and reached for the remote. "And we kill without remorse." She turned on the television, effectively ending the conversation.

Checking my watch and the light through the window, I figured I had at least an hour or two before Clive was up. Grabbing my e-reader, I went in search of a cozy chair.

I found one in the front room, angling it so I could watch the neighborhood stroll by. If any ghostly apparitions showed up, I planned to investigate. In the meantime, I kicked off my running shoes, folded my legs beneath me, and dropped into the latest in a series of mysteries.

Engrossed, I didn't notice the change in light until Clive walked down the stairs. He wore a beautiful charcoal suit with a snowy white dress shirt and a pale gray tie that matched his eyes.

"Hey there, sleepyhead."

Grinning, he leaned over and gave me a kiss. "How's the book?"

"Excellent, and I totally know who the murderer is."

"Do you?" He sat in the chair opposite mine.

"Absolutely. When the author was describing the killer in the beginning of the book, she used an adjective that was avian. I don't remember the word, but it made me think of him as having a birdlike aspect. And right here, she used the word 'hawkish' to describe the doctor's expression." Plus, I never liked the guy.

"You're basing your suspicion on a word?" Clive's eyes twinkled as he watched me.

"Words are important," I said.

"Indeed, they are."

Closing the e-reader, I gave myself a moment to appreciate the stormy gray eyes, short blond hair, chiseled features, and sensuous mouth. He was incredibly handsome in a suit, but I knew his perfect body was even better without one. How'd I get so lucky?

"I love you," I said.

"So I heard." He nodded. "Important words. I'll share some with you. I love you, too."

The sound of hurling came from the other side of the house.

"Shut it, Stheno!" I shouted. I got up and climbed into Clive's lap. "I missed you."

His voice was low as he held me tightly. "When I wake and you're not there, I experience a moment of panic. Every time.

Your scent is there, but you're not. I have to remind myself that you're not tied to the absence of sun, as we are, and that you are no doubt fine. Today, I heard your voice downstairs and forced myself to surface, to listen, to make sure you were all right."

"Eavesdropping's rude."

"True. I'd apologize, but I wouldn't mean it." He kissed me and I melted into his arms. "Stheno's right. We're self-serving and not to be trusted."

"Except you."

"Of course. Except me." He kissed me, long and slow. "But remember, I didn't survive this long by being kind and considerate. She was right when she called me a cold bastard. Before you came along, that was the most apt description. Be aware, these changes are new. I need to think about kinder and gentler decisions. My first impulse will always be lethal for others so that I might survive. Always. I want you to love and trust me, but you really shouldn't."

"Truer words," Stheno called from the family room.

"Rude," I called back.

Clive ignored us both. "I think, though, given how I feel when I wake and you're not there, that you have become necessary for my survival."

I dropped kisses all over his face.

"Immortality, though, is not at question. You stopped aging a few years ago. You're lethal all on your own. With me at your back, no threat, be it your aunt or my enemies, will succeed. We'll share our very long lives together."

I held out my hand. "Deal."

Instead of shaking it, he pulled it to his lips for a kiss. "Feel like exploring the French Quarter?"

"Yes!" Scrambling off his lap, I headed toward the stairs. "I've gotta go change into my badass wear."

"But I like the way you are now." His voice followed me up the stairs.

"Too bad."

"You don't deserve her." Stheno's voice floated up as I crossed the third-floor landing.

"I know," Clive said.

I shut the bedroom door on their words and went in search of my leathers. After a quick change, I went back, hair blown out straight and long, in black leather pants, steel-toed boots, and a different painted-on top. This one was a charcoal gray that matched Clive's suit, a subtle message that we were together.

I found Russell and Clive in the kitchen, drinking glasses of blood, while Stheno vegged on the couch, watching another horror flick.

"You're in a house with vampires and a werewolf," I said to her. "Is that movie scary?"

"Hell, no. These movies are hilarious. Watch. The asshole's breaking into a house where he believes a vampire lives. Spoiler: He does. And this guy's going in—at night, mind you—armed with only a wooden cross and a long knife." Stheno chuckled, seeming to relish the imminent bloodbath.

Clive and Russell had stopped talking, moving closer to the TV to watch. The hero on screen jimmied open a back window and climbed in.

"Is there something wrong with the door?" Clive asked.

"More sneaky-like," I whispered.

"More idiotic," Russell said. "Does he honestly believe the vampire didn't hear him walking down the street, let alone the scrape and groan of that window opening?"

The music changed, slower and more ominous. "Someone's about to become a juice box," Stheno cackled as Clive and Russell nodded.

Two black eyes shone in the dark room. The hero—or moron, depending on your perspective—didn't notice. He loudly tiptoed across the room before opening a squeaky door and peering out.

"Why hasn't the vamp attacked?" I asked.

"Playing with his food," all three said at the same time. It was creepier than what was on the screen.

Godfrey was suddenly beside me. "What are we watching?"

"A preview of tonight," I replied as the music crashed and the vampire sunk his fangs into the struggling man's neck.

"Gotcha!" Stheno chortled.

"Kind of a messy eater, isn't he?" Blood was dripping down the man's neck. It seemed like the vampire didn't have a good seal around the wound. Shoddy work, if you asked me.

The vampires in the room turned to me, their eyes vamp black. I took a wary step back. "Um, is this like porn for you guys?"

I saw movement out of the corner of my eye. Stheno had turned her back on the screen and was watching us, instead. "Step away from the woman with the heartbeat. The fuck?"

Russell and Godfrey left the room quickly. Clive turned his back to me. I glanced back at Stheno, trying to pretend my heart wasn't racing in fear.

"Sorry," Clive said. "We don't watch things like that for a reason." He cleared his throat. "Cold, bagged blood is not the same. We drink it because we must. That film reminded us of how it used to be. The warm, salty, coppery taste of blood fresh from a vein."

"Are you sure I can trust her with you?" Stheno eyed Clive suspiciously.

"Don't be ridiculous. Godfrey," he called down the hall. "Feed. We need to go make ourselves visible. I'm very interested in how Lafitte reacts to our presence."

THIRTEEN

A Lovely Walk Spoiled by an Ambush

The walk through the French Quarter was warm, even in the fall, and the leather pants weren't helping. Either the Quarter was heavily haunted or my eyesight was failing. Glimpses of hazy, white apparitions hovered at the corner of my vision. Every time I turned my head, though, I found nothing. It was making me crazy.

My nose was also proving to be too sensitive for a town like New Orleans. The swampy scent of the Mississippi River underlaid the light, heady scent of periwinkle, impatiens, and begonias flowering in window gardens. That was fine. On top of that, though, was sweat from the hundreds of people wandering through the Quarter. At alley entrances, my poor nose was abused by the scents of urine and vomit. Confusing my senses completely was the mouthwatering aromas wafting out the doors of the restaurants we passed.

The temperature vacillated between warm and cold as well. At first, I thought the chill was coming from air conditioning blowing out open doorways, but then I began walking through cold spots when there was nothing around. Overwhelmed and wondering if the cold spots were more ghosts, it took me a few blocks before I picked up on the vampires following us in a loose pattern.

I touched Clive's arm. "Have you noticed?" I asked in a normal voice and then gestured at the overflowing baskets of flowers hanging beside the entrance to a boutique hotel. There was no point in whispering. The vampires would hear us.

He nodded. "It won't be long now." Pointing up the road, he added, "The bistro is ahead."

"Let's pull the trigger already. Pick a place." I was getting itchy. If we were going to be swarmed and attacked, I'd prefer it was sooner rather than later. The presence of each was a pressure point in my brain. It wasn't painful, but I was aware of each and every one of them.

"Four restaurants up ahead," I said to Clive while subtly motioning up. "And another four behind. Pick a place. I'm starving."

"Sire," Russell said quietly, "there's one down this alley and around the corner that Miss Quinn might enjoy."

We stopped and contemplated the dark, narrow alley as a battle zone. It would get us away from the humans walking around the Quarter, and there were no windows facing the alley. Perfect.

"Yes," Clive said as he headed into the alley. "I know the one you mean. They have a crawfish étouffée I think Sam would enjoy."

When we were halfway through the alley, men appeared at either end, bottling us in. Clive moved in front of me while Godfrey and Russell moved to protect Clive.

"My second called the house when the sun went down. Lafitte was informed of our visit. We have observed the customs. This confrontation is not sanctioned," Clive said.

"Don't think they care," I mumbled.

"We're establishing that what they are attempting is unlaw-ful. If they proceed, it is at their own peril," Russell said.

"We'll chance it," a man chuckled, and then all hell broke loose.

The four vampires on the rooftop dropped down on us as the other four raced in from the other end of the alley. I didn't have time to blink before eight vampires were on us. Two came straight at me, both wearing matching expressions of smug disdain. They thought I'd be an easy kill.

I unsheathed my claws and swung. Both stopped a hairsbreadth from me, shock making their eyes go wide. I lunged forward as they slid away. One feinted to the left and I pretended to follow his movement, unaware that the other had moved in behind me. I felt his intent a moment before he acted, spinning, claws out, taking his head before turning back to the remaining attacker.

He didn't spare his friend a glance, his gaze intent on mine. He was trying to mesmerize me. I heard the message loud and clear: *Stand still. Don't fight back.* Face blank, I dropped my arms. There was a burst of elation and then disbelief as I winked, swung my arm up, and took his head.

When I turned back to the silent fight, I found Clive, Russell, and Godfrey watching me, piles of dust and a couple of headless bodies at their feet.

"Were the theatrics necessary?" Completely unharmed, Clive now sported a fine layer of powder on the sleeves and pantlegs of his suit.

"That was fun. Okay, boys, brush off the vamp dust and let's go have dinner." I really was starving.

Clive held up a finger and pulled out his phone to make a call. "Is Bélisaire available? This is Clive Fitzwilliam, Master of San Francisco."

While Clive waited I mouthed, "Who's Bélisaire?" to Russell.

Godfrey, who was standing closer to me, leaned forward and whispered in my ear, "Lafitte."

I felt the presence of another vamp above us. I studied the roofline, bracing for attack, but it disappeared. Closing my eyes,

I scanned the surroundings for vamps. No one, but I'd felt it. I was sure I had. It had even felt familiar.

A phone somewhere in the vampire dust and discarded clothes began to buzz. Russell's foot went unerringly to it and smashed it.

"Clive, *quelle surprise*. It's good to hear from you."

"Is it? I was under the impression you knew I was here."

"Someone may have mentioned something." Lafitte's French accent was flavored with a hint of Cajun singsong. "Have you come to petition me?" His voice took on a sly tone. Everyone knew exactly why Clive was here.

"*Non*," Clive responded, causing Godfrey to smirk. "Warn, not petition. And my mate expressed a desire—"

"Mate?" Lafitte ignored the threat, redirecting the conversation. "*Bon Dieu*, I had not heard you'd found a mate."

"Odd. Amélie met her. Didn't she tell you?" Nice. Would he outright declare war or try to slide out of the responsibility?

"Amélie? No. We haven't spoken. She was restless, wanted to travel. *C'est tout*."

Another phone began buzzing. Godfrey crushed that one before the second tone.

"Interesting. As I was saying, my mate expressed a desire to see New Orleans, and as I needed to talk with you, I thought we'd come together." Clive still sounded pleasant, if not distracted.

"*Avec moi?*"

"Yes. I wonder, why are you trying so hard—and yet so ineptly—to kill me?"

Two more phones buzzed. Russel got one but Godfrey needed to go into the pockets of a newly turned vamp who had retained his body in true death. Once palmed, he crushed it.

"I don't understand." Lafitte wasn't sounding quite so confident now.

"Amélie, along with twelve more of your people, visited me a few days ago and attempted to kill me." Clive's voice had turned razor sharp.

There was a long pause before Lafitte spoke again. "How do you know they were mine? As I said, Amélie is no longer a member of my nocturne. Perhaps these were outcasts she has gathered into her ranks."

"Possible. They did, however, carry your scent."

I kept most of my attention focused on their conversation, but part of me was continuing to scan for vampires in the vicinity. So far, it was only the three with me.

"There are ways to confuse scent," Lafitte said, a belligerent tone sneaking into his voice.

"There are. Unless you've been bled, though, and they then bathed in it, it's unlikely they would smell so strongly of you or your nocturne."

"I don't know anything about that," Lafitte argued.

"I can see Luc is no longer with you," Clive said, referring to Lafitte's long-term advisor who had recently died—or disappeared. We needed to find out what happened to that guy. "If he were, he'd never have allowed you to tell another Master that you had no knowledge of, nor control over, your own nocturne."

Another phone buzzed. This one was near me. I hopped half a foot to the left, taking it out of commission. Someone was trying very hard to contact this squad.

"I have done neither of those things. Those were not my people. I will not take this accusation light—"

Clive cut him off. "What about the team of eight you sent tonight? Were they yours? By the way," Clive added, "you have a mess to clean up in an alley off Royal Street."

"*Pardon?*"

"Another eight. With the attack in my city, you've lost twenty of your people in less than a week."

The sound of glass shattering could be heard over the phone line. "There seems to be some mistake, some confusion. I'd like you to come to my nocturne so we can discuss it."

I grabbed Clive's arm, willing him not to accept. It was a trap.

"I can have a car come for you now so we can get this straightened out."

Clive grinned. "Thank you for the invitation. We'll visit tomorrow, as we have plans this evening. It would be good, though, if we were left unaccosted. I'd hate for you to lose more people so soon." Clive pushed the end button and Godfrey hooted with laughter.

"He'll be smashing crockery off every wall now." Godfrey's eyes shone in the dark as Russell shook his head, a rueful grin on his face.

"What am I missing?" I asked. "Why are you all so happy?"

Clive caught my hand in his own, kissed my knuckles, and led us out of the alley. "Nocturnes have a special magic all their own. Entering one uninvited can leave one weak." He squeezed my hand. "It shouldn't have any effect on you one way or the other. For us, though, had he not invited us, he would have had the advantage."

"He should have invited us to meet him at a restaurant, not the nocturne," Godfrey explained.

"He's angry and doesn't have Luc to advise him," Russell said. "The frantic calls to the hit team, the glass shattering over the line. He's not used to making these decisions on his own. The seeming incompetence makes him more dangerous, not less."

Godfrey scoffed at that.

"He's powerful but doesn't act rationally. That makes him very dangerous." Russell stopped in front of an elegant restaurant occupying the small corner of an ivy-covered, brick building.

Clive nodded and held the door open for me, while Russell and Godfrey remained on the sidewalk guarding us. "He's right. Lafitte is not without power and influence."

A maître d' ushered us to a table in the corner. I had no idea if locals knew about vampires or if we gave off a dangerous—or maybe just wealthy—vibe, but we were seated at a private table with white linens and flickering candlelight.

Clive and I had a system for eating out. We each ordered a meal, both something I wanted. When I finished the first plate, we'd switch and I'd eat his, too. He was very good at occasionally cutting a piece of meat or rearranging vegetables so that it appeared he was eating, if not enthusiastically.

We started with a plate of charbroiled oysters that was delicious. I ate the crawfish étouffée Clive had recommended earlier while he rearranged items on his plate. When I was done, I gave him my empty bowl and took his plate of brisket with mac and cheese and baked beans. Both my dinners were amazing and made me fall a little bit in love with this city. I would have fallen harder without the vamp attack, but no city was perfect.

"Should we bring something back for Stheno?"

Clive nodded. "Good idea." He motioned to the waiter. "I'll order a meal to be delivered so we can walk around the Quarter." When the waiter scurried up a moment later, Clive explained what he wanted and then ordered me an incredibly decadent dessert of bread pudding with bourbon sauce.

After stuffing myself, I felt good and ready to deal with whatever was waiting out there for us. Godfrey held a to-go coffee cup while he appeared to be chatting with Russell. It was a ruse for the humans. Vampires didn't eat or drink. Technically, they could but didn't. Their bodies had a hard time processing it. Blood was all they needed. They considered everything else pointless and painful. It was a mark of Clive's strength— although I hadn't understood it at the time—that he drank whiskey when he visited The Slaughtered Lamb once a month.

Another thing I'd recently learned was those monthly visits from Clive, when he sat at a table, drinking whiskey, were anomalies. Clive didn't visit the other supernatural businesses. If one of the businesses under his aegis had problems, he had people to deal with it. His visits to my bar had been personal.

I'd been raped, tortured, and dumped alone in his city to

either recover or die. Clive had once explained that I'd touched a nerve in him. Long, long ago, when he was human, he'd had a sister whose head had been filled with stories. She'd often wander off, thinking up new ones to share by the fire at night. One day, though, she hadn't returned.

He'd waited until he'd finished both his work and hers before he'd gone to retrieve her. He'd assumed she'd lost track of time again and was sitting on a felled tree, daydreaming. When he finally found her body, she'd been raped and killed by what appeared to be—judging by their tracks—three men.

Clive never forgave himself for not going in search of her as soon as he'd realized she'd been gone longer than usual. His initial interest in helping me open The Slaughtered Lamb Bookstore & Bar probably stemmed from a need to help a brutalized teen find a future, to try to balance the scales. Russell had told me Clive returned once a month to assure himself I was alive and recovering.

It was my turn to help now. I had to be fearsome, not fearful, so that Clive's hard-earned reputation didn't erode. I refused to be seen as weak, to invite danger to Clive and all the supernaturals protected by him in our city.

FOURTEEN

Always with the Ancient Evil

Clive walked us deeper into the Quarter, my hand in his, as Russell and Godfrey followed. Godfrey ditched the coffee cup in the first trash can we passed, which was a bummer. It smelled good.

"Do we have a destination?" The neighborhood was such an interesting and eclectic array: restaurants, bars, tourist traps, jewelry stores, Voodoo shops, both cheesy and authentic, to-go windows selling cocktails to drink as you stroll.

"No. My being tied up during the day limits our sightseeing to after dark. I wanted you to get a feel for the city if you decide to go out tomorrow."

His phone rang and he paused to take it. Liang was checking in, giving him an update on the San Francisco nocturne. To give Clive some privacy, I moved to a nearby window and gazed at all the lovely jewelry. One in particular drew my eye. It was a large, square-cut opal ring, with triangular diamonds on either side. The color was stunning, a deep indigo with iridescent blues and greens battling the occasional flash of deep red. I moved this way and that to watch the colors race.

"Something interesting?" Clive was off his call and watching me.

Shrugging, I said, "No. Just pretty." I grabbed his hand and we continued down the street. "Everything okay at home?"

"Yes. Liang and Rémy are handling things. Cadmael had to return home to deal with a problem. It was overkill having all three of them, and he had better things to do than babysit my well-protected nocturne."

Interesting, especially as I was almost positive it had been Cadmael I'd felt above us for a moment in the alley.

"Liang and Rémy haven't been in the same place at the same time for at least a century. They've been catching up and keeping an eye on things." He squeezed my hand. "Anything?"

I cast out, searching for those now familiar cold blips in my mind and found them. "Three."

He glanced back at Russell and nodded. "Watching, then."

I could absolutely be mistaken. I'd only met Cadmael once and I'd only felt his signature cold blip in my mind for a split-second, but if it were true—if he were involved in a plot against Clive—it would devastate him. He was already questioning himself and his allies without my added suspicions. If I felt the old Mayan warrior again, though, all bets were off.

We passed a Voodoo shop that, unlike the one down the block, didn't have a front window filled with plastic skulls, brightly colored goddess statues, and spell cards. This one had books and candles and what appeared to be gris-gris bags.

I squeezed Clive's hand and paused at the doorway. "Give me a minute?"

He inclined his head, giving me space and moving toward Russell.

The shop was dimly lit, with long, dark hangings draped from the ceiling. I walked through a cold spot I didn't think had anything to do with the fan spinning lazily overhead. A bored-looking woman with long black hair and a filmy top nodded to me before returning to sorting necklaces. The walls in the narrow, claustrophobic shop were lined with display shelves crowded with figurines, skulls, and Voodoo dolls for the tourists. The back of the shop, though, was different.

I made my way down the close aisle, afraid I'd brush a display case and send hundreds of small potion bottles crashing to the floor. I'd seen shelves of books in the back and was determined to get to them.

"Where y'at?" The deep, raspy voice sounded from the far corner, near the wall of books. And old Black man sat on a stool, sewing a gris-gris bag. The scent of herbs tickled my nose. He didn't appear to be paying attention to me, but there was no one else around.

"Good evening, sir. I wanted—" I pointed to the books.

Nodding slowly, he continued his work. "What you want is over here." He inclined his head toward the shelf right beside him.

"But I didn't say…"

The old man hummed a tune, all the while sewing tiny stiches in the bag.

The shelf to his right contained books on necromancy and communicating with the dead. Glancing at him, I saw a gentle smile tugging at his lips.

"How'd you know?"

"Oh, now," he chuckled. "I know lots of things, like the one you want is that cracked red leather one at the end. That'll do for now."

I reached for the book and felt a quick static shock, causing the old man to chuckle louder.

"Now, now, no reason for you two to tussle. You open yourself up, Miss. Let it teach you what it knows."

The book felt warm in my hand. *The Rituals of Necromancy*. Flipping open the book, I saw a chapter on "Pulling Back the Veil" and one on "Communicating with the Dead." Yes, this seemed like the perfect primer for me.

"What you need to remember is that you're stronger than they are. Don't let 'em scare you. They're hanging on 'cuz they're hurting and need help. You do what you can to help 'em, yeah?" He lifted the small bag to his mouth and cut the threads with his teeth.

"Yes." I had no idea what I was agreeing to, other than not being a dick and creating an army of the dead to do my bidding.

"Good girl." He reached for my hand and placed the gris-gris bag in it. "This'll protect you some. Hold tight when you need it." He wrapped my fingers around the bag, causing a shiver to run down my spine. Tapping my closed fist, he added, "*Mouri.* You say that while you're holding tight. Don't forget now." He dropped my hand. "No charge for that. The book you can pay for up at the desk."

I stumbled away, thanking him, but he only nodded once and took up another piece of fabric to begin the task of creating another small spell bag. I didn't remember paying. What felt like a moment later, I was back on the sidewalk, the red leather book in my hand, a receipt peeking out the top. What was *that*?

Clive took my hand and we stepped off the sidewalk into the street to go around a ghost tour. I tugged on his hand, wanting to stop and listen.

"...guests have claimed to see a small boy running down the hall in the middle of the night. A night when no guests had children. See that window up there?" A woman in cargo pants with pockets bulging, a microphone in her hand, and a small, portable speaker hanging from a strap over her shoulder pointed to a darkened window at the end on the second floor. "Guests have woken up to find a woman standing at the end of their bed, watching them sleep. She never says or does anything. Just watches. Others have said they've seen her reflection in the large mirror at the end of the hall. A hall empty but for themselves."

"Maybe you'd like to try the vampire tour next," Godfrey whispered in my ear.

Rolling my eyes, we continued on, passing two more ghost tours, a vampire tour, and a history tour. If I hadn't been with a snarky vampire, I'd have joined each and every one. While these guys were dead to the world tomorrow, I'd try to find a couple. I'd never been here and yet I was feeling a strange kinship with the city. I wanted to learn everything.

"Still with us?" Clive asked.

I mentally scanned our surroundings again. Where had the third one gone? I reached out farther and found a huge cluster of them. I tugged Clive's hand again and tilted my head to the north. "Is the nocturne that way?" I whispered.

He glanced up at street signs and then shook his head. "It's outside of town, in that direction." He pointed north. "It's a former plantation."

"Of course it is." I shook my head and tried again. "Maybe they have a clubhouse in the Quarter, because there is a glut of them in that direction." I again pointed a couple of blocks northeast of where we were standing.

"Are the three still with us?"

I cast out around the Quarter again. Had the third one been recalled to the nocturne? "Only two, a couple of blocks back, following us." Slowly, I realized there was something else. The vampires felt like icy pinpricks in my mind. This something else was more of a chilly fog hovering a few blocks to the left. The closer I got, the more I felt a subtle pull. Following that pull, I eventually stopped in front of a huge white building. It was multiple stories in an L-shape. A large courtyard of manicured shrubs planted in a geometric design sat between the two wings of the building. A plaque was affixed to the five-and-a-half-foot wall blocking off the building and courtyard from the sidewalk. *The Old Ursuline Convent.*

"Problem?" Clive asked.

Nodding slowly, I backed up into the empty street so I could see the dark, distant building more clearly over the wall. A chill went down my spine.

"Is there anyone inside?" All three vampires shook their heads. They'd know, seeing as they could hear a heartbeat a block away. "There's someone trapped inside, imprisoned by something dark."

Clive turned to me and waited.

"I can feel a dark, sticky, molasses-like evil oozing from the floorboards, dripping from the windowsills." I involuntarily took a step back and bumped into a parked car. Clive wrapped an arm tightly around me.

"You're shaking," he whispered.

"Hell didn't feel this evil," I said.

"She went to Hell?" Godfrey asked.

"No," Russell responded. "Her aunt trapped her in a vision of Hell. You were never there, Ms. Quinn," he added.

He was right. I hadn't been. It had felt so damn real though. Maybe this was what the real Hell was like.

Clive reached up and touched my necklace, the one given every protective spell and stone my friendly neighborhood dragon shifter could come up with. This, however, didn't feel like a spell.

As much as I wanted to get as far away from the convent as possible, that chilly fog bank that had drawn me was nearby. It shimmered strongly in my mind and then I saw it—her—in a window on the third floor. Shuttered dormers were dotted along the roof line, five of them, with one small round window under the roof peak. She was a ghost. I was sure of it. A ghost stood behind the round glass, eyes locked on mine. She seemed young, maybe a teenager, and she exuded a sense of resigned pain. Her lips were moving, but she was too far away to hear.

"Can you see her?" I whispered to Clive.

All three men glanced around the property, trying to locate who I was referring to. Right. They couldn't see ghosts. The girl pounded against the glass and waved her arms. I'd stared right at her. She knew I could see her, and she'd become frantic.

"Who?" Clive asked.

"A ghost in the third-floor window, the round one beneath

the cross on the roof. She's trapped, desperate to get my attention."

"She can see ghosts?" Godfrey asked.

"Quiet," Russell responded.

A shiver ran down my spine. Something in the convent was watching us. Shadows moved. Waiting. I flipped open the book in my hand and scanned the chapter on contacting the dead. I had no idea what I was doing—I'd read the book properly later —but I got the general gist. I needed to access that part of me that was a necromancer, that recognized the dead. So, as I did with vampires, I reached out to her cold, foggy essence, opened my mind, and listened.

Bile rose to the back of my throat. I had to fight the urge to run, to get as far away as I could, and to forget I'd ever been here. Whatever was holding her had been feeding off her for a hundred years. The entity was strong, but that girl, silently screaming for help, needed me.

I handed the red book to Russell. "Take care of this, please."

When he nodded, I turned to Clive. "What do you know about this place?"

"The Ursuline Convent was a hospital of sorts, an orphanage, a school for girls." He shrugged. "I wasn't living here then, but I think wealthy men also brought over young women from Europe to be groomed here before they married." He glanced down the street at a couple making their way in our direction. "There's a legend that vampires came to New Orleans through this convent."

"What?" I was pretty sure that was called burying the lede.

"As I said, I wasn't here then. The legend goes that a group of young women—students, prostitutes, vampires, who knows— arrived in New Orleans with caskets."

"Translation error," Russell interrupted.

Nodding, Clive said, "Most likely. They arrived with boxes holding their belongings. The girls were delivered to the Ursu-line Convent and never seen again."

"It's said the third floor was locked up tight," Russell continued. "Windows nailed shut with blessed nails. Shutters sealed. The floor was locked. No one went in. No one went out."

"Odd." Godfrey, who'd seemed bored by storytime, studied the convent with new interest.

"There are many plausible explanations that don't involve vampires," Clive said.

"Disease," Russell offered. "If they'd arrived ill, they would have been quarantined. It could have been as simple as that."

"The church might have sold them off to the highest bidders and then needed to cover their disappearance," Godfrey suggested.

"The point is, it was over a century ago and we have no idea what happened to them, if they did in fact disappear." Clive studied the window I'd indicated. "Is this like the ghost that warned you about the attack at the nocturne?"

I shook my head, not sure I was right. "I don't think so. This doesn't feel specific to me. I think she's desperate because she knows I can see her."

"Meanwhile," Godfrey said. "Where's our tail?"

I stretched out my awareness. "Two around the corner. You guys take off. I have to try to help."

"No." Clive's hand shot out and grabbed my arm. "You are not exploring a building dripping evil—your words—to rescue a ghost."

I gave him a quick, hard kiss. "I can handle it. You guys hurry up. They're about to turn the corner. I'll meet you back at the townhouse." I broke away from Clive and vaulted over the wall, landing silently on the other side.

As soon as my feet hit the dirt, a wave of revulsion swept through me. I closed my eyes and concentrated. My guys were gone and the two following us were passing the convent now. I gave them a moment to turn the corner and then made my way across the dark courtyard, sticking to the deepest shadows.

When another wave of nausea hit me, I spat, wiped my

mouth, and moved closer to the convent. The main entrance had a portico with a balcony on top. Once on the balcony, I'd need to scale the facade to get to the uppermost window. Stomach flipping, I went momentarily light-headed. Good thing I didn't have a problem with heights.

My scalp prickled. I was being watched. Casting out again, I checked the area. No vamps. One ghost on the third floor surrounded by a dark, possessive evil. It knew I was here and why. I felt its intent to stop me. To kill and feed on me.

When I made it to the entry steps, I stared at the front door, which was probably armed. That wasn't what had stopped me, though. It was the dark need, pulling me toward the door. It wanted me in the building in the worst way. It wanted to swallow me whole.

FIFTEEN

Spit It Out!

In the deepest shadows, to the side of the portico, I jumped ten feet, grabbing a hold of the edge of the railing before pulling myself up and scrambling over. The balcony platform was about eight feet square, with pots of flowering vines in the four corners.

Hearing a tour group approaching, I dropped to a crouch, studying the twenty-five feet I'd need to scale to get to the window. I could barely see the top of her head from this angle, but I could hear her tinny wails for help. How the hell was I going to do this?

I sensed, rather than saw, movement in the French doors directly in front of me. Oh, yes. It was watching me. Bile rose again in my throat as black eyes blazed in the dark. A sound like long, sharp nails squealed against the glass. When the doorknob turned, I fell back on my ass, something sharp biting into my right hand as I hit the concrete.

Laughing. It was laughing at me. I was sure of it. I studied my palm in the dark. There was a small puncture in the center that stung like hell. A thorn from one of the vines beside me had broken the skin.

When I was sure the tour group had moved on, I stood and

brushed myself off. The malevolent entity didn't want to, or couldn't, come out. I felt its rage, its hunger at having me so close and yet out of reach.

Okay, enough dicking around. The French doors had open shutters, resting against the side of the building. I pulled one side a foot away from the wall and jumped, landing easily—albeit off-balance—along the top. Grabbing a decorative edge in the wall six feet above the door, I steadied myself and planned my next step.

Wedging one boot against a stucco frame around the French doors, I pushed myself farther up the wall, catching a hold of a narrow ledge beneath the circular window. I would not look down.

My boot slipped and my stomach swooped, dots floating before my eyes. I was hanging by my fingertips, thirty feet off the ground.

"Why do I smell your blood?"

I jolted at Clive's voice, almost falling to my—well, it was doubtful I'd die, but it would hurt like heck. "Jeez! Are you trying to give me a heart attack?" Stupid, silent vampire. "And aren't you supposed to be leading those vamps on a merry chase away from me?"

"I'm not leaving you alone at the convent of evil. And Russell and Godfrey have already led them back to the townhouse."

Clive hung over the side of the roof, staring down at me, one hand wrapped around the cross, the other reaching for me.

"So, that vampire-cross thing is a big lie, huh?"

His eyes darted to the religious symbol he was hanging from and grinned. "Give me your hand and I'll pull you up."

"Can't reach that far. I'm going to have to jump and you better catch me. We're only going to get one shot at this." My fingers were killing me, losing strength, but I held on, trying to find a foothold that could give me some leverage. After scrabbling a few minutes, I found it. It wasn't much, but the tips of my boots caught on it. "Here we go." Muscles bunched, I leaped up, arms extended, and prayed for a miracle.

I only had a moment to picture my skull cracked open on the cement below before Clive's hand was around my wrist.

Heart racing, I blew out a breath. "Please don't drop me."

"Never. Now, why do I smell your blood?"

"It's nothing." I didn't know what would happen if the sap-like evil ooze that had crawled up my fingers while I dangled from the ledge had made its way inside me, but I was pretty sure it would be really bad. I concentrated all my energy on the cut. Lydia, Owen's mom, had taught me to visualize my magic like a spool of glowing thread wound tight inside my chest, ready to uncoil when needed. I pulled on that thread and mentally wrapped it around my palm, casting the cleansing spell. A high-pitched gasp sounded in my head and the invisible ooze was gone.

"Can you pull me up a little higher? I think I can break the window with my boot." The ghost in the window was frantic, pounding at the glass, mouth open in a scream.

Clive lifted me until I was gripping the edge of the roof. My plan was to open the sealed third floor, freeing the girl. I hesitated, though, unsure. What if the trapped, suffering ghost was actually the public face of the evil inhabiting the convent, drawing idiots like myself in so it could feed? She felt like a ghost, though. If I broke the window, would I be releasing the evil spirit as well?

Holding tight to the edge of the roof, Clive's hands firmly around my wrists, I swung forward, my boot smacking against the round window below. Something screeched against the glass like little shards of pain in my mind.

I kicked out again, but my position made it difficult to do it with enough force. I needed to drop lower. "I'm going to let go of the roof. I need you to dangle me maybe six inches lower than I am now."

"Sam." The warning in his voice was loud and clear.

"What's the worst that can—"

"No. We don't tempt fate like that."

I let go and he lowered me until one boot was able to find the lip of the window frame. Movement caught my eye and I peered through the window. The young female ghost was staring up at me, hope and gratitude shining in her gaze. A moment later, her hazy light faded and something very different stared out at me from the dark.

Ooze inched up my boot, but I mentally wrapped that magical thread around it and recited the scouring spell I'd been taught. A pulse of magic burned the ooze away. That gave me an idea. I closed my eyes, pulling on that thread and wrapping it around the toe of my right boot. Chanting what I hoped were the words I'd been taught to a spell for opening things, I swung back my right foot and kicked with all my might.

The glass spiderwebbed but didn't shatter. Still chanting, I focused my power on the window again. This time when I kicked, the glass crumpled to the floor of the room. The ghost flew out the window. Right behind her was a shadow with malevolent intent. Flowing around me, it cut off my air before yanking me away from Clive with such force, he flew off the roof and down to the darkened courtyard below.

Slammed into the balcony, pain exploding in my head, I lost what little breath was still in my lungs. It wanted me dead. Wanted to feed on me as it had the ghost girl. I felt its intent. It knew I was a necromancer, as it had been in life. Doing what the book had said, I opened that part of me that had a talent for communicating with the dead to see my invisible enemy, to understand and defeat it.

The dark, hazy cloud took form. It was a woman. Lungs ready to burst, I focused all my energy on the entity trying to choke me out. Flashes exploded in my head: a woman in a nun's habit, vamp black eyes and glistening fangs, children, a grotesque rat-like man giggling, a teenaged girl offered as a gift… It was too much. I couldn't properly process the rapid-fire images.

Unable to breathe, I lashed out but couldn't grab hold of anything. She had no physical form. Then I remembered the old man in the Voodoo shop. I pulled the gris-gris bag from my pocket and held it will all my might, even as black dots danced before my eyes. And then Clive was there, trying to hold me. I pushed him away, kicking him back, fearing this magic would hurt him.

When he was crouched a few feet away, I did what the old man had said. I thrust the gris-gris bag into the dark miasma and shouted the word 'mouri' in my head, adding my own magical power behind it. Screeching tore at my mind and then my ears popped and I could breathe.

Gulping air, I dropped my arm. Clive crouched beside me, eyes vamp black. I sensed his desperate need to destroy what was hurting me and his frustration at being unable to.

Rolling to my side, coughing, I reached out a hand. A moment later, he was pulling me up, cradling me in his arms. Closing my eyes, resting my head against his chest, I took a moment to appreciate being alive. My head hurt like a mofo, but I was still here.

I slipped the gris-gris back in my pocket and tried to stand. Clive helped me up, hanging on when I swayed.

"What was that?" The anger in Clive's voice comforted me. I wasn't alone.

Wrapping my arms around him, resting my battered head on his shoulder, my breathing slowly returned to normal. "Thank goodness I stopped in that Voodoo shop. He gave me the magic —the word—to save myself."

Gently running his hands over my head, he studied me, concern clear. "He? You didn't speak to a man in that shop, only the woman at the counter."

"No. In the back, an old man was making gris-gris bags. He

pointed me to the right book and gave me the bag and the word I needed to use."

Clive shook his head. "Love, I may have been standing on the sidewalk, but I was paying attention to you. The woman at the counter nodded to you as you entered. You went to the back of the shop, took a book off the shelf, and brought it to the counter to pay."

"No." I shook my head and instantly regretted it, as it felt like my brain was sloshing around free inside my abused skull. I'd go back tomorrow, thank the man, and see if he had any other advice for me.

"Let's get you home." Concern colored his voice as he pulled me close and then dropped from the balcony, landing us easily on the path below. "Can you walk?"

"Yep." Probably.

He walked us slowly across the courtyard, which was good as I was having some balance issues. When we reached the wall surrounding the convent, he leaped, carrying us both over. The street was dark, but the streetlights were enough to make my stomach roil. I stopped, eyes closed against the light, and leaned on Clive.

He picked me up and swung me around so I was clinging to his back. Fighting back another wave of nausea, I rested my head on his shoulder and prayed for a dark room with clean, cool sheets and blessed oblivion. He wrapped his arms under my thighs, holding me up. I let my arms dangle over his shoulders and burrowed my nose into the crook of his neck. His scent leveled me. If Clive was nearby, I was all right.

"Can you sense anyone following?"

Right. I forgot we still had vampires to worry about. I reached out, but it was far more difficult. That thing had kicked my ass. I tried again. After a brief, barely there flash that felt like Cadmael, I found one following closely behind. "One, but he's a good guy."

Clive cursed. "I told you to leave this to me."

Russell was suddenly beside us. "And I vowed to protect you. I can't do that from the townhouse." He glanced at me as we turned a corner and wove our way through sudden foot traffic. "That was quite a fall, Miss Quinn. How's your head?"

"How long were you shadowing me?" Clive's voice betrayed a mix of pride and exasperation.

"I arrived when Miss Quinn began scaling the building."

We turned off a main street, the pedestrian traffic dropping to a few stragglers. "There was some kind of malevolent being in that convent."

"The ghost?" Russell asked.

"No. She was its victim. When I broke the window, the ghost finally escaped and the entity went for me as a replacement." Something stopped me from telling them the next part. I could be wrong—probably was—but the evil spirit felt like a necromancer, a wicche who had been made a vampire. There were too many questions and my head wasn't working properly at the moment. Given I was a necromancer surrounded by vampires, it felt like that was the sort of information that needed to be hidden at all costs, lest someone decide to experiment.

"Thankfully, I had the spell the old man in the Voodoo shop had given me," I explained, realizing Clive wouldn't have known what I'd been doing either.

Russell studied me as we turned another corner. "You spoke to no man in the shop. We were listening to make sure you were safe."

A visit tomorrow was definitely on the agenda. If the man had a spell that could hide him from vampires, I wanted it too. My hand stung. Remembering the vine, I held up my hand and studied the puncture on my palm. It should have healed by now. Instead, the small wound was open and had black at the center. Dirt or some of that evil ooze finding a way inside me? *Shitshitshit.*

"Clive, can you suck me?"

"With pleasure, but we should wait until we're back at the

townhouse." He turned another corner. The street was dark and quiet. He picked up speed.

"Ha ha. See that black spot? It's probably nothing, but that entity wanted inside me very badly." The thought scared the shit out of me. I wasn't like that thing. I'd never be like it.

He stopped on a dime and grabbed my hand. Studying it, he sniffed and then put his mouth against my palm and sucked at the wound. After the initial pinch, it had me wishing we were alone. *Wait!*

"Spit it out!" I smacked his shoulder with my other hand. "It wants a new host. Don't give it a Master vampire."

He leaned over a shrub, but then thought better of it, dropping one of my legs in order to retrieve a handkerchief. He spat into that. A black, tar-like substance was mixed with my blood. Clive pulled my hand to his mouth and repeated the process. It took three pulls before my blood ran clean.

"Why the handkerchief?"

He took a moment before he responded. "Didn't want to seed the earth with evil." He spat into the handkerchief again. "My mouth is numb, and—as you would say—I'm feeling very stabby."

"Bite me!" I scrambled down. Russell caught me and held me steady. "Clive, bite me. Right now, before it takes hold. My blood will clean out your mouth." Hopefully. How the hell would I know, but it sounded right.

"She may be right, Sire."

Russell held me up, my back to his chest. Clive's eyes went vampy black as his fangs lengthened. I was exhausted but I tried to push my magic out again in a pulse of white light as he bit into my neck. He drank long and steady, consuming far more than the little sips he'd occasionally taken in the past. I slumped against Russell.

"Sire, her heart is slowing. You're killing her."

Clive disappeared and the world went black.

W HEN I AWOKE, I WAS FULLY CLOTHED, INCLUDING BOOTS, AND lying on my bed. A bed that was empty but for me. The evening rushed back, including Clive trying to suck me dry. Had that black tar turned my gentleman caller evil or was magical blood catnip to vampires?

Standing on shaky legs, I went to the bathroom and studied myself in the mirror. My neck was fine. I didn't even see a bruise. Next, I studied my palm. Again, I didn't see a scar. Had I dreamed the night before? I glanced down at my clothes, felt the gris-gris in my pocket. Nope. It had happened.

I peeled off my top, checked for injuries, and found bruising. My back, in particular, was one big purpling bruise, yellowing at the edges. Struggling out of my leather pants, I wondered if I could put leather in the wash. Did this place have a washer and dryer? I had one more pair of leather pants, blood red. They were up for tonight.

I finally made my way into a gloriously hot and soapy shower. As I washed off the evil residue of last night, I wondered where Clive was. Head still muzzy, I reached out for him. He wasn't in the townhouse. Damn. Where was he?

SIXTEEN

And Thus Begins Our Sculpture Garden

Cleaned, dried, and evil-free, I put my hair up in a ponytail, dressed in my usual jeans, hoodie, and running shoes, and then noticed the red leather necromancy book on my nightstand. Grabbing it, I went downstairs to discover what fresh hell we were dealing with today.

The entry was bright—still day then—but there was a new sculpture standing at the base of the stairs. And another one in the front room. What the hell? And then it hit me. "Stheno, what have you been up to?" I called down the hall.

I found her in the same family room off the kitchen, kicked back on the couch, feet on the coffee table. She held a beer loosely in one hand while the other rooted around in a chip bag, a holiday romance playing on the big screen.

"Have you seen Clive?" He had to be fine, right? He'd survived for a millennium; surely last night wouldn't have done him in.

"Shh!" She pointed at the screen.

"Really?"

"Fuck off. I'm enjoying myself. You wanna be critical of my viewing choices, you can do it in another room. This is my room."

I sat down on the couch next to her and put my feet up. "Any chips left?" He was fine. He had to be.

"What did I say about fucking off? And quit talking over my show." She didn't sound angry, just annoyed to be interrupted. I probably should have been afraid of her, especially after seeing her handywork in the entry. She was like Dave, though, all snarling anger on the outside, not as angry on the inside.

At the commercial, I popped up and went to the kitchen in search of food. I was starving. My body had taken a lot of abuse last night.

"Did you like the dinner we sent?" I asked as I rooted through the refrigerator that finally had food in it. "You want a sandwich?"

"Hell, yes, I want a sandwich and dinner was good. Thanks." She finished her beer and threw the bottle over her shoulder. Thankfully, I'd seen the movement and caught it before it hit me in the side of the face.

"Did you want me to spit in your sandwich?"

She snorted. "You're closer to the recycling."

I dumped her bottle into the bin and then began taking lunch meats, cheese, a tomato, and lettuce out of the fridge. "Mustard, mayo, both, neither?"

"Horseradish."

"Okey dokey." I found bread in the pantry. "Do you like your bread toasted or not?"

"Commercial's over. Shut up," she growled.

I like mine toasted, so I did the same for hers. I walked back a few minutes later, carrying two plates, my own bag of chips, and two drinks under my arm. I handed her a plate and a bottle of beer and then settled in to eat and read my book while she watched true love triumph under the mistletoe on Christmas Eve.

I started with the introduction, which gave some good general information I needed. One passage stood out, though. It explained why I kept losing my sight.

Matter cannot be created or destroyed. It can, however, be altered. It is the same with magic. When we manipulate the natural world, we must pay the price of that manipulation. For small white magic spells, the payment for balance is so inconsequential, most fail to notice. That's not to say some payment hasn't been taken, only that we don't always feel it. For those gifted with strong magic, like the true necromancer, the payment is far heftier and often painful. Nature requires balance.

Balance. I was invading another's most private thoughts. I was using my powers to create an imbalance and the magical world was backhanding me for it with horrible headaches and blindness. My reasons were irrelevant. For every action, there was a reaction.

After the credits rolled, I put down my empty soda can and finally asked Stheno what I was dying to know. "Did Clive come back at all last night?"

"Walking out on you already, huh?" She smirked at me and took a swig.

"Don't be a dick. I waited until your movie ended. Did he get home okay and then leave?" Please, don't let him be caught out there in the sunlight. Did we purge the poison from his system?

"No, he didn't. And do you really want him back? He about drained you dry last night. I say good riddance." When she reached for my bag of chips, I pulled it away.

"No. And last night wasn't Clive's fault." When she glared at the bag of chips I was holding out of her reach, I relented and handed them over. "Now tell me what you know."

"Russell said you battled a convent of evil, rescued a ghost, got infected by said evil, and that Clive sucked the evil out—which would make a great porn title: Sucking Out the Evil."

"Stheno."

"Right. Anyway, Clive went all fang, you almost died, and Russell brought you back here." She stuffed her hand in the chip bag and started eating.

"That's it? I already knew all of that." Damn it. What happened to Clive?

"Then what did you ask for?" She picked up the remote and started flipping.

I needed to wait for Russell. Stheno was going to be no help. "What's with the new statues?"

She grunted a laugh at that. "Assholes thought they could sneak in here." She shook her head.

"What time did they break in?" I thought the vampires following us had gone back to the nocturne, but maybe they'd come here.

"One came a little after you four left last night. The other two showed up early this morning, right before first light. They were cutting it close, anyway. Now instead of a carpet full of dust, you get pretty statues to put in your garden." She paused a moment, her hand halfway from the bag to her mouth. "I wish they'd die in more interesting positions, though. They're always standing there shocked, like slack-jawed idiots."

"Three? I only saw two statues in the entry." Did I miss one?

"I put the first one in Clive's holding cell in the basement. They like to torture their prisoners for information. I didn't want to ruin anyone's fun. Since I'd saved him one, I figured I could have the other two." She belched, and I wondered if when she turned them to stone, she also consumed something of them. Hmm, question for another day.

"You said there's one in the basement?" I hopped up and then realized I had no idea where the basement was.

She pointed back toward the hall. "Door to the side of the stairs. It's day, though. He'll be dead."

I headed toward the entry. "He's dead even at night."

"I'm glad to hear you remember that," her voice trailed after me.

It took me a moment, but I found the panel in the wall that led to the basement. It was like the panels in Clive's house in San Francisco. I had to tap the wall in the right spot to get the door to release. Luckily, Daniel, Godfrey, and Russell had all tapped it recently, so I followed their scent markers to the right spot.

The cement steps smelled strongly of damp. I flicked on the light switch. Wait. How was there a basement in this house? I thought the water table was too high in New Orleans. It was why people were buried above ground here. Warily, I hit the bottom step, half expecting to wade to the holding cell. No water, but I did smell traces of magic in the air. For me to get a whiff, it had to be an active spell, one that was probably keeping my feet dry.

I passed six closed doors. They were closer together than they should have been, as though the rooms were a half to a third of the size of a regular bedroom, which, I suppose, made sense. Lying there dead didn't take up a lot of room. At the end of the hall, there was a door to what appeared to be a much larger room.

Opening it, I found a metal cage, solid on five sides with thick mesh covering the front. Inside, a vampire hung slack from shackles on the back wall. I had a theory about the whole dead-during-daylight-hours business, and it was one I was going to test.

If Clive could, with enough motivation, be awakened during the day, then he couldn't be dead. Well, not completely dead. Yes, only really old and powerful vamps could do this, but since they could, they weren't dead. And if *they* didn't die during the day, it stood to reason none of them did. It struck me as more of a state of stasis, rather than true death, like those frogs that could survive being frozen solid during the winter.

Putting this theory to the test and understanding I'd be paying a price for it, I sat cross-legged on the cement in front of the cage, leaned my forehead against the stiff mesh, and opened my mind to the dead. Swirling mist filled my mind. The dead were everywhere. I had no idea what I was doing but tried reframing my thinking. Not the long dead, moldering in the ground, not the newly dead in hospitals and mortuaries, not the ghosts who chose to remain on this plane. I wanted vampires.

Cold blips came to the fore in my mind, but they expanded,

slowly, unrelentingly covering the world. Could I touch the mind of a vamp in, say, Romania? I superimposed a mental map over the cold, faint blips and zeroed in on one in Romania. It could have been Hungary or Bulgaria. It wasn't an exact science.

It was evening there, and I could feel his hunger. He was going out to hunt. My head started to pound, so I pulled out quickly. I didn't have Clive to take away the pain, so I didn't want to waste time on an experiment, no matter how compellingly disturbing it was.

I narrowed my focus to New Orleans and searched for Clive. It took some time, skimming over blips, hunting for *my* blip, but I eventually found him. I had no idea where he was, but he was alive-ish, so I relaxed on that front.

Changing my focus, I narrowed in on the cold blip directly in front of me. Did vampires have thoughts or dreams when in stasis, assuming I was right about that? I could have tested my theory on one of the other vamps in the house, but I didn't know if any of them were old and strong enough to wake during the day. I didn't want my throat torn out before they realized who I was and that they shouldn't kill me. So, a prisoner in a cage seemed like a perfect test subject.

I reached into his mind and felt the immediate pounding in my head. Trying my best to ignore the pain, I squeezed my eyes closed and mentally pushed. It was like pushing on a thick wall of rubber. It moved with me but didn't allow me through. In frustration, I focused my energy into a pinprick of annoyance, trying to break the protective bubble around his thoughts. Pain sliced through my head, light flashed behind my eyelids, and I was in.

To say a vampire's thoughts were dark was an understatement. I felt as though I was lost in a thick fog on a starless night, forever wandering in circles. I would have pulled out to escape the crushing anxiety of that dark, suffocating weight, but a light flashed in the corner of my vision.

Turning, I mentally stumbled forward, searching for that

elusive flicker of light I'd seen a moment before. There was another flicker to my left, so I changed direction. At last, something flickered right beside me and I stepped into it before I had a chance to question the advisability of that.

I was consumed with hunger and thoughts of blood slaking my thirst, blood gushing down my throat, my fangs tearing at flesh. The need was mindless and all encompassing. I wasn't sure how to escape the hunger, but I tried mentally stepping back while pushing that vision away. It shouldn't have worked, but it did.

Back in the dark, muffling fog, I allowed myself one moment to panic. What if that hadn't worked and I'd been trapped forever in a vampire's thirst? Doing my best to shake it off, I wandered aimlessly, searching for another flicker of light.

Head pounding horribly, I finally saw one and dove into it before it went out. Cold, black eyes stared back at me. I couldn't see the rest of the face because the eyes trapped me in their gaze. Words. He was speaking to me—commanding me.

"…now. Follow Clive and his mongrel. Kill the others, but I want Clive and his pet taken alive."

"Sire, Clive will not be easy to overtake. Perhaps you—"

"*Absurdité.* I have it on good authority that he is weakened. He is no longer the golden one."

"Sire?"

"Gather your men and secure him *maintenant.*" There was more. It was unspoken, but I felt a hidden desire behind Lafitte's words, a desire to preen and assert his superiority before someone.

I mentally broke the connection and stepped back into the fog. My head felt like it had been stabbed with a railroad spike, so I tried to pull out of the vamp's mind altogether. It took longer than when I'd spied on Clive's vamps, but that might have been a combination of paralyzing pain and mounting panic. I wasn't listening in on thoughts, I was reliving memories.

When I opened my eyes, I was lying on the cold floor, the

smell of wet cement strong in the room. It was pitch dark. It wasn't that the lights were out. I'd lost my sight again. I was paying the price of invading another's mind as deeply as I had.

Heart racing at being vulnerable in the dark, as I had been seven years ago, I reassured myself that this was different. I wasn't alone in the woods. There'd been no snap of a twig. I hadn't been hit in the back of the head before I could turn. I wouldn't wake up, bound, in an abandoned shack.

Trapped in darkness now, I couldn't stop my mind from remembering then. No. It was different now. I was in a house surrounded by vampires, which shouldn't have been comforting but strangely was. Of course, they were resting now, but I also had a gorgon upstairs who would come if I called. Probably. Unless there was something good on TV, in which case she might investigate at the commercial.

I'd be okay. The light would return. I could still protect myself. I stood, searched for the door, moved through, and then closed it after me. I could find my way upstairs, but why fumble? My sight would return. It had before. Balance needed to be restored. I slid to the corner of the hall, so I had walls at my back. The threat—if there was one—would need to come at me head-on. I unleashed my razor-sharp claws and stood tense, listening for the slightest movement and waiting for the light.

"I could—"

I flinched at the sound of a voice. Adjusting, I put the voice directly in front of me.

"What's going on?" Stheno, thank God.

"Nothing. I'm fine. You can go back upstairs." I didn't need an audience.

"I could hear your heart racing from upstairs. I came down to make sure one of the bloodsuckers wasn't gnawing on you. And I find you standing in a corner, weapons drawn and sightless. What the hell, Sam?"

Was there even a point in lying? I didn't want her—anyone, really—to know my business. As Clive had said, if people knew what I could do, it would paint an even bigger target on my back.

"Sam?" The voice was inches from my face. It came in a cloud of Dorito breath.

"It's temporary. I need to wait it out. You should go upstairs. It'd be easier dealing with this alone."

"I see." The voice was farther away. "If you need me, call for me." A moment later, a door shut. Footsteps sounded above, heading toward the back of the house.

How long had it been? Did the length of time I was blinded correlate with how invasive I'd been or how deeply I'd subverted another's free will? Was it cumulative, getting worse every time? I worried this was the magical world's way of telling me I was very much in the wrong.

SEVENTEEN

Let There Be Light

In the end, it had probably only been five minutes, but a second was an eternity when you're terrified and trapped in the dark. I should know.

Still standing in the corner of the hall, I snicked in my claws before heading upstairs. Where was Clive holing up during the day? He'd survived for hundreds of years. There was no need to worry. He was fine. He'd lived in New Orleans long ago. He wasn't lost in an unfamiliar city. If anyone knew where to find a daylight resting place, it would be him. Still…

Stheno was lounging on the couch. I checked the clock, wondering how long I'd been wandering through that vamp's mind.

"Almost two hours," she said, voice bored.

"What?" The hell? Could Stheno read minds?

"You were staring at the clock." She turned to study me. "You seem okay." She turned back around to watch the TV. "Bring me a beer, will ya?"

I checked the time again and then peered out the window. The sun was setting. If he was okay, he'd be arriving soon. And then we'd be walking into the lion's den.

I grabbed a beer from the fridge and threw it at Stheno, who had her back to me. See how she liked flying projectiles to the head. Her hand flew up at the last second and snatched it out of the air. Impressive.

Wandering back through the house, I settled on pacing in the front room. It had a large window overlooking the street. If —*when*—he came back, would he come this way? Watching the street darken outside the picture window, I waited.

A door opened. I spun, searching for him. Russell moved into the doorway, Godfrey behind him. His second and third were awake, but Clive still wasn't back. Fear poked at me with sharp claws.

"He's on his way," Russell said.

A lock clicked open in the back of the house. I flew down the hall, desperate to find him. Rounding the corner into the kitchen, I saw him closing the back door. He was alive-ish! Thank all that was holy. I almost threw myself into his arms, but a horrible stench had me pulling up short.

"Where were—*what* is that smell?" He seemed fine, but the odor was horrendous.

"I found a tunnel in which to rest," he said. "As to the other, I'd rather not say. I need a shower." Clive made for the hall.

Stheno cackled behind him. "How many cats pissed on you? Ballpark."

Russell and Godfrey bowed as Clive walked past, but it felt like it had more to do with hiding their amusement than deference.

Following him—at a distance—I climbed the stairs and entered our bedroom. The bathroom door was shut, and the water turned on. I sat on the bed and waited.

When Clive emerged in a puff of steam, a towel around his waist, smelling significantly better, I stood. "Are you okay?"

Shaking his head, he reached out and pulled me into his arms. "I could have killed you. Would have, if Russell hadn't stopped me."

"We all make mistakes."

He crushed me against his chest, his lips at my neck, gently kissing where his fangs had been embedded last night. "I love you."

"I know."

What started as a snort became a full-body laugh. "And is it any wonder?"

"To me it is." I ran my hands down his broad back. "Although I'm grateful."

"We'll go to Lafitte's tonight."

"And be ambushed."

He kissed my forehead, my cheek. "No doubt. This is why we came, though. We will take out Lafitte and as many of his people as possible."

Clive dressed quickly in one of his charcoal gray suits with a snow-white shirt, open at the collar. Smart. No need to wear a tie and give your enemies an easy way to strangle you. I should have been changing into my badass wear, but I couldn't tear my eyes from the normal and mundane. When I realized I was watching him put on his shoes with far more intensity than the moment dictated, I turned away.

The bed depressed next to me. Clive's hand wrapped around mine. "Talk to me."

"We're in a hurry. I'll—" When I tried to stand up, he held my hand firmly, causing me to drop back down.

"We have time." His thumb brushed across the skin on the back of my hand. "Sam?"

"I was scared."

"Please forgive me. I could have killed—"

"Not about that," I said. "Though, I guess I should be." When I tried to stand again, he let me go. "It wasn't that. You disappeared and I passed out. When I woke this morning, I didn't know if that evil tar had poisoned you. I couldn't ask Russell or Godfrey anything during the day. I searched for you." I pointed vaguely at my head. "But I didn't know where you were. I was worried *for* you, not *about* you. And then Stheno said she had a vamp downstairs in a cell."

Clive's body stiffened, his expression intent.

"I tried to do what I did before when you were questioning your vamps. I went down to the cage and tried to push into his thoughts."

"We're dead during the day."

"I don't think so. I was testing a theory that you're actually in some kind of stasis, not dead." Clive opened his mouth to argue but I barreled on. "If you can be roused in an emergency situation, then you can't be dead."

"That's only because of my age and power," he protested.

"Doesn't matter. If you can do it at all, you can't be dead, not completely anyway."

"So, only mostly dead?" He smirked at me.

"Exactly. Anyway, it was far more difficult than before, but I pushed and prodded and eventually slipped in." I glanced around the room and then leaned in to whisper in Clive's ear. "Is this room soundproofed?"

"No. I need to hear what's going on around me." Clive's eyes never left my face, waiting.

Lowering my voice as much as I could, I continued, "It was different than before, more like a vast, foggy minefield I had to cross in the dark. Sometimes I stepped on important memories, sometimes I got caught in horrible ones. He and his buddies— the statues in the front room—were sent by Lafitte to kill Russell and Godfrey but capture us. Lafitte's been told you're weak and —I'm not positive, but it was a feeling I got, an emotion under the words—he's jealous of you and excited to win. I got the impression he was like a little brother who could never measure up to the older one. He was almost giddy at the idea of showing you broken to someone else."

Clive's grin was terrifying. "You have been busy today, haven't you? As to the rest, we'll enjoy proving him wrong." Studying me a moment, he added, "There's something else."

"Yes, but it's not important now. We can talk about it later. I need to get changed and you need to coordinate with your men." And I wasn't even sure how I did it or if I could do it again. Could I really tap into the mind of every vampire in the world? And if so, did I want any vampire—even Clive—to know?

"All right. For now." He leaned in and kissed me before heading downstairs.

This was it. It was time for my game face. I went into the closet to prepare for battle.

I found everyone in the kitchen a short time later. Clive, Russell, and Godfrey all wore impeccable dark suits. Unlike the NOLA vamps when they came to San Francisco, they weren't wearing uniforms. My guys were deadly handsome, but each in his own way.

In unison, all three turned to regard me. Russell spun away quickly. Godfrey grinned before following Russell's lead. Clive's glance turned vampy black as he strode across the room to me. His hands traveled down my naked arms, over the tight, black tank I wore, and landed on my blood-red, leather-clad hips.

"Gentlemen, we'll need to postpone the battle for an hour." He leaned in and skimmed his fangs down my neck, causing me to shiver. "Make that two."

"Unless we're throwing down for a five-way orgy, move that shit out of here. I'm choking on the stench of lust. And somebody get me a beer," Stheno snarked.

Laughing, I took a deep breath, shook off The Clive Effect™ and walked to the refrigerator to grab a beer. When I chucked it at her head, Russell flinched, like he wanted to snatch it out of the air before it hit her, but Stheno caught it a split second later. Winging shit at her head was my new favorite pastime.

Clive ran his hand down my naked arm again. "Are you sure?" he murmured. He knew how desperately I'd hidden my scars for the last seven years.

"Scars are cool. Let 'em wonder." No one was buying my

bravado. They could all sense my unease, hear my heart pound. I meant it, though. These scars told the world I was a survivor. You think you can intimidate me with haughty manners and cut crystal? Get the fuck outta here.

Daniel appeared in the hall. "Sire, I've brought the car around."

"Thank you. We'll be right out."

I caught a stray thought from Daniel. It wasn't words so much as a smug satisfaction. "Daniel, could you come in here a moment?" He paused at my words, wanting to ignore me but knowing Clive was standing beside me.

"Yes?" he inquired politely.

I backed farther into the kitchen, waving him toward me. When I got close to the couch, I smacked the back of Stheno's head. One of her long curls wrapped around my hand, fast as a snake's strike.

"Get ready," I breathed, feeling Stheno stand behind me, her hair slipping from my wrist.

Daniel turned the corner into the kitchen. Seeing me, he stopped. "Is there some other food you two require?"

"We could use more beer," Stheno said.

"We could, but that's not why I called you back." I paused, willing the other men to stay out of this. I didn't have Clive's ability to mentally speak with his people, though.

"I was wondering how long you've been working for Lafitte," I said, sitting on the back of the couch.

"I knew it," Stheno said, a smirk in her voice. "What kind of a douche buys light beer and mayonnaise and calls it food?"

"Right?" I said.

Clive, Russell, and Godfrey ranged silently behind Daniel. He wasn't getting out of here alive. Undead. Whatever.

"You're lucky you never had to drive with him," I said to Stheno, over my shoulder. "I've got whiplash from him jabbing at the pedals. I feel sorry for any lovers he's had. The man does not understand nuance."

"Bitch!" he spat out.

I gave an exaggerated cringe. On a laugh, I pushed my hair back from my face and subtly tapped my temple, next to my eye, hoping my guys got the warning. "Ooh, such a scary, weak-ass vamp."

That did it. He flew at me, hands extended like claws. My vamps had understood, turning away from us. A moment later, cold fingers rested against my neck. Daniel, in all his pissed-off glory, loomed over me, permanently turned to stone.

Sliding to the side, I turned to Stheno. "You said you wanted one that wasn't standing there slack-jawed. Here you go."

Stheno high-fived me, vaulted over the couch, and picked up the statue like it weighed nothing. "This little guy is going to keep me company." She placed him in the corner of the room, where he'd lean forward, arms reaching, fangs extended forever more.

"Bad driver?" Godfrey asked.

"I didn't know what would set him off. I was giving him a scattershot of insults, hoping something would stick." I shrugged. "Apparently, he feels a little insecure about his skills in the sack."

"Shocker," Stheno said, flopping back onto the couch.

Clive took my hand and led me over the polished wood floors toward the front of the house. "Apparently, we're driving ourselves."

After we'd all piled in, Russell behind the wheel, Godfrey asked, "How did you know he was in league with Lafitte?"

"I didn't. Not for sure."

Clive turned to study me.

"I mean, it wasn't like he was thinking, 'Boy, I sure am glad I get to deliver these guys to their deaths soon.' It was more of an impression. He felt too smug about something. Okay, sure, vampires are dicks to me all the time, but he was a dick to Stheno. Either he's stupid or he didn't know who she was." I raised my eyebrows to Clive.

He shook his head. "He ranked low in the nocturne. He was here to oversee some renovations."

"In that case," I said, "If I were you, I'd chuck the blood supply and make sure the window shutters are working properly."

EIGHTEEN

Ghosts of the Past

We turned a corner, moving away from the bustle of the French Quarter. "She's right, Sire," Russell said from behind the wheel. "If Daniel's loyalty was compromised, we are no longer in a safe house."

"I know. We may need to eat free range until we're able to replenish our stores." Clive squeezed my hand to regain my attention. I'd been watching the neighborhoods change. "How does his treatment of Stheno add to his duplicity?"

"It's all part of a whole. He pretended to be subservient but was a dick about it. Some of that can be written off to being a vampire. You guys can be huge, pompous dicks—"

"Thank you, darling," Clive grumbled.

Godfrey laughed, "She's not wrong."

"But he was a sly asshole with you guys, too. He'd bow or whatever, but always with either a sulky expression or a smug one." Shaking my head, I tried to figure out how to explain it. "Back home, your people may not like that I'm there, they may resent having to deal with me, but there is a healthy fear and respect for you guys that shows through. Daniel didn't have that at all. He was like that asshole who guarded the front of the nocturne, always giving me shit, smirking, hiding his reactions when he saw you but not completely."

Russell drove us farther from downtown. The streets broadened and the land opened up.

"I played the odds. We have a freaking ancient monster staying with us and he treats her like shit? Even after statues start appearing in the hall, he still buys her off-brand, lite beer and crap snacks. Either he's a moron or wants to die. *Or*, he believes himself to be separate from us, free from repercussions, and protected by someone bigger and badder."

"Yes, I see," Clive murmured.

"I never felt any loyalty to you in him. I was fishing when I asked about Lafitte. It was his reaction that I was waiting for. As soon as I said the name, his thoughts were consumed with escape. He hated my guts and wouldn't mind gutting me, but I wasn't the priority. It was all contingencies and escape routes and calling for help. I goaded him into attacking me to disrupt his planning but also to give Stheno the statue she wanted." I patted Clive's shoulder with my free hand. "Don't worry. I'm not wrong."

"I don't doubt you. Although, I'd prefer you didn't goad predators into attacking you," he said.

"Picky, picky."

Sooner than I would have thought, Russell turned onto a long drive. Live oaks lined the road up to a plantation house, glowing white in the moonlight. Hazy specters hovered in the distance, flashing and then disappearing behind trees as we made our way down the drive. Clive had said *plantation*. I'd heard the word, but it wasn't until we were driving on the property that it hit me. Generations of humans enslaved and tortured, their pain bleeding into this soil. My stomach cramped and seized as the weight of so many lives pressed down on me.

"Stop," I gasped, pushing open the door before Russell could brake. I needed out. Needed to breathe. Misery was thick in the air. Stumbling to the side of the road, I fell to my knees. Vision blurred with tears, I pressed my head to my knees and wept. It was hitting me from every side. Lost souls enduring the pain, anger, humiliation that held them tethered to the place that had broken them.

Distantly, I heard Clive's voice, felt his concern, but I shook him off. I needed to help if I could. Putting my hands flat on the ground, I pulled from the spool of magic reeled inside me and sent a pulse of healing and contrition through the ground. The pressure on my chest lessened. I could breathe now, but no one came to me. They were wary of a white woman offering help.

Most had passed on, had found a better place, but for the few souls who had remained on the plantation grounds, there was no getting past, around, or through what had been done to them. The trauma was soul-wrenching and they'd lost their way, unable to follow the light home.

Lifting my head, I surveyed the grounds. Three, four, five hazy specters hovered dimly in the dark, but they were farther away from me than they'd been. They didn't trust me, had been taught not to.

"Sam?"

The concern in Clive's voice cleared my head. I turned and found him kneeling in the dirt beside me, eyes glowing in the moonlight.

"What happened? Are you sick?" His hand ran up and down my back, comforting.

When I glanced back, I saw Russell and Godfrey behind us, both scanning the area for threats.

"It's a plantation," I said simply.

Clive nodded, as though to encourage me to continue the thought. It was Russell who turned at my words and studied me, understanding.

"How bad?" he asked.

Tears slipped down my face. "I'd been feeling sick in the car, but I'd thought it was nerves. When you started down the drive, it all hit at once."

"What did?" Godfrey asked while still turned away, keeping an eye on the house in the distance and any movement nearby.

"She's a necromancer," Russell stated. "We're on a plantation." He glanced toward the big house. "There's movement."

"I hear them. Can you stand?" Clive asked.

Nodding, I rose, brushing the dirt from my knees. When this was all over, if I was still alive, I was coming back, offering my help again. Centuries of pain lived in these places and the souls needed release.

When we climbed back in the SUV, I settled by Clive again. He took out a handkerchief and wiped my face. "I'm sorry," he said, kissing my temple.

I shook my head. "I'm not the one who's been hurt. They are."

"Yes," Russell agreed.

I needed to pull it together. I was going into battle already shook. That couldn't be a good plan. In the minute we had left of the drive, I closed my eyes and settled myself, checking the magic spooling inside me, checking the surroundings.

"Five vampires outside the house. Two in back, one on each side, and one at the end of the drive. Thirteen in the house. Ten of them in one room, first floor. The other three are spread out." Counting the cold, hazy patches around me, I added, "There are also twenty-three ghosts. Seven or eight seem strong enough that they may be sentient. Far more barely register. They're fading."

I snicked out my claws as a safety check and then slid them back in. Russell pulled up to the stairs and parked. The imposing double doors opened and a vampire stood to the side, waiting to welcome us in.

Swallowing down the nausea, I turned to my fellas. "Were we supposed to bring a hostess gift?"

Clive gave me a hard, fast kiss and hissed, "Don't die," before he stepped out of the vehicle and held out his hand to me.

Russell and Godfrey flanked us as we climbed the stairs, walked through the tall colonnade, and across the dark wood veranda. The vamp at the large white doors gave a polite nod that wasn't quite a bow to Clive, saying, "In the salon, please."

Clive led the way through a darkly ornate entry. The candlelit black marble foyer read like a movie soundstage for a vampire flick set in the 1800s. It reeked of WE ARE VAMPIRES, with a side of in-your-face goth. If it had been intended as camp, it would've been hilarious.

I fell in line behind Clive as we traveled down a side hall with a chandelier hanging above us, real candles flickering in the dim light. They were trying way too hard, and it was kind of embarrassing. Walking safely between Clive and the boys allowed me the time to do another quick check. There were now only four vamps in the room ahead and to the right. Wait. Six more cold pinpricks of light flickered like the candles overhead in a room beyond.

Russell moved up and overtook Clive, entering the salon before him. Godfrey stayed behind me as we filed in. The salon was not a large room. It was packed with antique rugs, art, and furniture that placed it firmly in the past. This was going to be a difficult room to battle in.

"Clive, how lovely to see you again."

My eyes shot to the voice. Fricking Amélie. She was gorgeous. Her dark, perfect, dewy skin glowed in a long white dress with a plunging neckline. She stood tall next to a man who sat in a high backed, throne-like chair.

"Amélie." Clive nodded to her, acknowledging her comment before addressing the New Orleans Master. "Bélisaire, it's been quite some time." He glanced around the room. "Is this the welcoming party?" he asked, gesturing to the two other vamps standing on either side of the salon door. Even I knew so few people would be rightly construed as an insult.

Lafitte finally rose, waving a hand dismissively. "My people are very busy. You and I, we are family, *n'est-ce pas?*"

He was shorter than I'd anticipated, maybe five and a half feet tall, with long dark hair pulled back and secured at the nape of his neck. Like his people when they'd visited San Francisco, he wore a long black suit that had probably been the height of fashion two hundred years ago. He slid his arm around Amélie, who stood almost a head taller.

Bélisaire sniffed the air, his brow furrowed. "You're right," he murmured to Amélie. "I do smell dog." He lifted his goblet to Clive amid sly chuckles from his men at the door. "If that is your —what's the word? Ah, kink—if that is your kink, well, who am I to cast aspersions? My tastes are varied as well." Laughing, he added, "I haven't yet sunk to the animal kingdom, but to each his own."

Resting his hand possessively on Amélie's hip, he continued, "I think you envy me my lover, *oui*?" He smirked, giving me a dismissive glance before putting all his focus back on Clive.

"*Non.*" Clive nodded to the woman in question, adding, "No offense intended, Amélie. I have great respect for your drive and intelligence. Your loyalty?" He made a small sound of disapproval in the back of his throat.

More vampires silently filled the room, the ones who had been behind some kind of muffling wall. Taking a quick check, we still had three in other parts of the house, with ten of his and three of mine in this small salon.

Lafitte grinned as he lifted his goblet and drank deeply. "Don't be a sore loser, my friend. Even the favored child eventually stumbles and falls."

"I've neither stumbled nor fallen. I think, perhaps, you've been given faulty information." His eyes flicked to Amélie.

"*Peut-être*, but I have heard that many of your people fought against you, *non*?" The gleam in Lafitte's eyes made me want to smack his head right off his body.

A vamp with a tray offered Clive a goblet. He flicked his hand, sending the man away.

"They were not mine. A cancer—one of your brother's making—had taken root, spreading lies and stirring unrest, turning the weakest amongst mine into tools for a poorly planned and pathetically executed coup."

Lafitte raised his eyebrows in disbelief. "So you say." He patted Amélie's hip. "Still. Perhaps you do not value and attend to your gifts as you should. I loaned you my beloved Étienne to be your protégé. Remind me, where is my brother now?"

"Dead."

"*Exactement*," Lafitte spat, eyes cold.

The vampire Clive had brushed off circulated around the room, offering burnished goblets of blood to Lafitte's people before approaching Russell and Godfrey. My guys declined. Smart.

"It could be said, then, that *you* are the one who does not value his gifts. You sent me a spy, determined to work against me. I protected myself and my nocturne. You then sent more of your people—including your lover—against me, knowing what would happen to them. And even more when we arrived in New Orleans. *Non, mon ami.* It is you who does not value what he has been given. Envy is unseemly in ones as old as we, *n'est-ce pas*?"

Lafitte fumed, his eyes turning vampy black. His vampires repositioned, ranging themselves around Clive, Russell, and Godfrey. No one seemed to care about me. That was interesting. Had Amélie not told them what I'd done? Hadn't she seen? She'd been standing right next to Clive, so I'd assumed. While the vamps not so subtly surrounded my guys, I moved closer to Amélie.

"You will die tonight, and I will piss on your ashes," Lafitte ground out, slamming down his goblet and shoving Amélie from his side.

"Your words stink of desperation." I tapped my nose. "We can smell fear." Swaggering ostensibly toward Lafitte, but really positioning myself closer to Amélie, I ran a hand up my opposite arm, highlighting my scars. "I've survived actual battles. These weak taunts remind me of the trembling whine of a lapdog cowering before a far more deadly predator. It's your party, though. Yap away."

Clive threw back his head and laughed as Godfrey grinned and Russell shook his head, a portrait in patience. "Is it any wonder I love you?"

Lafitte threw his goblet against the wall. "How dare—you have no voice here!"

I rolled my eyes at his rage. "Yip, yip, yip."

And then all hell broke loose.

NINETEEN

Heads Commence Rolling in 3...2...1...

Holding my hands up at the shouts of outrage coming from Lafitte's people, I backed up a few steps, needing to sidestep a small table with an antique lamp. A couple of Lafitte's people stepped forward, thinking I was retreating. Glancing at Clive, I found him watching me, expression thoughtful, clearly trying to follow my play.

Winking at him, I took one more step back, hearing Amélie's desperate thoughts right behind me. I wasn't going to let her get away again. Unfortunately, one of Lafitte's men slipped in silently behind me, blocking me from Amélie.

To the room, I said, "Damn, you people sure are prissy for a bunch of bloodsuckers." Dropping my arms, I flicked a hand toward Lafitte. "One yappy dog comparison and you lose your shit. And, seriously, you guys are a little overdressed for a brawl, don't you think?"

"What brawl?" the sneering one closest to me asked.

Clive tensed, a glare pointed over my shoulder as Russell's gaze snapped to the same spot. The coward was about to attack me from behind.

"This one," I said with a maniacal grin. I spun, claws out, and sliced through the vamp's neck as he dove for me, sending his head flying across the room and bouncing off the shoulder of the vamp standing next to Lafitte.

There was a pause of shock, and then Lafitte shouted, "Now, now, now!"

My jaws elongated to hold a wolf's teeth, my arms growing more muscular. A vamp attempted to tear my head off, but I ducked at the last moment and came up swinging. I plowed into his stomach, sending him flying. A vamp jumped on my back, his fangs tearing into my neck. Grabbing his head, I sunk my claws though his skull while sending a pulse of white magic through him. His fangs retracted and I flipped him over my shoulder, planted a foot in his groin, and wrenched his head from his body with a roar of my own. Damn, vamps did it the hard way. Ripping off heads was far more labor intensive than cutting necks. I liked my way better.

Blood ran down my neck and shoulder. It didn't feel life-threatening, though. It hurt like hell, but my skin would start knitting together soon.

More vamps raced into the tiny room, presumably the ones guarding the grounds and scattered around the house. I caught sight of Lafitte to my left. He wasn't fighting. His eyes were on Clive, who was battling two vamps at once, grappling for dominance before flinging their heads and bodies in different directions.

A hidden passage opened behind Lafitte, and he ran. Amélie and three of the vamps closest to him ran as well, the doorway sealing after them. Another vamp trying to follow bounced off the wall. Russell was there a moment later, giving the deserter his true death.

A vase flew across the room and then a vamp head hit the wall no more than a foot from me before turning to dust and sifting to the floor. Turning, I found Godfrey grinning.

"Don't throw heads at me!"

"Just following your lead, luv."

We surveyed the room. It had been brutal but quick. Piles of dust and dead bodies were littered around the room. My guys and I were the only ones left standing, although Clive was the only one who didn't appear to be bloody or gnawed upon.

"Is it me, or was that kind of anticlimactic?"

Clive was by my side a moment later, expression equal parts concern and amusement as he studied my neck wound. The pain disappeared. Lowering his head, he put his mouth over my injured neck and licked, vampire saliva helping to heal my wounds.

"Not just you," Russell said. "That was pathetic."

"Where did short and creepy disappear to?" Godfrey asked.

Russell tapped the wall at the same time I pointed.

"Can you sense them nearby?" Clive asked. "I'd like to finish this now."

Mentally reaching out, I searched for the little blips in my head that told me vamps were nearby. "Only you three. That hidden room must lead to an escape route or something."

Russell knocked on the wall again. "Metal, not wood or plaster."

I wandered out to the candlelit hall. There had to be another door to that room. Except there were no doors on the right side of the hall. I ran my hand over the wallpaper, black filigree flocked on mirrored paper. Their decorator seriously sucked.

Godfrey leaned against the doorway, watching me. "Anything?"

Shaking my head, I continued feeling for a seam or a catch. Nothing. Clive and Russell stepped out into the hall, watched me a moment, and then headed for the front door.

"Wait. Aren't we going to search the joint, all sneaky-like while no one's here?"

Godfrey paused. "She has a point, Sire. Perhaps we should go through Lafitte's things."

Clive shook his head. "It's all right, Sam. I know what I need to know. They were completely unprepared for us." He paused at the front doors and shook his head in disgust as we descended the front steps. "He ran away. Master of the City and he ran away." Pointing at the vehicle, he directed Russell and Godfrey to the SUV at the base of the steps while he walked me around the side of the house.

"Um, whatcha doing?" The grounds were beautiful—albeit haunted—but it seemed like an odd time for a stroll.

"They're checking for tracking devices and explosives. I want you out of the blast zone." Clive checked my neck again. "If he'd been faster, stronger…"

"But he wasn't." I patted his chest and glanced around. "They really liked columns, didn't they?" The plantation house had a veranda that ran around the entire ground floor of the structure, as well as regularly spaced, tall, white columns that rose to the roof three stories above. Galleries ran along the second and third stories.

Clive ignored the question, his focus on his men and our possibly compromised ride. Turning away from the house, I marveled at the huge oak towering overhead, its massive branches sheltering the corner balconies. How long ago must this tree have been planted?

Stepping off the path, I crossed the lawn, sidestepping gnarled roots pushing up through the grass. I rested my head against the thick, rough bark. Hazy, cold spots danced behind my eyelids. Leaning my head back and looking up, I saw the ghosts of four men hanging from the branches. These weren't the ghosts of enslaved people. Their clothes were more modern, maybe fifty to a hundred years old, rather than two hundred. These were Black men who had been lynched, their ghosts trapped where they had been murdered.

I climbed up the tree, strength, balance, and sharp claws making easy work of it. Tightrope walking out on the lowest branch, I stopped over the ghost of a young man who couldn't have been more than a teenager in life. I tried desperately to remember anything I'd read today that could help these men. Straddling the branch and reaching down, I placed my hand on the young man's shoulder, let magic pulse through my fingers, and prayed he found passage to the open arms of his family waiting for him on the other side. "Peace," I whispered.

When I opened my eyes, the ghost was gone and Clive was watching me. Hopping up, I moved to another branch and repeated the process. I had no idea if what I was doing was correct, but it felt right.

When I dropped to the ground a few minutes later, all three vampires were watching me. "We can go now."

Clive nodded and held out a hand. Russell cornered the house first, with Godfrey bringing up the rear.

"Did you guys find anything?"

"A tracking device. No bomb."

Eyeing the SUV warily, I asked, "You're sure?"

"Yes," Russell and Godfrey said in unison.

Glancing back and forth between the two, I smirked. "That was cool. You guys should always do that. Like those freaky twins in *The Shining*. You'll scare the crap out of everyone."

"No," they said in unison.

After we climbed in, I turned to Clive. "So what did you learn?"

"Lafitte is not the architect of these hostilities," Clive said. "He's being used and is too enamored of his own legend to realize it."

"Yes," Russell agreed.

"Who then?" Godfrey asked from the seat behind us.

"Perhaps Amélie," Clive murmured, staring out the window. "She saved herself again and didn't appear to have warned Lafitte that Sam was deadly in either form."

"I might have a clue," I said.

Clive's attention snapped to me. "What do you know?"

Russell turned, heading back to the Quarter. Stomach growling, I thought longingly of food. Tapping Russell's shoulder, I asked, "Can we stop somewhere fast? I'm starving."

Nodding, he took a sharp turn and headed in a different direction.

Turning my attention to Clive, I said, "I don't *know* anything. When I was standing near Amélie, I picked up some stray thoughts. She knew this was going to happen, had told Lafitte to be wary, but in a way she knew would egg him on. She was sorting through escape routes. What I thought was interesting, though, is she was trying to figure out how to let someone know more of the nocturne were dead.

"Again," I continued, "this is sketchy information at best. It was a few flashes and impressions that I'm trying to piece together now. There may be no connection, but it felt like it was two different people. She needed to tell someone about the brawl, but there was someone else, someone much farther removed, who was shuffling chess pieces on a board. No guarantee, but it felt like the chess master was female."

"Did you see her? Get a name?" Godfrey asked.

Glancing back at him, I said, "It was an impression, a flash, but...light hair, maybe blonde. Brown eyes. I'm not sure." I shrugged. "Ring any bells?"

"Too many, but not one in particular," Clive said as he stared out the window, dark streets racing by.

Russell pulled up in front of a burger joint that was still hopping at—I checked my watch. "Seriously? We wiped out a bunch of vamps and sent their Master running in under an hour? Damn, we're good." I opened the door and slid out. "Be right back."

The red and white building was filled with people. It was the smell, though, that pulled me to the open station at the counter. Scanning their menu board, I ordered four bacon cheeseburgers, two with A1 and jalapenos and two with barbeque sauce and mushrooms. I added a couple of bacon dogs and a whole slew of fries.

I glanced over my shoulder at Russell. I'd felt him shadow

me in. "Are we close enough to home that I can get Stheno a shake?"

His tense expression relaxed.

"What?"

"I'm worried. If that's how much you normally eat, we've been horribly underfeeding you." His voice was so quiet, I doubted anyone heard him, and yet his presence drew stares.

I turned back to the poor, sweaty teen working too close to the sizzling fry station. "Add two milkshakes, one coffee and one chocolate."

The cashier's eyes were glued to Russell, so I repeated, "Two milkshakes."

Shaking herself, she said, "Yeah. Got it."

I dug into my pocket for cash, but Russell was already passing the money around me to the cashier.

"I can pay for my own food."

He ignored my protest, pulling me to the side to wait. "How many were in the tree?" he asked softly.

"Four."

Nodding, he stood beside me like a large, protective wall.

"Can you do me a favor?"

He stopped scanning the room and focused on me.

"When we're done with all this, can you take me back there? I want to try again. With the others." I'd never find that plantation on my own.

Nodding, he went back into Secret Service mode.

I'd do what I could—assuming I survived whatever was coming, that was.

TWENTY

Dinner and a Movie

G odfrey entered the townhouse first and came to a stop almost immediately. "There are more," he said, and then got to work hauling the vampire statuary aside so we could enter.

Moaning and grunting echoed down the hall, accompanied by pretty crappy instrumental music.

"Um." I stopped in my tracks. Clive barely raised an eyebrow. If I didn't have food and a melting shake for Stheno in my hands, I would have left her to her porn.

Russell appeared at the door a moment later, having garaged the SUV. He paused, assessed the situation, and then pushed me toward the kitchen. "I think Sam should check."

That statement earned instant approval from Clive and Godfrey.

My mouth dropped open. "I fought with you. Was injured on your behalf. And you're going to send me off to deal with a horny gorgon?"

"Yes," they said in unison.

"Well, that sucks ass," I grumbled, making my way down the hall. When I reached the corner, I closed my eyes and raised my voice. "We're home and I have food." Hopefully, she'd be less likely to death-ray me for breaking up her self-love time if I came bearing burgers and fries. Nothing.

Sliding around the corner, I kept my eyes closed and said her name. Still nothing. Squinting one eye open, I searched for the back of her head. Wow, okay. There were a lot of orifices getting hammered on the big screen, but I didn't see Stheno. Dropping the food bags and drink cups on the counter, I made my way hesitantly toward the couch.

"Stheno? I have food." Flashing lights from the screen illuminated a vampire in the corner. *Fuck!*

Clive, Russell, and Godfrey were standing around me a moment later. "Sorry, guys. Heartbeat returning to normal now. It was our statue in the corner. I thought he was the real deal."

When I peered over my shoulder, all three were staring at the screen with varying expressions of concern.

"Leave you guys alone for a minute and you turn on the porn. What are you, twelve?" Stheno walked in the kitchen behind us. "Food. Nice."

Godfrey turned off the television, thankfully, while I sorted out our burgers.

"How many more tonight and when did they arrive?" Clive asked.

"The first wave was right after you left." Stheno took a bite and moaned, not unlike the people on the screen Godfrey had silenced. "Two more arrived about five minutes ago. One's out in the hall and the other's in your cage downstairs." She sucked on the shake straw. "Go play with your prisoner," she said, waving her hands at the vampires. "We're trying to eat."

After the men left, the feast began in earnest. I'd finished my second burger and was digging into the fries when I heard Clive's voice from downstairs.

"When you have a moment, Sam, we could use your assistance."

"She's eating," Stheno said before I could respond. "She's probably dropped five pounds since I first saw her. You want her to fight, you need to feed her." She rolled her eyes. "Fucking bloodsuckers."

Clive stood at the kitchen entrance a moment later, watching me. He crossed to me and then crouched by my chair, his hand on my hip. "She's right. You have lost weight."

Shrugging, I ate more fries. "The asshole in the corner didn't stock the kitchen with real food."

"Fucker," Stheno agreed.

"But I've seen what's stocked for you in the nocturne's kitchen. It doesn't seem that different from here." His hand ran up and down my thigh.

"There's usually real food there, not condiments and random ingredients that don't go together. Plus, I know San Francisco. I know where to go to get something to eat. When I'm in The Slaughtered Lamb, I have a fully stocked kitchen, one Dave uses to feed me and the rest of our patrons every night. There, I don't have bands of vampires trying to kill me every time I step out of your nocturne doors. Here, we had to rely on that idiot Daniel."

Clive tipped forward, his head against my shoulder. "Things. I bought you things, thinking I was providing for you, and you were starving." His hand went around my waist. "God, she's right."

"Not starving. Just really hungry. After we're done interrogating your prisoner, can I borrow one of the guys to—" I checked my watch. "To find a late-night market so I can buy more food for Stheno and me? I mean, we appreciated the addition of lunch meat and chips and whatnot today, but that was enough for one meal, maybe two, not a few days."

"Of course. Do you want to do that now?" He seemed so upset with himself, I ached for him.

"I'm fine. Really." Leaning forward, I kissed him between the eyes.

After finishing my fries, I went downstairs. The guy chained up was one of the vamps that ran with Lafitte. Interesting. Like his boss, he had long dark hair pulled back and tied at the nape of his neck. Jaw clenched, he stared down his long nose at me before turning his head away, as though I was more than his delicate sensibilities could take.

I dropped to the floor and leaned against the mesh opposite the chained vamp. Closing my eyes, I found the four cold vamp blips in the cage. "Hey, what happened to the last guy you had chained in here?"

"Didn't need him anymore," Godfrey answered.

Good point. With my eyes still closed, I began worming my way into our prisoner's mind. When I caught a fragment of a thought, wondering if my face was thinner, I asked my guys to move to the edges of the cage. I didn't want any of them messing up my reading.

Lafitte's face floated in front of him in a memory. 'I'm trusting you, Gérard. We need this taken care of. Take Charles with you and wait for them at their townhouse. We must end this tonight.' Something crashed and then Lafitte's face was back, his eyes vampy black and crazed. 'I'm not taking the fall for all of these screwups. Competence,' he said, stalking away. 'Is that too much to ask?'

Lafitte paced back, his voice hushed, 'She took his head. *Mon Dieu*, she's a woman. How is she able to perform…' Rubbing his hands over his face, he continued, '*Comment ça s'appelle? Sommet transformation*. Who is she? I thought only the strongest Alphas from the original line could do that. Talk to the wolves. We need to know who we're dealing with. Maybe we have *them* take her out. Yes. Threaten them. Unless they kill the bitch, we'll destroy their whole pack.' He seemed lost for a moment and then whispered, 'Her claws…'

Great. Now I had to worry about wolves, too? This trip was getting better and better. "Who is Lafitte taking his orders from?" I was trying to direct his thoughts where I wanted them.

Gérard ignored me, naturally, but his mind went to a whispered phone conversation. He hadn't known who was on the other side of the line, but after that phone call, Amélie had moved up the ranks, taking over Gérard's rightful spot as second. Their focus had also turned from local matters to destroying Clive.

"Did you contact the wolves before you came here?" With any luck, he might not have made that call yet.

I felt his shock at the question and then the immediate answer. He'd made the call and the local Alpha had told him to fuck off and kill his own enemies. They weren't the bloodsuckers' guard dogs and if she was taking out vampires, good. I grinned. Leading with a 'Fuck you' was so very werewolfy.

"Why are you smiling?" Clive's voice came from right beside me.

"This asshole called the local Alpha and asked the pack to kill me. The Alpha told him to fuck off. He was cool with my killing bloodsuckers." I laughed. Wolves were so much more straightforward. Vamps were all about ancient grudges and plots within intrigues within convoluted machinations. It was exhausting.

Gérard didn't know what was going on, but he was putting up every mental block he could think of. My head was already killing me. I didn't know if I had it in me to push past them. Waving Clive closer, I snagged his hand and placed it on top of my head, hoping he'd remember what I needed. I heard a low curse and then blessed pain relief was flowing through me.

I shoved hard against a mental barrier and slipped further in. Filtering past memories of lovers, of feedings, of battles, I found the brown-eyed woman I'd sensed in Amélie's thoughts. It was a fragment, floating in the depths of his memories, but she was there. It was a memory filled with pain and wonder and a fiery thirst that broke through Clive's pain relief. I gasped at the excruciating agony and pulled out.

Clive crouched before me, both hands cradling my head. His mental powers barely lapped at the ocean of pain roiling through me.

"I'm going to be sick." Clive picked me up and raced me upstairs to the bathroom. He knew I'd be blind after what I'd done, so he positioned me over the toilet, pulling my hair back as I lost my dinner.

Later, after Clive had wiped my face and put me on the bed, my vision slowly returned. He sat in a chair by the bed, shirtsleeves rolled up, watching me.

"I'm fine." I needed him to lose the solemn expression. I hadn't died.

"You're not, no." He ran his hand over my hair. "I can't seem to properly get my feet under me. I'm making mistakes and others are bearing the brunt." He ran a strand of my hair through his fingers. "I've failed my people and I've failed you."

"Stop," I said, grabbing his hand and holding tight. "No one wants an emo vamp."

He squeezed back, one corner of his mouth kicking up. "Sorry."

"You're not screwing up. You're under attack. It's a layered offensive from multiple directions." Scooting over, I patted the mattress next to me.

Nodding, he rose and then stretched out beside me. "It is, but that's how vampires war. I should have seen this coming and prepared long ago."

"Were you, maybe, distracted by an annoying werewolf who kept getting herself almost killed?"

Sliding his arm under me, he pulled me closer so I could rest my head on his chest. "It started long before that. Plots like this are years, sometimes centuries, in the making." He paused. "And I had no idea. I was focused in the wrong direction while my people were being turned against me."

"Do you know who's behind this now?"

He made a quiet sound in the back of his throat in the negative. "Did you learn anything from our friend downstairs?"

"His name's Gérard. He was Lafitte's second, but then Amélie sailed through the ranks and took his spot, pushing him down one rung. That had him bitter. He didn't know who was pulling the strings, but believed it was someone older and more powerful than Lafitte. He overheard part of a whispered phone call that Lafitte wouldn't discuss and then Amélie showed up."

"Interesting."

"Lafitte is flailing, throwing vampires at us. Losing tons of his people. Trying to recruit the werewolves. He's desperate. Are we sure this was aimed at you? Maybe someone wanted him taken out and pointed him at you so you'd do the work for them."

He nodded slowly, lost in thought. "That makes more sense than anything else. Perhaps Amélie wants to break Lafitte and take over the nocturne. We still have no definitive answer on Luc, Lafitte's strategist who's missing and presumed dead."

"Could they be working together? Using you to take out the most powerful in the nocturne so they needn't worry about internal rebellion when they ascend to the throne?"

"Could they? Absolutely. Are they?" He shrugged a shoulder. "I've been going over every battle and grudge, trying to think of anyone strong enough and angry enough to set something like this in motion. I have enemies and yet, of those I can recall, none who actively want me dead—or, at least, want it enough to go to this much trouble. And why would they care about killing or capturing you, except as a means of hurting me." He blew out a breath and stared at the ceiling. "If the motivation is to hurt me, to make me question myself, they're doing a fine job. But why?"

I ran my hand over his chest, trying to comfort him. "It seems petty, doesn't it? Vindictive. Do you have an ex who's been stewing for a while? Someone powerful enough to orchestrate this?"

The arm around my back tightened as he drew me closer. "I wouldn't have thought so. I don't mistreat my partners."

"It wouldn't need to be mistreatment. It could be someone you broke it off with who took offense at you not loving them forever."

Sighing resignedly, he said, "I couldn't even fathom to guess. Their numbers are legion."

I punched him in the side. Hard.

"Oof. Do you remember how old I am?" He rubbed his hand over my shoulder and down my stiff back.

"Right."

"Scores upon scores of lifetimes, Sam. A needle in haystack would be easier than finding one disgruntled former lover."

If he was alive during William the Conqueror's reign, he was almost a thousand years old. I was twenty-four and had had one lover. One thousand divided by twenty-four... Wait. That wouldn't work. That would mean he took one lover every twenty-four years. So, best case scenario, if it was only one a year. Nope. Never mind. Not going there.

"Sam?"

"Can vampires get STDs?" And what if it was a five-hundred-year-old strain of something horrible that modern doctors had never heard of?

"What?" He palmed the back of my head and tilted it up so he could see my face.

"Nothing. Imagining bubonic syphilis and scaring myself." Shuddering, I added, "Luckily, a vampire, werewolf, or wicche will probably take me out before I start showing symptoms. Bright side, I'd rather die in battle than languish away, quarantined for the ick."

Kissing my forehead, he rested my head back on his chest. "We don't have STDs. That was a fascinating little jaunt, though."

"But how would you know? It's not like you guys go to doctors. You're probably the original disease vectors for all of history's plagues."

"Interesting point," he responded seriously, but I could hear the humor in his voice.

Rolling me over, he settled between my legs. "In the mood to be exposed to something infectious?"

I snorted. "You seriously need to work on your sweet talk, because that was pathetic."

Murmuring in French, his ran soft kisses up and down my neck before his fangs grazed down the same path. Shivering, I wrapped my legs around him. "I take it all back," I said on a sigh.

"*Je t'aime. Je t'adore. Tu es mon seul,*" he rumbled low in my ear.

"Better."

"Give me time, darling. I'm just getting started."

TWENTY-ONE

Distractions and Other Embarrassments

Once I'd rushed to the bathroom to brush my teeth, because eww, Clive proceeded to show me, with every kiss and caress, how much he adored me. We needed this. After all the scares and battles and betrayals, we needed to have this time alone, to remember why we were fighting so hard. When his lips brushed my own, I plunged my fingers into his thick hair, holding on, never wanting to let him go.

He made short work of our clothes. I ran my hands down the soft hair on his chest, over the ridges of his abdomen before he slipped out of reach, tasting my body, making me quake and quiver. When he finally settled back between my legs, I was a sweaty, blissed-out mess who was strangely grateful to the legion who had come before me.

Sliding a hand over my hip and down my leg, he wrapped his fingers around my knee and pulled it up to his waist. Groaning at the fullness, I gasped as he changed the angle. Fingers splayed over the back of my thigh, he pushed my leg up, holding me open. My back arched off the mattress, reveling in him, in us. I heard a high-pitched keening and then Clive's mouth was on mine. When I exploded a moment later, I took him with me.

"Shut up! You two are worse than the porn. I'm trying to sleep down here!" Stheno's voice made me jump.

"*Pardon*," Clive said in a normal voice.

"You should be! Fucking, French-spouting vampire," she grumbled.

Giggling, I whispered, "Is her hearing really that good?"

"Yes! Now shut up."

Dying of embarrassment, I tugged a pillow over my head, trying to hide from the memories of every private conversation we'd had and noise I'd made.

Clive pulled the pillow away and rolled me again so I was lying on top of him, his hands resting on my butt. "I got distracted before," he said, squeezing my bottom. "Did you get anything else from our prisoner?"

"But Stheno's trying to sleep," I whispered back.

"She knows as well as I how to put up mental barriers. She's on guard duty now, so she's not doing it. She can sleep during the day."

Talk of barriers reminded me. "Are you sure Daniel didn't sabotage your sun shields?"

"He didn't have access to those controls. I checked the systems. They're reading operational." Clive shrugged. "Do me a favor, though. If they malfunction, drag me into the closet and close the door. Russell and Godfrey will be fine. There are no windows in the basement."

"Deal."

"Back to our prisoner," he prompted as the shields slid down behind the bed.

"I saw that woman again, the one with long blonde hair and big brown eyes. She was *way* back in Gérard's memories. It was murky, but this time when I saw her, I felt a horrible, scalding need and a fiery thirst. It was excruciating. Like my skin was being peeled off and my lungs had turned to stone. I was suffocating while burning to death."

"First thirst," Clive murmured.

"What?"

Shaking his head, he said, "Continue. The sun is approaching the horizon."

"That was it. My head felt like it was splitting open. I pulled myself out of the memory before it killed me."

"She was his maker. Interesting." And then Clive was out.

Did all new vampires go through that agonizing thirst? Every time or just the first? I needed a field guide to vampires.

I slept for a few hours, but hunger woke me up midmorning. After showering, tying my hair up in its usual braid, and putting on my normal jeans and a hoodie, I jogged downstairs to see if food had miraculously appeared overnight.

No new statues in the entry. That was good. I left my running shoes on the stairs and padded down the hall to the kitchen and family room. If Stheno had finally fallen asleep, I didn't want to wake her. A dim light glowed from under the kitchen cabinets, but the TV was off. I tiptoed to the couch and peered over the back. Stheno was sound asleep.

"Fuck off."

Mostly asleep. "Sorry. I'm going to run out and get food. I'll be right back."

"Beignets," she grumbled, rolling over.

"You got it." I swung by the refrigerator. Still pitiful.

Heading back down the hall, I heard Stheno slur, "Coffee," followed by a snuffling snore.

"You betcha." I checked my hoodie pocket for cash and the alarm password Godfrey had handed me when we'd arrived. I think he'd intended me to memorize it and then eat the evidence, but really, were alarms even needed? We had three vampires, one werewolf, and a gorgon. I was pretty sure we were good.

It was a gorgeous morning in the French Quarter. Too warm for the hoodie, I took it off and tied it around my waist before jogging toward the center of the Quarter. If Stheno wanted

Beignets, that meant Café Du Monde in the French Market. Even I knew that much.

As I moved from homes to businesses, the scent of the river was overpowered by a musty underlying odor of spilled alcohol and mold. Parts of New Orleans were below sea level and those above weren't much above, so flooding was a recurring reality. It was a gorgeous gem of a city, though, so I understood why they kept rebuilding. Some things were too magical to abandon.

My sense of smell was much closer to an actual wolf's than a human's, so I wasn't sure how much the people living here even noticed. Shops were opening as I passed, and the delicious scents of bacon and maple syrup floated out of restaurants. Stomach rumbling, I stopped in front of one that smelled particularly amazing. The beignets were relegated to second breakfast.

The restaurant was lovely, with white linen tablecloths and waiters in uniform jackets and pants. I stood to the side of the host's stand, surreptitiously checking to make sure I had my thin wallet in my jeans pocket. I usually only carried cash on me, but since we were traveling to a new city, I had pocketed a thin leather fold, carrying the credit card Clive had given me and some cash.

I didn't have a driver's license, since I'd never learned to drive, and I didn't have my own credit card because—well, I didn't know why. I'd never needed one, living in The Slaughtered Lamb. Dave, my half-demon cook, had been with me since I'd opened The Slaughtered Lamb Bookstore & Bar's doors when I was seventeen. He'd volunteered to take care of the banking, dropping off the cash at the bank. I transferred funds online for wages, supplies, and payments on the business itself.

Since all my patrons were supernaturals, I didn't interact with the human world much. When I did, I used cash. After my beautiful bookstore and bar had been destroyed and I'd started living at the nocturne with Clive, he'd given me a credit card. The first time I'd used it had been for the clothes for this trip. I was on a vampire mission, so it seemed fair. If the prices in this restaurant matched the décor, I'd be using it again this morning.

The host, a very distinguished Black man, graying at the temples, returned to the stand. "May I help you?"

"I don't have a reservation. Do you have a table available?" Pausing, I added, "You can shove me in the back by the kitchens. I don't mind." He studied his reservation book, his gaze snagging on my scars. I'd pushed up the long sleeves of my tee when I'd been jogging and had forgotten to pull them back down before I'd walked in. I'd never done that before. Never. I'd been hiding my scars for seven years. I'd bared my arms in public last night for the first time and I'd forgotten to cover them this morning. Pulling my sleeves down now, I realized something in me was changing.

When he glanced back up, his expression had changed, softened. "Follow me," he said, picking up a tall, leather-bound menu. He led me through a beautiful room, with pink velvet chairs. Green lattices striped the walls between charming murals of nineteenth century Mardi Gras floats. I followed him through the main room and into a courtyard dining area. It had a pitched glass roof and greenery everywhere, with vines climbing the brick walls. Twinkle lights crisscrossed above.

He stopped at a small table next to a water fountain. The people around me were wearing suits and dresses, their Sunday best. Pulling at the hoodie sleeves knotted at my waist, I asked, "Are you sure?"

"Lovely young ladies such as yourself shouldn't be hidden. Would you like some coffee?"

His words tightened my throat. I sat and said, "Yes, please."

"Very good." He nodded once before handing me the menu. "Your server will be right with you."

My stomach rumbled as I read over the options. I wanted one of everything on the menu, preferably now. I hated that Clive felt guilty about it, but Stheno was right. I'd lost weight since I'd been here. I had to fasten my belt over a notch and my jeans—a new pair that fit perfectly last week—were now a little baggy.

A waitress set down coffee and cream on the table. Her hair was shorn close to her head, making her big hazel eyes stand out. She had the most beautiful golden-brown skin. It glowed against her white uniform jacket.

"Welcome. Is this your first time with us?"

Nodding, I said, "First visit to New Orleans."

"Sightseeing on your own today?" She wasn't rushing me, not harried and checking her other customers. White coats were weaving between tables, dropping off food, picking up dishes.

"For now. I travel with late sleepers."

She laughed. "I know. Most visitors think of New Orleans as a nightlife city, and it is, but we have lots to do during the day as well. Make sure you go to Jackson Square, the French Market, Bourbon Street, Preservation Hall." She rolled her beautiful brown eyes. "I could go on and on. But don't forget Café Du Monde for beignets before you leave. If you time it right, you might see the Jazz Funeral band."

"I appreciate the tips, and beignets were next on my list."

She pulled out a small notepad. "Perfect. Well, what do you feel like trying today?"

"I'll start with the crab and avocado toast, a bowl of the seafood gumbo, and then the Creole beef tenderloin."

She nodded, not even raising an eyebrow at my ordering so much food for breakfast, brunch, whatever this was. "Would you like anything to drink besides coffee?"

"Water."

She nodded again. "I'll go put your order in." She was turning when I stopped her.

"Sorry, one more thing. Do you deliver?"

"We can, sure. There is a delivery fee."

"Great. Can you make it two of everything?" I gave her the address and sent a text to Stheno to open the door when the food delivery guy knocked.

The quiet din of many conversations, with plates and silverware clinking in the background, had an oddly calming effect on me. Food was coming and no one was trying to kill me. The bright splashing of water falling in the fountain nearby added to an overwhelming sense of peace.

The waitress was back a few minutes later with my first course. The crab and avocado toast was delicious, but I finished it too quickly. Now I'd have to wait for the next course with my stomach all churned up and ready for more. The waitress seemed to be keeping an eye on me, so I only had to wait a short time before she was dropping off the gumbo and taking my empty plate.

Too soon, I hit the bottom of the bowl, and in no time at all, she was dropping off the tenderloin. This waitress was my new favorite person in the whole wide world.

"I hope you don't mind," she said. "But I ordered you a double portion. You remind me of my cousin. She's thin and fit, like you, but needs lots of calories during the day."

"Not only do I not mind, I was actually trying to think of a polite way to ask you to start at the beginning and repeat the meal."

Nodding, she said, "That's what I thought. Like my cousin." She had a knowing glint in her eye that made me wonder if her cousin was a member of the local pack.

"Listen," I said before she could leave, "if some snooty, vintage-clothes-wearing goths ask your cousin to hunt down and violently encourage an out-of-towner to leave, maybe you could tell her I'm okay and she should ignore the goths."

Snickering, she echoed, "Goths." Patting my shoulder as she walked by, she murmured, "I'll pass it on," knowing I'd hear her.

The tenderloin was amazing, the bill exorbitant, but it was all worth it. When I paid, the waitress lifted her eyebrows at the matte black credit card.

"Friends with deep pockets."

She ran my card through a reader on a small tablet and handed it back to me to sign. "The delivery went out a little while ago."

"Perfect. Thank you so much for a lovely meal." Standing, I took back the card and pocketed it. "It occurred to me—I don't travel much—do I need to check in with your cousin's boss?"

"I don't know for sure," she said in a hushed voice, "but probably. If you want to leave your number with me, I'll pass it along." She gave me her pen and I scribbled my cell number on her order pad before handing it back. "415?"

"San Francisco."

"I'll pass it along."

TWENTY-TWO

A Day of Sightseeing Spoiled by a Kidnapping

I left the restaurant feeling nicely full, with more than enough room for beignets. The day had warmed while I'd been eating. Walking along Royal Street, I passed art galleries and cigar shops, vintage clothes stores and bakeries. Jazz and blues floated out of clubs opening their doors.

Wandering up one street and down the next, I meandered my way through the Quarter, searching for the Voodoo shop I'd visited my first night. It only took a few wrong turns before I was walking through the door again. The same woman was at the counter, showing a customer necklaces secured beneath the glass counter.

Dodging a group of friends discussing who they should get Voodoo dolls for, I made my way back to the wall of books. The old man was gone. There was no stool, no fabric bags waiting to be sewn. I saw movement out of the corner of my eye. Turning, I watched a book slide off the shelf and fall to the floor.

I picked it up. *Communicating with the Dead.* If I'd been wearing a hat, I'd have tipped it. "Thank you," I whispered and went to the counter to pay. It was a slim, black volume that fit perfectly in the back pocket of my jeans.

After doubling back, I finally arrived at Jackson Square, sitting in the shadow of St. Louis Cathedral. A green area encircled the courtyard in front of the cathedral.

Coaches pulled by horses were lined up near the entrance to the square on Decatur Street. Artists and palm readers sat at card tables, waiting for tourists. I had almost made it to the Decatur exit when a psychic waved me over.

She had long blonde hair with small sections braided. Her eyes were blue and guileless, her skin too fair for this bright sun. She pointed to a sign that read *Donations of $10 or more accepted.*

Holding up a hand, I demurred, "I'm good, thanks."

"No, you're not." She waved me forward again and pointed to her chair. "Something dark is following you. Let me see," she said, gesturing for me to give her my hands.

Deciding I'd chalk this up to a New Orleans tourist experience, I sat and gave her my left hand. She pulled my right hand toward her so she could study both. I knew this was probably a scam, but I felt a jolt when she touched me.

Staring at my left hand, she said, "You have great potential. It's"—she glanced up at me and then back down—"kind of terrifying, actually. In another age, kingdoms would have bowed before you." She ran her thumb back and forth over my palm, seemingly lost in thought. "It's trying to burst out of you while you try to pen it in."

Gripping my hands, she said, "It won't work, you know. It's your destiny." Turning her focus to my right hand, she said, "You'll do much for love, but it will be given back to you in kind." Rubbing her thumbs over both palms, she closed her eyes. "The darkness that has walked in your wake your whole life is getting closer, stalking you. You'll meet it when the time comes. I don't know if you'll win or lose. Only you know that. It's your birthright, though, to stand on the field of battle, to challenge the darkness."

Pulling her hands back, she waited for payment. I stood and

pulled a twenty out of my pocket. After dropping it into her jar, I turned to go.

"Oh, and Sam?"

I pulled up short, peering over my shoulder.

"Watch your back."

"How did you know my—"

"Hello." She turned from me and motioned to a couple walking by, waving them over for a reading.

Unsettled, I left the square and the psychic behind. I didn't need to check the map on my phone. My nose led me across Decatur and to the door of Café Du Monde. It was large and airy and filled with people eating, drinking, and chatting with friends.

I was headed to the front door when my phone rang. Unknown number. "Hello?"

"Need to speak with you," a deep, gravelly voice said. He had the lyrical accent locals possessed.

And then I smelled it. Wolf. The coffee, grease, and powdered sugar had blunted my senses to anything else. I'd had too relaxing of a day. So, of course, wolves.

"I see." Pausing, I moved toward the edge of the sidewalk, out of the flow of traffic. I'd heard his voice in stereo. I'd smelled wolf. He was nearby. Forcing myself to steady my suddenly galloping heartbeat, I glanced up the street. A man on a phone leaned against a motorcycle thirty feet away.

Staring at me, he crooked a finger and ended the call.

Shit. Okay. I could handle this. I'd killed vampires. I could deal with my fear of wolves. Straightening my shoulders, I tried for a saunter. I'd killed my wolf torturer. He was dead and I was still here. I could handle this guy too. Fuck him if he thought he could intimidate me. Throat tight, I stood directly in front of him.

He studied me and then grinned. "Not the tough guy I was expecting. You seem more like a ballerina than a killer."

I was in love with Clive and all that, but once I stopped sweating over an unknown male wolf in close proximity, I could acknowledge that this guy was hot. Dark hair a little too long, deep brown eyes in a suntanned face. Muscles bulged in arms that were crossed over a broad chest. He wore a black t-shirt straining at the shoulders, black jeans, and scuffed motorcycle boots. When he grinned, my heart may have galloped for a different reason. He was potent as hell.

"Careful. I'll plié your ass to the ground."

He threw back his head, laughing. Was this a meet and greet, or was I about to fight a pack of wolves? I was really hoping it was the former and not the latter.

"You're cute, ballerina. Why was I tipped off about a badass in leathers, covered in scars? One who's already taken out at least four vampires?" His gaze was assessing, still sexy, but assessing. "Do we have two unannounced visitors in our territory?" He'd dropped the jovial tone.

"Just me," I replied, pulling up a sleeve to show him my arm, some scars light and silvery, some thick and corded, some jagged. The torture had lasted a lifetime or almost a day, depending on whether or not you were the one being tortured and raped.

"Huh," was all he said.

Doing the math in my head, I added, "And my vamp kill count is more like eight." Jeez, I was becoming a serial killer. Or a vampire hunter. Yeah, that sounded better.

Eyebrows raised, he studied me again. "You don't say."

"Listen, I'm jonesing bad for beignets." I shot a thumb over my shoulder. "Can we do this quickly so I can eat?"

"You already ate," he said, watching me.

"Your point?"

"My point is that you're not starving. You can come with me, meet my Alpha. If he says you're okay, I'll bring you back and buy you a dozen."

"Two dozen. Final offer." I knew this had to happen. I didn't want werewolves hunting me too.

He climbed on his motorcycle and tipped his head in invitation to climb on. I'd never ridden a motorcycle before. This was equal parts terrifying and exciting.

Pulling my cell phone from my pocket, I called Stheno.

"What?" As Stheno's default was pissed off, I didn't know if I had woken her up or not.

"Sorry to disturb, but I needed someone to know that the local pack has summoned me. I'm being escorted to a meeting with the Alpha by…" I raised my eyebrows and waited for the wolf to answer.

"Gabriel," he growled.

"A man named Gabriel. He's driving a motorcycle with the license plate CCP02."

"Wait for me. I'll be right there." Stheno's voice had turned angry.

"It's okay. I think I'm fine. If you don't hear from me in thirty minutes, call in the cavalry, though."

"This is a bad idea."

"Probably, but I want to talk with the locals. I'll call you back in a few." I hung up and turned back to the wolf on the motorcycle. "What time does this place close?"

"I'll get you back in time." He revved the engine when I climbed on behind him. "Hold on." And then we were weaving in and out of traffic, following the Mississippi River away from the Quarter. Concentrating on slowing my breathing and my heartbeat, I held on to his belt loops so I wouldn't have to actually touch a male wolf.

Assuming he didn't take us a few towns over, I could find my way back if need be. We drove through an industrial area, finally slowing down as the terrain changed from concrete to dirt roads up against forests and marshes. Turning through a gate at the end of a long drive, he parked in front of a ramshackle house that was a year away from being reclaimed by the wilderness.

"Wow. This place isn't covered in red flags or anything."

"All right, princess, off," he grumbled.

Warily, I stepped off the bike. "You guys don't keep a pet gator or anything, right?"

"Ha." Grim-faced, he walked me across the dirt yard, up the rickety steps, and to a door that didn't hang straight; its wooden planks water warped.

"You're ushering me into some kind of kill room, aren't you?"

He shoved me when I paused on the doorstep.

Oh. The inside was more rich-guy-country-cabin and less psycho-killer-body-dump. The floors and walls were polished wood; the furniture was a rich, brown leather. A huge stone fireplace dominated the wall opposite the door. Nice.

A wiry guy with dark brown skin and intelligent eyes that shone behind glasses sat on the stone hearth in front of the fire. He wore his hair in short twist outs and seemed more like a nerdy college student than a werewolf. A couple more men, bigger, with flexing muscles, leaned against the walls. Four male wolves surrounded me. My skin went clammy and my heart raced. Gritting my teeth, I talked myself down. I could protect myself now. They weren't trying to hurt me. I was okay.

The only wolf in the room not posturing and trying to intimidate me was the bespectacled one, so I assumed he was the Alpha. Desperately trying to mirror his badass reserve, I walked toward him, causing the wall leaners to tense. I stopped halfway across the room on a huge forest green rug.

"I'm Sam, a lone wolf from San Francisco, visiting your territory. I'm not here to cause you any trouble. I'm here on vampire business." Pausing, trying to get my panic in check, I thought about it. "I've never done this before. What am I supposed to say?"

The man in the glasses glanced at the others. "You're not what we were expecting."

Shrugging, I shoved my hands in my jeans pockets. When I realized I'd turned my ankle on its side like an embarrassed six-year-old rather than a stone-cold killer, I changed my stance, adopting something closer to a Wonder Woman pose.

The wolf who brought me started laughing. Whatever.

The guy in the glasses peered over my shoulder at the motorcycle dude. "She killed four bloodsuckers?" The disbelief in his voice made me want to smack him. Hard.

"She says eight," he sneered, causing everyone to laugh.

Okay, now they were pissing me off. "I introduced myself. Can you please give me your name so I can stop referring to you as *the bespectacled guy* in my head?"

Bespectacled guy stood. "I'm Mathieu, Alpha of the Crescent City Pack. The man who brought you here is Gabriel. And why, little wolf, are you here on bloodsucker business?"

"As with all vamp business, it's convoluted. The short answer is that Lafitte's vamps came to San Francisco and attacked our nocturne. They started it. We came to finish it." I didn't think I was giving away anything confidential.

"That explains why the bloodsuckers are killing each other off, and good riddance. That does not, however, explain why *you're* here."

This could get ugly. "Okay, from all the bloodsucker talk, I'm pretty sure I get how you feel about vampires. The thing is"—I glanced over my shoulder to see where Gabriel was—"I'm with the Master of the City." I took in the furrowed brows watching me. "A vampire."

Growls surrounded me on all sides. Goosebumps ran down my arms. I did *not* want to fight all these guys.

"Say it ain't so, princess," Gabriel groaned

Angling myself so I could keep everyone in view while acting like I was responding to Gabriel, I said, "I love him. Whaddaya gonna do?"

"Kill yourself," one of the guys against the wall said.

"Really?" Mathieu asked. "You go for dead guys?" The disgust on his face was clear.

"Not all of them. One in particular." I crossed my arms over my chest. They were all staring at me like they weren't sure if they should feel sorry for me or kill me. "And he's only mostly dead."

Mathieu shook his head, but it reminded me of what a wolf does when he shakes his coat, shaking off the unease or discomfort. "Necrophilia aside, why did he bring his little pet wolf to a bloodsucker battle?"

I stiffened, my jaw tightening, my claw tips biting into my palms. I knew my eyes were lightening as well when the men around me came to attention. "I'm no one's pet," I ground out.

Gabriel took a step forward, ready to attack to protect his Alpha. I unleashed my claws, my jaw changing shape to accommodate a wolf's fangs. I was not dying in their clubhouse.

Shock. The only reaction that registered from every man in the room was unmitigated shock. They thought they were dealing with a ballerina in jogging shoes and they got a survivor with six-inch razor-sharp claws. One of the men whined, dropping to the floor to shift. The other followed a moment later. Gabriel was sweating, holding off the change, while Mathieu studied me, more thoughtful than menacing.

"Apex transformation. I've heard stories. We all have. But I've never seen it." He walked over to the men, struggling to shift and placed a hand on each of their heads. "Peace." The struggling stopped, although each continued to slowly shift to wolf.

"It's a legend. And yet here you stand in partial transformation." He moved closer to me but I didn't get a whiff of aggression from him, merely curiosity.

I relaxed my jaw, allowing it to shift back to fully human. "I'm no one's pet, nor am I an oddity to be stared at."

He bowed. "I apologize. I had no idea a descendent of the origin existed. Your name is Quinn?" he asked.

"Yes."

"Well, then." He fell gracefully to his knees and bowed his head. Gabriel followed a moment later, either following what his

Alpha was saying or because he couldn't stand while his Alpha was kneeling.

Pulling in my claws, I asked, "What's going on?"

Mathieu leaned back on his knees, gaze awed as he took note of my retracted claws. "You are our queen."

TWENTY-THREE

Does a Crown Come with the Gig?

"Not that this isn't nice or anything." I was feeling decidedly awkward as the only one standing in the room. The two wolves who had been shifting trotted over and sat on either side of me like furry guards. "But the clock's ticking on those beignets. So if nobody plans to kill me, I'd like to go back now."

"Of course," Mathieu said, rising but still keeping his head canted slightly forward in deference. "Gabriel can take you wherever you need to go." Pausing, he thought a moment. "In fact, perhaps Gabriel could serve as your guard as long as you're in our city."

Gabriel stood behind me. "It would be my honor."

"Not being threatened with death is a nice change of pace for me, but I don't really need a guard." After all, I had three vampires and a gorgon watching my back.

Something passed between the men. "As you wish. If there is any way the pack can assist you, you need only ask. Gabriel will give you my number when he takes you back." He stepped forward and held out his hand. "May I?"

I took it to shake, but he bowed over it, pressing his forehead to my wrist. I'm not sure what prompted me to do it, but I laid my other hand on his shoulder in a kind of blessing. When he let out a breath and seemed to curl around my hand, I hoped I'd done the right thing.

Straightening, he released my hand. He seemed taller and broader than a moment ago. Of course, he'd been on his knees a moment ago. After nodding to Gabriel, he said, "You have a pack at your command. You need only call."

"Um, thanks for that." I needed to work on my ceremonial phrases.

"Miss Quinn?" Gabriel waited at the door for me.

"Mathieu, may I consider you my champion?" I'd pulled that idea from a medieval romance I'd read last year, but it felt right.

A huge grin spread across the Alpha's face. "Yes, my queen."

Nodding at them in a benevolent ruler way—or at least my best impression of one—I backed out of the cabin.

Gabriel held out his hand to help me down the rickety steps. Seeing as he'd shoved me through the door on the way in, I stared at his hand until he dropped it and then leaped from the porch to the dirt yard.

He drove me back to the Café Du Monde, slower and more carefully than he'd driven before. This being a queen thing wasn't bad. He parked his motorcycle between two other cars in front of the café.

"Yay! They're still open," I said, hopping off.

"They're open 24/7," he said, glancing around, already behaving like my bodyguard. "I think you should stay here. There are police across the street and you'll be in plain view. I'll go get you whatever you want and then drive you where you need to go."

"Nope." Waiting for a group of people to pass, I headed for the front door. Coffee, fat, and sugar had me salivating as I walked in. Multiple employees were taking and filling orders behind the counter, so the line didn't take long.

Gabriel stood at my back, protecting me as I stared at the very short menu: beignets and coffee. That was it. I made a vow to come here as often as possible before we flew home. Or I died. One or the other.

I grabbed two cans of their ground coffee with chicory to take back to the townhouse. The couple in front of me moved aside, revealing a short, middle-aged woman who exuded calm in the middle of chaos. "Hello, dear. What can I get for you?"

I placed the two cans on the high counter. "Is it possible to order three dozen beignets or is there a limit?"

"Only limit is your appetite." She glanced over my shoulder. "Is he helping you?"

"Oh, no. These are all mine."

She cackled, "Atta girl."

When she told me the price, I tried to hand her my card, but she shook her head. "We're cash only."

Three twenties passed over my shoulder to the woman.

"He does have his uses, now doesn't he?" She chuckled to herself while she made change. A moment later, someone from the back brought out three white bags filled with sugary goodness and placed them on the counter in front of me. I almost fainted.

Back outside, Gabriel walked me to his motorcycle, taking the coffee cans from me and putting them in storage boxes, one on each side. He tried to stuff the bags in there, too, but I wasn't letting them go and certainly not to be put in a box that smelled like motor oil.

Once we were both on, he started the engine and asked over his shoulder, "Where to, ma'am?"

"I think I liked princess better." I gave him the address and we were off. I must have puttered around the galleries and shops in the Quarter for longer than I'd thought; it was starting to get dark when Gabriel pulled up in front of the townhouse.

I got off, hugging the beignets to my chest. He pulled the cans out of the storage boxes but rather than hand them to me, he offered to carry them in.

I held out my free hand for them. "I appreciate it, but

vampires and an unknown wolf are probably not the best combo."

The front door opened and Clive stood in the doorway. "I disagree. I think your friend should come in."

A woman walked her dog down the quiet, tree-lined street, completely oblivious to the tension amping up over here.

"Clive," I said in hushed tones. "This is Gabriel, second—" I paused, eyebrows raised to Gabriel. He gave a quick nod. "Second in the Crescent City Pack. He's offered himself as my bodyguard while we're in the Big Easy.

"Gabriel"—I gestured to the angry vampire in the doorway —"this is Clive, Master of San Francisco and my gentleman caller."

Clive shook his head at my moniker for him and waved us both inside.

I was barely in the door when I heard, "What's that smell?" Stheno appeared at the end of the hall, her curls moving in a nonexistent breeze as she stared intently at the white bags in my hands.

Gabriel slid in front of me, not even knowing what this new threat was. Good bodyguard.

Stheno's eyes narrowed as she took in the gorgeous man who'd stepped in front of the baked goods. "Well, well, well. I gotta say, Sam, you are racking up points right and left today."

Her heated gaze traveled up and down Gabriel's cut body and chiseled face. Slowly. "When the delivery kid came with food this morning, I thought, 'She's good people. I'd probably protect her even if I wasn't getting paid.' But now? Beignets *and* a hot wolf? I will get off this couch and kill indiscriminately for you."

I felt it when Russell and Godfrey came up the steps behind us. Gabriel didn't flinch, so the gorgon in front of him must have had his full attention. "Thanks. And while I will be sharing my beignets with you, the wolf isn't mine to offer. You'll have to do your own wooing there."

When I tried to get past Gabriel, he moved, keeping himself between me and the strange woman undressing him with her eyes. If he got closer, she'd start doing it with her hands.

"Stheno, step back. Let him pass. Yes, he's gorgeous." At that, he looked over his shoulder at me and grinned. A strange angry growling sounded down the hall. Hmm, probably shouldn't have said that out loud. "Consent is important. The hot wolf decides who he sleeps with."

"The hot wolf has a name," Gabriel offered.

"Sorry," I said as Stheno purred, "Who said anything about sleeping?"

Once all six of us were in the kitchen, I grabbed two plates from the cabinet and split the beignets in half. We each got eighteen. Gabriel was still holding the coffee cans, his expression somewhere between uneasy and defiant when he realized we had two more vampires with us. I wasn't going to call attention to my bodyguard missing their arrival, though. Stheno can be overwhelming.

Gesturing to the coffee maker, I asked, "Can you make us some?"

He seemed relieved to have a task. "Of course, my queen."

Four sets of eyebrows raised at his words.

"That's right!" I gloated. "It's about time I started getting the respect I'm due."

"Queen?" Godfrey asked in a tone that was about to incur my royal wrath. "Does that make Clive the king?"

Scoffing, I bit into a beignet and moaned softly. Truly, they were food of the gods. "He's my consort."

Clive was leaning against the wall, arms crossed over his chest, gaze fixed on Gabriel. "I suppose that's better than gentleman caller."

"Everyone, this is Gabriel, second in the Crescent City Pack. Gabriel, you've met Clive. The two vampires with him are Russell and Godfrey." Each nodded when I said his name. "And this is Stheno. I'll let her tell you more about herself when she sees fit."

"We know his name and his place in the pack," Russell said, watching Gabriel make coffee. "Can you tell us, Sam, why he's here?"

Hitting the button on the coffee maker, Gabriel turned around. "I'm here to protect my queen."

Stuffing another beignet in my mouth, I nodded regally at the vampires. That's fricking right.

Godfrey stared at Clive and then Russell. "I feel as though we've missed a few steps. Are either of you following this?"

I unleashed the claws on the hand not currently stuffing another beignet in. I really needed that coffee; I was about to choke on powdered sugar. Gabriel's response was like that of a tuning fork. He vibrated with intensity, fixated on my hand.

No one, besides Gabriel, paid any attention to me. They'd seen me do that trick before. Well, maybe not Stheno, but she'd already been watching Gabriel. Her perusal now was more focused.

Choking down the beignet, I got up to check the fridge. Milk? Anything? Since I had no desire to wash down the powdered sugar with mustard, I grabbed a glass from the cupboard and filled it with tap water.

Once my mouth was clear, I explained. "Apex transformation has only ever been done by members of the Origin's line. Mathieu, the local Alpha, had thought it was only legend. As my father, uncle, and cousins are all dead, I am probably the last of the Quinn line and the only one able to achieve apex transformation. Ergo, I am the Werewolf Queen! All bow!"

Gabriel bowed while the others stared at me with varying levels of disbelief.

"Rise, my Knight of the Beignet." I needed a scepter, a big gaudy one I could slam on the floor while making pronouncements. The coffee machine beeped, so I popped up to pour a cup for Stheno and myself. "Do you want one?" The poor guy seemed confused, but he nodded.

"Gabriel, do you know how many are in the New Orleans nocturne?" Clive asked.

"Before we began our reign of terror, that is." My eyes rolled back in my head as I took my first sip. Hello, darkness, my old friend.

Gabriel leaned against the kitchen counter close to the coffee machine and across the room from the vampires. "We never had an exact count, but we believe it's somewhere between fifty and sixty."

"Whoa." I thought our nocturne was big. That's a lot of fricking vampires. "How is this town large enough to support that many vampires?"

Russell said, "It's not," at the same time Godfrey said, "Bagged blood."

"Speaking of which, don't you guys need to…" I waved at the refrigerator.

"Not until we're sure we're dealing with an untainted supply," Clive said.

"Oh, right," Stheno said. "Beignet, hot wolf, coffee, I forgot. A cooler arrived earlier. I ditched the blood bags in the fridge and replaced them with new ones." Stheno took another gulp of coffee. "I'll have no trouble staying awake tonight." She caught Gabriel's eye and winked.

Godfrey prepared glasses of blood for the vampires in the room. I kept my focus on the last remaining beignets on my plate, deciding if I had it in me to finish them. Gabriel, though, never took his eyes off the vamps.

"If the pack's estimates are correct, we've taken out half the nocturne," I said. Gabriel turned sharply at my words. "Will Lafitte lick his wounds and lie low," I continued, "or try to hit us with what he has left?"

"Regardless of what he directs his people to do, Lafitte will go into hiding," Russell said, his deep voice commanding the room. "He is a preening coward. We saw that last night. He likes to goad and taunt. When the battle begins, though, he runs."

"Lafitte ran?" Gabriel's expression was one of disbelief. "But he's the Master of the City. He left his people to fight without him?" Shaking his head, he scanned the room. "The pack acknowledges no one above our Alpha. We offer no allegiance to the bloodsucker, but other supernaturals do, even though he ignores all but his own nocturne. How did he become Master? How has he kept it for centuries?"

"Reputation, a huge army, tacticians at his ear, and—we believe—a much stronger individual hiding behind the curtain," Clive said.

TWENTY-FOUR

I Think I Might Have Peed Myself

When Gabriel finished his coffee, I sent him away. I was covered and the guys weren't going to talk freely with a random wolf in the room, no matter how often he bowed or called me queen. Stheno was annoyed with me until I reminded her about the food and coffee.

"Your Highness," Clive began, "you and I are going to visit someone who is a bit like vampire royalty. With luck, he will still be feeling neutral toward me. I doubt he involves himself with the local nocturne, so I don't think there will be reprisals there."

"Sire, no," Russell said. "If you must go, take one of us." Russell's gaze darted to me for a moment before returning to Clive. "The Count enjoys—" He gave me another uneasy glance. "She'll be like catnip to him."

"Do you question my ability to protect my mate?" Clive's voice was deceptively calm, but his eyes had turned vamp black.

Russell bowed. "Never. I only worry for your mate's safety. Please forgive my insolence."

Clive closed his eyes. When they opened, they were back to his normal stormy gray. He patted Russell's shoulder, releasing him from his bow. "It's I who am sorry for overreacting to your valid warning. My mate smells of a strange male wolf, one she must have been pressed against on that motorcycle. And now I must take her into danger in order to get information."

"You could piss on her if you think it'll strengthen your claim," Stheno said.

"Thank you, Stheno," Clive said before focusing on me. "Russell is correct. The Comte St. Germain is a philosopher, a scientist, a musician, and a *very* old vampire. He claims to be the son of a Transylvanian prince, but who knows? He has lived many lives, used many names, but three things have always been true, no matter who and when he is: He is very powerful, extremely intelligent, and utterly depraved."

"Awesome." The beignets sat like rocks in my stomach.

Clive remained tense as he explained. "I don't want you anywhere near him. Ever. And yet I have to ask you to accompany me." Running a hand down his face, he shook his head. "I'll be wrapping you up in a glittering bow for him." He glanced at Russell. "I know that."

Turning back to me, face pained, he continued, "The Comte and I have known each other for a very long time, and he owes me. I *will* be using you, though. He'll be so excited to meet you that more might slip out than he's intending. Doing so means informing him that you exist, though, making you the new plaything he desperately wants."

"Bastard," Stheno spat.

"Yes." Clive sat down heavily in the chair next to me. "I want you to storm off, have your wolf friend drive you far away from here and treat you like a queen."

"Will my being there help?" Lord knew, I had no desire to put yet another target on my back, but if this would help Clive, Russell, and Godfrey figure out who was plotting against them, it might be worth it.

Watching Russell and Godfrey, their expressions stoic as hell, broke my heart a little. The emotions in the room were battering me from all sides. Russell was shouting 'No!' at me. Godfrey was hoping I'd help but feeling like a right bastard for hoping. And

Clive was painfully conflicted. The fact that I could read him at all meant he was either too torn up to shield or that he wanted me to know what he was feeling.

On one hand, he really did wonder if I'd be happier and safer if I found a nice, protective wolf to love. I might even be able to have children and not be the last of the origin line. On the other hand, he wanted to gnaw off the first hand and then set fire to it. He knew he wasn't selfless enough to let me go.

What he also knew was that the Comte St. Germain kept himself aloof from the rest of vampire society and yet heard everything. If there was anyone in town who knew who was pulling Lafitte's strings, it would be St. Germain. Clive was torn between his need to protect me and his obligation to protect his people.

"How can you be sure St. Germain isn't the one directing Lafitte?" He seemed sure, but we knew a powerful vamp was working behind the scenes. Why did St. Germain get a pass?

"He has other interests," Russell offered.

Clive nodded. "He does. St. Germain has neither the interest nor the patience to involve himself in political maneuvers. I said earlier he was like royalty. What I meant by that is he is the mad king who indulges his every whim while his people starve in the streets. He's the ultimate narcissist. He cares nothing for others. I could be wrong, but I don't see the benefit to St. Germain. What does he get by involving himself with Lafitte?"

"We don't yet know, Sire," Russell replied.

Clive inclined his head, acknowledging the point.

I took his hand and squeezed. "So, tell me what I need to know and when we're going."

Stheno swore and went back to her couch, making sure to turn the volume on the TV *way* up.

Clive stood and led me down the hall, Russell and Godfrey following. We settled in the front sitting room, cutting down the noise from the family room considerably.

"As I said, St. Germain is quite old and powerful."

"And ugly," Godfrey cut in. Russel gave him a bland look. "What? He is. She should be prepared. He's like a hairless rat but bafflingly vain."

"Yes," Clive said, pulling my attention back to him. "Old, powerful, and ugly."

"You mentioned twisted before. Twisted in what way?"

"Every way," Russell grumbled.

Clive inclined his head in agreement. "Pain is an intoxicant to him. One moment he might be discussing a performance at the opera, and the next he's gutted a servant and is playing with her intestines. I would say he's insane, but that's not quite right. He's a brilliant sadist with impulse control issues."

"Well, that sounds lovely. Sign me up." I was starting to break out in a cold sweat. I couldn't believe I'd agreed to this. "Can you take him? If push comes to fangs and he tries to eat me, are you stronger?"

"Yes," Godfrey said at once while Russell remained silent.

Shit.

"I believe so," Clive finally responded.

"Okay. Well, if we're off to meet with a legendary psycho, I best get changed." Leaving them, I went upstairs to freak out, shower, and change.

I was halfway through the shower when I heard Clive open the bedroom door. Damn, I hadn't finished my freak-out. How was I supposed to curl into a fetal ball and shake if he was watching me? I took my time drying and dressing so I could more firmly affix my warrior face.

When I emerged from the bathroom, I had my hair blown out long and wore a robe over my undies. I had no idea how to dress for the ancient sadist. Clive sat on the edge of the bed, waiting.

"You don't need to do this. No one will think less of you for it. In fact, I was speaking with Russell. We wonder if he might not behave more poorly than usual in order to entertain himself by terrifying you."

Nodding, I sat down next to him. "True. Which I believe was

the original point. He'll be so distracted terrorizing me that you'll get info you might not. Remember?" I patted his knee. I knew what he was doing and a plausible excuse to stay home should have made me happy. I could sit on the couch next to a gorgon and watch bad TV, safe and sound.

"I'm scared, okay? I'm not going to lie. But I have to go. Partners, remember? We're in this—whatever it is—together."

"Yes, but I'm placing you in peril far more often than you have ever endangered me. In fact, you have never—"

"Oh, it's coming. Don't worry. It's coming."

Standing, he said, "I still don't think that makes us even."

"That's okay." I stood and wrapped my arms around him. "No one's keeping score."

"I am!" Stheno shouted from downstairs.

"Shut it, you!" I shouted right back. That woman needed to work on her boundaries. And her filters. I liked her.

"So," I said, walking to the closet. "How do I dress for this? If he's vain and sort of a royal, should I dress up? I brought one fancy dress with me. Or do I put on my leathers again?"

Clive thought about it a moment. "Neither. *You're* what's unique. Everyone else dresses up. You wear jeans and running shoes." He kissed my neck and then walked out. "I'll wait for you downstairs."

A few minutes later, I trotted down the stairs in jeans and my *Pride and Prejudice* hoodie, with my hair tied up in a braid. If I was getting gutted tonight, at least I'd be comfortable.

Russell drove, with Godfrey in the passenger seat. They'd wait for us in the SUV while we went in. Even in a soundproof house, Clive said he could communicate with them if we needed help. Russell stopped in front of a tall townhouse on the fringes of the French Quarter. It was painted charcoal gray with white trim. A nondescript house that raised my hackles, nonetheless.

Clive took my hand as we slid out of the backseat. The house appeared abandoned. No light peeked out through any window.

Great. This was going to be like the NOLA nocturne, with antiques, ancient clothing, and guttering candles.

Clive raised his hand to knock but before he made contact, the door swung open, bright light spilling out of the doorway. An attractive young Asian man in bare feet, faded jeans, and a black silk shirt open at the collar held the door and beckoned us in.

"St. Germain is in the sitting room. He's expecting you." The young man led us down the hall to the last door on the right. "I'm Li, if you need anything." Extending a hand toward the open door, he said, "I'll leave you to your visit." Turning, he traveled back down the well-lit hall.

The house seemed to have been remodeled, so while the exterior appeared forbidding, the interior reminded me of a society garden party. Did he intend for the interior to disorient? I'd been warned that he was a rat-like sadist, but the townhouse screamed maiden aunt with money and a partiality for pastels. Chandeliers dripping with crystals hung from the ceiling. What was it with vampires and chandeliers?

Clive placed a hand on my lower back and guided me through the door into a sitting room of dusty pink and green with lush floral paintings on the walls. A fire burned in the fireplace, and unlike the front of the house, the curtains were open to the backyard.

A man who, yes, had certain rat-like facial features was sitting in a high-backed chair next to the fire. He seemed familiar. I'd never met him, but there was something… Had I seen him in someone's thoughts? Dressed in a European-cut, deep teal suit, he placed the goblet in his hand on a small but ornate side table and rose.

"Clive, an unexpected pleasure." The two inclined their heads toward one another before St. Germain turned his attention to me. "And who have you brought me?"

The hairs on the back on my neck prickled. "I'm Sam Quinn."

When he took my hand in his own, I had an overpowering desire to scream, 'Get it off! Off!'

A slow smile curled his thin lips as he squeezed my hand rhythmically. "It's lovely to meet new friends, isn't it? So many delicious possibilities."

The dark, feral eyes, the leer, it was all too much. I unleashed the claws on my free hand, causing him to blink. Eyes gleaming, he studied me, more intrigued than concerned. I yanked my hand free of his grip and glared. The bastard clapped and chuckled, as though I were an adorable child performing a new trick.

"Deadly, not delicious." I knew my speeding heartbeat was giving me away, but I refused to be cowed by this creep.

St. Germain turned to Clive. "Do you agree?"

Clive gave a barely perceptible shrug, saying, "I've found her to be both."

With a laugh like nails on a chalkboard, St. Germain's attention stayed fixed on me, which was what we wanted. Mostly. When he stared a little too long at my claws, I snicked them in.

"Fascinating," he purred. Twirling his finger, he said, "Turn for me."

"No."

At my reply, his eyes hardened, going vamp black. Lowering his eyelids coquettishly, he murmured, "Precious." When he raised his eyes a moment later, they were back to brown.

Shit. I was about to die, wasn't I?

TWENTY-FIVE

Kill It!

"Sit, sit. Let's get to know one another." St. Germain took the spring green, high-backed chair to the side of a tufted pink velvet settee. Gesturing to the cushion closest to him, he invited me to sit.

Ignoring his request, I sat in the middle of the settee and Clive took the chair identical to St. Germain's at the end opposite our host.

"Li," St. Germain called.

The young man appeared at the door a moment later. "Sire?"

"Our guests need refreshments." St. Germain spoke to his servant—boyfriend, underling. I couldn't get a handle on the relationship—but his gaze never left me. The man excelled at being unnerving.

"Of course." Li crossed the room to hand St. Germain the goblet he'd left by the fire before turning to Clive and me. "May I get you a goblet?" he asked Clive, who nodded. Then Li turned his attention to me. His eyes sparkled, as though this was all extraordinarily funny. "Miss?"

I was feeling distinctly like a mouse being toyed with right before the cat pops it in his mouth and bites it in half. "Nothing for me."

"As you wish." With a slight bow for all assembled, he left the room.

"I don't remember meeting Li the last time I visited," Clive said conversationally.

St. Germain tipped the goblet up, finishing his drink, and then placed it on the coffee table in front of him. A pale tongue darted out to snatch a drop of blood left on his upper lip.

"Because you didn't. Li is a recent addition, aren't you?" St. Germain said as Li returned with a silver tray bearing an ornate goblet like his master's.

"I am, indeed," Li said, offering the goblet to Clive. Once the tray was empty, Li picked up St. Germain's cup and placed it in the middle. "The Comte and I have so many shared interests." His gaze strayed to me a moment. "It's been a mutually beneficial relationship."

As Li turned to go, I poked in his head. It was getting easier to push through natural defenses. Li was thinking about a woman they had tied up in the cellar. Head pounding, I was bombarded by a barrage of images involving sex, pain, and blood. St. Germain and Li enjoyed themselves with the willing and unwilling alike. Some craved the pain, some the dark kiss, others had wandered in unaware of what lay in store. Clive must have guessed what I'd been doing, because cool pain relief washed over me.

"Now *what* caused that?" St. Germain asked quietly, almost as though he were talking to himself. "It's lovely, though, isn't it?" he asked Clive. "The racing of that strong heart. The blood pumping in that lithe body. Simply delicious." Eyelashes lowering, lips curling, he added, "Oh, but you don't like that word, do you?"

I wished I could say I sprawled on the settee and gave him the finger, completely at ease with his creepiness. Unfortunately, that would be a lie. What I wanted to do was climb on a table, point at him, and shout, 'Kill it! Kill it!' like an old cartoon heroine while someone else disposed of the vermin. What I actually did was sit stiffly, scared shitless, and brace for an attack.

"What brings you by?" His question was directed at Clive, but his gaze never left me.

"I was hoping you might lend some light to the situation. I haven't been in your town for quite some time, so I'm sure I've missed developments."

"Hmm." St. Germain nodded, his gaze languidly caressing me, his expression alight with delicious plans.

"Lafitte has become uncharacteristically hostile toward me, treating far too many of his people like cannon fodder. I'm sorry to say, we've handed half of his nocturne their true deaths."

That got St. Germain's attention. For the first time since we'd entered the room, he was focused on Clive. "Is that so?"

"It is." Clive nodded. "Sam here has even killed—how many now—well, she's close to double digits."

St. Germain's attention swung right back to me, expression giddy. "With those sharp little nails of yours, I'd bet."

"That's right."

"You'd be a formidable opponent, wouldn't you?" He giggled. "Such fun."

Desperately fighting off a full-body cringe, I met St. Germain's stare. "Most vamps don't find it fun when I slice their heads off."

Turing to Clive, he whispered conspiratorially, "They're adorable when they raise their little fists, aren't they?" Crossing his leg, he brushed nonexistent lint from his knee. "Now, Miss— Quinn, was it?" His eyes lit up. "Quinn?" He turned to Clive for confirmation.

Clive nodded. "Yes, Quinn."

St. Germain laughed long and loud. He rose and held out a hand to Clive. "Only you."

Clive shook it, a small, self-satisfied smile tugging at his lips. If I didn't know better, I'd beat the crap out of Clive for that smile. We were playacting. I knew that and I had a role to play.

Feigning ignorance, I asked, "Is my name funny?"

"No, my dear. Most assuredly not." He sat back down, tapping a finger on the arm of his chair, expression flitting from amusement to resentment and back again. "I do so love unique treasures."

Clive drank deeply from his goblet, giving our host time to study me. "Has Lafitte lost interest in holding this city?"

"Hmm? Oh." St. Germain waved a hand. "The man is a popinjay, desperate to be seen as royalty when what he is is a mediocre pirate given the veneer of sophistication through a bite. Tedious." His gaze traveled over me again, from ponytail to running shoes. "Now you wouldn't be tedious, would you?"

Turning to Clive, I asked, "Is he asking to get his face sliced?"

"Sam, we're guests," was all Clive said, but when I returned my attention to St. Germain, his eyes were vampy black and he was leaning forward in his chair.

Shit, shit, shit.

Expression annoyed, fingers drumming forcefully, he said, "Someone's been whispering in his ear, puffing him up. He had the nerve to slight me. *Me.* He was overheard in a restaurant commenting on my proclivities." A high-pitched giggle bubbled out of him. "I sent him a big box tied with a loopy silver bow containing the dust of the men who had laughed at his joke."

"Between the two of us, we're decimating his numbers, aren't we?" Clive sounded bored.

"He's nothing. I'm surprised you bothered to respond. I'd have thought his people not returning from your nocturne would be message enough."

"Like you, I was annoyed."

"And you brought a friend on your journey, which makes everything so festive, doesn't it?" St. Germain was back to studying me. Thankfully without the anger.

"She does keep things interesting. Why isn't Luc protecting him from his own idiocy?" Clive asked. I remembered Clive saying that Luc was missing. He must have been fishing for info.

"Ah, Luc. Now that is sad. I've heard that Lafitte flew into a rage and killed him. That's the story being actively spread. Piffle. Lafitte could never defeat Luc. My guess, if you're interested?" At Clive's nod, he continued, "My guess is that someone else took him out, someone who wanted an easily manipulated Master of the City. Something's afoot, but I don't actually believe it involves our kind."

"No?" Clive asked.

Shrugging, St. Germain said, "I may be wrong, but Lafitte had been dabbling in Voodoo before Luc disappeared. He knew he was no match for me, or you for that matter, so I think he was trying to become more powerful. The nocturne?" He waved a hand, unconcerned. "Whoever is manipulating the poor idiot may not care for us. A few dozen fewer of us in the city might be a perk rather than a goal."

"Interesting."

St. Germain gave Clive a disinterested nod before focusing his considerable creepy attention back on me. I took a chance, trying to push into his mind. If he was actively thinking about Lafitte and a Voodoo practitioner, maybe there was more in there he wasn't saying.

Staring into the fire, I immediately found the little, cold blip in my head that was St. Germain. Trying to be cautious, I imagined myself curling around the blip and slowly seeping in, rather than pushing at one point. Nothing. I squeezed the blip, searching for a weak spot while Clive asked if St. Germain knew who might be whispering in Lafitte's ear. There. A soft spot. I pushed and wriggled, trying to get through.

Part of my brain was trying to pay attention to the conversation and any possible threat, but the rest of me was mentally boring through the barriers, of which there were many. I hadn't tried this before, but in my mind, I unsheathed one claw and tried to slice through the barriers. St. Germain's voice faltered midsentence. I saw only a flash of an image, but it had my stomach dropping and my body going cold.

Clive, hair long, clothing dated, and eyes vamp black, reaching for a struggling, disemboweled woman. Barriers snapped back into place. Pushed out, I found St. Germain's black eyes glaring at me, his fangs descended.

Shitdamnfuck. I popped off the couch and braced for battle.

"What have you brought into my home?" he demanded, rising slowly and taking a step toward me. "You two must stay." His rage sucked up all the air in the room. "For dinner."

When that pale tongue peeked out of his mouth again, I unleashed my claws and felt my shoulders shift, broadening. My arms bulked with stronger muscles as my jaw distended to make room for great big fangs of my own.

He blinked, eyes brown and thoughtful again. "Well, well, well. What have you been hiding?"

I had no idea which of us he was speaking to, whether or not I was still being spoken of as Clive's pet. Mostly I wanted to take a swipe at every vampire in the joint for scaring me senseless, including Clive for dangling me in front of this sadist like a cat toy.

Clive watched me, his eyes vamp black, a self-satisfied smirk on his face. "You can hardly blame me for keeping her to myself. She's quite the prize, isn't she?"

The front door crashed in and footsteps pounded down the hall. Mathieu, followed by Gabriel and six other wolves, four in wolf form, stormed the room and encircled me. Three of the wolves, teeth bared, growled at St. Germain. One directed his aggression at Clive. Li ran in a moment later but skidded to a stop at the doorway, fear and excitement battling in his eyes.

Shifting my jaw back, I said, "I'm leaving now. I've had about all the vampires I can deal with for one day. Don't talk to me. Don't follow me. Any vampire who gets within arm's reach is losing his head. I'm done with your shit."

When I turned to leave, Clive backed away, his expression closed. Li had already disappeared. My saviors and I walked over the broken door, out onto the empty street. I didn't give more than a passing thought to Russell and Godfrey being MIA. I loved Clive with all that was in me, but I needed to get away from vamps. The fact that I was willingly fleeing with were-wolves said exactly how much.

TWENTY-SIX

I Really Needed to Work on My Royal Pronouncements

Wrapping my arms around Gabriel, I tried to put the whole evening out of my mind. The roar of the motorcycle helped muffle the memory of high-pitched giggles crawling over my skin. The heat emanating from Gabriel was different, but soothing. So was the heartbeat I was listening to, my ear to his back. Eyes closed, blocking everything else out, I swayed with the motorcycle and listened for the next beat of his heart.

Thirty minutes later, narrow city streets had given way to long, open expanses of road. Gabriel turned off the main boulevard, following a narrow, overgrown gravel lane that cut through tall trees and scraggly underbrush. At the final turn, a large clearing appeared with a sprawling warehouse sitting in the middle. The front of the building had a hand-painted sign over the closed cargo door. The paint, weathered by decades in the elements, was barely legible. *Matt's Canoe Repair.*

Climbing off the bike, I asked, "What is this place?"

"Pack house." He pocketed his keys and pointed toward one of the bay doors that was sliding up. The rest of my rescue party ducked under the door while we stood in the clearing.

"Where are we?" We'd traveled far from the Quarter and seemed to be out in the middle of nowhere.

Gabriel paused to take in the waxing moon above. "It won't be long now." When he glanced back at me, his brown eyes had lightened a few shades. He was closer to his wolf. He answered by gesturing everywhere east of where we were standing. "Jean Lafitte National Park."

"Nice backyard."

"Twenty-two thousand acres. We still have to be careful, but we know how to avoid the random human." He shrugged. "Superstitions run deep 'round here. People may not believe that werewolves exist, but they all know to stay out of wooded areas on a full moon."

I was feeling the full moon too and longed to run.

"Come on. Let's go in."

Following, I ducked under the door and found myself in an industrial chic living room with a huge state-of-the-art kitchen. Metal stairways on both sides of the cavernous room led to an open gallery on the second floor. Doors opened off the gallery walk, presumably the bedrooms for pack members.

Gabriel put two fingers in his mouth and whistled. Those not already sitting on the couches or eating at the dining tables banged out of their rooms above and hustled down the stairs. In less than a minute, I was facing at least forty werewolves, most in skin, but some in fur. The Crescent City Pack was predominantly male, which was normal from what I'd read, never having been a member of a pack myself.

Mathieu appeared at my elbow and addressed the assembled wolves. "May I present Samantha Quinn, last of the Origin line and queen to us all." The pack cheered and howled, through both human and wolf throats.

"And Miss Quinn, this is the Crescent City Pack. We are honored to have you with us." To a one, they bowed.

Standing in a room full of bowing people is nothing if not awkward. "That's very kind but, really, you don't need to—um, at ease, everyone. As you were." Yeah, totally crushing this queen thing.

Mathieu came to my rescue. "Thank you, all. Miss Quinn needs a quiet place to plan her next steps. She'll be working in my office. If you need me, give me a few minutes to make sure she's taken care of first."

Everyone shuffled backward, making a path to what I assumed was the door to Mathieu's office. Gabriel got there first, opening the door and then following Mathieu and me in. Mathieu offered me a chair, taking the seat behind his desk.

"First, let me ask if you're all right."

"I'm fine, thank you," I said, grateful to both of them. "How did you know I was in trouble?"

Mathieu gestured to Gabriel, giving him the floor.

"I was following you, watching the house once you'd gone in. The bloodsuckers in the car were getting agitated. The smart one got out of the car and crossed the street to talk to me."

"Which one is the smart one?" And how had he made that judgment when they'd only nodded to him in the kitchen?

Gabriel held his hand above his head. "Tall guy, Black, when he looks at you it feels like he's seeing into your soul and taking inventory." Shaking his head, he dropped his hand and leaned against the wall. "Anyway, I think you said he was second, but I don't remember his name."

"Russell." I thought it a good description of him. Still waters and all that. He spoke rarely, but was *always* thinking, usually a few steps ahead of everyone else. There was pain there too. Sometimes it was so deep, so vast, I almost choked on it.

"Yeah, him. Anyway, he told me to call the pack. Said you were in trouble and needed an extraction. I called my Alpha right away. The bloodsucker walked back to the car and then they both took off."

I knew we'd done it for the greater good, but I couldn't shake the sick feeling of being used to dazzle a sadist with my scars.

"Miss Quinn?" Mathieu's tone told me he must have repeated this phrase a few times.

"Please, Sam is fine." I was getting better, stronger. I knew I was, and yet, when confronted with St. Germain, I'd lost it. Knowing how desperately he wanted to add to my scars had stripped away my shields. All I wanted was to hide in The Slaughtered Lamb, away from all of this.

Mathieu opened his mouth to speak and then grinned. "I'm afraid I can't. Highness may be more than you can handle, but Sam is far too little for me. So, I believe we'll settle in the middle with Miss Quinn."

I gave what I was sure was an anemic smile. "Fair enough."

"We would be honored to have you stay with us."

I nodded before he'd finished his invitation. I wasn't ready to go back to the townhouse. I needed time and space to think, to work through tonight.

"*Bon.* Gabriel, can you show Miss Quinn to the guest room?" Mathieu pushed back in his chair and stood. "Whatever we can do, we're at the ready."

I held out a hand and shook his. "Thank you. You've already helped more than you know."

Gabriel walked me out by way of the kitchen. "I'm starving. Figured you might be, too, if all you've eaten today are a pile of beignets and some breakfast twelve hours ago." He opened the refrigerator, shuffled containers, and pulled out a platter covered with foil. Underneath was a mountain of ribs and fried chicken.

Stomach growling, I said, "Gimme, gimme."

Chuckling, he got plates, napkins, and a couple of sodas for us. Once we were settled in, I grabbed a piece of chicken and bit in. Spicy, crispy, succulent, it was a work of art. I groaned.

A few of the wolves who were sitting at a nearby table playing poker chuckled. A woman with short brown hair, wearing cargo pants and flip-flops tilted her head up and called, "You hear 'dat, Jacko? Queen like your chicken."

"'Course she do." A voice from the second floor floated down to us.

Gabriel and I made quick work of the platter. Feeling wonderfully full, I followed him up the metal stairs to a room at the end of the gallery.

A young woman was leaving towels on the bed. When she saw me, she gave a shy, flustered bob of a curtsy. "Yer Highness."

"Thanks, Lolly. It's real pretty in here," Gabriel said, glancing around in approval.

"You've certainly made me feel welcome," I said, earning another shy smile.

"Go on, now," Gabriel said. "Get some rest. That alarm goes off early."

"Yes, sir." She scurried past and disappeared around the corner.

Gabriel scanned the room again as though assuring himself it was ready for a guest. "You still have the numbers I gave you earlier, right?" I nodded and he continued, "Good. My room is on the first floor. If you need anything, though, call out and you'll have the pack at your door."

"I'll be fine. I just want a quiet place to think and sleep."

Perfect, white teeth flashed. "Happy to be your port in a storm, princess."

Once I was alone, I closed the door and rested my forehead against the wood. What was I doing? The only reason I was in New Orleans was to help with vampire shenanigans. I said I'd fight side by side with him, and I had, until fear made me a liability. Clive had had to call the wolves to rescue me. He'd worn the façade we'd needed, controlled the conversation, but what had I done? I'd taken a stick and poked the bear, revealing my secret weapon to our enemy, while also making him desperate to possess me.

All the vampires I'd met to date had been varying shades of powerful, aloof, and disdainful. The guys in Clive's nocturne who hated me had been dicks about it, but I hadn't worried any of them fed on babies. St. Germain was evil. I felt it. Being in close proximity to him felt like standing in sewage.

And then it hit like a lightning strike. I remembered why St. Germain had seemed familiar when we'd met. I'd seen him in the memory of that dark entity trapped in the Ursuline Convent. They were connected. He'd turned her or been her hunting buddy. I didn't know the relationship, but he exuded the same unspeakable cruelty that she had.

I'd tipped our hand to a monster. How the hell was I going to be Clive's partner in life when I couldn't get through one meeting with a bad guy without losing my shit? I could admit, at least to myself, that I'd hoped to win the respect of the vamps with this trip, hoped to finally put an end to their inexhaustible store of snide comments and dismissive glances. So much for that idea.

My phone buzzed in my pocket. When I pulled it out, I saw I had a missed call from Clive and a new text from Stheno.

Stheno: The bloodsuckers are home but you're not. Do I need to kill them? Where are you?

Apparently, the offer to kill indiscriminately for me was still good.

Me: Don't kill your paycheck. I'm fine. With the pack. You want to get something to eat tomorrow?

I needed to talk to someone who wasn't a vampire. Stheno was ancient and didn't understand the concept of sugarcoating. She'd help me gain some perspective and maybe lend me some of her bravado.

Stheno: Remember that hot wolf is mine. Are you asking me to shirk my protective duties and leave the corpses without a guard? Hell, yes, I want to go get food! Text me where and when.

Me: Gabriel's all yours and I'll see you tomorrow.

I returned Clive's call but got his voicemail. Damn.

Fear was getting the better of me. St. Germain scared me deeply, profoundly. They'd been carving up a woman in their basement before we'd arrived. The moment I met him tonight I'd known why he wanted me. I was a rarity, yes, but I was a strong supernatural who could last through hours and hours of torture. Had and could again. His need had eaten up the air in the room. I had suffocated in fear while Clive kept the façade in place, smirking with our guest. He'd maintained. I'd fallen apart.

Needing to check, I closed my eyes and searched New Orleans for Clive. He was with Russell and Godfrey. They were okay. Wrapping myself around his consciousness, I thought, *I love you.* Wiping my wet face, I curled up around my dark phone and willed myself to sleep.

TWENTY-SEVEN

It Kills Me to Say It, but Sometimes Beignets Are Not the Answer

By three, I gave up on getting any sleep. I silently made my way across the gallery and down the stairs. Not wanting to leave without saying goodbye, I grabbed a piece of paper and a pen from a communication area at the end of the kitchen counter. Sitting at one of the tables, I wrote a quick note to the pack.

Mathieu and the Crescent City Pack members, thank you all for opening your home to me. I had to leave early to deal with some problems, so couldn't thank you in person. If I can in any way repay your kindness, please don't hesitate to contact me. Sam Quinn

I attached the note to the refrigerator and then turned to go, bumping into a broad, hairy chest.

Gabriel stood in nothing but sleep pants hung low on his hips, reading over my shoulder. Nodding, he said, "They'll like that." Focusing on me, he added, "Give me a minute to grab clothes and then we'll go."

"Wait," I whispered. "You don't need to come. I can find my way back."

"Good. Still taking you, though."

He jogged back to his room to change while I sat waiting on the arm of a sofa. He was right. This was safer. I pulled out my phone and found a message waiting.

Clive: I love you too.

Needing to hear his voice, I tapped call but got his voicemail again. Still, even that helped to settle my stomach. Clive was a master tactician. He'd survived vampire politics for almost a thousand years. He'd understand this was all new to me. Hopefully.

Opening my texts, I put on a bright voice and shot one off to Owen.

Me: Morning, Sunshine! How's it going back there? How's my home coming along? I miss you guys. Hey, it's totally normal to be a huge disappointment to your partner, right? Just checking. Anyway, say hi to Dave for me :)

Gabriel came out a few minutes later, keys in his hand. "Okay, princess. Let's hit it." He opened the door, waiting for me to go through, and then closed it after me, leading the way to his motorcycle.

Pausing, I pointed at the door. "Aren't you going to lock it, alarm it, something?"

Starting the engine, he revved it once, rolling his eyes. "If they can handle a pack of wolves, I don't think a lock is gonna keep 'em out."

I got on the bike behind him. "Good point."

"Where to?" He drove down the gravel road.

"French Quarter."

"Beignets again?" I could feel his chuckle, rather than hear it. "And after that?"

I'd been formulating a plan while lying awake all night, but his suggestion was a good one. "Sugar and coffee first. Then we'll see if my idea still makes sense." I'd promised to help Clive, so I would.

Thirty minutes later, when Gabriel turned a corner into the French Quarter, a chill ran down my spine. Someone was watching. Leaning my forehead against Gabriel's back, I closed my eyes and reached out with my mind. My stomach lodged itself firmly in my throat at the thought of St. Germain lying in wait.

Fear may have amped up the mental pulse, or maybe three in the morning was the true wicching hour, but cold blips and hazy clouds were everywhere. Amélie was close, and, yes, a vamp was racing up the street behind us.

Squeezing Gabriel's waist, I said, "Vamp on our tail. Coming in fast. Don't slow down or stop, no matter what I do."

"Princess," Gabriel's voice warned, but there was no time.

Grabbing Gabriel's shoulders for balance, I hopped up and spun around, standing on the seat. The vamp was there, not a second later, arms reaching, fangs glistening in the streetlights. I leaped toward him, claws out.

His arms were around me, crushing bones, trying to break me. He'd caught one of my arms at my side, but with the other, I slashed at his face. When we hit the pavement a second later, he was on top of me. My right arm hurt like hell, but I could still move it. Without thinking, I grabbed his mind, yanked hard, and then slashed my claws across his neck, sending his head spinning toward the curb.

Gabriel was there a second later. "Princess, are you okay?" I felt his hands checking for injury. Unfortunately, I couldn't see anything, having lost my sight again. I'd caused a vamp to go brain dead. Right before I took his head, his eyes had gone back to blue and his fangs had disappeared from his slack face.

"Yeah," I said. "I'm fine." Other than a vicious headache and not being able to see, I was totally cool. I held out my hand, hoping he'd assume I was wobbly after slamming into the pavement.

Gentleman that he was, he helped me back to the bike and had me sit down first so he was at my back, ever the guard. Once he'd revved the engine to life, I turned my head and whispered, "Did we leave a body or dust in the street?"

After a moment, he responded, "Dust."

"'Kay."

While Gabriel drove, I tried to reach out to see if more vamps were closing in. My head was currently on the fritz. Glass was grinding in my skull, but I kept trying. Eventually, I saw faint blips, but nothing nearby or moving toward us. The hazy clouds, though, seemed to have coalesced around me, like my own ghostly bumper zone.

Gabriel shivered at my back. A few minutes later, he pulled to the side and stopped, the bike idling. The pause lengthened until he finally asked, "Do you still want beignets?"

Right. I'd forgotten. "Depends. Am I covered in blood or dust?"

I felt Gabriel lean forward, no doubt peering over my shoulder. "No blood. Wind on the drive here probably took care of the bloodsucker dust."

Perfect. "Can you rev it?"

While he complied, revving his engine a couple of times, I twisted my head and whispered, "I can't see, but I need to eat. Are there a lot of people here? I can hear voices."

With his mouth at my ear, he breathed, "Two tables of six to eight. Probably on their way home from the bars. Another seven scattered tables of singles."

"Can you guide me so no one can tell I'm blind?" I whispered.

Turning off the engine, he put down the kickstand and helped me off the bike. "Come on, *cher*," he said in a normal voice. "*Laissez les bon temps rouler*, you said." He wrapped his arm around me and pulled me close. "We'll get a little fat and coffee in you and you'll be right as rain."

I kept my arm around his waist, eyes closed, head resting on his chest. Drunk and sleepy would hopefully cover any missteps.

"Morning, ma'am. We'd like two dozen beignet, one large black coffee, and—" he turned to me. "What do you feel like, *cher*?"

Pretending to squint up at the menu board, I said, "Hot chocolate."

"Large, please." He shuffled us over the side to wait.

I felt his mouth on the top of my head. To anyone watching, it would look like a kiss. "We have a medic in the pack. Did blood-sucker dust get in your eyes?"

I shook my head.

"Here you are, dear." The voice of an older woman seemed to be directed at us.

A moment later, a cup was brushing against the back of my hand. I grabbed it, hoping it had a top and I didn't spill.

"Are we staying or heading home?"

"Let's sit for a bit." I really did want to eat something before we headed out and I wanted to give my vision time to return. Yes, bacon and eggs would have hit the spot better, but I wasn't going to complain about beignets.

Gabriel kept his arm around me, skirting us around tables until we seemed to be right next to the two raucous ones. He guided me into a chair and then the intoxicating sent of sugar and fat were in front of me.

"The plate is on the edge of the table, directly in front of you. Lean forward because they're messy." He kept his voice barely audible, the loud conversations around us covering his words.

Fumbling, I found the edge of a beignet, lifted it to my lips, and bit in. Still as heavenly as I'd remembered. I washed down the bite with cocoa and realized that the darkness I'd been trapped in was starting to lighten. The world had gone a deep charcoal gray, but the edges seemed to be brightening.

"Can you tell me now?"

Could I? I'd known the man one day and our relationship had begun with a kidnapping, in the mildest sense possible. Still, he'd already proven he'd protect me. Well, it was less dangerous for the werewolves to know than the vampires, and three vamps —four, if I counted St. Germain, which I probably should— already knew.

The gray was lightening and forms were taking shape. I spoke to the big blurry blob in front of me. Where to start… "My father was a Quinn, as you know, but my mother was a wicche."

I heard a quick intake of breath. Apparently, they didn't like wicches down here. "Is this going to be a problem for you?" Vision finally clearing, I saw shock and disgust mingling in his eyes.

"Gabriel?"

Face going blank, he said, "No."

"See, I'm not buying that." I glanced around the room and then leaned forward. "I release you from your word. You don't need protect me or even eat with me. Go ahead and go."

"You can see now?" He studied me with far less adoration than before. You never knew what you'd miss until it was gone.

"It's back. I'm fine. You can go." I bit into a beignet and shooed him away with my free hand. The doughy goodness felt like paste in my mouth. It had been cool having a pack on my side for a while. They *had* helped with St. Germain. So there was that.

Standing up, I offered my plate to the noisy table beside us. "Eyes were bigger than my stomach. Would you guys like them?"

"Hell, yeah." A young woman in a black tank top with hair piled on top of her head clapped. Glancing at Gabriel as she walked past, she reached for the plate. She came much closer than necessary and whispered, "Do you need help? Are you okay?" Taking the plate, she moved to block Gabriel from my line of sight. "We'll see you get home safe."

Kindness. Out of nowhere, kindness. My throat tightened as I shook my head. "Thank you, sincerely, but I'm fine. I know how to protect myself."

"Good." She nodded approvingly. "And thanks for the beignets."

Grabbing my cocoa cup, I saluted Gabriel. "Thanks for the ride." Weaving between the small tables, I crossed the mostly empty room. We were still a couple of hours from sunrise, so when I was close to the exit, I did a quick scan for vamps in the vicinity. There was a congregation of cold blips maybe a half mile away. Interesting.

Finishing the last of the hot chocolate, I dropped the cup in a trash can on the way out. The streets were wet in the lamplight. At the sound of a loud drone, I glanced up Decatur. A street cleaning truck was making its way slowly toward our dead vamp's ashes. Perfect.

The streets were mostly empty so I strode across the wide road, making my way around Jackson Square. Once away from the lights of Café Du Monde, I began to jog. How many vamps were left in New Orleans? By our count, there should only be maybe twenty or so left, and yet it seemed like at least that many were all gathered together a block away. We were nowhere near the nocturne. Who were these guys?

Slowing, I approached the corner, senses on high alert. Cadmael. *Damn it!* I felt him again. There and not, he was gone before I realized who I was sensing. Again. What was he doing in New Orleans? He'd said he had to go back to his own nocturne and yet he was here. Was there a connection to Lafitte, St. Germain, Amélie? I needed to talk to Russell. He'd know. I didn't want to tell Clive yet. If the attempts on his life had been directed by Cadmael, Clive would be devastated.

Casting out again, I found only the glut of vamps I'd sensed earlier. They were all together in the squat little building across the street. Sticking to the shadows cast by streetlights, I approached a sign hanging by the main door. *Lafitte's Blacksmith Shop Bar*.

"You shouldn't be here."

TWENTY-EIGHT

I Make a New Friend

Pulse stuttering, I turned toward the voice. Nothing. I reached out again, all the cold dots were still inside. There was, however, a hazy specter hovering beside me.

"Why shouldn't I be here?" I whispered.

"They'll hear your heartbeat." A cold hand clamped onto my wrist. The ghost of a thin man became more visible. He lifted a hand and waved me back across Bourbon Street, toward an alley between two two-story brick buildings. Apartment houses or hotels, maybe. Either way, he wanted me farther away from Lafitte's Blacksmith Shop Bar.

He walked with me, the contact making him seem more whole. I stopped at the mouth of the alley, watching the darkened bar.

"Your heartbeat will blend with the people sleeping over here. Too close, and they'll wonder why someone is standing outside their door. Curiosity kills around vampires." Glowing with white transparency, he appeared to have died recently. Jeans and a t-shirt hung from his frail body.

"Listen, would you like me to help you, you know." I fluttered my fingers. No idea why. "Move on? I can help."

His hand promptly left my wrist and he winked out of sight.

"I'll take that as a no." I cast out again. My ghost helper was still there, hovering out of reach, and the vamps hadn't moved. I closed my eyes and concentrated on the cold blips. I didn't want the world to go dark, standing across the street from a swarm of vamps, but I wanted to know who they were and what they were doing. Nosy? Probably, but also a fan of survival.

My stomach swooped and I realized the vampires were underground, beneath the bar. I mentally touched the blips, one at a time, not trying to delve in so much as get a feeling or a taste for each, for someone familiar. I found him almost at once. Lafitte was in there.

"What are you doing?"

I spun toward the voice. This wasn't the gaunt ghost. "What are you doing here?" I hissed. "I told you I didn't need a body-guard and I can do without the disapproval."

"Sorry," Gabriel said. And to his credit, he appeared contrite. "I have a thing about wicches. Long story. Doesn't matter. Point is, you shouldn't be here." He nodded toward the Blacksmith Shop Bar. "Bloodsuckers lurk in that place. We can smell them."

"He's right," my ghostly friend said.

"What's your name, anyway?" I heard Gabriel open his mouth to say something but then he stilled on my other side.

"Why?"

"Where's the trust? I don't like thinking of you as that skinny ghost guy."

He chuffed a laugh. "Henry. My name's Henry."

I offered my hand. "It's nice to meet you. I'm Sam."

The vague, cloudy mist didn't react. I was ready to drop my outstretched hand when he suddenly took it and shook. And like that, he was back, transparent but visible.

"You glow," Henry said.

"I do?" I glanced down at myself, confused. "Huh." I turned to Gabriel. "Do I seem to glow to you?"

He studied me and shook his head. I think my talking to and shaking hands with nothing was flipping the poor guy out.

"Oh, sorry. Gabriel, this is Henry. Henry, Gabriel." I closed my eyes and focused on the cold blips under Lafitte's. Hopping from blip to blip, I found Lafitte again quickly, and then Amélie. She must have been on her way here when I felt her on the street earlier. Wait. Was she on the street to meet with the now-you-sense-him-now-you-don't Cadmael? I didn't know the histories and connections with all these people.

I pulled out my phone and shot a quick text to Russell, letting him know I needed to talk with him. When there was no immediate response, I pocketed the phone.

Closing my eyes, I scanned the vamps again. Godfrey. Godfrey was with Lafitte in his underground lair. Why that son of a—

"Ow."

"Sorry." I'd been crushing Henry's hand. I'd consider the fact that ghosts could feel pain later. Right now, I was pissed.

I pulled out my phone and texted Clive.

Me: Godfrey is with Lafitte.

No dots. No response.

Me: On a mission? Traitor? WTH?!

Nothing

"How do you know who's in there?" Gabriel whispered, peering over my shoulder at my phone.

"In a minute." I turned to Henry. "Can you go down where they're gathered and listen? Is it warded to keep you out?"

He let go of my wrist again, becoming invisible. "I guess." His voice was faint. Had it not been so quiet on the deserted predawn street, I never would have heard him.

"Is it dangerous for you?" There was a hesitancy in his voice I was trying to pinpoint.

"He's already dead, right? How dangerous could it be?" Gabriel asked.

Elbowing him in the gut, I focused instead on the haze hovering to my right. "Henry?"

"It's—My brother is one of them. I don't like seeing him like that."

"I'm sorry. Did—Is that what happened?" Poor guy.

"He didn't know what he was doing! It was an accident." Voice straining, he defended his brother.

"When first thirst hits, it's all mindless need for blood. Rational thought is gone."

"Yeah," he sighed. "That thing wasn't my brother. His eyes turned black. He was like a demon. And so fast. He was across the room and then he was on me, slamming me to the floor. Those fangs tearing at my neck." He cringed.

I reached out a hand. I was sure he wouldn't take it but needed to try. "I'm so sorry."

"Yeah." The sound contained a world of disappointment and sorrow.

When I felt a tentative touch on my wrist, I tried again. "Is spying right out or would you be willing?" I didn't want to spook him but needed the help. "The New Orleans vamps came to San Francisco. They tried to kill our Master of the City. We came here to find out what was with the dick move."

"War," Gabriel said.

"Probably, but why? The three vamps I came with are all good men. Godfrey is funny, more irreverent than most vamps. Russell is honor personified and loyal to the bone. Clive has known both men for hundreds of years." I turned my attention back to Henry. "If you can, can you listen in for a while? I need to know if Godfrey is a prisoner or a willing co-conspirator. And if possible, how to get in."

Reluctantly, his fingers slipped from my wrist. "I'll listen." And then he was gone.

After a minute of silence, Gabriel asked, "So, did he go?"

I nodded, continuing to monitor the blips.

"Can I ask now?"

"What?" Making my mind like a gelatinous goo, I encased

Godfrey's cold blip, testing the strength of his barriers, trying to catch a stray thought or emotion without pushing all the way in.

The blindness was really beginning to worry me. It was lasting longer each time it happened. Was I pushing farther each time, overriding their will more, or was it cumulative? Every time I decided my needs should supersede their free will, I added to the imbalance I'd learned about from the necromancy book. Would I eventually lose my sight forever?

"Princess?"

I started at his voice. Right. Forgot. "Yeah?"

"How do you know who's in there?" he asked again.

A jogger turned the corner and a woman walking her dog passed on the opposite side of the street. Leaning against the brick wall, I focused on Gabriel. "The last time I tried to explain this, you got your knickers in a twist over wicches. Are you sure you want to know?"

Crossing his arms over his chest, he nodded.

Shrugging, I glanced at the Blacksmith Shop Bar. Nothing yet. "My mother was a wicche. I didn't know that growing up, but it explains some things. Anyway, I have both werewolf and wicche blood in me. Apparently, my wicche gift is necromancy." I stopped. "Do you know what that means?"

He nodded, his jaw clenched tight. "You can raise the dead."

"I haven't tried that, so no idea. What I can do is read the thoughts and emotions of vampires, who are—depending on your point of view—dead or mostly dead."

His arms dropped as he gaped at me.

"Right. Came as a shock to me, too. This vamp was trying to kill me and I stopped him, made him shoot himself. It was like an Alpha challenge for dominance. It was instinctual, and it worked. After that, I tried doing it on purpose. It hurts like hell and gives me a splitting headache, but I'm able to pick up emotions and thoughts."

"This morning. With that bloodsucker."

Nodding, I said, "Right. He had my arm pinned. I didn't

have time to block the kill strike. I had to—I'm not sure how to explain it—I guess I yanked his mind out. He went limp and I took his head. What I did, though, was so much worse than reading a mind. What I did meant going blind for a while."

"Your eyes are different, too." Gabriel leaned in to study them.

"What?" Different how?

"When I first saw you—"

"Yesterday."

He thought a moment and then gave a quick head shake. "Right. Anyway, your eyes were green."

"They *are* green, like my mom's."

He shook his head, leaning in closer. "No. This one," he said, pointing to my right eye. "This one's a brighter green than before. But this one," he said, pointing to my left, "is more like hazel now. There are brown flecks."

"What are you talking about?" Not only was I going blind for longer periods, my eyes were changing colors? In the grand scheme, it didn't matter, except it did. I was changing, inside and out, and that was terrifying.

"Earlier, that was why you couldn't see?" All of the strained anger or fear regarding wicches was gone.

"Wicches are supposed to do no harm. When we impose our will over another's, we're causing harm. We've upset the natural order and so something must be done to regain balance. That something comes back at the wicche who performed the spell, or whatever it was he or she did. Most of the time, the payment required for balance is so minor, the wicche barely feels it. What I do causes such a huge imbalance, I'm blinded."

"But you're doing good. Why are you punished for ridding us of a plague?"

"From a different perspective, wolves are the plague. I don't want to get into a big philosophical discussion about predators versus monsters. I'm explaining how I know who's under that bar and why I was blind earlier."

"Okay, but I'm here now. If you lost your sight, I'd watch out for you." He gestured toward the bar. "And they're all a bunch of unnatural demons. What difference does it make what your ghost hears? Bloodsuckers lie when they speak."

"Still dating one over here." Probably. Man, that werewolf-vampire grudge ran deep.

"Right," he said, breath gusting out. "I try not to think about that."

Keeping my attention on the bar across the street, I explained, "I need to read a vamp who's scary powerful, and I don't want to be weak before I start."

He swore. "Please tell me we're not going back to see that bastard St. Germain again."

"You don't have to go." Although a guard would be super helpful when the world went dark.

"Sure. I'll let our queen get killed on my watch." With another curse, he shook his head, pulled out his phone, and started texting.

I would have told him keeping me alive was a losing battle, but the poor guy took his job so seriously, I didn't have the heart.

TWENTY-NINE

St. Germain, part deux

As the sky began to lighten, Henry returned. "He's not a prisoner."

My heart dropped into my stomach. It wasn't possible. "How do you know?"

"He was sucking up to Lafitte, and that guy was eating it up. Robert, my brother, was with them. He paler, thinner than he used to be." Sighing, he continued, "That English guy mentioned someone named Russ, I think. Lafitte has him in a cell."

"Under the bar? He's holding Russell there?" I was going in.

"Uh. Don't think so. Not the way they said it. Sounded more like someplace else. Didn't say where. Just got the impression it was somewhere else."

How could I have been so wrong? I'd been in Godfrey's mind. He genuinely cared for Clive and Russell. "How could he do this?"

"Do what?" Gabriel asked.

"Godfrey betrayed them. He gave Russell to Lafitte." Feeling sick, I reached for my phone again and then rethought it. Clive wouldn't wake for some time. Maybe I'd find out something that would help this make sense before then. Leaving my phone where it was, I turned back to Henry.

"Is there a trapdoor, hidden lock, anything that would allow me to slip in?"

"Tunnel." His grip felt less substantial on my arm. He was fading.

"How is there a tunnel that's not underwater? That makes no —sorry, never mind. Where's the entrance?"

"Storeville…" he slurred, strength gone.

"Henry?" What was that word? Closing my eyes, I searched for his hazy form. Nothing. Had I worn him out? I knew nothing about the stamina of ghosts. "Thank you."

"Okay," I said to Gabriel. "The sun is rising. That means it's time to visit our friendly neighborhood sadist again." I started walking down Bourbon Street to St. Germain's townhouse.

"No." Gabriel looped an arm around my waist and pulled me up short.

"Hey." I pushed him off. "What gives?"

"Real food first. I'm starting to get how this works. The apex transformation, ghost talking, bloodsucker snooping, it takes a lot out of you. That means we need to fuel you up before your next mission." He started walking in the opposite direction, toward his motorcycle. "Come on. I know a place."

Gabriel drove us to a tiny diner on the edge of the Quarter. It was closed. He drove us around back and parked near an open door.

"Dude," I said. "They're closed. You can't just walk into a kitchen and demand food."

He grabbed the back of my hoodie and dragged me with him through the door. "Woman, make us food," he growled. "Now."

I gasped, but the woman stirring something at the stove only glanced over her shoulder and then went back to cooking. "You're not too old for me to put over my knee, you know." The woman went to the sink and washed her hands before turning back to us. "And who are you bringing into my kitchen this early in the morning?"

"*Tante*, this is Miss Quinn. She's visiting. Princess, this is my *Tante* Élodie."

As she dried off her hands, she studied me. I became painfully aware that I hadn't slept or showered recently. "A little early, don't you think?" She raised her eyebrows at Gabriel. When his face flushed, I realized she must have thought he was bringing in the woman he'd spent the night with.

I had no idea how much she knew about Gabriel's furry issues, so I couldn't say anything. I stuffed my hands in my hoodie pocket and let him take the lead.

Glancing at the man who was priming the grill, he said, "Miss Quinn is a guest of Mathieu's. She was having trouble sleeping, so we're out early. I need to get her fed before she starts her day and we got an *envie* for your grillades and grits. Maybe some of those sweet potato biscuits? I told her these were the best eats in all Nawlins."

"He did," I chimed in.

At the mention of Mathieu, she stopped giving us the stink eye. "Shoo. Go sit down. You'll get what you get."

We detoured to the coffee maker, each pouring ourselves a cup, and then sat at the table closest to the kitchen.

"*Tante.* That's aunt, right?" I'd only taken French one semester in high school. When mom and I moved a few months later, the new school had put me in a Spanish class instead.

"*C'est vrai.* Élodie is my mama's sister. Now," he said, leaning forward and lowering his voice, "why are we going back to that devil's house?"

"I want to make up for last night, find out what he knows, and, if possible, I want to see if I can erase his memory of me." I had no idea if I could. Honestly, I kind of doubted it, but I was doing all kinds of weird crap these days, so it seemed worth a try.

Gabriel sipped his coffee, watching me. "You can do that from across the street? We don't have to break in?"

"Holy no. We're not breaking into a vampire's house. Who

knows what kind of creepy stuff he's got in there? And they can move around during the day."

Gabriel almost choked on his coffee. "What?" he whisper-shouted.

A garbage truck lumbered down the street; sunrise pinkened the windows.

Glancing back at the open door to the kitchen, I leaned in and said, "The older, more powerful ones can move around during daylight hours. It's why I don't think they're actually dead. They're not alive, but it feels more like a kind of stasis, a waiting period while their cells regenerate or something. I have no idea. I only know that when I was in trouble, Clive came to rescue me. After sunrise. And I know he sometimes hears conversations in other parts of the house during daylight hours." I felt kind of bad. Gabriel's tan face was turning decidedly green.

"They're active during the day?" He stared out the window, lost in thought. "That actually explains a few things."

"Not all of them. The older and more powerful ones, like St. Germain."

Gabriel's Aunt Élodie placed two heaping plates on the table, a basket of biscuits dropped in the middle. She gave us ham and eggs, with what I assumed were grits and an amazingly fragrant concoction of beef, tomatoes, onions, bell peppers, and who knew what else. My stomach rumbled at the feast before us.

Gabriel kissed his aunt on the cheek.

"A little *lagniappe* for my favorite nephew." She grinned down at him as he dug in. "Go on," she said to me.

"Thank you, ma'am." I dug into the brown stuff first. I couldn't control the groan as rich, spicy flavors burst in my mouth.

Chuckling, she patted my shoulder and returned to the kitchen.

Gabriel and I didn't bother talking. We both ate with the single-mindedness of predators.

When we were finally done, I sat back, well and truly full. "Can I pay?"

He waved away the idea. "You want to offend my *tante*?"

I pulled out the black credit card Clive had given me. "But a vampire would be footing the bill. Seems the least he can do, seeing as we're risking ourselves on vamp business."

"This is your bloodsucker's?" He snatched the card from my fingers and then picked up a menu to check prices.

He ran the card through the reader attached to the register, proving he'd spent some time working behind his aunt's counter. When he handed me the slip to sign, I added a huge tip for his aunt and received an approving nod from Gabriel.

His aunt gave us both hugs on our way out, which was a nice surprise. As the sun rose over the Quarter, we wended our way through slowly filling streets. When Gabriel pulled over, two houses down from St. Germain's, I felt my stomach cramping with nerves. Chances were, this wasn't going to work. I needed to be prepared for that.

Leaning my head against Gabriel's back, I closed my eyes and cast out with my mind. There were no other cold blips nearby other than those in St. Germain's house. There weren't even any ghostly hazes hovering anywhere around. Interesting. Was that because they steered clear of him or because they lost strength during the day? Question for another time.

One cold point on the second floor, while… five cold dots were ranged around a large basement. Clive had said St. Germain was a loner, not involved in nocturne business, so why did he have vamps living with him? Li, sure, but who were the others? And how the heck did vamps get basements in New Orleans? Like Clive's, St. Germain's must have been spelled to stay dry.

Deciding it was best to check first, I mentally touched each of the five below. One of the cold spots was Li and one I recognized from Gérard's memory, when we'd been interrogating him in Clive's cage. He was one of the vamps being ordered to capture

Clive and me. I didn't recognize the other three. This meant, though, that Clive was wrong. St. Germain did involve himself in nocturne politics. What the hell was he up to?

Hands fisted, I pulled my arms up against my chest, curled in on myself as I kept my head firmly against Gabriel's back. Mind circling St. Germain's cold, glowing orb, I tried not to touch it. Being even this close had my stomach roiling. Breathing deeply, I willed my stomach to settle.

"Listen, if I throw up, don't take it personally. This hurts like a mofo in the best of situations. Diving into evil is likely going to make me sick."

He wrapped his big, warm hands around my knees. "Not to worry, princess. I'll keep you safe. And sick washes off."

Absorbing one last moment of comfort, I wrapped my mind around St. Germain and searched for a weak spot, a way in. A sour tang hit the back of my throat. My whole being recoiled. I was swimming in sewage. The blip felt more porous than the others had been. Because he was older? Insane? Pushing in, though, was far easier than it should have been. The black, foul-smelling slime coating his blip was now covering me.

"Your scent changed." Gabriel's voice was small and far away.

"It's him," I said, or maybe only thought. God, please don't let contact with him change me forever.

With the other vamps, I could see dim visions in the dark, synapse trails connecting memories. Here, there was no light, only putrid, inky suffocation. Head pounding, bile rising, I tried harder to see, sending out a pulse of white magic to clear the way. It worked. I saw something, shadows in the dark that weren't there before. A chill ran down my spine. It felt like someone was watching me. I could feel myself shuddering against Gabriel's back. *Shit.* Did St. Germain know I was here?

Ignoring the prickling of my skin, I dove into the first memory I came upon. He and Li were torturing a woman in their basement. Pulling out as quickly as I could, I moved on to the next one. After what seemed countless memories of bloody, horrific acts, I found a memory of St. Germain sitting in his parlor, talking with Lafitte.

"Why do I *still* not have the wolf?"

"Not much longer, Sire." Lafitte's voice tipped toward a whine.

"So, you've been saying. Too many times to count." St. Germain's lip lifted in sneer.

"My people, *mon Dieu*. He killed them all. Only Amélie—"

"Must I do this myself? Is that what you're telling me? You're not equal to stealing one deliciously scarred little wolf?" St. Germain tapped the arm of his chair, lost in thought. "If you can no longer be useful to me..."

"It shall be done. Right away. Leticia has sown the seeds." He swallowed. "On my orders. We couldn't have stolen her before. Now? His people will clear the way. *Ça sera facile.*"

"And I'm sure your people thought it would be easy right up until their heads went flying."

"Comte—"

St. Germain cut him off with a wave of his hand. "Send another party. Capture her when she's away from him. Kill whoever you need to but bring me the wolf."

The memory changed. One went dark while another lit up, like spotlights on a stage.

"He brought her to me?" St. Germain threw back his head and laughed, relishing the irony.

"My people. He is destroying my nocturne. I need—" Lafitte's pleading was cut short.

"There are always more who crave the dark kiss. He'll come to me," St. Germain stood, pacing in front of the fire, Lafitte's problems ignored. "He'll try to get information, and he'll come to me. You said Godfrey and Russell are with him. Russell is worthless. Godfrey, though, could prove useful."

"But the woman—"

And who do we have listening in on my thoughts?

The voice boomed, pushing me out of the memory. *Shit-damnfuck.*

Is that you, little wolf?

I backed out, fear making me incautious. I stepped into a memory that felt as though it had been placed in my path. This one was different. St. Germain's clothing was older. This wasn't his townhouse salon or basement. The light was odd. Torches flickered against stone walls.

A wail rent the quiet, dragging me fully into the memory. Suddenly the room was filled with sobbing, desperate cries of agony, and the drip, drip, dripping of blood on a stone floor. Screams, harsh and throaty because too many had come before, tore at me.

The woman chained to the table wasn't me. This wasn't me. I'd never been here before. These weren't my memories. Those weren't my screams. The man leaning over the tortured woman turned to me and smiled with blood-stained teeth while his hands continued their work, disemboweling his victim.

"Welcome. I was wondering when you'd join me."

He couldn't be talking to me. I wasn't here. This wasn't me. Glancing over my shoulder, I saw him. Clive stood in the doorway.

Listen to that delicious heart racing. What are you up to, little wolf?

Fighting off the panic, needing to get as far away from this memory as possible, I closed my eyes to the horror and backed out quickly and quietly, wading through sludge. I focused on the feel of my head against Gabriel's back, the sound of the voices walking by, and I was back in my own head.

"Gogogo," I chanted, needing to get as far away as I could, away from that poor woman, away from the blood and stench, away from knowledge I couldn't reconcile.

The motorcycle roared to life and we were weaving down the narrow roads. At the first corner, I changed my grip, grabbing at his waist to keep from tumbling off. Still, though, I kept my eyes closed and my face pressed against him.

"Where to?"

"Townhouse," I choked out. I needed to shower. I needed to feel clean, if only on the outside.

"You sure?"

Oh, yeah. If ever I needed a gorgon, it was now.

THIRTY

Gorgon Mating Rituals

The house felt strangely empty and vamp-free as we entered. Clive wasn't upstairs. It was daylight. Where was he? I walked down the hall toward the kitchen, Gabriel at my side. When I turned the corner, I found Stheno facing me, hands on her hips, expression furious. I almost closed my eyes in case she decided to let me have it.

"Where the hell have you been?"

"I told you, I was with the pack." My mom had been killed when I was seventeen and we'd moved around so much, I'd never really had friends to stay out too late with, but this felt like a mother's scolding.

"Liar!" She yelled, finger stabbing the air. "That Mathieu called here looking for you. Where *were* you two?"

I wasn't sure what kind of terrified expression I wore, but Stheno couldn't hold it any longer. She busted out laughing, falling back onto the couch. Clutching her side, she gasped, "Your face."

"Ha ha. What the hell?" I walked around the back of the couch and flopped down. "It's already been a miserable day and it's only—" I checked my watch. "How is it only 7:32?"

Gabriel handed me a glass of orange juice and then sat down.

Stheno sobered up and studied us. "What happened?"

The quiet concern in her voice tightened my throat and brought tears to my eyes. The enormity of the morning was pulling me under.

She focused instead on Gabriel. "Talk."

He turned to me, checking. I nodded. "We were chased by a bloodsucker. She yanked out his mind. Killed him. Went blind for a while. Then she jogged over to Lafitte's Blacksmith Shop Bar. Stared at the building. Discovered a group of bloodsuckers, including Lafitte himself, hidden under the bar. That guy Godfrey was there. She said he betrayed Clive and Russell. Russell's being held somewhere. She befriended a ghost who did some recon for her. We had breakfast. Then we went to St. Germain's place and she dove deep into his mind. She's been shaking ever since."

"Are you shitting me?" Stheno spit out. "You got breakfast and didn't bring me anything? Bitch."

I choked out a laugh. "Sorry. It was really good, too."

Stheno leaned forward, her elbows on her knees. "What happened at the bloodsucker's?"

When I shook my head, she pinned Gabriel with a stare. "You. Go away."

"I'm her bodyguard." He sounded two parts outraged, one part hurt.

"I can handle it from here on out," she said.

"How do I know that, and who the fuck are *you*?" He did not appreciate being dismissed so easily.

"All you need to know is I'm a hell of a lot more deadly than you are. I can take on any who come for her. And," she winked, "I'm great in the sack. Think about it." She shooed him away. "Somewhere else, though. We're busy here."

I patted his arm. "I really appreciate everything you've done for me, but she's right. She's the scariest thing around. You should go back and get some sleep. I'll contact you later if I need you. I promise."

He stood reluctantly, clearly trying to think of an excuse to stay.

"And you'd know who I was if you'd bothered to Google me." She rolled her eyes. "I'm hoping you're more thorough in bed than you are with research."

That did it. He strode down the hall, slamming the door on his way out.

"Wait." Stheno held up a finger until we heard him gun the motorcycle and tear off down the street. "Nothing like an angry werewolf," she sighed. "Now, spill."

"First, do you know where Clive is? I don't feel him upstairs." Why hadn't I considered Clive being in danger? Godfrey had betrayed Russell and I hadn't made the very logical leap that Clive would be in trouble, too. I'd been off my stride ever since we got here. I wasn't normally this dense.

"No idea. They came home last night, then went out again." She shrugged, completely unconcerned.

"Apparently, all of this is because of me." All the dead people, vamps, whatever. And now Russell was in a cage.

She leaned back on the couch. "How so?"

"St. Germain knew about me. Before Lafitte sent people to us, before all that, he knew about me. Wanted me. That party was sent to San Francisco to kill everyone *except* me. I was to be delivered to him. When that didn't happen, St. Germain was absolutely giddy to learn that Clive had actually brought me to New Orleans." I stopped, feeling sick again.

Stheno lowered her voice. "Did he bring you here *for* him?"

I shook my head. I didn't pretend to understand vampire politics. They were masters of the long game. They plotted revenge schemes centuries in the making. It may have been naïve of me, but I didn't believe it.

"Then why are you more sad than scared?"

"I could be wrong." I thought about that last memory. "I was in St. Germain's head, sorting through memories for information. In one of them, he was torturing a woman, blood and guts dripping on the floor around her. He smiled right at me, welcoming me. Excited to share. When I spun to see who he was talking to—" I swallowed the bile rising up my throat.

"It was Clive."

I flinched at her words. "How did you know?"

"Why else would you be upset?" She put her feet up on the coffee table and stared at the black TV screen. "Did you see him join St. Germain or stand at the door?"

"Door. But last night when we met with St. Germain, I tried to poke around in his head. I saw one flash before he shoved me out. It was Clive. He appeared the same in both memories, hair long, old clothes, and he was reaching for a disemboweled woman on a table.

"I backed out of the memory right away this morning," I continued. "St. Germain knew I was there, though, poking around." I'd made myself an even bigger target. I wasn't just a scarred wolf who was strong enough to withstand prolonged torture. I was a wolf who could read the minds of vampires. That made me quite the prize, indeed.

"Okay." Stheno stood. "Let's get the fuck out of here. We'll go get a hotel room, away from the bloodsuckers. We'll sleep—you look like shit, by the way—and then we'll eat and plan. Get whatever you need and let's go."

"I desperately need a shower. St. Germain's mind—" I cringed. "Give me a few to get cleaned up and then we'll go."

The shutters on the windows were sealed tight when I flicked on the lights in the dark bedroom. I grabbed some clothes and then made my way into the bathroom. Adjusting the water to scalding, I stood in the spray, willing the mental muck to wash away. Then I began soapy scrubbing in earnest.

Faced with dirty leathers or clean jeans, I opted for my usual, a long-sleeve tee, running shoes, ponytail, and a hoodie tied around my waist, in case I was up all night again.

Checking my phone for the millionth time, I stared at Clive's text telling me he loved me. Where was he? I sat on the bed, closed my eyes, and searched for him again. Nothing. Panic was edging out concern. It wasn't like him to disappear. He always let me know if he was going somewhere and who to contact if I had an emergency while he was gone. I'd thought it was adorably sweet, if a little over the top. Now, my world seemed to hang in the balance, waiting for a quick check-in. I tried yet again, focusing all my power on locating vamps. The cold blips shimmered in my mind, weaker than usual, but there. My head pounded as I searched for Clive and then Russell. Nothing.

Stheno was waiting for me at the bottom of the stairs, "You ready to go?"

"I can't find Clive." I tapped my forehead. "He's not there." Dread was creeping into my voice.

"You're exhausted. You'll find him after you get some rest. Remember, he's survived centuries, wars, plagues, murder attempts. I'm sure he's fine."

I desperately wanted to believe her. "Maybe if I walked around the Quarter... Proximity might help." I really wanted to get out of here and search for him.

"I get that, but you need sleep. Hell, I need sleep. I work the graveyard shift, remember? We'll find a hotel, get a few hours, and then head to lunch, okay?"

"A hotel won't keep us safe. We might as well sleep here."

Stheno thought about it a moment and then said, "*Mi couch es su couch.*"

I followed her down the hall and stretched out on one side of the huge sectional. My thoughts circled around the question of Clive, but before I believed possible, I was out.

I was awakened hours later by keys dangling in front of my face. "Where do you want to go, kid?"

"If you're driving, wherever you want."

"Well, shit." She tossed the keys on the coffee table. "I guess we're walking."

It was another warm day in the Quarter. Perhaps I was just used to the chill skating off the ocean back home. The streets were properly busy now, not like the predawn deserted ones I'd traversed earlier. We passed a group of people gathering, getting ready to start a historic walking tour. I wished I could join them, that all I had to worry about was the rising heat and whether that couple was going to talk loudly the whole tour.

"I'm fine with wherever you want to eat," I said. I had yet to have a bad meal in the Big Easy.

Opening myself up, I tried again to locate Clive. Nothing. Could he cloak himself, like Cadmael seemed to be doing? I clung to that thought because the alternative was more than I could handle. I'd find him. He was fine and I'd find him.

"Where was that place you ate yesterday morning?" Stheno looked amazing. I'd become so used to the sweats she always wore while lounging on the couch, I hadn't considered how she'd look if she cleaned up. She was wearing a short black tank dress and sandals, showing off golden brown skin and drawing stares. Her long, tightly curled hair bounced on her back, coppery strands in the dark hair glinting in the sun.

When we arrived, I asked to be seated in the courtyard again, hoping we'd end up in the same section with the same waitress. She understood ordering large portions. I'd had a huge breakfast, but I was hungry again. Mentally battling evil took it out of a person.

We ended up with a different waiter, who thankfully didn't raise an eyebrow at our large orders. The food was, as I had come to expect, amazing, and we scarfed it down quickly, even ordering dessert. Blissfully full, we were back on the streets in the bright sunlight. Bars were filling, music trailing us as we meandered around the Quarter.

While Stheno window-shopped, I searched for Clive and Russell. Still nothing. The realization gave me hope. They said they were holding Russell in a cell, but I couldn't find him. Either they were lying or they had the ability to cloak Russell, to hide his vampy blip. If they could do that, they could hide Clive, too. They were both alive-ish and well. I held on to that thought with everything in me.

My phone buzzed in my pocket, a text from Owen.

Owen: What's going on?

Me: Nothing. How's my baby?

Owen: I'm fine and I don't buy it. Did you and Clive have a fight?

Me: Everything's fine and you know I was talking about my bookstore.

Owen: Oh that. It's good. The bookshelves are in, angled like I wanted. Sam, you can tell me. What happened? You've never done anything to disappoint Clive. Ever. So, did he do something? George and I can come get you if you want to come home.

Me: Thank you, but no worries here! I'm shopping on Royal Street. Give everyone I love a hug for me, okay? I've gotta go now.

I snapped a pic of the busy street and sent it along, hoping that would satisfy him. I didn't want him dragged into all the vamp killings. I wanted to be able to think of him and Dave overseeing The Slaughtered Lamb renovations, arguing about how the bottles should be organized behind the bar. Stheno was happy to be out in the sunshine, so instead of pushing for an immediate battle strategy, I picked up souvenirs for Dave, Meg, Owen, and George.

As we walked, I related everything that had happened the previous evening and this morning. I played with boas and chose long-sleeve tees for my new collection while explaining to Stheno in hushed tones no human would hear why I'd spent the night at the pack house and what I'd learned from Henry, my friendly neighborhood ghost.

"Do you want my take?" Stheno asked.

"I guess I must." I stopped at that same jewelry store window I had a couple of days ago, searching for the indigo opal ring. Damn. It was gone. Judging by the exorbitant prices in the window, I never could have afforded it anyway.

"Clive called the pack because he needed you away from the rabid bloodsucker and he didn't want to be the one to do it. He trusted you to hold your own with a pack of werewolves, so"—she pinned me with her gaze—"Not weak."

"To be fair," I interrupted, "they bow every time they see me, so they're not much of a threat."

"Nice." She ran a hand through gold chain necklaces. "I miss the bowing. Anyway, he needs St. Germain to see him as another dirty old man preying on innocents in order to get some info out of him."

I thought about that, the knots in my stomach starting to loosen. "Yeah?"

"Stands to reason. If he was honestly worried about your safety, he would have dumped the whole meeting and gotten you out himself. It was getting dicey in there. He trusted you to take care of yourself and any random werewolf or bloodsucker attack. Since he trusts you, he can sit it out and *not* intervene, thereby avoiding war on two fronts, Lafitte and St. Germain—"

"But Lafitte is working for St. Germain."

"Clive doesn't know that. The easiest way to get you out is to call in the wolves, taking the conflict out of bloodsucker hands." She turned a corner and walked into a shop. I followed along, considering.

She tried on a pair of sunglasses. "These are nice, don't you think?"

Nodding absently, I said, "You should get them."

We left the shop with Stheno sporting new sunglasses, courtesy of Clive's card, and me feeling hopeful. Maybe I wasn't a failure as Clive's partner.

"We need a plan," I said, hurrying to walk beside her.

"For what?"

"I can't find Clive and Russell in my head. They must have a place that's been spelled against"—I don't know, what?—"psychic interference, a place to keep people and thoughts hidden. We have to break in and rescue them. So we need a plan."

Stheno patted my shoulder. "Hold it together." She stepped off the curb a moment later and pulled up short. A certain sexy werewolf sat on his motorcycle across the street, staring over the tops of his sunglasses at her. Sauntering across the road, paying no attention to traffic, she stopped in front of him, her gaze molesting him. I followed in her wake, cheeks heating at the blatant come on.

"Think you could give me a ride?" Her voice was a throaty purr.

I quickly turned, focusing anywhere but on the two of them. Mathieu stood in the shade of a balcony, leaning against the side of a shop, watching. Deciding he was the better one to approach while Stheno and Gabriel discussed the nature and timing of rides, I nudged his shoulder with my own and leaned by his side. Adopting his crossed-arms stance, we surveyed the unfolding negotiation

"My lady," he murmured, nodding.

"My champion," I returned.

His lips quirked up at that, but then his expression went stony. "Is this going to be a problem?" He pointed at the two whose discussion had them leaning closer together.

"Stheno's cool. She won't—"

"Stheno?" His eyes went wide, dark skin paling. "That's the real Stheno?" Excitement with a healthy dose of fear had him standing straight and blocking me.

"Dude," I said, pushing him from in front of me. "She's here to protect me. Relax. Could she kill everyone on this street? Yes. Will she?" I shrugged.

"Jury's still out," she called to us.

Gabriel glanced back and forth, clearly missing some key pieces of information.

"She told you to Google her, you slacker." I turned to Mathieu. "He's a good bodyguard, but he needs to up his research game."

Gabriel took out his phone. Stheno leaned over the screen, no doubt helping him to spell her name correctly. As if on cue a moment later, he flinched. She pulled her glasses down her nose and winked. The smile she gave him had me turning away again.

"That vampire hired a gorgon to protect you?" Mathieu was awestruck. "I did my PhD in Mythological Studies with an emphasis in East African myths, but I've been reading the Greek and Roman ones since I was a kid."

I nudged him with my elbow. "Maybe she'll let you interview her."

His mouth dropped open. "Do you think she would?"

"I might," she called to us. "Depending on how good of a mood I'm in."

"Stheno, no," I scolded. "We don't blackmail bed partners."

"Since when?" she asked, honestly confused.

Smiling and nodding at the woman walking by who seemed to have heard that last part, I hissed, "Since forever, you psycho. Borrow Gabriel's phone and look up consent next."

Dropping the seductress ploy, she strode over to Mathieu and me. "Fine. I'll leave him alone. You lost all the brownie points you earned bringing me food, though," she snarled, disgusted with me. "I think you should try to find that Henry ghost again. See if he's learned anything. Then you can dive deep into a couple of bloodsuckers while they're out of it. We need intel. Creating a plan without it is a waste of time and resources."

THIRTY-ONE

Who Knew Ghosts Could Be Worse Than Vampires?

W hich was why, very soon afterward, the four of us were sitting at a corner table in Lafitte's Blacksmith Shop Bar. After a lengthy and impassioned argument as to where I'd be safest, it was decided I would put on Stheno's new sunglasses and sit with my back against the wall, the other three surrounding me.

Closing my eyes behind the dark shades, I tried to block out overlapping conversations and clinking glasses. I cast out and found the cold blips beneath me. There was also hazy smoke at my shoulder.

"Henry? Is that you?" Mathieu, Gabriel, and Stheno continued their conversation, as though they hadn't heard me.

Nothing from the ghost.

"Henry, touch my hand. I can't hear you."

Cold hands covered my nose and mouth. Jolting at the touch, I twisted away, struggling to breathe.

"Miss Quinn? What's the matter?" Mathieu whispered. It was a ghost, so they couldn't see what was happening.

"He told us to search for you," a cold, tinny woman's voice hissed in my ear. "Instead you walk right in. How lucky for me."

I clawed at her hands but couldn't grab hold. They went right through hers, and yet her insubstantial hands blocked my breathing completely. She wasn't like Henry, nor like the entity at the convent. My lungs started to burn.

"We're to capture you if we can, kill you if we must. Personally," she said, cold lips at my ear, "I'd rather kill you," she hissed. Her hands were clamped down like steel, cutting off all air.

She smelled faintly of wicche and was going to suffocate me if I didn't figure out how to stop her. Was I a necromancer or not? Ignoring, as best I could, what was happening to me physically, I focused my mind on her. I could see her, eyes slitted as she sneered, using her residual power to smother me.

As I had done with the vampire this morning, I lashed out. Imagining my hands crushing her head, I gouged my thumbs in her eyes. When she shrieked in pain, she loosened her hands, allowing me to breathe. I didn't stop, mentally unleashing my claws and stabbing them into the back of her head. Her hands went straight to my throat, her grip an icy noose. I ripped through her head, slashing her into pieces. Her screams broke off as the haze dissipated into nothing.

Falling forward, elbows slamming against the table, I struggled for air, rubbing at my sore neck. What the hell was that?

Mathieu was crouched beside my chair, his hand sliding up and down my back. "Miss Quinn, please, tell us what we can do."

Taking a slow breath, trying to calm my breathing, I sat up. Gasps came from the men as they stared at my neck in horror. Stheno, on the other hand, appeared lost in thought.

"What happened, my queen? Who hurt you?"

I glanced around the room, but no one seemed to be paying us any mind. There was a rowdy group at the bar drawing any stray attention.

Patting Mathieu's shoulder, I said, "Sit. I'm fine now." I drank from the glass in front of me, swallowing fire, and started choking again.

Gabriel shot up and went to the bar. He was back a moment later with a glass of water. I drank it down and then pointed to the other one. "What the hell was that?"

"Vieux carré," Stheno said, gesturing to the now near-empty glass. "I thought you might like it."

"God, I thought it was iced tea." I glared at her, my throat still burning from gulping the whiskey cocktail. "And you knew I wouldn't like it. You were getting back at me for before."

"Cockblocker," she coughed.

"Stop," Mathieu snarled at Stheno before returning his focus to me. "Please tell us how you were hurt? We can get you out of here now."

Mathieu couldn't see Stheno's glare, but I could. I patted him on the shoulder and whispered, "Pro tip: Don't snarl at a gorgon. They don't like it."

To his credit, he didn't back down. That's why he was the Alpha. "She's been hurt," he said to Stheno, "and you're making jokes. We need to know if she's in immediate danger. If you're not serious about her safety, we'll take over guarding her."

After a moment of charged tension, during which Stheno no doubt considered killing us all, she downed her drink and said, "Whatever."

Mathieu's focus returned to me. "Can you tell us?"

Sliding what was left of the vieux carré across the table to Stheno, I said, "That wasn't Henry. I think she was the ghost of a wicche. She was suffocating me, hands on my face, but I couldn't touch her. With Henry, I was able to touch him like he was still living. This one could physically hurt me, but I couldn't do the same."

"Because she was a wicche?" Gabriel asked.

"No idea. I need to find another necromancer who can explain this stuff to me. Maybe there's a section on it in one of my books." I shrugged. "She said he told them to hunt me. Capture me if possible and kill me if not." I spun the empty water glass on the table. "So, definitely excited about random ghosts choking me."

"Then what happened?" Poor Gabriel was starting to lose it.

I mimed grabbing two sides of something and ripping it apart.

"Niiiiice." Stheno nodded in approval.

Mathieu stood. "We'll leave. Take you to the pack house."

I patted his arm. "Where's safe from a ghost?" Shaking my head, I gestured to his chair. "Sit. I haven't even tried to read the vamps yet. All we've learned is that 'he' sent ghosts after me. We don't even know who 'he' is."

Staring at my neck, Mathieu leaned in. "We can't protect you from that. Your bloodsucker has a plane at the airport. Are you sure we can't convince you to fly home, given none of your protectors can even see them, let alone fight them?"

"That's okay. *I* can." Safely behind my dark glasses, I closed my eyes again and reached out. A clot of cold blips convened beneath my feet. Thankfully, though, no hazy shapes hovered nearby. Letting out a long, slow breath, I dove down.

It took a few tries before I found Lafitte. Consequently, my head was already pounding before I pushed myself through the thick, gelatinous membrane of his mind. Unlike St. Germain's, Lafitte's mind was similar to other vampires, with dim pulsing memories glowing in the dark.

I stepped into the one closest that seemed to pulse more quickly than the rest. Standing in front of me was an enraged blonde woman. I couldn't put my finger on it, but her scent was familiar. Then it hit me. Leticia.

"He killed Ètienne, Master!" she spat while pacing in front of him, fury making her movements stiff.

"Ètienne? *My* Ètienne?" Lafitte's voice was quiet, disbelieving.

"Gave him true death because of some mongrel bitch," she continued.

"*Arrêtez.*" Lafitte rose from his chair and crossed to the

woman. Fingers digging into her arms, he lifted her six inches off the floor. "Explain to me why Clive would hurt *mon frère*. Why he would take the gift I'd loaned him and spit it back in my face?" Lafitte screamed the last words.

Oddly, Lafitte becoming unhinged seemed to settle her. "He'd insulted Ètienne, made him guard some scarred, teenage wolf."

Lafitte dropped her back to the floor and paced away. "And?"

"It was a slap in the face, giving guard duty to man like Ètienne. He did it, though, for as long as he could stomach it." Hands fisted at her side, she continued. "Clive ordered us all to protect her. No one was allowed to hurt the little—"

"*Pourquoi?*" Lafitte broke in.

"Who knows?" Face screwed up in distaste, she added, "He visits her. Stops in to make sure she's all right. Is helping to build her a bookstore."

Lafitte leaned forward, a gleam in his eye. "He cares for this little wolf?"

"He must. He forced Ètienne to guard her. And one time. *One* time, he left early to see me, and the bitch is attacked by a kelpie." She shook her head. "She lived. She's covered in scars anyway; what's a few more? She's a werewolf! Why can't she protect herself?"

"What happened?"

"She screamed. Clive came running—"

"Clive was *listening* for her?" Lafitte spoke slowly, the implication of Clive's interest in me changing his expression. "*Continuer.*"

"Clive rushed in. Saved her. Killed the kelpie. But instead of putting vampire welfare ahead of a stray dog, he summoned Ètienne, torturing him to find out if he'd left her with the intention of her being attacked. As though he'd have given one thought to that stupid girl."

"He hurt *mon frère*? Not a quick, clean death. *Torturé.*"

Snatching the black vase from the fireplace mantel, he fired it across the room. It exploded against the closed door, shards flying.

"You will go back," he said.

"Master, no." The rage had dropped from Leticia's expression. "Please."

"*Oui*. You will go back. You will undermine him. Subtly. Slowly. You will win back his trust and then little words here, expressions there. You will sow the seeds of doubt. You will make his own nocturne question his fitness to lead. Quietly. Over years."

"Years? But I hate—"

"We all hate. It's how we put that hate to use that separates us. Will you walk away and let Clive lead his people, Ètienne forgotten, that wolf enjoying a nocturne's protection? Is that how you show your love for *mon frère*? Your loyalty?"

"No," she breathed.

"*Non*. You will return. Be a model member of the nocturne, subservient to your Master, and then you will start to pull the threads that will unravel him." He moved closer, placing a finger beneath her chin and tilting her head up. "We will destroy him. Think how much sweeter it will be when those he holds dear start turning against him, *n'est-ce pas?* When we give him his *morte finale*, he will be unlamented and forever forgotten. That is how we will put our hatred to use."

Turning his back on her, he strode across the room and settled back into his chair, expression thoughtful. "Go," he said absently. "I have plans to put in motion as well."

The memory went dark as another close by lit up. I stepped into that one and found myself back in St. Germain's sitting room. He stood by the fire while Lafitte sat in a chair. This wasn't the same memory I'd visited earlier in St. Germain's head. The art on the walls was different, the color scheme more severe. This was an older memory and I was viewing it from Lafitte's perspective.

"He has a wolf he's grooming? An abused adolescent?" St. Germain's lips turned up in a wicked smile. "Those are my favorite. If he does it right, she'll do anything for him." A high-pitched giggle escaped before he sat by the fire. "And I do mean *any*thing."

"He killed *mon frère!*"

"Yes, yes." St. Germain waved that concern away. "He wasn't very promising, was he? This, though. This is delicious. Clive has a weakness, and such a pedestrian one. Oh, this is delightful news you've brought me."

"Ètienne?" Lafitte's voice had taken on a wheedling tone.

"You'll get your revenge. I'll help with that. In return, I want to witness the great Clive brought low, and I want that wolf." St. Germain stared into the fire, eyes alight with malicious intent.

"*Le loup?*"

"Yes." St. Germain shivered. "Oh, yes. A tortured girl who's been taught to cower, but one still young enough to respond to pats. One I can train to crave the whip. One strong enough to survive and serve me in all things." Eyes turning vamp black, tongue darting between thin lips, he fisted his hand on the mantle. "When it's time, I want the wolf."

THIRTY-TWO

An Unforgivable Bargain

Head ready to split open in pain, I stepped out of the memory, willing myself out of Lafitte's head. I needed Clive nearby, taking the pain away, in order to do this effectively. I stopped that thought, remembering what St. Germain had said about grooming victims.

No. He was wrong. St. Germain didn't know about Clive's sister. He couldn't understand helping someone for honorable reasons. I refused to allow St. Germain's voice to take up space in my head.

Stomach roiling, I considered calling it for the day, but Godfrey was down there. I needed to know if he was still an ally or if he had betrayed us. The search didn't take long, as the vamps weren't moving down there.

I'd been in Godfrey's mind before, but this felt different. Likely, it was the cumulative effect of everything that had happened today, but his mind was oddly difficult to enter and far murkier than I'd remembered.

The memory pulses were hidden. I stumbled in the dark, unsure of which way to go. Like walking in a minefield, I braced at each step for something horrible. I'd been in more than enough truly ghastly vampire recollections to put me off vamps for life. Except for one. Mostly.

"Aren't you sick of being third? He doesn't appreciate you." Amélie's soft, insinuating voice came through Godfrey's phone.

Godfrey stood in the room in the townhouse basement with the prisoner cage, the only room in the house that was sound-proofed. "Yes," he breathed.

"I know you, Godfrey. Have known you for centuries. I've fought by your side and shared your bed. I know you. You can't possibly be happy being Clive's third. With your age and strength, you could be a Master and yet he keeps you under a younger vampire, one without your… flexibility."

"Honor," Godfrey translated.

"Yes, yes, but look where that got him. You cannot be that rigid in our world. His entire nocturne was destroyed because he chose to be honorable. No, a Master must be able to transfer loyalties in order to better benefit his people. Clive took him in and made him second because he knew Russell would never betray him. He's strong and loyal." Scoffing, she added, "So's a dog."

Godfrey let out a heavy breath, agreeing with Amélie without saying the words.

"You and I could rule New Orleans together. We'll hold the largest and most powerful nocturne in the New World. Lafitte is a joke, and everyone knows it. Clive will take him out and then you and I will step in to restore strength and prestige to this nocturne."

"Not as many left as there used to be."

"To be taken out so easily means they weren't trained and utilized properly. We'll rebuild and create a force to be reckoned with."

Godfrey paced the room, listening intently.

"It is such a waste," Amélie's disappointment was palpable. "Sitting around in that foggy, little nothing of a town, no real power, waiting for Clive and Russell to give you something to do. It's insulting."

Slowing his stride, Godfrey moved to the outer wall, rested his head against the plaster,

and released a sigh of defeat. "Yes."

"Side by side, we'll rebuild this nocturne. They will all finally see our true power and they will tremble in our presence."

Amélie's words had Godfrey straightening, his shoulders drawing back. "Yes," he breathed.

"Not the afterthought. The leader. Be my second. We will rule the most powerful nocturne in the world."

Godfrey paused, thinking. "What would I need to do?" And then Amélie laid out the plan for imprisoning Russell and killing Clive *after* he'd taken out Lafitte for them. Godfrey nodded along and my heart turned to stone.

"What about Sam?"

"The dog?" She laughed. "St. Germain is desperate for her. We give him the wolf and he'll ignore us while we transform this city."

Head pounding painfully, I opened my eyes to nothing. Hearing the bar bustling around me, I desperately willed my stomach to settle. When I tasted the sour tang of bile at the back of my throat, I knew I was in trouble.

"Stheno, bathroom. I'm gonna be sick."

A moment later, her strong arm was around me as she rushed me across the small, cramped bar. Bouncing off chairs, I gave strangled apologies along the way. Miracle of miracles, there was no line. She shoved me into a tiny bathroom and pushed my head down.

Tears were running down my face when I finished. Stheno was unexpectedly gentle, helping to clean me up and flush the toilet.

"All that beautiful food gone. It's a damn tragedy." Stheno put her arm around me again. "Come on, kid. Let's get you out of here."

A line must have formed because Stheno was shuffling us sideways down what felt like a narrow hall.

"I need to find Clive," I said.

"Why?"

"He needs to know. They're coming for him from all sides."

"Yeah, well, you too. Want me to grab the wolves?"

"Probably a good idea. Can we start walking, though? I need air." I heard Stheno give a quick, shrill whistle and figured the guys had been alerted to our departure.

We walked awkwardly down the crowded sidewalk, Stheno's arm around me, directing me. "How long does the blindness last? Gabriel said it took ten minutes this morning."

"Not sure," I said, as someone's shoulder knocked me back. "It's been taking longer each time."

"That ain't good; the sun's beginning to set."

Shitshitshit. "Promise me something?"

"What?" she grunted as I stumbled down a curb.

"If it comes down to being taken by St. Germain or dying, you do it, okay? A quick flash and I'm done. I won't be a victim, not again."

"If it comes to that, take yourself out. Why're you involving me?" Stheno's voice was hard.

"I can't do much damage to myself when my claws are yanked out and my hands are tied. A lot can be done to a person while her claws are growing back." I would know. The world was turning gray at the edges. It wouldn't be long now.

"You're a survivor, kid, not a quitter. This is a stupid conversation. You're upset about whatever you saw in those bloodsuckers' heads. Do yourself a favor and find a nice wolf to settle down with. Not my wolf, though. I have plans for him."

I huffed out a laugh, as shapes formed in my vision. It felt like I was underwater, but I could see. "I thought the guys would have caught up with us by now."

Stheno checked over her shoulder. "Yeah, me, too. The Alpha

was on the phone when we left, but Gabriel nodded. He saw us go."

"Maybe there's pack trouble," I said as we turned down a narrow side road, headed for Dauphine Street. Darkness fell all at once, sound from the Bourbon and Dauphine Streets muffled. "Wicches," I whispered, clutching at my necklace. "Get ready," I warned.

"I'm always ready."

When the first vamps dropped in front of us, she hit them with her high beams, turning them to very toothy statues. Four more dropped a moment later, one directly to the side of Stheno. Before she could turn, he threw powder in her eyes. Screaming and tearing at her own face, she didn't see it coming when he backhanded her against the brick wall. Head slamming hard, she crumpled to the street.

I killed the one who'd dropped down next to me while Stheno was screaming. The other two flew at me and I ran to meet them, taking them off guard. I killed one cleanly, his head flying, but I missed the second one. My claws tore across his shoulder and chest, not his neck.

Stheno's assailant and my bloody vamp moved in together, stopping before getting too close. I had a moment to think they were wary of me before two more dropped directly behind me.

I spun, claws out, but they were faster. One kicked my leg, breaking it, while the other punched the back of my head.

***

PAIN. MY WHOLE BODY SCREAMED IN PAIN AS A HARD BOOT connected with already broken ribs. I heard the unmistakable sound of phlegm being gathered and then a wet glob of mucus hit my cheek.

"What is taking so long?" I recognized Amélie's voice as heels clicked on the pavement. "Let's go. The wicche who hid the alley only guaranteed us ten minutes at the most. You've had your fun. She needs to be alive when I hand her over."

Of course. That was part of the deal. Godfrey had agreed to hand me over to St. Germain to torture. Rage and terror exploded in my head. Never again. I could barely move any part of my battered body, but Stheno was right. I wasn't a quitter. I wasn't going to take myself out.

"Grab her so we can go." He heels clicked away.

"Cunt," one sneered as he kicked my hip.

Unable to see, I focused my energy, drawing inward. I rested my hand on my hip, as though covering the pain. My fingers brushed against the soft burlap of the gris-gris bag the old man had given me. A calm settled over me as they discussed what more they could do to me that wouldn't anger the Comte.

Sliding two fingers into my pocket to settle firmly on the gris-gris, I opened my mind, wound my magical thread around the four cold blips that stood over me, and with unfettered rage, growled, "*Mouri,*" as I yanked their minds free of their bodies.

A wave of fiery pain washed through me. The magical world was taking payment for the four lives I'd taken. I may not have been able to see, but my senses were still as sharp as ever. I'd given them true death and heard the dust fall to the ground in piles around me.

I had to get away before Amélie returned. The broken bones had started to knit, but there was no way I was walking out of here. I rolled to the side that hadn't been kicked to see if crawling was an option.

Dragging myself through a pile of dust, I aimed for the mouth of the alley opposite of where Amélie had gone. One leg still worked, mostly. I crawled, two hands and one knee, blindly toward escape.

"Stheno?" I whisper hissed. "Are you okay? Stheno, wake up." My heart pinched. *Please let Stheno be alive.* She'd survived for millennia and then a few days with me....

The broken leg was dead weight as I edged as quietly as

possible away from the dead vamps and toward help. Sound was beginning to return. I heard traffic noise and conversations. I was close.

A vehicle screeched into the alley behind me. A moment later, a door flew open and footsteps pounded. I was yanked up and thrown in the back of what must have been a van. The panel door slid shut and the van squealed out of the alley, making a sharp turn and causing pedestrians to shout curses.

THIRTY-THREE

Oh, Good. I've Heard Such Lovely Things About the LaLauries

I tried using my necromancy to kill these guys as well, but I'd fried my circuits with that last stunt. I couldn't even see their cold blips. Resigned to bide my time, I took inventory of my physical injuries. It wasn't only that I hurt everywhere; it was that I didn't have the strength to fight. I was being given to St. Germain utterly vulnerable.

One vamp stayed in the back with me while the other drove. Amélie sat in the passenger seat, bitching about the vamps in the alley fucking up the mission. At every turn, I rolled, jolting my injuries over and over. If we didn't get wherever we were going soon, I'd be vomiting back here. With any luck, it'd be on the vamp watching me.

In what seemed forever but was probably only a few minutes, the van pulled over. We had to still be in the Quarter, given the short straightaways, frequent turns, and extended waits at stops. If I'd thought the pedestrians on the street would have heard me through the walls of the van, I'd have yelled, but the Quarter was filled with live music and the din of many overlapping voices.

Before the door opened, Amélie said, "Gag her."

Something ripped and then thick tape smelling of motor oil

was slapped across my mouth. The back door opened and a vamp grabbed the ankle of my broken leg and yanked before throwing me over his shoulder again.

A door of a building opened and we rushed inside. The vamp climbed two long flights of stairs to the third floor and then strode down an echoing hall. Another door opened and I was dropped to the floor and left, the door slamming shut, a lock sliding into place.

I still couldn't see, but my nose told me I was in a room filled with dust, one that vermin had made their own. The whole house sounded empty. Footsteps and indistinct voices bounced off wooden floors and empty walls. Carpets and furniture muffled sound. This house seemed to have neither of those things.

My bones would start knitting together soon, so I needed them positioned properly. I tore the tape off my mouth and felt my leg, making sure I didn't have a bone jutting out of the skin. It hurt like hell, but I didn't feel anything I shouldn't.

I tried taking a deep breath next. It felt like an elephant was sitting on my chest, but I could breathe. Taking stock, my left leg and chest throbbed painfully in dozens of spots where I'd no doubt been kicked. I was sore as hell and I still had a splitting headache. The world had gone gray around the edges, though. My sight was coming back. I could do this. I'd lived through worse. I'd rest on the gritty floor and let my body heal. With any luck, St. Germain would take his time getting here.

If the vampires were attacking, Clive must be up. Ignoring the pounding in my sluggish brain, I tried again to cast out for him and slammed into some kind of barrier. Everything outside the walls was cut off from me and what was inside them barely registered. I had no idea if it was due to a spell or my battered noggin. It felt, perhaps, like there was one vamp downstairs and a multitude of hazy forms floating in the building. Was this like wherever they were keeping Clive and Russell, a house spelled to mute psychic signatures? Where the hell was I?

As the room became clearer, the hazy shapes did as well. The windows were boarded over, but I could see. Ghosts watched me from across the room, insubstantial but visible. There was something odd about them that took my brain far too long to understand and accept.

I knew where I was. My stomach roiled at the horror. This had to be the LaLaurie Mansion, and these were the ghosts of the enslaved people that Madame LaLaurie had tortured and disfigured. In the 1830s, there'd been talk of the LaLauries, Madame LaLaurie in particular, abusing slaves. Which, given the fact that they were okay with enslaved human beings, was saying something.

Apparently, there'd been a fire, and when townspeople had broken in to make sure everyone had escaped, they'd found the cook chained to the stove, found a room with emaciated people missing limbs, bearing the marks of hideous torture.

And a little girl. There was a story about a girl. I tried to remember what I'd read. Something about her brushing Madame LaLaurie's hair, hitting a snag, and LaLaurie coming after the child with a whip. The little girl jumped off the roof to avoid the lash again.

When the townspeople understood what was going on, a mob set the house on fire and put LaLaurie on a ship bound for Paris. I studied the room I was in. Someone must have rebuilt what was lost, the ghosts forever tied to where they'd been killed.

Throat tight, I held out a hand, but they drifted farther away.

"I can help," I whispered. "You don't have to stay in this place. You can go where your family and friends are waiting."

A man with no arms glared, distrust a living thing in his eyes. A woman with a thick metal collar around her neck tried to hold back a child. A man tottering on one leg, the other missing, made a grab for the girl as she darted away from the woman who'd been holding her.

The child, small and painfully thin, appeared to be about

eight or nine. She studied me, edging closer. I wondered if this was her, the one who'd jumped to her death. She opened her mouth, but nothing came out. Many had had their tongues cut out so they couldn't tell anyone what happened in the LaLaurie Mansion. The girl pointed at me and waited.

"I'm Sam. I own a bookstore. I'm also a werewolf and a wicche." At my words, they moved as far away as they could, the one-legged man disappearing. "I know. Those both sound scary." The little girl was still watching me.

"They beat me up and dumped me in here because they want to hurt me again. I'm strong, so they don't have to worry about me dying too quickly."

The little girl moved the neck of her oversized dress to show me the scars the whip had left. Responding in kind, I lifted my t-shirt so she could see my scars. "I have them, too."

She moved in closer to see, as did the ghosts behind her.

"Can you do me a favor?" At the distrust in her eyes, I continued, "It's nothing bad. I'm going to do my best to get out of here, but it's probably going to take me a while to do it. When the vampires come, you should go. I don't want you to see what they do, okay?"

She thought a moment and then nodded.

"Good. And if you want to leave this place, go see the people who love and miss you, I can help."

Another nod, this one much slower.

At the sound of footsteps on the stairs, I hissed, "Go. Some-one's coming."

A minute later, the door swung open and there stood Amélie. Before I could flinch, her boot slammed into my head. Light exploded behind my eyelids and then a bloom of darkness consumed it all.

When I woke, she was standing over me.

"How do you keep screwing up my plans?" She paced to the wall and came back, seeming more annoyed than angry. "I thought you were a wolf, a scarred, pathetic excuse for a wolf, but St. Germain thinks you're more." She studied me. "How did you kill my men in the alley? You were too broken to stand. How did you do it?"

"Not me. They got into a fight. Killed each other."

A few of the ghosts faded, clearly uncomfortable in the company of a vampire.

"Hmm." She crossed her elegant arms, eyes narrowed. "Do you love him, little wolf?"

I knew who she meant, and I wasn't having that conversation with her. I let my middle finger do the talking.

"I'm sure he's sorry he's not here to rescue you. Quite chivalrous, that one."

"It would be impossible for me to overstate how much I don't care what you think."

Ignoring me, she continued, "He said he loved you. He meant it; I could tell. He stood in front of all those vampires and proclaimed his love for you." She shook her head, uncomprehending.

"I have my good points."

Dressed a long, slim dress, she crouched beside me. "You may. I made a critical error in judgment. I thought you were a fling, a distraction." She sounded thoughtful and more than a little sad. "I thought I could promise you to St. Germain and Clive would move on. I was wrong." She shrugged. "I can't stop what's already in motion. There are too many players."

She sighed. "My patroness will be disappointed, but perhaps it's all for the best. I'd hoped he'd help me take over this nocturne, be at my back when others attacked."

Sighing again, she stood and smoothed down her dress. "Ah, well. Godfrey's not Clive, but that can be a good thing. He'll be easier to use."

Footsteps ascended the stairs and then a silhouette filled the doorway. St. Germain stared down on me, eyes vamp-black, fangs peeking through curled lips.

"I'll let you two get acquainted," Amélie said as she departed.

"My child, it's so lovely to see you again. Li," he said over his shoulder, "pick up our guest and show her to her new quarters."

Li stepped around St. Germain, leaned down to curl an arm around my neck, and stood, dragging me across the room.

"Oh, Li, really." In contrast to the censure in his words, St. Germain's voice was positively giddy. "We've added silver manacles to the wall for you."

Grinning maniacally, he watched and waited as Li yanked my arms over my head and snapped the tight new cuffs around my wrists.

The new position had my leg throbbing like a mofo. Ribs jarred, my breath became even more labored. Black dots floated in front of my eyes in the dimly lit room. I was about to pass out. My left leg buckled and I dropped, hanging from my wrists, my chest on fire.

St. Germain ran his cold fingers over my face. "Ew. Sweaty. Fix it, Li," he whined.

Li pulled my top up so it covered my head. "There."

St. Germain giggled breathlessly, fingers skating over my flesh, tracing the extensive scarring. "She's a work of art," he crooned. "And I get to add my signature."

When Li unbuttoned my jeans and pulled them down, I searched the corners of the room for ghosts. The man with no arms stayed to watch, the little girl at his side. *Go!* I thought and she was gone.

St. Germain moved closer. "Look at her beautiful skin." He dragged a sharp nail down my side. "I think a little drink to fortify us before we begin," he said, and then two sets of fangs were plunged into me, one above my bra and one at my waist.

Panic and pain were clearing my head. Not again. I tested the strength of my leg. Would it hold my weight? Pain shot through my body. It wobbled but it held. Good enough. I was getting the fuck out of here.

There was no other way. St. Germain had to die. He'd never let me go, never stop hunting me. It had to stop now or I'd be running scared the rest of my life.

Transforming hands to paws, I slipped through the cuffs before shifting back to hands with lethal claws. My jaw distended and lengthened like a wolf's, with incisors like blades.

Now or never. Breathing deeply, focusing, I stabbed one hand down, four claws stabbing through Li's neck as he knelt, drinking from above my hip. Blood spurted as I cut through flesh and muscle. Squeezing, twisting my fingers, I shredded his neck, sending his head rolling.

At the exact moment my left hand was beheading Li, my right cupped St. Germain's head, lifting him to me. Momentary confusion and blood lust gave me the time I needed to lunge and snap. Blood, my blood, gushed from the holes I'd gouged in his neck. Jolted, he flailed and fought. His arms wrapped around me like iron bands, crushing me. Before he could break more ribs, I shook my jaws viciously, snapping his neck. I bit through his spine and watched him turn to dust.

Transforming my feet to paws, I stepped out of my running shoes and ankle cuffs. Once I was free, feet restored, I leaned against the wall, spitting vampire dust from my mouth. I pulled up my jeans as best I could with only one working leg and then shuffled away from the dust piles. This whole scene would come back to haunt me, but there was no time now.

The little ghost girl was standing next to me as I slid to the floor to put my shoes on. She pointed to where I'd been chained up.

"Yeah. But in my defense, they had it coming." I pushed up on one leg, the other too weak to hold me, and cast out. There were hazy ghosts throughout the house and one cold blip down below. Great.

THIRTY-FOUR

In Which Sam Learns That Getting Up Requires More Strength Than She Currently Has

Hopping across the room, hurting everywhere, I searched the dusty torture chamber for anything that could serve as a crutch. I couldn't hop across New Orleans. Technically, I probably could, but I'd fall a great deal.

Cracking open the door as quietly as possible, I listened intently. If the vamp downstairs were paying attention, he'd hear. Of course, no matter how stealthily I hopped, the impact would be heard. A door opened below, admitting quiet voices.

Lafitte and Godfrey talking. The little ghost girl appeared next to me, pointing across the room to a tall, wooden cabinet. The doors were hanging open, revealing whips and knives and all manner of torture devices, both ancient and modern. My stomach dropped at the sight. That was what had been planned for me. Those were what had been used on the poor people whose souls had never moved on from this cursed place.

The little girl pointed again, more urgently as the voices moved up the stairs. Did she want me to know what had been used on her? Moving toward the cabinet, she urged me to follow her. Closing the door as silently as possible, I hopped after her.

The girl stabbed her finger in the space between the back of the cabinet and the wall. Hoping I was getting it right, I lifted one side of the heavy, old cabinet and swung it out. The girl was standing in the space I'd created, pointing at a spot on the wall between two wooden planks. Hoping desperately, my hands flew over where she had pointed, searching for a catch or a release.

The girl pointed again and I saw it, a knot in the wood grain that was actually a release button. I hit it and a small panel swung inward, revealing a narrow stairway. I dove in, turning to pull the cabinet back into place. The main door of the room opened as I was quietly pressing the hidden panel closed.

Standing in the dark, cobweb-covered passage, I pressed my ear to the wall and listened.

"*Merde*. Where is she? Oh, *mon Dieu!*" Lafitte's shoes slapped hard against the floors as he muttered in French.

I heard the zing of metal slicing through air and then a thud. A moment later, the faint, tinny ring of a phone could be heard.

"He's dead," Godfrey said, his footsteps traversing the room. Chuckling, he added, "I may have mixed up the order of my kills, but did it really matter whether Clive or Lafitte went first?"

I lost my breath. It felt as though my good leg had been kicked out from under me. No. It had to be a lie. A mistake. Clive wasn't dead. I cast out, searching, but my mind bounced off the walls of this building again. I couldn't find him. He hadn't been at the townhouse, hadn't responded to my texts.

Nonono. This was some murky vampire intrigue. I was sure of it. No one could kill Clive.

I dove into Godfrey's mind, not caring if I'd be blind in this passage, not caring about anything. "You must be mistaken. Russell wouldn't leave without speaking with me." Clive paced a few steps down a dark, narrow alley before turning back to Godfrey. "You should have seen Sam this evening. She was magnificent, claws out, threatening to cut off St. Germain's head." His gray eyes glowed in the lamplight before he turned to pace away again.

Godfrey pulled a short sword from behind his back and

swung with such speed, there was only the flash of metal slashing through the air and then Clive crumpled, turning to dust.

The memory went dark and jumped to Godfrey standing in Lafitte's entryway. "It is done, Master."

Amélie stood behind Lafitte, hiding a smile.

Lafitte clapped Godfrey on the shoulder and crowed, "The arrogant bastard is dead! *Enfin!*"

I pulled out and dropped to the ground. It wasn't true. He wouldn't have turned his back on Godfrey, not after Russell had disappeared. He hadn't survived a thousand years by making mistakes like that. He was too smart, too ruthless.

But then I thought about the last week. The attack on the San Francisco nocturne had shocked him. He hadn't been prepared for rebellion and had faltered afterward, unsure of who to trust, questioning himself most of all. He'd held himself so stiff that day in the library when I'd tested my new mind-reading gift on Russell and Godfrey. I think it would have gutted him if I'd told him his oldest and dearest friends had plotted against him.

And I'd been *wrong*. I'd assured him Godfrey was loyal. Godfrey, with whom he'd fought side by side with for centuries, had taken Clive's head. For what? It made no sense. If he'd wanted to be a Master, Clive would have supported him, helped him find the right city to take over. He hadn't been mistreated or belittled. Clive trusted him as he trusted very few.

Cracked ribs and a desperation to hold in sobs meant the elephant had returned to sitting on my chest. I should have slammed back into the room and killed Godfrey where he stood, but my limbs refused to move. Shattering grief had put me down and I wasn't sure I had the strength to get back up this time.

In my mind's eye, Clive's golden image lit the darkness. The way he'd grin and roll his eyes at me caused a painful sob to burst free. Only me. Only I got relaxed, adorable Clive. I'd thought him so damn scary and aloof for years and then he'd let me see behind the mask.

He'd visited The Slaughtered Lamb every month, sitting silently at a table and having one drink. He'd been checking up on me, making sure I was all right. I'd been nothing to him at the time, an abused teen who'd survived what his sister hadn't. But that had been enough for him to stride into my bar every month to make sure I was safe.

When things went sideways and I couldn't seem to cross the street without someone trying to kill me, it was Clive who came to my rescue. He protected me when he could, but more importantly, he encouraged me to overcome my fear and defend myself. Clive, who was the first to touch me after… everything, the first to accept me, all of me, and love me.

Maybe I really was cursed. Father, mother, uncle, cousins, and now Clive. Too many people had died because I'd been born.

The house fell silent around me. How long ago had Godfrey left? It didn't matter. I'd find him. Funny how the thought of killing no longer bothered me.

First, though, I needed to find Russell. If he wasn't under Lafitte's bar, perhaps he was in a cage like the one at Clive's townhouse, somewhere in the New Orleans nocturne house. The thought of battling my way through all the vamps, heads flying, brought contentment to my broken heart.

Logically, though, I knew that wasn't the best way to rescue Russell. That was suicide by vampire. I didn't have the time to fantasize about going down in a blaze of claws and fangs. Russell needed help. I'd honor Clive by saving his best friend, not by dying.

And while I was convinced that vampires—at least the ones like Clive and Russell—retained their souls, Clive never believed it. So, on the very slim chance we didn't meet again on the other side, I had shit to do before my time was up.

Getting my good leg beneath me, I pushed up and tested my weight on the bad one. It held, barely. At some point, my vision had come back and I hadn't noticed, trapped as I was in this dark passage.

The stairs led down. Holding tight to a rail, I gingerly made my way down two flights of rickety stairs, hopping over a few missing boards along the way. I was so busy checking the steps, I hadn't noticed the wall of cobwebs until I broke through it with my face. A frantic, cringing, swatting dance ensued.

When I got near the bottom, I cast out again. Ghosts and that one lone vampire blip I'd sensed earlier. It was right on the other side of the wall ahead of me. The stairs stopped, dead-ending into a wall. I searched for the door, ready for whoever was waiting for me on the other side of it.

When I finally found the catch, the door swung wide open, no cabinet down here to hide it. The room was dark and musty, with an overlay of mold. I ducked out of the passage and shut the short door behind me. The room felt empty but my spidey senses were telling me a vamp was in here with me.

Claws out, I limped as quietly as I could through the room. And then I saw him, hanging from manacles in a cage across the room. Russell.

"Good evening, Miss Quinn," he croaked.

I ran to the cage. "Oh my God, what have they done to you?" I'd never seen a vampire this beaten and still alive.

"No need for tears. I'll heal." It looked like twenty vamps had all taken turns beating him.

I hadn't even realized I'd started crying again. "Why?" The sun had gone down when they'd attacked Stheno and me in the street. How long ago had that been? I'd seen vamps heal while they slept. For these wounds to be so fresh, they had to have just happened.

"My allegiance was requested and denied."

"How do I get you out?" I searched the walls for keys.

"You don't. You leave now, before they return. Have Stheno protect you and tell Clive where I am. This house has been spelled in some way. I can't hear him in my head."

A floorboard creaked above and we both froze. I cast out to see who'd joined us. "It's okay. It's the ghosts." A few of whom, I'd noticed, were in here watching us.

I tried the door of the cage, yanking with all my werewolf strength. The door flew open. "They didn't lock it?"

Russell appeared surprised by that information.

I rushed in, wanting to hug him but afraid to hurt him. "Keys?" I tried to find anything that would get him out of those manacles.

The little girl ghost stood inside the cage and pointed to the floor. I searched where she pointed and found a set of keys dropped in the corner. Grabbing them, I raced to Russell. I had to get him out of here before I explained what Godfrey had done.

I unlocked the first cuff and he groaned, his left arm falling to his side. The right arm dropped a moment later on the same note of pain.

"I'm sorry. I know how much that hurts. Can you move them?"

He tried, not quite stifling another grunt of pain. They moved, but not easily or well. I unlocked the metal around his ankles next and then the chain around his waist. He almost fell forward but caught himself.

"Can you walk?" If he couldn't, I didn't know how we were getting out of here.

Swaying, he tested his legs, fierce determination all that kept him upright.

"Okay. This isn't going to work." I held up my arm to his mouth. "Feed."

"Thank you, but I can't. Clive would never approve," he said, clutching a chain to balance.

"I'm the boss of my blood. You're no good to me if you can't walk." When he remained unmoved, I added, "I have a fractured leg and possibly broken ribs. How am I supposed to carry you? Feed so you can help me, please."

That worked. As gently as he could, he held my arm and

pierced my skin with his fangs, drinking deeply. When I started to get light-headed, he caught himself and stopped. He was already standing taller, his face less battered. Good, because I was definitely going to need help getting out of here.

Arms entwined, propping each other up, we staggered to the door. We were on the first floor, an empty hall leading toward a main entryway. Ghosts waited for us in the foyer, the little girl in the front of the tortured group.

I leaned Russell against the wall. "Give me a minute." I limped to them and waited. "The offer still stands. I can help you cross." My words were met with varying degrees of hope and distrust. "It's an evil place. Please, let me try."

The little girl came first, holding out her hand. I took it in mine, closed my eyes, and pictured freedom and sunshine, loved ones and rest. I searched for that store of magic my mother had left me, dug deep, and sent out a pulse of white light. When I opened my eyes, the girl was gone.

More came and one by one, I helped them cross over. Unlike reading minds or shifting forms, this caused me no pain or fatigue. This brought only joy and bone-deep gratitude.

For a few, though, hope had been beaten out long ago. They turned their backs and faded into the house.

THIRTY-FIVE

Dead Men Tell No Tales

Russell and I staggered out the front door of the LaLaurie mansion, arms around each other, to silent, deserted streets. I cast out. No vamps besides Russell were nearby. Lots of ghosts, though.

"By the way, if I start choking inexplicably or something, it means I have a ghost trying to kill me."

Russell stopped moving and stared down at me. "Excuse me?"

"Long story." I pulled him to keep moving. A safe house in New Orleans didn't seem to exist, so I headed in the direction of the townhouse. I was in desperate need of sleep and healing.

"I believe we have time while we walk." Russell seemed better. Horribly beaten, but better. The blood perked him right up.

"Good point." And as we both had sensitive hearing, we didn't need to worry about disturbing others on the way. "So either Lafitte or St. Germain—or, I guess, someone I don't know about yet—set the ghosts on me. Not sure who. It was a 'he,' anyway."

"Charming."

"Right? You knew those guys. Could either of them see ghosts?"

Russell was silent for a long time. "I don't know, but Lafitte has always been interested in the occult." More thoughtful silence. "He had a theory he spoke of—perhaps a hundred years ago—about drinking the blood of wicches, psychics, occult practitioners, of those who were gifted in some way. He believed he could inherit their gifts, even if only briefly, through the blood."

We turned up another street, zigzagging through the Quarter. "Well, that's a terrifying thought. You drank my blood. Are you feeling wolfy? Can you see ghosts?"

"I see no ghosts. I do, however, feel stronger than I normally would. As for Lafitte, it is possible that he's found a necromancer, like yourself, and has absorbed some of her abilities." He paused. "May I ask; you've been speaking about Lafitte and St. Germain in the past tense. Was that purposeful?"

Oh, right. "I took out St. Germain and Li when they came to torture me. And then Godfrey got Lafitte,"

"Godfrey? You've seen him?"

"It's kind of a long story. Is it okay if I wait to tell it when we get home?" My bad leg was shaking from the strain. It was making it hard to concentrate.

"Of course. I've recovered enough to carry you, Miss Quinn."

My initial impulse was to say no, to suck it up and keep going, but the pain was becoming overwhelming. "Thank you," I said instead.

"Where was your leg injured?"

I pointed to the outside of my thigh, right above the knee.

"Then I can't carry you on my back, as I'd be gripping your leg right at your injury."

"And no over the shoulder carry. They messed up my ribs, too. The assholes at the torture house kept throwing me over their shoulders and bashing my already-battered ribs."

Russell's expression was pained. He almost touched my face but stopped himself. "We should have left you at home. The pain you've endured because of us is shaming." He sighed. "You're so young," he said, scooping me up in his arms. "Your pain will be added to our final tallies."

"Hey, I've held my own. I got you out of that cage. And with the attack on Stheno and me, I've probably killed more vamps than you guys since we arrived." I crossed my arms over my chest, feeling stupid for being carried like a baby while arguing my ability to keep up.

I prayed Stheno was all right, that being my guard hadn't cost her her very long life. I'd been fighting my own vamps at the time, but I'd seen something thrown in her face, something that had caused her to scream before she had her head slammed into a brick wall. My chest constricted with pain. I wasn't sure I could take much more.

We were silent for a few blocks, streetlamps glowing in the misty dark, before Russell spoke again. "You misunderstand. I am shamed by taking one so young and brave, who has had to fight for survival her whole life, and dropping her into these pointless, indulgent battles that force her—you—to choose between death and murder. You'd never taken a life until we showed up. And now you're trying to impress me with your kill count. I'm horribly shamed to have had a part in doing this to you."

Arms relaxing across my chest, I was at a loss for words.

"What you did for the dead at the nocturne and the LaLaurie Mansion, that is a rare and beautiful gift. I hate the idea of dragging you down into the blood and muck with us when you can do that.

"But," he continued, his lips curling up. "I'd also hate for Clive, for the rest of us, to lose you. You've helped him to remember who he was long ago. You've stripped away the ennui and cynicism he'd clothed himself in."

Clive. The grief washed over me, tightening my throat. I had to tell him.

"Russell," I began. "About that—"

"Finally, I'm near enough to hear him. He's sensed me as well." Russell grinned down at me. "He's on his way."

My mind went blank. "What?"

A moment later, Clive dropped to the ground in front of us. It was him and yet not. He wore jeans, basketball shoes, and a hoodie pulled up, obscuring his face. I'd never have recognized him if I hadn't known, deep in my bones, it was him.

He grabbed Russell's shoulders, a grin blazing across his beautiful face. "You're alive."

"For the most part."

He paused a moment, smile dimming. "Godfrey?"

Russell shook his head. "I don't know."

Nodding, Clive focused on me, pulling me from Russell's arms, crushing me in his embrace. "And you," he breathed. "You were amazing, threatening St. Germain right to his face." He shook his head. "Master vampires are too afraid to do that. Before we're done here, I'll deliver his true death for you. You won't spend the rest of your life looking over your shoulder for that one."

"She already took care of him, Sire," Russell said, patting Clive on the shoulder and walking around us.

"Here now, why are you crying?" Clive wiped at the tears washing my face. "Are you hurt?"

"Leg and ribs," Russell's voice floated down the street to us.

Clive swept me up in his arms and carried me, catching up easily with Russell. "And why do you appear to have been set upon?" Clive asked him.

I couldn't stop staring. He was alive. Was I dreaming? "You died. I saw it." I ran my hands over his face as tears streamed down my own. "Godfrey killed you. I saw it in his memories. You turned to dust."

Clive stopped walking. "You've seen Godfrey?"

"He killed you."

"No, darling. I'm only mostly dead." And then his lips were

on mine, comforting, reassuring. "Explanations can wait until we're home. Are there any of us about?"

He meant vampires. I cast out again, searching. "You two. That glut at the bar. A couple at St. Germain's place. And I think there are a few out at the nocturne. They're dim, but I'm counting three. The bigger problem is the parade of ghosts following us."

"Why would that be a problem?"

"They've been weaponized. You should run," I said, staring at the horde following us.

"You'll be jostled. I'll hurt you."

"Trust me on this."

Clive and Russell ran while I put out a hand and sent a pulse, pushing them back.

As soon as we were in the door, I smacked Clive's shoulder to let me down. Hands and forehead resting against the door, I asked the powers that be to keep the ghosts from entering the house, protecting all inside, then sent multiple pulses of white magic through the exterior of the house, picturing it in my mind like a coating of paint, running over the roof and down the sides, seeping into the earth, pooling beneath the basement, cocooning us.

Turning, I found Clive watching me. I shrugged. "We'll see if that works."

Bellowing filled the hall, coming from the family room.

"Stheno?" Oh, thank God! I was afraid she'd been killed. Limp running, I turned the corner a moment later, Clive and Russell at my heels, and found Stheno in a screeching battle with Meg, as Dave, Owen, and George leaned against the kitchen counters, watching.

"What the hell?" I shouted.

The screaming abruptly stopped. Stheno turned, grinning. She wore a t-shirt that read *Dead Men Tell No Tales* written across her chest and was sporting an eye patch. "Did you bring me anything to eat?"

"Not this time." I pointed at my own eye and asked, "Are you okay?"

"Eh." She flopped down on the couch. "One doesn't work at all and one is always on. Now I have to flip up the patch to turn people to stone." She propped her socked feet up on the coffee table. "When I'm done with this shit job, I'll go home and heal. Be right as rain in a couple hundred years. No worries."

"Sorry." A couple centuries to recover from a few days with me.

"It's okay, kid. Not your fault. I should have been prepared for the asshole. I was too used to being the baddest bitch in the room. Like this one," she said, motioning to Meg.

"The difference being, I *am* the baddest bitch in *any* room." Meg studied me a moment while Stheno flipped her off. "What's the matter? You're standing like you're in pain. What happened?"

"Super long story. Can we start with why all you guys are here? How did you know we were in trouble?"

"That text," Owen said, glancing at Clive.

"I told you this was a bad idea," Dave grumbled. "Did I not tell you to sit your ass down and leave the vampire shit to Clive?" He shook his head, disgusted with me.

Limping, I made my way across the kitchen, stopping directly in front of him. Poking him in his broad chest, I said, "And you were the one who told me I had to be a partner, fighting side by side with him, not a scared rabbit hiding away, needing protection."

"Stupid demon," Meg said.

I leaned in and hugged Dave. "I'm okay. Really."

"Yeah, we can all see that. You look like you've lost ten pounds since you've been here. You've got dark circles under your eyes, so I'm guessing no sleep. You have a leg you're not putting weight on, and you're holding your ribs like they've been bruised, if not broken. And your aura's changed."

I stood straight and stared. My aura had changed? I turned to

Owen and George for confirmation. They both nodded. "Changed how?"

"It's not bad." Owen's weak reassurance had alarms bells going off in my head. "Not like a black wicche's or anything. It's mottled now."

"Mottled? Is that a nice way of saying stained?" I'm not sure why this piece of information was the one making me panic, but it was. Like Gabriel telling me my eye color was changing. It seemed many things about me were changing and it was terrifying.

"No." George put his arm around Owen. "It's richer. When I first met you, your aura was a bright and shiny gold. There were little ragged tears in places, but it was uniformly glowing. Now it's a deeper, richer, burnished gold. You've had difficult decisions to make and you've made them. The bright innocence is changing, as it needs to. Welcome to the world of moral ambiguity and making the best decision you can, given the circumstances that you're in."

When he put it that way, it took some of the sting out. In a kill or be killed world, innocence was lost quickly. Which was what Russell had been saying. He was sorry I was facing those decisions. Yeah. Me too.

"Will someone please tell us what the hell has been going on?" Meg complained.

"Only if I can sit," I said, limping to the couch. Owen followed me and helped me lie down, propping a pillow under my head. He then held his hand over my leg, performing a healing spell.

"It's not broken," he said. "Or, at least not anymore." He studied me a moment. "Anywhere else?"

"Her ribs," Clive said, and the pain disappeared.

I groaned in relief. "Thank you."

"You have to tell me when you're hurting. I could have done that when I met you on the street." Clive had his angry face on, but I knew he was worried.

While Owen held his hands over my ribs, I glanced around the room at everyone's concerned expressions, feeling blessed. "Well, since I've been awake and in the middle of most of it, I guess I'm the one talking." I started the story from when we landed and right up until Clive found Russell and me on the street. There was some hissing and pacing as I told them of St. Germain and Amélie, the convent, and the killer ghost.

"What I don't understand, though, is how you're standing here," I said to Clive. "I saw Godfrey kill you."

THIRTY-SIX

Tonight We Dine in Hell!

"I planted that memory in case Lafitte had developed the ability to read him. He's never possessed it before, but he seems to have picked up new tricks," Clive explained.

"Russell told me about that, about Lafitte's theory on drinking the blood of wicches or psychics in order to gain their gifts."

"You can alter people's memories?" Owen asked, more than a little concerned.

The two vampires in the room regarded him blankly. Finally, Russell responded, "Of course we can. It wouldn't do to have our donors running off to tell the authorities about us. We can muddle the last few minutes. Have them focus on something else so what we're doing doesn't register and become a memory. Little things," he said with a shrug.

"As Sam's current lack of pain can attest," he continued, "Clive is gifted among us in his mental abilities. To create a memory with such clarity and implant it in one of us... I don't know of anyone else who could do it."

"Cadmael can," Clive said, referring to his Mayan friend who may or may not be behind all of this. "And I've heard rumors about an ancient Romanian. There could be more. It's not as though we advertise." He crossed the room and crouched beside me, brushing a stray hair from my face. "I'm sorry you saw that and thought it was true. You were with the pack. Stheno was set to take over if you left them. Godfrey was with Lafitte. I hadn't anticipated you two crossing paths."

"There's been a lot of crazy shit going on." I patted his shoulder.

"So, you've said." He sighed.

"Speaking of Cadmael." I squinted in sympathy. "He may be involved in all this."

Clive stood slowly. "Why do you say that." His voice was carefully measured, but I could feel the turmoil inside.

"I keep feeling him nearby. It's a wisp of awareness and then gone. That first night, after the alley fight, I got the impression he was somewhere close, but it disappeared before I could put a name to it."

I reached for Clive's hand because I knew this was hurting him. "I've felt that barely-there-but-not-really feeling twice more. I've searched New Orleans and can't find him, but I also couldn't find you or Russell earlier, so he may be someplace spelled to hide him."

Sitting down heavily on the coffee table, he studied our joined hands for some time. "I don't think that means what you think it means," he began slowly. "I haven't felt him." He turned to Russell. "Have you?"

"No, Sire."

"Cadmael is very old and very powerful. I felt it when his plane landed in San Francisco. I don't think he could mask his power so completely that I wouldn't be aware of his presence." He paused. "Regardless of what he said as we left, he doesn't trust you. I think, in his own misguided way, he was keeping tabs on us, making sure you weren't working against me."

"But—"

"I believe he is able to do what you do." He gently tapped my head.

I knew it was hypocritical of me, but the idea of that old vampire rummaging around in my head had me panicking and cringing away from Clive. "He's seen…"

"I don't know." The sorrow on his face belied those words. "Please don't cry."

I hadn't realized I was. I wiped my face, but the tears wouldn't stop. That old vampire, who hated me for what I was, had sorted through my memories, had seen what had been done to me, had watched… Bile rose. I reached for Stheno. "I need—"

A moment later, she had me in her arms and raced me to the restroom.

Afterward, she handed me a cold, wet wash towel. "I gotta say, not a fan of watching you puke. Of all the people in that room, how did I end up the lucky one?"

I wiped my mouth and then laid down on the cold tile floor, feeling sick and lost and painfully, unforgivably exposed.

Stheno crouched down next to me. "Come on, kid. Don't give him that kind of power."

The cold tile felt good against my heated cheek. "I thought if I dressed a certain way, people would see me as strong. I wanted to be the tough guy, not the victim." I held the wash-cloth to my leaking eyes. "No wonder Clive said it didn't matter what I wore. Do they all know?" I asked Stheno. "Have I been some pathetic idiot, swaggering around in leather pants?"

"Come on, kid. Get up. If you wanted coddling, you picked the wrong person to watch you puke." She pulled me to my feet and held me in place by my jaw. "They don't get to say who you are. Only *you* can do that. So, are you someone who cries on bathroom floors or someone who kicks bloodsuckers' asses?"

I sniffled. "Both?"

The corner of her mouth turned up. "Yeah. And, you know, that's what makes you special. I don't like many people—in fact, any—but I like you. You know why? Because you're both. You'll take on a nocturne of bloodsuckers and then worry about putting ghosts to rest. You always remember to send me food when you're out, but love throwing shit at my head."

I huffed out a laugh. "I really do."

"You risked your life at the convent to release a dead girl. You came on this trip to do something that scares the shit out of you, but you did it anyway because you wanted to keep Clive safe. You've risked your life over and over to keep a thousand-year-old vampire safe." She shook my face. "Most of us have tragic pasts, kid. It's what we do afterward that matters."

She dropped her hand. "Come on. Let's go get a beer. You can wash the taste of puke out of your mouth and I'll let you throw the empty at my head."

I nodded. "Deal."

When we went back to the kitchen, I was hit with the realization that Owen was probably the only one who hadn't heard all of that. Dave was standing at the refrigerator with a bottle in one hand and a glass in the other.

He handed the glass to me and the bottle to Stheno. "She's not much of a beer drinker," he explained.

"Lemonade?" I took a swig and almost choked.

"Lemon drop. A quadruple." He patted my shoulder and shoved me and my huge cocktail toward the couch. "Go sit your ass down. Your limp is still bad and your breathing's gotten worse. Puking probably rebroke the ribs that were healing."

He was right, so I limped back to the couch. "Know-it-all demon," I grumped.

Stheno turned to visually assault my studly, half-demon friend. "Really," she purred.

He barely spared her a glance and said, "Taken."

Stheno blew out a disgruntled breath and flopped onto the cushions.

While Dave offered drinks to everyone else, I whispered to Stheno, "His girlfriend's a banshee. She'll cut a bitch."

Dave chuckled. "That she will," he murmured before grabbing beers for himself and George.

My head was so screwed up, I'd forgotten. "We have to go get Godfrey. The ghosts may have recognized you, Clive. If Amélie knows Godfrey lied, they'll kill him."

Clive sat on the back of the couch and rested his hand on my head. "I know. The sun will be rising in a few minutes, though. We couldn't possibly find him, extract him, and get to safety before it does. Russell and I will head out at nightfall and search."

"I know where he is, remember? They're beneath Lafitte's Bar."

"Still?" Clive leaned forward, instantly intent.

"Let me check." I cast out for all the vamps in the city. Ignoring the two with me, I searched farther afield. "There's one across the street, watching the house… There are still three at the nocturne house."

"Is this new?" Dave asked.

"Holy crap," Owen responded.

"There are two at St. Germain's… There's something in the bayou that glows like you guys but isn't you, and there are… twenty-two vampires under Lafitte's bar. Give me a minute. Yes, Amélie is there. And Godfr—" I opened my eyes to find Clive watching me.

"Amélie knows what Godfrey did. He's—Godfrey's in a lot of pain."

Clive stood and turned to Russell. "Shall we?"

Russell nodded. "I'm ready, my liege."

"Wait. You said it's almost sunrise."

"We'll make it if we go now." Clive moved toward Russell.

"Stop." I sat up straight. "Henry told me there was a tunnel leading to their underground clubhouse. He said the tunnel started in Storeville or Storvel. Anyone here familiar with New Orleans geography?"

"Sam, we don't have time for this."

"You're right. *You* don't. The sun is coming up, meaning the vamps are going down. We'll rescue him while you guys are mostly dead. So," I said, glancing around the room. "Storeville?"

"There's a Storyville," Russell said as he moved closer. "It was the red-light district in New Orleans a hundred years ago."

I put down my drink. "Good! Now is there a building there, maybe a brothel, that's associated with Lafitte?"

"Josie's?" Russell turned to Clive, who nodded. "Josie and Jean Lafitte—Bélisaire's cousin—were lovers. The bar they're under is Jean's. Josie Arlington ran a brothel in Storyville. If there's a tunnel running from Storyville to the Blacksmith Shop Bar, I'd guess it originates at Josie's."

Russell turned to Clive. "She's right, Sire. I can feel the sun pulling me down. We'd never make it. Attacking during the day would be safest for her and allow her time to heal."

Clive's gaze found mine. "I don't want you involved in this. You've done more than enough already."

"Look around you," I said, rolling my eyes. "I've got a Fury, a gorgon, a half-demon, a wicche, a dragon shifter, and I'm a freaking werewolf. I think we've got this covered."

"Which one's the dragon?" Stheno whispered.

Owen wrapped an arm around George. "Taken."

"Shit. I'm not getting any this week," Stheno grumbled.

"I need rest. Russell's right about that. We all need to rest. And then we'll head out while the sun's up. By sundown, we'll have Godfrey back and we can head for the airport and our ride home."

"All right," Clive said. "Everyone, find rooms." He scooped me up off the couch and carried me upstairs.

"If you're about to take a nap, it might be best if you weren't carrying me upstairs at the time."

"I'm crawling out of my skin. I need to do something. I've spent the last day in a cold room." He was about to drop me on the bed when I tapped his shoulder and made him put me down.

"Do you have any idea how filthy I am?"

"That's what I'm talkin' 'bout!" A shout came from downstairs.

I limped to the door, opened it, and shouted, "Shut it, Stheno!"

Closing the door at least gave us the impression of privacy, faulty though it was. "I have to shower. Can you talk to me while I do, tell me why you were in the cold room?"

Nodding, Clive followed me into the bathroom and then helped me undress and step into the steaming shower.

I stood under the water jets a moment, letting the heat sink into my sore muscles. Before I had a chance to move, Clive's hands were in my hair, taking down my braid. "Dude, if you pass out in here, you'll drown."

"You have to breathe in order to drown. And I'll be fine for a while longer."

It was glorious. I stood in the hot, pounding spray while Clive washed my hair. "Cold room?"

"I own mews apartments. Years ago—must be over a hundred now—I bought a row of stables on a narrow alley near the port. Eventually, I had them remodeled to make low-income apartments." He massaged shampoo into my scalp and I found it difficult to focus on anything other than his fingers.

"They've since been remodeled again and have been sold as luxury condos. I saved one for myself, though. When I visit town, I prefer this townhouse, but that apartment has something this house doesn't."

"A cold room?"

"A cold room. No sounds, no signals, nothing escapes that room."

He paused a moment, running his hands through my long hair. "Since I was supposed to be truly dead, I sat in that room after I sent Godfrey off with his false memory." He rested his head on my shoulder. "It was miserable. I couldn't do anything. I was trapped in that room with my thoughts and regrets. Russell was missing, Godfrey was with Lafitte's people, and you were so angry with me."

"But how did Russell hear you in his head if you were in a cold room?"

He tilted my head, rinsing the soap from my hair. "I was going crazy, not knowing where you all were and what was happening. The last couple of hours, I'd taken to stepping into the hall for a few seconds to search. When I received no responses, I went back to the room."

I wrapped my arms around him. "I'm sorry. That does sound miserable."

"Bloody worthless, that's what I've been."

"Sometimes you need to trust us to carry the load."

His hands moved up and down my back. "You've had to carry too much of the load. And it's not even your load to car—"

I shut him up with a hand over his mouth. "We're in this together, right? When I have to deal with my aunt once and for all, should I tell you to sit it out, as it's not your fight?"

He nipped at my fingers until I moved them. "Try it."

After rinsing and toweling off, we made our way to the bed and settled in. He wrapped me in his arms and curled himself protectively around me. Within moments, we were both out.

I awoke sometime later to the sound of whispering outside the door.

"What?" I called groggily.

The door opened a sliver and Owen's voice floated in.

"Sorry. We drew the short straw. We tried to let you sleep as long as we could, but it's two and we should really get moving. None of us is excited about walking into a nest of vamps after the sun goes down."

I shot up in bed, tapping my phone for the time. 2:03. Shit. I had meant to set an alarm for noon. "Sorry, sorry. Getting up now. I'll be down in a couple of minutes."

"Thanks," George said.

By 2:15, I was dressed, teeth brushed, hair braided, and

heading down the stairs. My leg was sore, twinging in pain when I moved the wrong way. I took a deep breath. More soreness, but nothing like yesterday. The sleep had helped.

Owen and George were sitting on the bottom steps, waiting for me. "You look better," George volunteered.

"We were worried," Owen added, pointing to the front sitting room. "Can you sit down for a minute? I'll do another healing spell. I'm not a healer, but I can help."

I went to the settee, making room for Owen beside me. George watched worriedly as Owen did his best to aid my natural healing. When he was done, I stood and took a deep breath. "Better," I said, and he smiled.

"Sorry I'm late," I shouted down the hall. "Let's hit it."

"Food first," Dave bellowed back.

As if on cue, my stomach rumbled. "I could eat," I said as I headed for the kitchen.

"Ready your breakfast and eat hearty, for tonight we dine in hell!" Stheno roared.

Seriously? "Were you watching *300* again?"

"I've got two words for you," she said. "Gérard Fucking Butler."

"Actually," George began.

"Shut up, kid."

THIRTY-SEVEN

Graves and Long-Dead Secrets

The afternoon was still and warm as five of us piled into the SUV, with Dave behind the wheel. Meg and Stheno weren't happy about being in an enclosed place together, even for a short time, so Meg took to the air. Chameleon-like, she can blend with her surroundings to the point that she goes unnoticed when she flies.

"Does anyone know where we're going?" I asked. They'd wedged me into the middle seat in the second row. They seemed to be taking this whole we-must-protect-Sam thing a little too seriously.

Owen, from the front passenger seat, held up his phone. "I have a map."

Siri, with a male Irish voice, began directing us to Storyville. I wished we had one of those walking-tour guides with us so we could learn while we rescued.

"Does Josie's place still exist or do we just have a general area to search?" I was feeling pretty guilty for sleeping through the planning session this morning.

"No," George said from beside me. "It burned down in 1905 but was rebuilt almost immediately. Problem is, Josie retired a few years later, and then the Storyville district was shut down in

1917. Prostitution was made illegal. Most of the original buildings were demolished and the whole area was turned into a low-rent housing district."

Bummer. "I was really hoping we'd get to break into an old brothel and search for a trapdoor, not unlike Scooby and the gang."

Owen turned, grinning. "You know that makes you Scooby, right?"

"I am totally cool with that." I patted Dave on his beefy shoulder. "Will you be our Fred?"

"Fuck off."

"Very un-Fred-like, but we'll take it." I glanced between Owen and George.

"Not it!" George said before Owen could. "I'm neither Daphne nor Velma. If I have to be anybody, I'd rather be Shaggy."

I shot my thumb toward Stheno on my other side. "If anyone is Shaggy, it's her. She's obsessed with food and sits around all day watching TV."

"Hey," she began, thought a moment, and then shrugged. "Fair."

"Scooby, shut up," Dave said. "We're here." He pulled the SUV over, parking in front of a large, nondescript apartment building. We piled out onto the sidewalk and studied the unadorned rectangle of apartments.

A six-foot fence surrounded the building and its parking lot. The neighborhood, a mix of historic and modern, had a huge crane towering over new construction a few blocks away. I'd become so used to the French Quarter, I'd forgotten not all of New Orleans was a historical site.

I clapped my hands. "Okay, gang. How do we do this?"

Dave stood with his hands on his hips, surveying the neighborhood. "Fuck if I know. This is modern construction," he grumped, gesturing to the apartment building. "They wouldn't have left an intact tunnel when they were pouring concrete and laying the foundation."

"That place," Owen said, pointing to the market on the corner. "That looks old."

"Hell, if that's our only criteria, we should ransack every original building on the street." Dave studied the nearby buildings, frustration lining his face.

"The brothel was huge, though. At least those pics we found made it seem like it was. It's possible that market was one of the original outbuildings. A barn or something," Owen said.

I heard an impact and then Meg appeared on the sidewalk beside Dave. Like him, Meg could alter her appearance when she needed to. Her naturally gray, scaly skin was a softer olive, like Stheno's, and her long scraggly gray hair was now black.

"The St. Louis Cemetery #1 is two blocks that way." She pointed down Basin Street. "And Cemetery #2 is five or six blocks that way," she said, pointing behind the apartment building. "We know they were here before Storyville. I was thinking about it," she said. "Pirates, vampires, booze, prostitutes; where would it be safe to transport people or goods if you didn't want anyone to see you?" She shrugged. "A cemetery. Especially in this town, people stay away from those places at night."

"Who's got a phone I can borrow?" Having lost mine sometime during my ass kicking and abduction. Five people held out their phones. I grabbed Stheno's, since she was right next to me. I tried to hold it up to her face, but she grabbed it back and keyed in a code.

"Damn thing doesn't recognize me anymore because of the eye patch."

"Right. Sorry." I pulled up her search engine. "Let's see who's buried over there." I pulled up a site dedicated to the Saint Louis Cemeteries and scrolled through the famous names.

"Meg, you're a genius! Dominique You is buried in Cemetery #2. He was Jean Lafitte's brother, sort of. Marie Laveau is in

Cemetery #1. Now, I don't know of any connection between Laveau and Lafitte other than St. Germain saying that the current Lafitte was interested in Voodoo. Of course, St. Germain was a big ol' liar and a creep to boot, so maybe his input can be ignored." I glanced around at the blank faces. "What? I have a lot of time on my hands while vampires sleep. Book nerd. I research stuff."

Handing Stheno back her phone, I turned to Owen and George. "Why don't you guys check out the market and then meet us over at Cemetery #2." I checked with the other three. "Is it okay if we spread out and walk? We may pass something on the way, some clue or whatever, as to where the tunnel is."

"I say we tear the damn Blacksmith Shop Bar apart until we find a trapdoor, but if Scooby wants to search for clues, okay." Dave shook his head and started walking. "I'll check out Laveau."

"Am I being stupid?" Maybe Dave was right and this whole tunnel search was a waste of precious daylight.

"Screw him," Stheno said, patting me on the back. "He didn't see what happened when the ghost in that bar tried to kill you."

"She's right," Owen said. "This is a good idea. George and I will check out this place and then head over to your cemetery." He glanced between Meg and Stheno. "Which one of you is staying with Sam?"

"I am," Stheno said, a hand on my arm, claiming me. Glaring at Meg, she added, "Fly away, you harpy. No one needs you around here."

"Fury, not harpy. I'm a goddess, you ignorant beast." Meg flipped her off and disappeared, the sound of huge wings beating the air in her wake.

"We totally need Meg. Why are you stirring up shit?"

"She's an asshole. Let her go brood. Come on. Dave went that way. We'll head up the block and turn down Iberville Street," Stheno said, completely dismissing Owen and George.

Since Stheno was still holding on to me, I stumbled to keep up. "Be careful, you two," I shouted over my shoulder.

Apartment complexes and parking lots seemed to be the name of the game in this part of New Orleans. I held my tongue for two blocks before I finally asked, "So, what is it with you two?"

"She's an asshole."

"So, you've said. Anything else you'd care to share with the class?"

She shrugged. "I thought we had something good going. She dumped me for a prettier face with more divine relations. That beast comment was a dig. She and her sisters grew from the blood of Titans. My sisters and I were created as monsters, pure and simple. Fuck her," she said, her words dripping in bitterness. "I was her walk on the wild side."

"Oh." I was making her deal with the woman who broke her heart. "I'm really sorry."

"It was a long time ago. I was young and going through an emo phase. That whole dark, brooding thing got to me. Whatever. There have been scores of gorgeous, witty, sexy as hell men and women since. What do I care what that bitch thinks about me?"

We walked another block in silence. Finally, we passed the last apartment building and were crossing the street toward an ancient brick wall surrounding the cemetery. We had to travel another half block before we came to the open, iron-gated entrance.

The water table is too high in New Orleans for anyone to be buried underground. Consequently, their cemeteries were like small cities of the dead. Row after row of tombs, some towering overhead, with ornately sculptured angels shining in the bright light, others barely two feet high and so plain as to be ignored.

"See if you can pull up a map of this place. It'll take forever if we have to check every monument."

"Look at this," she said, pointing to an information plaque by the entrance. "It closes at three."

I checked my watch. "We've got twelve minutes to find the

grave. Then we can hop the wall after they close and we won't have to deal with tourists in our way. This is perfect."

"And what do we do about all those apartment windows staring down on us?" Stheno asked as she gazed up at multiple buildings along one side of the three-block-long cemetery.

Standing with her, I studied the housing outside the walls too. "Most are only two-story. They probably can't see much."

"Enough. They'll see enough." She pulled up a map to the cemetery on her phone. "He's down here. Let's find him before we get tossed."

We turned off the main path and bumped into a walking tour.

"And this," the guide said, "is the grave of Dominique You, a privateer. He served in the French Republic's artillery corps. In 1802, he sailed with General Leclerc to Saint-Domingue to quell a slave revolt. Yellow fever killed many of the soldiers, including the general." He wore khaki shorts and a wide-brimmed straw hat. Unlike the guides I'd passed in the French Quarter, this one didn't use a microphone.

"If any of you are familiar with You's name, it's probably in conjunction with Jean and Pierre Lafitte. In *The Diary of Jean Lafitte*, he was referred to as a brother to the Lafittes. There's no evidence that's true. What we do know is that You was a privateer along with Jean and Pierre."

"What's the difference between a pirate and a privateer?" a teenage boy asked.

The guide grinned. "Very little. A privateer is a pirate sailing under the government's authority. As long as the vessels they plundered were foreign, no one swung from a rope." The guide checked his watch. "This cemetery is closing in a few minutes. Let's all move outside the walls and we'll continue the tour."

Once they were gone, Stheno and I began to study the monument in earnest, searching for anything that might unlock a tunnel entrance. A bell rang. I checked my watch. Damn it.

"Time to go," she said. We waited for the others outside the wall on the far side of the cemetery near a highway underpass.

"Should we text them or something?" I had held out my hand for Stheno's phone when I felt an impact and the brush of a wing. "Meg, anything?"

She popped into existence beside me, wings hidden. "No." She watched Stheno for a moment, her expression unreadable, while Stheno texted away. "Laveau makes no sense. She was about twenty when Jean died. What, he built a tunnel to where her grave was going to be? Besides, that tomb has been gone over by a million different people over the years. If there was something to find, I'd think it would have been found by now."

Well, damn. "You're right. I've been thinking of Bélisaire as younger than Jean and Pierre. He's alive and looks like he's in his thirties while they've been dead for a hundred years." Idiot. Sometimes it was really hard to wrap my mind around people who didn't age. "If he was a contemporary of theirs, why would a tunnel go to the grave of You, who died a few years after Jean?" *Shitdamnfuck.* Dave was right. We were going to need to tear up the bar.

The SUV pulled up to the curb beside us a few minutes later with Owen and George in the back seat. Dave got out and slammed the door, scanning the apartment buildings on the opposite side of the cemetery.

"Sorry, guys," I started when Owen and George joined us on the sidewalk. "Dave was right."

"I usually am. What was I right about this time?"

"The graves. I forget. I—it breaks my brain thinking about you guys living as long as you do."

"Not just us, Scooby," Dave said, arms crossed over his chest. "You stopped aging too."

I was already starting to panic, thinking about our need to break in through the bar. I was not adding my own possible long-ass life into the mix. "Considering what my life's been like recently, I don't think I need to worry about that."

THIRTY-EIGHT

Premature Burial Is a Definite Possibility

"We're here anyway," Dave said, ignoring my comment. "Owen, cast some kind of don't-look-over-here spell so we can hop this wall and do some sleuthing."

Owen cast a spell under his breath and then shrugged. "Never tried that before. I think it worked."

"Good enough," Dave said before grabbing the top of the wall and vaulting over.

I realized only Owen would have trouble jumping over it. George seemed to have come to the same conclusion, so he held Owen tight and leaped. When I was the last one on the sidewalk, I checked to make sure no one was around and then hopped over.

Stheno had led everyone to Dominique You's grave. They were tapping and pushing, trying to find any way in.

"Remember," I said, "they didn't have our strength. They couldn't move a thousand-pound slab." Since there was no room for me around the monument, I studied the names of the people entombed around him.

The ones on either side of You's were quite large, but the one opposite his was plain, easily overlooked. The engraving had been worn by time, the name of the dead lost. Saddened, I crouched down and brushed away surface dirt. If I tilted my head, viewing it from the right angle, the letters appeared.

Nicolas Touze. I tapped the top of the plaque and stood. "Rest well, Nicolas."

"What?" Dave asked.

"Nothing. I was—" I stared at the name. I knew that name. How did I know that name? "Can somebody search the name Nicolas, no H, Touze T-O-U-Z-E? I know this guy from somewhere."

After a few minutes, Owen said, "He built the bar. Lafitte later bought or won it, but Touze actually built it in the early 1700s."

"Huh. Well, isn't that interesting." Could I feel the dead? Not ghosts, not vampires, but those well and truly dead? I cast out and altered what I wanted. I ignored the glowing blips that were far away. I brushed the hazy images of ghosts out of my mind's eye and searched for something else.

And then I realized I was seeing them, the dead. They were the black that made up the void I was gazing into. I narrowed my focus to this section of the cemetery. Each of the monuments held a flat black oval, a portion of the void separated. You's tomb had one. They all did. Except the one I was standing beside. No one rested in Touze's tomb.

"Hey, guys. I think I found our entrance."

It took us twenty minutes to discover that the latch required a series of actions to trigger. Owen, Stheno, and Meg were all going over the stone, inch by inch. Each of them found an area that was smoother than the section around it. Each tried pushing. Nothing.

It was Dave who figured out that they all had to be pressed at the same time. When they did, the top of the tomb opened a hair, releasing stale, musty air. I jumped up and down, clapping, while Dave got his fingers under the lid and slid it to the side. We all gathered around and peered into the gaping maw.

"Does anyone else kind of wish we hadn't found this?" Owen asked. George nodded his agreement.

"I'm smelling earth and damp," I said. Leaning my head through the opening, I tried to block out the daylight, hoping my night vision would kick in. The inky blackness was impenetrable. "I'll go first. If I end up plunging into an icy underground lake filled with prehistoric monsters, I expect someone to throw me a rope."

"Sam," Owen began. "Maybe we should—"

"Too late." I braced my hands on either side of the opening and then dropped through. I hit the ground far sooner than I'd feared. "It smells like magic down here. That must be what's keeping the tunnel mostly dry."

"Is there room for us?" George asked.

The light from above allowed me to see a few feet into the tunnel. I tilted my head back before calling up to them. "Either people used to be a lot shorter or they really enjoyed walking hunched over."

"Shit," Dave said, and I think we all agreed.

"New plan," I said. "I'm going to shift and run through the tunnels. You guys go back, grab a table at the bar, and lay low. When I get there, I'll open the secret doors for you, and then we'll—"

"Rain hell down upon the soulless bloodsuckers!" Stheno bellowed.

"I was going to say rescue Godfrey, but your way works too."

"No," Dave said in a tone that refused discussion. "You are not going alone into an ancient tunnel that could be underwater or collapsed while we drink in a bar."

I gazed down the tunnel warily. I hadn't considered being buried alive in a cave-in. "Seriously, though. It's like five feet tall, maybe three feet wide, at least right here. And it's gotta be a mile to Lafitte's."

The light above was blocked and then Dave was standing next to me. "Close it up," he called. "We'll meet you there."

The stone lid was shoved back into place and Dave and I were plunged into complete darkness.

"Give me your clothes. I'll carry them."

I stripped quickly, handing off my stuff to Dave, and then shifted to my wolf. The darkness was so absolute that night vision didn't help. It was more that I had an impression of where the walls were than an ability to see them. Not wanting to race into an unseen danger, I trotted, all senses on high, while Dave made his way behind me.

My paws padded over the hard-packed earth, occasionally hitting muddy spots where the spell must have been thin. When I hit those spots, I huffed so Dave would be aware something was coming.

About a quarter of a mile in, something ran down the length of my body. Yipping and spinning, I sniffed furiously, growling.

"What is it?" Dave demanded.

I couldn't smell anything out of the ordinary. I took a few hesitant steps back and felt long, thin fingers brushing through my fur. I snapped my jaws around a finger and tore at it. The taste in my mouth was dry and dirty. Spitting it out, I shifted, feeling the top and sides of the tunnel.

"That ought to provide nightmares for years to come. Sorry. There are roots coming through the tunnel walls here."

"Great."

"Shifting back." Stomach growling, I continued, unable to stop the full body cringing every time a long root brushed against me in the dark.

Dave muttered curses ceaselessly behind me. "We're probably under a fucking park."

I stopped right before I went nose-first into a wall of dirt. *Shit.* I shifted and felt what I was dealing with. When I heard Dave draw close, I said, "Hold it. We have a cave-in. Wait. Don't you have your phone?" What the hell? Why didn't he have his flashlight on?

"Yeah."

"Turn it on. Night vision doesn't work in absolute darkness."

"Cover your eyes. It's going to fuck with your sight." The beam lit up the cave-in as well as my naked, scarred body.

I shifted back to wolf as we both studied the wall of dirt. The right side of the tunnel had collapsed, blocking the passage. There was a section, high on the left, that I thought I might be able to squeeze through if it was for a brief time. If it was more than a few feet long, I was pretty sure I'd flip out.

Dave nudged me out of the way and cast the light into the small opening. "I can't see how far it goes. At a guess, it's at least twenty or thirty feet. It might open up at that point or it might be completely collapsed." He rested his hand on my head. "It was a good idea, but we can't keep going. We move the wrong section of dirt and we're looking at a premature burial."

I retreated a few steps and shifted back, my stomach rumble echoing in the quiet. "How do we get him back?"

"We might not. He knew what he was risking. He chose to endanger his immortal life for Clive and Russell. We respect and honor his sacrifice." He pushed out a hard gust of breath. "We're still going to break in and kill all those candy-ass bloodsuckers, but we might not make it in time to save him. Make your peace with it, Sam, because this tunnel plan isn't going to work."

"Where is Henry when I need him?" I didn't want to give up, but the thought of being unable to move, being buried alive, was making me light-headed.

"Who's Henry?" Dave kept his back to me since I was naked and his light was still on.

"The ghost who told me about the tunnel." Maybe he hadn't followed it all the way through. He'd only seen one end of it under Lafitte's bar.

As I brooded about whether or not the ghost had been fucking with me, a hazy form shimmered near me. "Henry?" I'd made this mistake once before.

"Yeah," he said.

"I take it your ghost is with us?" Dave asked.

"Not sure which one, but yes, we have a ghost. If I start choking, give me a minute to shred the asshole."

"It's me," Henry said. "Sorry. I tried to tell you about the cave-in, but I couldn't get it out before I faded." He took my hand, his form taking shape, and stared. "You're naked."

"Unfortunately. Can you see how far this narrow passage goes?"

"Sure. I've been following you for a while. I tried to push you toward the Touze monument. I didn't think it worked, but then you called people over."

"Thanks for the effort." I pointed to the narrow passage. "Can you check?"

He let go and was gone. Dave kept his back to me as we waited.

Henry returned a few minutes later. "It's not far. After this, it's clear to the bar."

"How far is not far?"

"Maybe twenty-five feet."

"He says twenty-five feet and then clear sailing to the bar."

Dave started to stand and then cursed, remembering he couldn't. "I don't like it. We have ghosts trying to kill you, but we're believing this guy. Didn't you say his brother is one of the local vamps? And he appears right after I say we're gonna kill all of them." He shook his head. "I don't trust him."

"It's the truth," Henry said and then faded away.

Shifting back, I laid down and gave a quiet woof so Dave would know. After glancing over his shoulder, he turned and sat next to me, his big hand on my shoulder.

"This isn't smart. I know you're going to try anyway, but I wish you wouldn't."

He was right.

"They've been trying to capture or kill you since—hell, since you were born. The players keep changing, but the goal has been the same. You're going to take the word of this ghost that the passage is clear and short. Even if that's true, we have no idea what's waiting on the other side. And let's say he's telling the whole truth and you make it to the bar; how are you going to get past their security? How are you breaking in?"

Knowing everything he said was absolute truth, I whined. I couldn't turn around and hope for the best. They weren't just going to kill Godfrey. They were going to torture him first. I couldn't live with myself if I didn't try to stop it.

Dave's hand dropped away when I stood. "Fine. Be stubborn. I'll wait here until I can't see or hear you, then I'll head back and meet you at the bar."

Chuffing an agreement, I started to climb the hill of dirt. As piles moved, more rained down from above. I turned my head, found Dave, and barked.

"Nope. I'm standing right here until you make it through."

My paws lost traction as more dirt slid, but I scrambled up quickly and dove into the hole. It was a tight squeeze as I crawled forward on my stomach. I was strong. I could do this. Dirt rained down on me as my head and shoulders dislodged large chunks. Blowing hard, I cleared my nostrils of the soil I was breathing in. If the tunnel collapsed on me, I could power through, digging myself out with long claws.

A hazy mist appeared in front of me, seeming to swoop in from the far side of the cave-in. *Henry?* And then I felt strong hands around my neck, trying to choke me. I flailed, bringing down more earth, burying myself while I struggled.

"Sam!"

I couldn't breathe. My body shook, fear crushing me. I ignored Dave's shouts and stopped moving, focusing instead on the ghost with her arm around my neck. Was she another weaponized ghost sent to kill me, like the one who'd tried to choke me in the bar? I saw her in my mind's eye and imagined my claws shredding her to death. Lungs burning, I sent out a magical pulse, ripping her from this world.

When I could breathe again, I realized I'd been buried. I blew the dirt out of my nose and kept crawling with my eyes closed.

Desperate to free myself, heart hammering, I tried to be calm and logical. If I had to crawl a half mile through this, I could do it. I was doing it.

Dave's shouts followed me. I barked once, to let him know I was okay, and got dirt in my mouth. Head down, I continued to dig my way out until I was tumbling through the air and landing on the hard-packed earth.

I shook myself ferociously, blew dirt out of my nose again, and opened my eyes. Henry was right. The tunnel continued unobstructed. Shifting, I turned back to the fallen passage. A narrow beam of light made it to me.

"Dave! I'm okay! I'm out!"

After some profanity-laced muttering, he shouted back, "Keep going. We'll meet you there."

"Wait. They sealed the tomb before they left. How are you going to get out?" I could shift and start digging again, but I'd probably bring the whole tunnel down this time.

"Keep going. I can move a slab of stone."

"But—"

"Go!"

And then the light went out, plunging me back into unrelieved darkness.

THIRTY-NINE

Wherein Sam Learns That Personal Charnel Houses Are a Thing

The rest of the passage was clear and easy. I trotted through more than a few sections under a half-foot of water, so I wasn't sure how long the magic would continue holding, but for right now, I was getting through.

The tunnel finally opened into a large, cavern-like room. Barely perceptible light seeped through boards above, enabling me to pick out details. Crates and barrels were stacked in the corner, but it didn't seem as though anyone had been down here in a very long time. Once Storyville was closed, once Prohibition ended, there probably hadn't been a need for the underground tunnel.

Rickety stairs led somewhere on the far side of the cavern. Closer was a slide or a chute. This was probably how the crates and barrels were moved down here. Peering up, I tried to find an entrance to the bar, but I couldn't make anything out.

Shifting back to human, my stomach grumbled again. I was putting my body through too much. Also, I was way too naked to be taking on bad guys. The stairs creaked as I hesitantly climbed. One stair cracked underneath me, but I'd been holding the rails and leaped to the next stair before it collapsed.

When I reached the platform at the top, I searched for a way in. There was no door, no locks, no keypads. The storage room had been abandoned and I was faced with a solid brick wall. Unleashing my claws, I tore at the mortar between the bricks, hoping to find a weak spot. It worked, but only a few crumbling pieces at a time. This would take all night.

The chute it was. I scrambled back down the rotting stairs and studied what I could see of the slide. The chute had a hood starting about ten feet up. I couldn't see beyond that.

The boards of the slide were rotting in places, splintered in others. If I'd still been wearing shoes, I'd have chanced it. As it was, I shifted back to wolf, more slowly than normal. The constant shifting was wearing me out. I needed a huge meal and sleep. Since neither were in my near future, I climbed the slide, claws digging into the wood.

When I got to the top, wedged between the slide and the inside of the hood, I found another wall. This one was wood, though, not brick. Bracing myself as best I could, I used my front paws to tear at the wood. A few rotted boards crumbled but others held.

Shifting one paw to an arm, I punched at the board until it broke and then yanked the broken pieces out. Behind the boards was another wall, though this one appeared to be more like sheetrock. Hoping for the best, I punched again and didn't end up with a busted hand.

The inner wall gave way easily. I gouged a hole big enough to squeeze through and found myself in a dark room filled with rotting corpses and scattered bones. A full-body shiver ran through me. I'd found where they dumped the bodies of their victims.

My paws slid off decomposing skin as I tried, as gingerly as possible, to step around the moldering bodies. It was a losing battle, though. There were too damn many, the bastards.

Something covered my nose as another strong arm wrapped around my neck, choking me. Damn it. Why the hell were they working for their killers? Exhausted, I tried to shred it like I had the last ones, but my claws went right through it. Too many shifts, too many psychic battles. I was drained.

Suddenly, the ghostly muzzle was off and I could breathe. What—and then I saw her. The ghost I'd rescued from the Ursuline Convent was here, grappling with the other ghosts. She made short work of them. She was a strong one, all right.

Shifting again, slowly, I eventually stood before my rescuer. "Thank you." I rubbed my sore throat. "They always go for the neck. Assholes."

Nodding, she inclined her head toward me in response, I assumed in thanks for freeing her.

"Okay." I slapped my hands together, strangely revitalized at having someone new on my side. "Let's get the heck out of here."

Studying the walls, what I didn't see was a door. There had to be a way out of the mass grave. Unless this was a *"Cask of Amontillado"* deal, there had to be some kind of entrance, if for no other reason than to throw bodies down here. Throw bodies… I glanced at my fading ghost friend and saw her pointing up. There was a hatch in the ceiling.

It was only about eight feet up. I could jump that. Crouching, I held my hands fisted over my head and leaped. I'd expected a lock or a bar to keep the hatch closed. Apparently, they weren't worried about the zombie apocalypse. The hatch flew open and I landed on the carpeted floor next to the hole.

Listening intently, I could hear voices and glasses clinking. I was close. Peering back through the hatch, I searched for my new friend. She'd faded again, so I kicked the hatch closed and padded down the darkened hallway, on the hunt for secret passages. I turned a corner and found a metal door with a keypad. Casting out, I searched for the vamps and found them all on the other side of this door. Hidden lair found, I needed to locate my friends and my clothes.

At the end of the hall was another door. This one was like the panel in Clive's room that led to the sidepiece bedroom. There was probably a release button somewhere close that allowed this section of the wall to open. I felt all around the door, the wall, the ceiling, the panel itself. Nothing.

Getting down on my hands and knees, I studied the carpet, searching for a spot more worn than the rest. I was close to giving up when my fingertips felt the depression. I pushed at the worn spot and the panel released. Sound from the bar increased. The door was still closed, but if I pulled, it'd open.

Scrambling up, I used a fingernail to pull the panel open, peering through the small break. A woman walked by and I almost jumped out of my skin. A toilet flushed nearby, and I knew where I was: the hall to the restrooms.

Waiting until it was silent outside the bathrooms, I whisper-shouted, "Dave! Stheno! Meg! George!" They all had hearing like my own. Hopefully, someone heard me over all the noise of the bar.

Straining, I heard a tentative, "Sam?"

"Yes! The passage is in the restroom hallway. Get over here and bring my clothes."

A minute later, five people were rushing for the bathroom. I opened the panel and ushered them in before anyone saw.

"Please, tell me someone brought me—"

Dave handed me my clothes and a wrapped sandwich. Hallelujah! They kept their backs to me while I dressed. It wasn't until now that I realized how filthy I was. To my elbows and shins, I was covered in dried mud and things I didn't want to think about again. Ever. The rest of me looked as though I'd been dragged through dirt, which I guess I had been. My hair was a long, tangled mess, since hair ties fall out when you shift.

I dove into my clothes and then sat to put on my shoes and eat. "You can turn around now," I said as I put on a sock. "And thanks for the food. I'm starving."

"I know. The sound of your stomach growling in the tunnel was deafening." Dave was down the hall, checking out the keypad on the door to the vamp lair, Meg beside him.

"You're a mess, kid." Stheno finger-combed my hair and then started to French braid it.

"You know how to do that?"

"You'd be amazed the shit you pick up over thousands of years."

Once my shoes were on, I tried to force myself not to inhale the sandwich. It was a large sub, double high with meat, and it was glorious. I made sure to hold it so my fingers only touched the paper it was wrapped in because... of reasons I was never going to think about. I meant it, damn it!

"Dave said you had to burrow through a cave-in to get here. Any other problems on the way?" Owen sat on the floor across from me, George at his side.

Swallowing, taking a breath, I put down the sandwich for a moment. "A couple of ghosts tried to kill me—"

"Her neck." Owen sounded more upset than I felt.

I was too exhausted to care about anything but food and an eventual nap. "But the tunnel itself was fine. A few wet spots where the spell was giving out. Once I got to the cavern below, though, I was stuck. There was a brick wall at the top of these rotting stairs, so that was a no go."

"How did you get in?" George asked.

I took another bite and then answered. "There was a chute for barrels and crates to get down there. I crawled up that and found another wall, but that one was wood. I busted through and ended up in their on-site charnel house."

The expression on George's face was priceless.

"Exactly. I had to walk over... things I'll never think of again and then jump through the hatch in the roof." I was going to tell them about the ghost girl from the convent, but I wanted to eat. Taking another big bite, I watched Dave walk around the corner, no doubt hunting for the bone room.

Having properly horrified Owen and George, I finished the sandwich. It was nowhere near enough, but it helped immensely. I jumped to my feet, ready to begin our rescue mission.

"Hey, what time is it anyway?" I walked to the security panel Meg was studying. "How long did that take me?"

Dave walked back around the corner, patting me on the shoulder. "Sunset's in about twenty minutes."

"That's a problem. Clive can get up before sunset." *Shit-shitshit.*

"That's Clive. These guys aren't Clive." Dave turned his attention to Meg. "Any ideas?"

"Hard to tell. Bloodsuckers don't have oils on their fingers. I have to go with the keys that seem more worn than the others. At a guess, I'd say it's the numbers one, four, and nine."

"One, four, nine," Owen echoed. "A, D, I… aid, dia? It could be a French word. Maybe an acronym?"

"Some of those numbers could be doubled too," Stheno suggested. "Like 1941 or 1494. Do we know any significant dates in Lafitte's life?"

"Jean or Bélisaire?" George asked, prompting frustrated curses around the room.

"Or," I began, remembering my research, "it could be this address. 941 Bourbon Street."

"Sam," Stheno said, grinning, "if you weren't filthy, I'd kiss you."

Meg had her fingers poised before the security keypad. "Everybody ready?"

I released my claws and moved to the front of the group, nose inches from the door. Dave muscled in next to me. Owen's hands were moving as he readied a spell. Stheno stayed to the back.

"I'm lifting the eye patch," she said. "No one look at me from here on out."

"No problem," Meg muttered as she keyed in the code.

The door slid open, revealing a large, dark room. The dim light in the hall illuminated little in here. "Meg, stay on the door so we have the light and can get out," I whispered.

The rest of us slowly made our way into the room. I felt like that idiot in the horror movie Stheno had been watching when we'd arrived in New Orleans. I was trying to be stealthy in a dark room filled with vampires. I really didn't want to end my life as a juice box.

Vamps were sitting on couches and lying on the floor. Knowing they could pop up and attack at any moment had me jumping at shadows. Stepping over vamps, I searched for Godfrey. It wasn't that large of a room. Where the hell *was* he?

I flinched at the tap on my shoulder. Dave's big arm pointed to the far corner, where a body was hanging. Hurrying around furniture and dormant vamps, we made our way to the corner and found a badly beaten Godfrey hanging from shackles.

I pulled at the cuff on his left hand but couldn't move the metal. Dave grabbed the right cuff and pulled, muscles straining. After a moment, the silent room was filled with the sound of metal squealing and then Godfrey's right hand fell limp at his side.

Dave moved to the left side and did the same. Godfrey had a thick chain around his neck. There was no way Dave would be able to bust through that.

"Owen," I whispered, "do you have a spell for loosening this chain?"

"I got it," George said. He set a chair down beside Godfrey, hopped up on the seat, and grabbed the chain in both large hands, biceps bulging. An ear-piercing screech filled the room as George busted the thick links.

Godfrey fell forward but I caught him. Dave and George made short work of the cuffs around his ankles, and then George was carrying Godfrey out of the room.

"Do we back out or do we start taking heads?"

No one had a chance to answer before a door on the far side of the room slid open. Amélie stood in the dim light, two vamps beside her. "Rise, my children. Enemies are among us."

FORTY

Flying Heads Have Become No Less Disconcerting

Almost as one, the vamps rose and attacked in a full-fanged frenzy. Stheno scored our first kills, turning two to stone at the jump. Almost immediately, another one jumped on her back, arms around her neck, poised to rip off her head. Meg was there, iron-tipped scourge in hand. With a flick, the vamp was ripped from Stheno's back and was missing the flesh from his head.

"Owen, get out of here!" I didn't think his magic could save him from this.

Meg, in all her winged glory, moved back to the door, protecting Owen, bloody whip in taloned hand, ready to kill any vamp who tried to escape. Owen ducked under a wing and stood behind her, casting his spells.

Dave roared and pulled a vamp's arms off before twisting the head off as well. Stheno caught another vamp in the eye, freezing him on the spot. I, on the other hand, made my way toward Amélie. When she was down, the rest would stop. Probably.

A vamp leaped toward me and I swiped my claws across his neck, sending his head flying. George and Dave were working in tandem. George, cut and bloodied, used his overwhelming strength to crush vamps before tossing them to a battered Dave, who set them alight.

The battle raged on, with vampires slashing and biting all within reach. They seemed to be coordinating a campaign of weakening us through blood loss. At one point, both Dave and George each had two vampires clinging to their backs, trying to behead them. Owen screamed from the hall, making my heart clench. I sliced through the neck of the vamp flying at me and then turned, terrified I was about to lose a friend. Dave reached up and unerringly grabbed both vamps by their necks. I watched as each was slowly blanketed in flames, ash settling to the floor around him.

George, since he didn't have his demon counterpart's gift with fire, threw himself back, slamming into the table behind him and knocking loose the vamps who were trying to behead him. Like a flash, he flipped over and drilled his fists straight through the vamps' heads, his powerful dragon muscles making mush of the vamps' faces. Owen cheered as George tore the head off each.

Stheno high-beamed another one as Meg took out any within reach of her scourge. Having the two of them saved us. The vamps had to keep their distance from Meg and their eyes closed. Without them, we wouldn't have had a fighting chance against twenty vamps.

A vamp tried to make it to the door, but with one flick of Meg's scourge, the clothes and flesh were torn from the vamp's body. Surveying the pile of skeletal vamps in front of her, Meg threw back her head with a screeching war cry.

A vamp jumped on my back, teeth in my neck and hands tearing at my face. I stabbed my claws through his head and yanked him over my shoulder. Holding him in place with one set of claws, I used the other to swipe through his neck. Blood dripped into my eye as I searched the room for Amélie.

She shoved her two guards toward me and then retreated into the secret room. Before the door secured behind her, I saw a blur and then one of the guards crumpled to the ground, head rolling to my feet. I only had a split second to wonder who got that one before the second attacked. Leaping toward him, I dragged my claws across his chest, spun, and took his head on my next turn.

"Pretty," Dave said admiringly.

"If by pretty you mean vicious, hell yeah. Nicely done, kid." Stheno patted my back while I wiped the blood from my face.

"Everybody okay?" I frantically counted the upright. Were all my people alive and well?

Owen searched for the light switch while Meg beheaded the fleshless vamps at her feet. When the overhead light—a chandelier, naturally—flicked on, we saw the carnage around us. Antiques smashed, gold-flocked walls spattered while blood dripped from the crystals above.

"Who used a table leg to stake a vamp?"

"Asshole wouldn't look at me," Stheno complained.

Along with the piles of ash, dust, and clothes, we had lots of vamp bodies. Amélie must have been down to her youngest people. And she'd left them to fend for themselves while she hid.

"Amélie's still alive, or undead anyway. She's in that room," Owen said, pointing to the section of the wall that had opened earlier.

Dave kicked the headless corpse in his way. "I'd say let's throw these guys down the hole with their victims, but I don't want to touch them."

"Right there with you," George said.

I'd made my way to the section of wall Amélie had disappeared behind, searching for the security panel. It appeared to be a smooth, papered wall, like the other four. Casting out, I searched for Amélie. I didn't want us to waste time trying to get through the door only to discover she had a back way out.

Closing my eyes, I sought out the cold, glowing blip of a vamp. It was difficult to see beyond the wall though, my brain sluggish. I desperately needed sleep. Faintly, finally, I sensed two blips.

"I only saw Amélie retreat. Did someone go with her? There are two vamps behind the wall." I tapped the wallpaper under my hand.

"It was only Amélie," Owen confirmed. "I was watching."

"Maybe there had been four in the room originally, but only three had shown themselves?" George ventured.

"Possible. Either way, they're both still in there. So, how do we get in?"

We all started running our hands over the wall, trying to locate a catch or a depression, anything that would trigger the release. After long minutes of fruitless searching, battle adrenaline waning, we gave up.

"It could be a remote she carries," I offered.

"She's gotta come out at some point," Dave said, dropping onto a nearby couch. "We'll wait her out."

Not finding anything, the others roamed around the room. Meg studied what was left of the manacles that had recently held Godfrey while Stheno went through dead vamps' pockets.

Owen drew George out into the hall and had him sit so he could treat his wounds. Owen's head suddenly pivoted to the right. "Hey, when did you get here?"

We'd all turned to the hall when the wall slid open right behind me. *Shit!* Spinning, claws out, I barely managed to stop myself before taking Clive's head. Then I realized his hand was holding my wrist six inches from his neck. Yeah, his reflexes were definitely faster than mine.

Unruffled, he grinned. "Darling, mind the claws."

I threw myself into his arms, knowing it was finally over.

"How the hell were you in there?" Dave demanded.

Clive ran his hand down my back, comforting me. "I can wake before nightfall, if pressed. When I was close, I sensed Godfrey like a homing beacon. I arrived as Amélie was closing the door."

"You were the one who beheaded the guard." Of course. I knew he was fast, but that was ridiculous. "I take it Amélie is no longer among the living-ish?"

"You take it correctly. Russell," Clive called, "how is Godfrey?"

Russell had an arm around Godfrey as he helped him walk through the door. Neither was looking his best at the moment.

"There has to be a blood fridge in here. You two need some help healing," I said. Russell was much better than last night, but still. Godfrey, on the other hand, appeared to be barely clinging to his undeath.

Godfrey pointed to a panel near the door. Clive swung it open and brought out blood bags for him and his men, two each for Russell and Godfrey.

Owen walked in a few minutes later carrying beer, water, and soda.

"How'd you do that?" I asked.

"George waited at the door for me while I went out for provisions." After passing out the drinks, he pulled a bag of chips out of his pocket and threw it to me.

"You're a prince among men," I said, tearing open the bag.

"Can you tell us what happened?" Clive asked. "Russell has no memory of being captured. He said he was standing on the street in front of the townhouse and then he was in a cell."

Godfrey finished his second blood bag and then spoke. "Amélie bragged about having St. Germain in her pocket because he could fog a vampire's mind the way we can a human's. The problem, of course, was that he was entirely unstable. She crowed that he'd been able to slip into some of our people's minds to turn them against you. The goal, obviously, being Sam. Destabilize the power structure in San Francisco and we're too busy to notice our lone wolf is missing. Give the sadist his wolf and she takes New Orleans."

"Yes," Russell said. "The vampires who beat me kept asking about Sam. There was a desperation behind their brutality. She must have been worried it was all falling apart. We'd taken out most of the nocturne she wanted to lead. And then she lost the lynchpin: Sam. No wonder."

"Which meant," Clive said, "she needed you to push me toward killing Lafitte for her and then separate Sam from me."

Godfrey nodded. "Loyal, she's not, but she has a chess player's mind. She lost it last night. Clive was missing, Russell had escaped, and instead of Sam being tortured by St. Germain, he was dead and Sam was gone." He tried to laugh but the pain cut it short.

"She had a wicche, a Voodoo priest—I don't know—on the payroll," Godfrey continued. "He sent the ghosts after you," he said to me. "He called last night, tipped her off about Clive being alive, and thus began my evening of torture."

I moved to them and placed a kiss first on Russell's cheek and then on Godfrey's. "Thank you. You both endured unspeakable pains to protect me. Clive, you're sworn to protect. Me, not so much. And yet you did. Thank you."

"It is held that valor is the chiefest virtue, and most dignifies the haver," Clive said.

Godfrey shook his head and elbowed Russell. "He's quoting Shakespeare at us now. We'd prefer raises, maybe a couple of nice villas in Tuscany," he joked.

"Done." Clive slid his arm around me and kissed the cut over my eye, stopping the blood, and then glanced around the room at the carnage. "Lafitte is no more. Amélie has been vanquished. St. Germain has been given true death. We can't go home, though, and leave New Orleans without a Master."

"Mathieu," I said. "He's the local Alpha. He's smart, fair, and tough. He'd make a great Master."

Nodding, Clive said, "Yes. That would work well. I can point him to the other werewolf Masters in the US, if he'd like advice. Perhaps it would be better, though, if you broached the subject with him. I'm sure he'd rather discuss it with his queen than a filthy bloodsucker." Leaning back, he took me in from head to toe. "Speaking of filthy, have you been playing in mud puddles?"

"Long story. I'll tell you about it later." I *really* wanted a long, hot shower, a huge meal, and an extended sleep. In that order.

"Fair enough. What say we depart premises and head back to the townhouse? As much as I'd love to fly home tonight, it makes sense to stay an extra day and get everything settled before we put New Orleans behind us."

He paused a moment. "There's no reason for all of you to stay, though. Sam and I need to, but if the rest of you would like to leave now, my plane is at your disposal."

"George and I have never been here, so we'd like to sightsee tomorrow," Owen said.

Wiping blood from his bald head, Dave added, "I'll stick."

The others nodded their agreement.

When I woke the following day, I kissed a sleeping Clive, rolled out of bed, hit the shower again, and was ready for my last day in the Big Easy. Aside from the near-constant threat of imminent death, I loved this town.

Recruiting Dave's help, I had him drive us to the Crescent City Pack house. They were still cleaning up from their vamp attack. Mathieu turned as we came around the last bend in the road. Dave and I climbed out. He went to help a man struggling under the weight of a destroyed metal bay door and I walked to Mathieu.

"Is everyone okay?"

Mathieu shook his head. "They attacked right after sundown. We'd been warned." He glanced away from his people for a moment to regard me. "I have a psychic on retainer. She called when we were in the bar with you and Stheno." Shaking his head, he returned his focus to his people.

"We called." He gestured at the warehouse. "But they didn't

have time to get everyone out. We still had two adolescents, who'd been helping to barricade windows, racing down the road when the bloodsuckers attacked. They were the first to be killed." Mathieu crossed himself and said a silent prayer.

"I'm sorry." I rested a hand on his shoulder and he clutched it.

"It was a diversion. There were only three of them. They killed our children and then caused as much damage as they could to keep us busy. When Gabriel and I arrived, we found three more of our wolves dead and one pile of bloodsucker dust. The last two circled us, like they were planning to fight, and then they disappeared into the night."

I didn't know what to say. *Sorry* didn't begin to cover the death of five of his pack members. "I'm not sure if this is good news or not, but the position of Master of New Orleans has recently opened up."

Everyone in the yard stopped what they were doing and turned. People inside the warehouse strode out, focused on Mathieu and me.

"And we thought you might want to fill it." Mathieu blinked at my words, face blank. "I mean, if you'd rather keep to yourselves, I get it. All the powerful vamps are dust, though, and I think this town could use a Master who actually protected *all* the supernaturals."

Like a match to gunpowder, the mood in the pack exploded from mourning to rejoicing. Howls and whoops filled the air as Mathieu allowed himself a small smile. Gabriel came around the side of the pack house and pounded his Alpha on the back, a huge grin splitting his face.

"I have no idea how any of this stuff works, but Clive said he'd pass along the names of other werewolf Masters in case you wanted any advice." Before I turned to go, I pointed at Gabriel. "And Stheno is waiting to hear from you."

"We're getting together tonight, but thanks for passing along the message." He winked, and I could only hope they both survived the experience.

Dave was waiting for me by the SUV. "All right, gentlemen. Take care and if you're ever in San Francisco, stop by The Slaughtered Lamb to see me." Waving, I got in and Dave drove us to our next stop: the nocturne.

I'd promised myself I'd come back before I left. I knew it probably wouldn't be any different than before, but I had to try. As we drove down the long lane, sheltered by a line of huge oaks, I asked Dave to wait in the SUV for me. I wanted to walk the old plantation grounds by myself.

Parking in front of the big house, he waved me off. I hopped out and followed the dirt path back toward what had been the slave quarters. Stopping within view of the cabins, I sat. This world wasn't mine. I didn't pretend to understand the pain and indignity that had bled into this ground. But, like at the LaLaurie house, I opened my senses to the spirits of the enslaved trapped here, offering a conduit to a better place.

I'm not sure how long I sat, eyes closed, arms open. It was quite some time before I felt the hazy shapes of the dead moving toward me. Eventually some came to take what I offered, but not all. Of course not all. Hope and trust had been destroyed long ago. Before I left, I put both hands on the dirt path and sent out a pulse of magic, of healing, contrition, and peace.

When I circled around the big house, I found Dave leaning against the driver's door. He opened his arms and I walked into his burly hug.

"I could feel what you were doing. You're getting better at this stuff." He patted my back and ignored the fact that his shirt was getting wet.

Sniffling, I wiped my face dry and headed to the other side of the car. "Self-taught."

"We need to find you a teacher." He got in and started the engine.

"You're telling me. I'm making this up as I go along. I need some peace and quiet so I can at least read my necromancy books."

Dave chuckled. "Good luck with that. So," he said, turning onto the main road, "where to next?"

"I'm done. Do you want to pick up a souvenir for Maggie?" His banshee girlfriend and I hadn't started off on the best of terms. In her defense, though, she'd thought I was sleeping with her man. So, understandable.

We wandered the Quarter for a bit and ran into Owen and George. I took Dave to the jewelry store with the amazing rings in the window. He went in to shop while the guys and I chatted, sucking down to-go cocktails.

Dave emerged empty-handed but with a suspicious lump in his pocket. After picking up a few bags of beignets, we headed back to the townhouse to pack. The sun would be setting soon and then we'd be flying home. I couldn't wait to see the progress on my Slaughtered Lamb.

Clive was still asleep so I pulled out my suitcase and starting stuffing clothes in. My leathers were trashed, but hopefully I could find a place back home that could fix them. When I walked out of the bathroom, toiletries collected, I found Clive sitting on the side of the bed.

I stuffed the last of my things in the suitcase and then walked over and sat next to him. He took my hand, squeezing hard, as he leaned in and kissed me. The kiss heated up quickly and when it finally broke, I realized I'd crawled up onto his lap. Embarrassed, I tried to move, but he held me right where I was.

"How was your day?"

"Good. Mathieu and the pack are pretty stoked about fewer vamps in New Orleans."

"It won't last long. More will move in, but I hope they enjoy it while they can. What else?"

I needed to ask him about that memory I'd seen in St. Germain's head. I was sick to my stomach, though, dreading the answer.

"Sam?"

"When I was slogging my way through a multitude of depravities in St. Germain's mind, I saw you."

He tilted his head, waiting.

"He was in a torch-lit stone room. He had a woman strapped down and was gleefully eviscerating her. Giggling—and, God, he's terrifying when he giggles—he invited someone to play with him. When I turned to see who he was talking to, I saw you."

Clive nodded slowly. "I remember. It was Paris, in the… eighteenth century, I believe. The woman on the table was Rémy's maker. Remember I told you to ask me about the harrowing story of how I met Rémy? Élise, the woman you saw, had insulted St. Germain. That's why she was still alive as he played with her intestines."

When I shuddered, he rubbed a hand up and down my back. "Suzette, a friend at the time"—at my glare, he kissed the tip of my nose—"asked me to find Élise, who was maker to both her and Rémy. I discovered them as you saw in the memory." He sighed. "At the time, he had no defense against me, against what I can do with my mind. While he writhed on the floor, I made him promise to keep a tighter rein on his proclivities or I would give him his true death. To behave as he did was to expose us all to discovery. I gathered Élise and returned her to her nocturne. I have no idea if she survived. I left Paris shortly thereafter."

Huh. "What did she look like?"

He studied the ceiling a moment, thinking. "As I recall, she was petite and brunette. Innocent, almost childlike in her aspect. Why?"

I shrugged. "Trying to find our blonde-haired woman."

"Ah. Considering I saved her undead life, I'd think she'd be more inclined to help me rather than plot against me."

"What about Suzette? Maybe Élise died and Suzette blames you."

A leer flashed before he sobered up. "Doubtful. We've run

across each other quite a few times over the years and she's never been angry with me. Besides, she's a tall redhead."

"It's like you're begging me to stab you," I muttered as I tried to stand up and put some distance between us.

Clive wouldn't let go, though. "Sam," he murmured, his lips hitting that spot behind my ear that drove me nuts. No. Screw him and his endless parade of gorgeous women. Crossing my arms over my chest, I decided to wait him out and then finish packing. When his fangs slid down my neck, I went limp and gave up. Stupid, sexy vamp.

"We'll figure it out," he said between kisses. "Meanwhile, I want to hear about you and your day."

Blowing out a breath, I continued my recitation of the day, "The guys and I wandered around the Quarter. Dave was supposed to be getting Maggie a gift. He *says* he didn't get anything, but I think he's a big ol' liar."

Clive grinned. "Speaking of gifts for women we love," he said, reaching into his nightstand drawer, "I have something for you." He held up a small, red leather jewelry box. When I stared at it, he rolled his eyes and opened it himself.

It was the ring from the store I'd taken Dave to, the one I'd fallen in love with on the first night. A large square-cut indigo opal, iridescent blues and greens racing across the stone, framed by two sparkling triangular diamonds. It took my breath away.

"It has long been obvious to me that I simply cannot do without you, not well, not happily." He took a deep, unnecessary breath. "This is rather unnerving. I've never done this before," he grumbled. "Yes, so, I love you is the thing. I don't foresee a time when I will ever not love you. That being the case." He took the ring from the box and held it up. "You can have it either way, but will you marry me?"

Dear Reader

Thank you for reading ***The Dead Don't Drink at Lafitte's***. If you enjoyed Sam and Clive's second adventure together, please consider leaving a review or chatting about it with your book-loving friends. Good word of mouth means everything when you're a new writer!

Love,
Seana

Acknowledgments

First, let me thank you, the readers. I started writing The Slaughtered Lamb thirteen years ago. I was pregnant, the doctors saw problems, and I shunned reality, diving deep into all things fantasy. I read obsessively and then I started to write. Sam and The Slaughtered Lamb were there for me when I needed them. There's an adage in writing: Throw away the first book. It's crap. Consider it practice as you learn how to write. I couldn't, though. Sam had saved my sanity. I wasn't going to abandon her because an a-hole of an agent I'd met early on told me he didn't even need to read it to know it was garbage. I ignored him and rewrote the book more times than I can count, learning and getting better with each version. So, thank you for buying and reading Sam's story. Your kind support and lovely reviews mean I get to keep telling Sam's story.

Thank you to my gifted, hilarious friend and critique partner C.R. Grissom. This poor woman has read ever iteration of everything I've ever written. She also introduced me to Nora Roberts books, so there's eternal gratitude on multiple fronts. She writes charming, heartfelt, sexy sports romances set in college. Do yourself a favor and pick-up *Mouthful,* the first in her series.

Thank you to my beta readers! Roseann Rasul, who was a mentor when I started teaching and then a first reader when I began writing, always gives me the nuanced feedback I need. Norma Jean Bell, a former student who spent much of her free time talking about books with me in the library, has become a gloriously wonderful adult who is still willing to talk books with me. The only difference is that some of the books are mine.

Thank you to my family! My parents Phil and Barbara Kelly could not be more excited and proud. I got my dad a ball cap with The Slaughtered Lamb logo. He wears it all the time so he can tell strangers about his daughter's books. My mom goes the other way and is quietly tearful. Thank you to Greg and the girls who are endlessly supportive, ready to cheer every milestone, whether they understand its significance or not. I have been blessed with you.

Thank you to my wonderful editor, Peter Senftleben, an incredibly talented and insightful editor who understands there's a person on the other side of that editorial letter. When I read his feedback, I'm excited to get back to work. Thank you to Susan Helene Gottfried for taking a huge load of my mind. Her proofreading expertise means my book reviews won't be filled with comments like, *Has she ever met a comma she didn't like?*

Thank you to the amazing team at NYLA! Natanya Wheeler, a goddess among women, has made every step of this process easier for me. Cheryl Pientka, a super star, made sure the Sam Quinn stories were also available as audiobooks. My fabulously brilliant agent Sarah Younger understood how much this story meant to me and never stopped trying to bring it to the world.

<u>Want more books from Seana?</u>

If you'd like to be the first to learn what's new with Sam and Clive (and Owen and Dave and Stheno…), please sign up for my newsletter *Tales from the Book Nerd*. It's filled with writing news, deleted scenes, giveaways, book recommendations, and my favorite cocktail and book pairings.

The Slaughtered Lamb Bookstore & Bar
Sam Quinn, book 1

Welcome to The Slaughtered Lamb Bookstore and Bar. I'm Sam Quinn, the werewolf book nerd in charge. I run my business by one simple rule: Everyone needs a good book and a stiff drink, be they vampire, wicche, demon, or fae. No wolves, though. Ever. I have my reasons.

I serve the supernatural community of San Francisco. We've been having some problems lately. Okay, I'm the one with the problems. The broken body of a female werewolf washed up on my doorstep. What makes sweat pool at the base of my spine, though, is realizing the scars she bears are identical to the ones I conceal. After hiding for years, I've been found.

A protection I've been relying on is gone. While my wolf traits are strengthening steadily, the loss also left my mind vulnerable to attack. Someone is ensnaring me in horrifying visions intended to kill. Clive, the sexy vampire Master of the City, has figured out how to pull me out, designating himself my personal bodyguard. He's grumpy about it, but that kiss is telling a different story. A change is taking place. It has to. The bookish bartender must become the fledgling badass.

I'm a survivor. I'll fight fang and claw to protect myself and the ones I love. And let's face it, they have it coming.

The Wicche's Glass Tavern
Sam Quinn, book 3

Whether I've learned enough or not, the time has come. I need to face off with my aunt, the woman who's been trying to kill me ever since I was a baby. In her mind, I'm an abomination. My father's werewolf blood sullied the long, pure line of Corey wicches. Whereas I think she's a total psycho who trucks with demons to get what she wants. Unfortunately, what she wants is my death.

I've put together the Fellowship of the Sam, with werewolves, vampires, wicches, a gorgon, a Fury, a half-demon, a couple of dragon-shifters, and the fae. It'll be one hell of a battle. Hopefully, San Francisco will still be standing when we're done.

And for something completely different…
Welcome Home, Katie Gallagher
This romantic comedy was my first book published. Remember, don't judge a book by its (truly hideous) cover.

Nobody said a fresh start would be easy

A clean slate is exactly what Katie Gallagher needs, and Bar Harbor, Maine, is the best place to get it. Except the cottage her grandmother left her is overrun with woodland creatures, and the police chief, Aiden Cavanaugh, seems determined to arrest her! Katie had no idea she'd broken his heart fifteen years ago…

Um, What the Hell?

The new engagement ring sparkled as I wiped down the already gleaming bar. Today was the day. My Slaughtered Lamb Bookstore and Bar was reopening. The construction crew had done much of the work while we'd been in New Orleans. It wasn't the same. It'd never be the same, but The Slaughtered Lamb 2.0 gleamed in the light of the setting sun.

Thankfully, the wolves who had destroyed the original hadn't compromised the window wall looking out over the San Francisco Bay and Pacific Ocean. Seawater splashed against the thick glass. Kelp bobbed and swirled as large fish swam by.

"Hey, boss. I put away those last two carts of books. Got a call, though. We have another shipment being delivered tonight." Owen, my friend, assistant, and wicche extraordinaire, was helping me get ready before we opened up for the first time in two months. "The shelves are pretty light, but they'll be full soon."

Dave, my half-demon cook, came out of the kitchen carrying a plate of treats. He knew me so well. When he dropped the chocolate, coconut, caramel bars in front of me, Owen dove for the plate as Dave turned back to the kitchen.

"Wait. Don't you want a drink?" I held up his preferred brand of cinnamon schnapps.

He paused at the swinging doors and glanced over his shoulder. Dave's shark-like black eyes zeroed in on the bottle in my hand. "Later. I don't want that scent in my head while I'm cooking." The door swung closed a moment later.

"Have you been in the kitchen yet? Do you know what he's making?" Owen snatched the bottle from my hand and returned it to its spot in the colorful, sparkling wall of cascading bottles behind the bar, aligning it so the label faced perfectly forward, as he had with every other bottle on the wall.

"No idea. I've been banished from the kitchen today." I took a bite of the five-layer bar and groaned.

"Makes it difficult to get to your apartment if you're not allowed in the kitchen." Owen glanced around the bar for anything that needed doing. I knew because I'd been doing the same thing all day.

I'd been in business for seven years before my home had to be gutted and rebuilt. This wasn't my first day on the job, but I was nervous as hell. Instead of opening at noon, as we normally did, we had postponed the grand reopening to five in the evening to make more of a party of it.

Checking my watch, I admitted, if only to myself, the fear that had been keeping me awake. What if no one came? It had been months. Habits changed. Maybe they'd found new places to hang out that they liked better.

"It's time," Owen said.

Nodding, I pasted on a smile, braced for silence, and opened the wards protecting my bookstore and bar. A moment later, many footsteps pounded down the stairs and something tight and scared in me disappeared. Owen grinned, kissed me on the cheek, and went to greet our customers.

First in was Grim, the aptly named dwarf who had been

sitting at the last seat at the bar every evening since I'd first opened. He wasn't a drunk. He was a man who enjoyed a tankard of mead at the end of the day. As he hopped onto his regular stool, I slid the tankard in front of him. And just like that, things were back to normal.

The bar filled quickly, with patrons overflowing into the connected bookstore. They collected scattered chairs and positioned them around a sofa in front of the glass wall. I wasn't the only one excited to see and talk with friends.

The first hour was a rush. People who never would have thought to hug Sam 1.0 were squeezing my hands, embracing me, even kissing me on the cheek. To say the last few months had been life-altering was not an exaggeration. Whether by necessity or design, I'd kept myself separate, isolated. And now… well, right now, Owen's gorgeous boyfriend George was swinging me in a circle as his sister Coco shook her head, a grin pulling at her lips.

Not as tall as George, she had his broad shoulders, warm brown skin, and piercing green eyes. She was also a recovering alcoholic, which was why she had never visited before. Once George had set me back on my feet, Coco shook my hand.

"It's even more beautiful than I'd imagined." She kept her back to the bar, her gaze on the view. "I can't stay. Just wanted to wish you well on your first night."

"To thank you properly, let me get you something."

When I reached behind her toward the bar, her eyes jittered. "No, thank you. I'm fine. I should probably—"

I held out the plate of bars Dave had made, offering my last two to George and Coco.

Releasing a gust of air, she nodded, taking a bar and a bite. The groan made me smile. George took the last bar and finished it quickly, all the while keeping a strong arm around his sister.

"I'm going to take Coco home. I'll probably be back near closing to pick up Owen."

Coco elbowed her brother. "You don't have to babysit me. I'm fine. Stay and have fun."

"Are you crazy? It's Springboks versus All Blacks. It's rugby night, woman." George gave me another kiss on the cheek, his arm never leaving his sister's shoulders. He waved at Owen before escorting Coco up the stairs and out.

An impact tremor reverberated behind me. When I turned, I found Meg glaring at the person sitting on the barstool she normally occupied. This was the drawback to having incredibly powerful patrons. They weren't used to waiting their turn. Meg was one of the Furies. She was an ancient Greek goddess of vengeance. I needed to get her a whiskey and a stool before a scourge appeared in her taloned hand.

Motioning to Owen, who was making a drink behind the bar, I pointed at the stool I kept in the corner. It was the one I sat on behind the bar on quiet nights. He picked it up and passed it over heads to me. I set it down at the end of the bar, near Grim. As neither Meg nor Grim were talkers, I figured they could tolerate each other well enough. I waved Meg over to the empty stool as Owen slid a double of her favorite whiskey in front of her. Annoyed but placated, Meg sat.

The kitchen door swung open and Dave started scribbling on the menu board we'd recently installed. It was best for all involved when Dave didn't directly interact with customers.

In honor of Sam's recent trip to New Orleans, tonight's menu is Po'boys—crab, shrimp, hot sausage, or roast beef, served with fries or onion rings. No substitutes. Don't piss me off.

When Dave went back in the kitchen, Owen began circulating, taking orders. A low, fierce 'Fuck' was breathed to my right. When I turned, I found Meg glaring at the bottom of the stairs.

"Nice place, kid."

I spun to find Stheno scanning the bar with her one good eye. With a yelp of excitement, I raced around the bar and hugged my favorite gorgon. She was stunning in a long white tank dress with high slits on either side that showed off glowing, golden brown skin. Her black corkscrew curls fell to the small of her back. She was still sporting an eye patch, but this one matched her dress.

"You came!"

"Said I would." She gave Horus—who may or may not have been the Egyptian sky god. I didn't like to pry—a long look. I'd never seen him anything but stoic. At Stheno's lascivious gaze, his dark skin colored. "You remember," she murmured, causing Horus to choke on his black and tan.

"I'm so happy to see you! Do you need a place to stay? My apartment is in the back."

Patting my arm, she said, "Thanks, but we're good."

"We're? Is Gabriel with you?" I was surprised he'd leave New Orleans when his Alpha was taking over as Master of the City.

"No, but that is one hot wolf. The things he could do with—well, this probably isn't the place to get into it." She winked. "Ask me later. No, 'we' is my sisters. Every century or so, we get together for as long as we can stand each other."

"Wait. Both sisters? I thought Perseus cut off Medusa's head."

Cackling, she said, "He wishes. Men. Do they ever stop exaggerating their exploits? Or the size of their dicks?" She rolled her eyes. "Not including that wolf, because oof."

I stepped back behind the bar. "What can I get you?"

Nial, a tall, dapper elf with grass-green eyes and long, silvery blond hair, stood and offered Stheno his stool.

She studied him from head to toe, a hand trailing over his arm as she thanked him. "I think I'd like something tall and cool." She winked at Nial and then sat.

Nial put his lips to Stheno's ear and whispered something that had her eyes dilating.

"Yes. I'd like that very much. I need to talk to my girl first. After that, you're on." She fanned her face as he bowed formally and then moved to the steps to wait for her.

I slid a tall, pink drink in front of her. "So, that whole beheading Medusa story was a lie?"

"Mostly. He saw her reflection in his shield and then wet himself and ran." Shrugging, she took a long sip. "Mmm. So anyway," she started, glancing over her shoulder at the hot elf waiting for her. "I need to go, but I wanted you to know we rented a house in Sea Cliff, a mile or so away. I'll bring Euryale and Medusa with me next time. Make sure you have lots of wine on hand. It's all they drink."

She hopped off her seat. "I'll be back." Flipping off Meg—who I didn't even realize she'd seen—she dropped a twenty on the bar, collected her elf, and headed out. I'd missed her.

Later in the evening, the place was still crowded, but they'd settled in. I was cutting lemon wedges when I noticed Liam, a selkie and one of my regulars, push up through the water entrance. I'd been wondering where he was. He removed his sealskin, shifting to human. Ignoring the privacy robes I kept hanging by the ocean entrance, he walked toward the bar.

People called out greetings, a few whistling, but Liam didn't respond. Confused, I pushed aside the cutting board and grabbed a pint glass, drawing his favorite lager from the tap. This wasn't like him. True, much of the supernatural world had no issue with nakedness, but I knew for a fact that Liam did. He was the main reason I kept robes available for patrons.

"Is everything okay?" I slid the beer in front of him.

Head cocked to the side, he stared uncomprehending. A split second later, he snatched up the knife I'd dropped and dove over the bar, knocking me down. My head slammed against the hard wood floor. Momentarily stunned, I didn't react until I felt the knife slice into my neck. Claws drawn, I knocked his arm away, breaking it. Eyes still blank and uncomprehending, he wrapped his good hand around my neck and squeezed.

His eyes were wrong. I knocked his other arm and again heard the bone break. Not a second later, he was yanked off me and was hanging from Dave's meaty grip. Flames ran down

Dave's arm, burning Liam, but still he hung limp and unresponsive.

"Stop! Drop him."

Dave complied but pinned Liam under his foot. "What the fuck was that?" he snarled.

I hadn't realized the bar had gone quiet until I stood and heard the collective gasp.

"Sam, you're bleeding!" Owen raced around the bar, clutching a bar towel. He pressed it to my neck, trying to stem the flow of blood.

Holding my hand over his, adding pressure, I studied Liam. "Look at him. He's not in there."

"Mom," Owen waved over Lydia with his free hand. "Is it a curse?"

Dave dropped to a crouch and laid his hand on Liam's unblinking face.

Lydia appeared to be readying a spell, so I stopped her. "He's tracing it. Don't do anything."

A moment later, Liam jolted, curled into the fetal position, and shook.

Dave stood, his expression grim. "She's back."

About the Author

About Seana Kelly

Seana Kelly lives in the San Francisco Bay Area with her husband, two daughters, two dogs, and one fish. When not dodging her family, hiding in the garage to write, she's working as a high school teacher-librarian. She's an avid reader and re-reader who misses her favorite characters when it's been too long between visits.

She's a two-time Golden Heart® Award finalist and is represented by the delightful and effervescent Sarah E. Younger of the Nancy Yost Literary Agency

You can follow Seana on Twitter for tweets about books and dogs or on Instagram for beautiful pictures of books and dogs (kidding). She also loves collecting photos of characters and settings for the books she writes. As she's a huge reader, young adult and adult, expect lots of recommendations, as well.